Also by Linda Dowling

Red Dust Novel Series
Splintered Heart
Sinister Intent

FATAL
ENVY

LINDA DOWLING

NEW SOUTH WALES, AUSTRALIA

Praise for the Red Dust Novel Series

'Both Splintered Heart and Sinister Intent had me mesmerised. The first book was quite confronting in the beginning and was so brilliantly written and described that I could feel every emotion that Lisa felt and endured. Her rescue was such a relief and the subsequent events added to the excitement and total enjoyment. Sadness, tension, beautiful relationships, joy and triumph made both books amongst the best I have ever had the pleasure to read. Thank you for your skill and ingenuity and making these books come to life.' Anne Murdoch

'Wow...Wow...Wow. I could not put my Kindle down. I read it while having breakfast, lunch & afternoon coffee time & then in bed at night...lol. Omgoodness... what Lisa went through. I cannot wait for the sequel, Linda, as you have left me with a story unfinished! I need to know what is to follow! I hope you continue with your writing. Where on earth have you been hiding!! Love your work, Linda.' International Amazon Customer

'When you read as many books as I do in a year, it takes something special to make a real impact on you emotionally. Splintered Heart is exactly such a book. Author Linda Dowling has created a scenario that was not only heart-wrenching and in places gut-churning, but sadly incredibly real and true for the time. The author pulls no punches when describing the level of depravity faced by this poor teenager but she also gives us real hope and inspiration as to the indomitability of the human spirit to rise above such terrible injustices and to seek to right the wrongs. Her portrayal of the indigenous people, the much-maligned Aborigines, was sensitive and deeply moving. Their understanding of the human spirit and its needs comes shining through every page.

In many ways, I found myself comparing this work to that of one of the great Australian authors, Colleen McCullough, and it did not suffer in comparison. I found the relationship between Lisa and her aunt and uncle to be the highlight of the story. I loved their liberal, caring, and loving attitudes, not to just Lisa but to all those around them. Alan especially typified the Australian hard-working sheep rancher of his time but his attitude toward the Aborigines was certainly rare for the period. In the lexicon of the time, one would probably describe him as a "real good bastard". This is a fantastic story and I cannot wait to see where this goes in the next iteration of the tale. I particularly look forward to Book Two, as Lisa faces seeking justice for the crimes committed against her along with possibly finding love in the arms of Billy and what problems that relationship would have to endure in 1960s Australia. I cannot recommend this book highly enough. It is an absolute cracker.' Grant Leishman for Readers' Favorite

'Having read and absolutely loved Linda Dowling's first novel Splintered Heart, I felt very privileged and excited to read and review the sequel, Sinister Intent. I was not disappointed. This story is as powerful, sweeping, and deeply emotional as the first. Sinister Intent picks up right where Splintered Heart left off and the character of Lisa, who I had become deeply invested in, continues to mature, grow, and develop in the second iteration. A good sign of an excellent sequel is in answering the question "Do I need to read the first book, before reading this one?" The answer to this is no. The author beautifully wove the events of Lisa's early life into this story to ensure the reader has no trouble garnering the full story. Having said that, I would recommend reading the two books in order for two simple reasons. First, you will gain greater context of the pain and suffering this poor young girl had to endure and second, both books are such fantastic reads, why wouldn't you want to read them both?

I love that the author addressed head-on the inequalities and damage done to the proud and great civilization of the Aborigines. In just over two hundred years, Europeans have tried desperately to eradicate 60,000 years of Aboriginal culture and the author does them a real service by recognizing and highlighting the wonderful aspects of their music, their spirituality, their simple joy of life, and their healing powers. The author's descriptive prose is vivid and sweeping, allowing readers to totally immerse their minds in the beauty and serenity of the Australian outback. For me, this is one of the best series I've read all year and I cannot recommend this highly enough, especially if you are a fan of romance with a touch of the exotic. I loved it!' Grant Leishman for Readers' Favorite

Cover design by Judith San Nicolas
Typeset in Estrangelo Edessa 18/36 pt and Goudy Old Style 9/12pt
Prepared for publication by Dr Juliette Lachemeier @ The Erudite Pen: theeruditepen.com
Printed and bound in Australia by IngramSpark

A catalogue record for this book is available from the National Library of Australia

Fatal Envy: A Red Dust Novel Book 3/ Linda Dowling. — 1st ed.
ISBN 9780648714859
E-ISBN 9780648714866

Paperback ISBN: 9780648714859
... ...

'Everything you've ever done, every person you've ever met, every experience you've ever had is a part of who you are today.' K Salmansohn

For my father, who married us to the bush.

For our Aboriginal people who believe we are all visitors to this time, this place. We are just passing through. Our purpose here is to observe, to learn, to grow, to love . . . and then we return home.

Author's Note

This is a work of fiction set in Australia in the 1970s, 80s and early 90s. The attitudes towards Indigenous people were different back then compared to the codes of conduct and morals of today, and particularly our more recent anti-discrimination laws.

Discriminatory laws against Indigenous people and multi-ethnic immigration were dismantled in the early decades of the post-war period. A 1967 Referendum regarding Aboriginal rights was carried with over 90% approval by the electorate. Legal reforms from the 1970s won by Aboriginal and Torres Strait Islander people have re-established Aboriginal land rights under Australian law, 200 years after the arrival of the First Fleet.

However, racist, offensive and derogatory language abounded when referring to Indigenous people in the 1970s and 80s in Australia. Please be warned that the novel's dialogue and character attitudes are reflective of that era.

The 1970s and 80s also saw major changes to mental health. Community-based care and smaller inpatient units located within general hospitals replaced stand-alone psychiatric hospitals. Alongside this was the evolution of talking therapies or psychotherapies. The development of anti-depressant, anxiolytic and anti-psychotic drugs cemented the role of psychiatrists as the experts in the treatment of mental illness.

However, the single most important development in the treatment of mental illness was the discovery of Chlorpromazine in 1951, an anti-psychotic medication that revolutionised the treatment of schizophrenia. The ability to stabilise and manage the symptoms of psychosis and mood disorders offered those with mental illness hope of discharge from the asylums.

Psychiatry and mental illness have come a long way. Fortunately, in today's society we openly discuss depression and mental disorders and some, but not all, of the stigma has been removed.

Although this novel does make reference to mental illness, psychiatric interventions and institutions, please note this is for fictional purposes only, and the content and characters do not depict any person, either living or dead.

CONTENTS

NEW BEGINNINGS

THE ARRIVAL 1

HOMEWARD BOUND 13

JESSE AND JEDDA 21

THE WALKERS 29

THE MEN RETURN 45

OUT OF CONTROL 51

A FATHER'S LOVE 57

EMU IN THE SKY 67

UME 75

DARKNESS COMES

GRIEF DESCENDS 91

A TROUBLING DIAGNOSIS 101

CHANGING OF THE GUARD 117

RIVER RIDE 123

A MONSTER COMETH 129

THE NEW DAM 135

GOOD FRIENDS RETURN 141

OLD HABITS DIE HARD 151

DEATH COMES CALLING 157

TWO STRANGERS 171

OPENING NIGHT 179

THE AFTERMATH 191

BAD FEELINGS 197

A KNIFE ATTACK 207

MURDEROUS INTENT 213

FRACTURED SPIRIT

CHAOS REIGNS 223

WALKING ON EGGSHELLS.. 229

DOWN BY THE RIVER 233

DESTRUCTION 241

LOVE AND GRIEF 249

A NEW INVESTIGATION.. 255

MAKING PROGRESS 259

LAYING LOW 269

FATAL ENVY

GRIFFO RETURNS 277

INVOLUNTARY PATIENT.. 285

HOMEWARD BOUND 289

OLIVIA AND JESSE... 299

JEALOUSY REARS ITS HEAD 307

AN UNSUCCESSFUL ATTEMPT.. 317

FORENSIC PSYCHIATRY UNIT... 325

FATAL ENVY.. 331

ANGELS SING THEE TO THY REST 341

EVIL COMES KNOCKING 347

A YOUNG MAN RETURNS 357

EPILOGUE 367

ACKNOWLEDGEMENTS.. 373

PART ONE

NEW BEGINNINGS

ONE

THE ARRIVAL

It was just before dawn. Still and quiet. Lisa Garrett rubbed her belly as she felt the movement within. Seven months ago, she had married Billy Garrett, the beautiful man who lay next to her. She smiled as she recalled the marriage that took place on the 8th December 1974. It had been a peaceful and beautiful ceremony. Lisa O'Connor had stood proudly next to the man she loved and had become Mrs Lisa Garrett. A new life had begun. Now heavily pregnant with twins, Lisa and Billy eagerly awaited their arrival.

Binna's daughter Ningali had said at their wedding that the great ancestral spirits would always be with Lisa and that they lived within her, in her heart, surrounding her with protection. Lisa remembered those words and knew her friend was right. Something not of this world was with her. She felt it. Not every day, but now and then something spiritual would occur. It might be the feeling of a presence, a sudden bright light, an eagle soaring or a whisper on the gentle wind. But something was there watching over her and her picaninnies.

Billy would openly speak of the spirits and tell Aboriginal stories, sharing his beliefs with the unborn twins who grew peacefully in Lisa's womb. He was fascinated by their movement and would place his hands gently on Lisa's belly, smiling as he felt them move.

Laughter was now a part of their daily life, a welcome reprieve after horrors that had befallen them just before Woori burned to the ground four years ago, let alone the horrors Lisa had endured as a young teenage girl. But justice had been served, and although she would sometimes have intrusive thoughts and flash-backs, she had healed over the intervening years. Lisa still sometimes pondered what would have happened if her aunt had not believed in her. She would never be able to thank her Aunt Zena and Uncle Alan enough after rescuing her from the Parramatta Girls Home. Nor all the wonderful people who had rallied around her, supporting her and helping to mend her splintered heart. Lisa had for years now felt a quiet calmness when Billy was around. He loved her deeply and gave her strength and courage. She could not wait to introduce her picaninnies to the man who had awakened and nurtured her soul. Her pregnancy and marriage had been the beginning of everything new and wonderful.

It now was July 1975. Lisa was thirty-seven weeks pregnant, and this morning something told her the babies were ready to meet the world. There had been a great deal of movement overnight. She swung her legs over the bed and gazed out through Wooribilly cottage's large bedroom window at a full and bright silvery moon with the twinkling stars illuminated against the breaking dawn sky. Not a creature stirred.

Lisa loved watching the sunrises as every sunrise was different: a majestic spectacle and powerful force ablaze with brilliance that filtered across the vast plains, energising and renewing. This morning, the golds and pinks swirled their colours like her own personal horizon, slowly erasing the stars. When she felt her first contraction, she knew it was time to wake Billy.

As she stood, Lisa momentarily had the profound sense of a presence. A spirit. Something otherworldly was with her. A deep peace and an immense feeling of wellbeing enveloped her. She softly stroked her stomach as her eyes scanned the room. *Is it you, Binna?*

'Billy,' Lisa called softly as she reached across the bed and let her fingers trace his muscled back.

Billy murmured and then turned to face his wife. He knew in an instant. Lisa smiled as his eyes grew wider.

'Yes, I think we best make a move,' she said.

'My beautiful grasshopper.' He placed a soft kiss on her lips. 'We meet our picaninnies today?'

Billy dressed quickly before pulling Lisa's hospital bag from under the bed. 'I call Zena now?'

'Yes. She knows I'm not far away from these two wanting to make an appearance. Zena guessed this week sometime. I'll get dressed. Can you make the call?'

Billy came over to her. 'I love you,' he murmured as he brushed her hair away from her face.

'I love you too,' said Lisa, waddling across the room to put on her clothes in the bathroom. So many emotions were running through her: overwhelm, excitement and intimidation. Over the months, as a young woman preparing for motherhood, she had grown stronger and fiercely protective. She thought about her own parents and childhood and knew in her heart that the lives of her children would be vastly different. She took a deep breath as she looked at her reflection in the mirror, sending a prayer to the spirits. *If you can hear me, please let my babies arrive safely.*

◊

The phone rang in the main house, and Zena quickly picked up the one on her bedside table. Alan's eyes sprang open. It was just on 5:15 a.m. After watching Lisa move about the previous day, Zena had expected a call. Her bump was suddenly looking low and there was much more movement, which meant labour was not far off

'Is our girl on her way, Billy?' asked Zena excitedly.

3

'Yes,' Billy replied, strong and confident. 'Lisa pretty sure of it.'

'Right then. I'll meet you at the front gates.'

'Do you want me to come with you?' asked Alan, now fully awake and sitting up in bed.

'No, you have so much to do here. We'll be fine, but thank you, my love. I'll call you once we get to Walgett Hospital.' She kissed Alan and made her way to the bathroom, reappearing moments later.

Alan slipped on some trousers and followed her to the front gates. 'Wish Lisa and Billy good luck. I'm thinking of them.'

'Can you call the hospital and let them know we're on our way? They'll get in touch with the doctor, who hopefully will be there when we arrive. Oh, and when it's a decent time, certainly not now, can you call Des and Mark to let them know?'

Alan nodded. He could see how nervous she was. He felt the same. Like everything else, Zena had done her homework and found the best obstetrician for her niece. She knew that other women were happy to have the local GP and a midwife, who were faultless, but Zena wanted a specialist because of the sexual trauma Lisa had endured as a teenager. So her niece had had months of perfunctory check-ups with Dr Rosemary Catlin, the obstetrician. She was a good fit, warm and caring, with a long career of delivering babies. The utmost professional.

Zena blew Alan a kiss as she raced to the front gates upon seeing the approaching car's headlights. Billy moved over as Zena hopped in and took the steering wheel.

'Morning, my darling girl,' Zena said as she looked at Lisa in the back seat propped up with pillows. 'Hang on, Lisa. We've got just under an hour before we get to Walgett. I hope that everyone who needs to be at the hospital is there.'

'What do you mean?' queried Lisa.

'Well, you know, after you fell pregnant, we elected to have a specialist, an obstetrician, which is why you have been seeing Dr Catlin. But as you also know, they are usually assisted by a midwife and a nursery nurse. These women study to be midwives and actually deliver babies as well. They have a double certificate, so they are extremely competent if the local GP or obstetrician doesn't make it to the delivery room. So, I'm just saying, I hope everyone is there.'

By the time they got to the hospital, the contractions were coming faster. Lisa practised the breathing she had learned in the antenatal classes and focused on the forthcoming labour and birth.

Zena headed to the sign that said 'Emergency Department' as Billy assisted Lisa out of the car. 'Over this way, Billy.' Zena pointed to the doors.

'Can I help you?' asked a nurse, glancing at the young couple with an almost disapproving look.

It was nothing they had not witnessed before over the years. Dark boy, white girl. Zena cleared her throat loudly and noticed her name badge: Nurse Bray.

'Nurse Bray, has my husband called? Alan Smith. He would have called close to an hour ago, maybe more, advising that my niece, Lisa Garrett, was possibly going into labour. It's only early stages but there are signs that the babies are on their way.' Zena looked across at Lisa, who had closed her eyes and was now leaning on Billy's shoulder, panting with another contraction.

'How far apart are her contractions?' Nurse Bray officiously shuffled her paperwork.

'They are erratic but closer together, and there was a clear pinkish discharge, which is why we are here now.'

'Ah, yes, I have a file here. Dr Catlin is the obstetrician and there is a note here. Your husband did call. The other duty nurse has already called Dr Catlin.' Nurse Bray looked at her watch. 'She should be here any minute now. Can you follow me, please.'

Billy a put his arm around Lisa to support her, and they followed Nurse Bray through a door, which the sign marked as the Labour Room.

'Put this gown on, please Lisa, and try to relax until Dr Catlin gets here,' said Nurse Bray. She then turned to Billy. 'Can you please wait outside?'

Momentarily confused, Billy looked at Zena, who was assisting Lisa.

'No,' Zena replied sternly. 'Mr Garrett, Lisa's husband and the father-to-be, is staying right here. We will both be present during the birth just as we have discussed with Dr Catlin.'

Nurse Bray's face flushed, and she left the room quickly.

Zena let out a sigh of disgust. 'It's okay, Billy. We'll wait for Dr Catlin.'

Billy moved to Lisa. 'Not long now, my grasshopper.' He gently squeezed her hand.

'Lisa, if the pain becomes too much, we can get something for it,' said Zena, feeling so helpless.

'No, Aunty. No drugs. I want to feel everything. But there is very little pain.' She squeezed Billy's hand. *Please let this be smooth. I can bear the pain, but I want my babies healthy. So many things can go wrong.*

The doors opened and a nurse in her mid-thirties, carrying gowns, introduced herself as she approached the bed. She was tall and slim, with blonde hair peeking out from under her cap. She exuded a warm and friendly aura, and her mere presence indicated self-confidence and control. This woman knew exactly what she was doing.

'Hello, Lisa, I'm Kate, your midwife-slash-obstetric nurse. I'll be with you all the way until the babies are safely delivered. I see you have your support team here.' She smiled.

'Yes, I'm Zena and this is Billy Garrett, Lisa's husband.'

Billy extended his hand, and Kate grasped it in both of hers. 'A beautiful gift awaits you, Billy.' She laughed. 'Actually two!'

Kate turned to Lisa. 'I think the initial contractions are erratic and that your cervix is probably dilating. You may have lost your mucous plug. We have a way to go yet, Lisa.' She slipped a cuff on Lisa's arm and took her blood pressure. 'A little high,' she said as she made some notes. 'Okay, I need you to relax and practise your breathing.'

Kate passed two more gowns to Zena and Billy. 'You don't have to put these on right now. I will let you know when. We may have about four to six hours ahead of us, maybe more, before active labour starts. So, for now, we just have to wait. I'll be back and forth to monitor you, Lisa. Try and get some rest, and as I said, practise those relaxation techniques you have been taught.'

It was just after 1:00 p.m. when the pain became stronger and Lisa's water broke.

'How are you coping, Lisa?' asked Kate the midwife as she came to her side.

'The contractions are coming more frequently and I'm feeling this pressure in my back, but I can manage the pain,' Lisa said honestly.

'I think we are on our way.' Kate turned to Billy and Zena. 'Best go and scrub up now and put the gowns on. Dr Catlin is here and will not be long. She's up in the maternity ward doing her rounds.'

Zena breathed a sigh of relief. Thank God Dr Catlin was here.

The doors suddenly swung open, and Dr Catlin strode towards Lisa's bedside with another young woman in tow. Both were in hospital gowns.

'Well, Lisa, the time has come. A little early, I see, at thirty-eight weeks. Your babies are in a hurry, but twins usually come a little early. This is Caroline, my nursery nurse, who will assist both Kate and myself with the procedures during and after birth.'

'Lisa, this is an exciting time for you and Billy,' said Caroline as she went about her business. 'I will also care for your babies in the nursery.'

Dr Catlin placed the stethoscope on Lisa's stomach. 'How are you feeling?'

'The contractions are now regular and much more painful, and I feel slightly nauseated.'

'All normal, Lisa. We are all here to help you bring these beautiful babies into this wonderful world.'

Billy and Zena stood at the head of the bed, fascinated as the events unfolded.

'I'm so relieved you're both here.' Lisa clutched Zena's hand.

'The contractions are coming from the back of her body and moving to the front. I don't think she is that far off. These movements open the cervix and help push the baby into the birth canal. Lisa, just put your ankles up into these stirrups. Kate, can you give her a hand, please. Remember your breathing, Lisa,' said Dr Catlin.

Billy, like Zena, had seen so many births from a variety of animals, but fear now stabbed at his heart. Lisa was in so much pain now as the contractions tore through her. She gripped his hand tightly as well as Zena's.

'Lisa, you are in the transition phase,' said Dr Catlin, concern now showing on her face. 'You will feel stronger contractions and pain in your lower back and rectum but wait until I tell you to push. Pant or blow your way through the contractions.'

Lisa nodded, her face white with pain.

'Just let me know if the pain is too much. I can give you something for it,' said Dr Catlin.

'No. I don't want any drugs. None!' she puffed.

Lisa felt the next contraction, and Dr Catlin's voice filled the room. 'Push, Lisa! Go with it. Your body knows what to do. Trust it.'

She panted in out as she gave her first push, bearing down as her body flowed with the force of the contraction. Her hair was now drenched with sweat. She searched in her mind for something to give her strength. Thoughts of Binna and Burnu and their beautiful souls began to uplift her weary body.

Zena looked at her watch. It was nearly 2:00 p.m. She felt the tears welling. She was so proud of her niece, who pushed so hard with every contraction. She knew Lisa was exhausted, but her body was incredible, like it had a life of its own. Billy was encouraging her every step of the way.

'Push, Lisa,' said Dr Catlin. 'I can see the head. Push, bear down with each contraction.'

Lisa pushed with all her might, her body taking over as she groaned with the effort. She was almost there.

Billy's face was awash with tears as a small bundle with dark hair suddenly slithered into the world. There was a little cry as Dr Catlin held the tiny boy, passing him to Kate.

'Let the baby rest on Lisa's chest, Kate. Skin on skin. Start that bonding process.'

'Oh God, Billy, isn't he just beautiful,' said Zena, a slight tremble to her voice.

'Does he have all his fingers and toes?' Lisa asked as the baby boy was placed on her chest. His brown eyes squinted at her. *You are my Jesse. Jesse Burnu. Your name means gift, little one.*

'He's so slippery, Billy,' said Lisa, wiping the tears from her face as she stroked the baby's soft, buttery cheek. *I am a mother now. I'm so filled with love, I could burst.*

Billy leaned to kiss Lisa's forehead and whispered, 'Grasshopper, my heart soars like the spirit bird. We have a son.'

'Quickly Kate, we must move now. There is another one in there,' said Dr Catlin.

Kate moved to clamp and cut the infant's umbilical cord, then Caroline took the baby to clean his airways and be weighed. The boy began to suddenly wail loudly.

'My boy? He alright?' asked Billy, concerned.

'Yes, he's fine,' replied Caroline. 'He's just shouting to the world that he is here.'

'Lisa,' Dr Catlin said. 'I know you're exhausted, but there's one more to come, so concentrate, breathe and push. You must push when I tell you.'

Dr Catlin knew she had to act swiftly as she was aware how very fast wondrous joy in a labour room could explode into immeasurable grief. She knew she had monitored Lisa's pregnancy aggressively, mainly because of her traumatic background, but now she needed the second baby out.

'Push again, Lisa, push, bear down. Good woman, that's it, we're nearly there,' the obstetrician commanded as Lisa groaned, trying to make it through one more long, strenuous contraction.

Lisa was beginning to feel she was on the verge of collapse as the contraction ripped through her. She closed her eyes momentarily. *Binna, please be with me. Please help me to bring my baby safely into this world.*

'Lisa, hold on, one more push. Come on, little one, don't stop now, you need to come out.' Dr Catlin reached for her stethoscope. The second baby was still in the womb, the head only partially in the birth canal. The heartbeat was slowing, indicating the foetus was clearly in some distress. A sudden light momentarily filtered into the room.

'Kate, did we need more light?' asked Dr Catlin, quickly looking up.

'I'm not sure where that light came from,' said Kate as she looked around the room, puzzled.

Billy leaned into Lisa's ear, whispering words only she could hear, 'Spirits, dey with us, Lisa. Our babies safe.'

'Don't worry about the lights now,' said Dr Catlin, the urgency in her voice apparent. 'Quickly, pass me the forceps and call down to Theatre. Get them ready for a C-section.'

Billy's face turned ashen as he felt every twinge of Lisa's pain. His heart went out to her, but he was helpless. He remembered Burnu telling him how his mother had died giving birth to him. How could anything be so wonderfully fascinating, magical and surreal but at the same time so truly terrifying?

His eyes grew wider as what looked like two giant spoons were handed to Dr Catlin. Everything was moving so fast, but it also felt like slow motion and that time was standing still.

Lisa whimpered as she held on tightly to Billy's hand.

'Come on, little one,' Dr Catlin persuaded as she tried to gently pull the baby out of the birth canal. The air crackled with tension.

'Lisa, push. That's it, one more!' And the tiny baby wailed her entry to the world, her lungs filling with the outside air. Lisa began to cry with relief. Billy had been holding his breath, robbing him of his ability to speak. He let it out in a huge whoosh.

'It's a girl!' exclaimed Dr Catlin, lifting the child up so they could all see. 'Look at the umbilical cord, there is a knot. This is what we call a true-knot baby.' Dr Catlin took a deep breath. Thankfully the knot was loose and posed no problems. 'You have one of each, a boy and a girl, and they are beautiful, Lisa.'

Zena's throat constricted as she failed to suppress a sob.

Kate placed the baby girl on Lisa's belly, and she stroked the baby's tiny head. There were marks on her forehead from the forceps. She cried like a duck, and Lisa smiled through her tears. 'My beautiful daughter.' *Jedda, little wild goose.*

After the umbilical cord was clamped and cut, Caroline whisked the baby away and did the same procedures.

'You need to push, Lisa, gently, one more time for the placenta,' instructed Kate.

After being whisked away, the little girl made no further noise. Lisa watched Caroline intently. 'Is she okay? Why is there no crying?'

'Yes, Lisa, no problem,' replied Caroline. 'This is a very odd thing to say, but she has a peaceful look on her face, like, I don't know, I can't describe it. Her eyes are peering up at me, like they are following me, which is quite extraordinary as babies really cannot see, just fuzzy images really. So this is remarkable.'

Both babies, now wrapped in blankets, were then handed to Lisa who gazed lovingly down at her children. It was an instant and intense love. She had heard women speak about this immediate love for their newborns, and now she knew.

'They are gorgeous, Lisa, and you did so well,' said Zena, their eyes meeting and holding.

''Thank you, Dr Catlin, for everything,' Lisa croaked.

'It's always a joy to me, Lisa, bringing new life into this world. You'll be in here for a few days and then I will call in on you before discharge. Make an appointment to see me in my rooms in six weeks' time. If you have any concerns in the interim, please just contact me. You should recover from the birth nicely, being young and fit. And you'll be pleased to know that you didn't even require any stitches.

The babies were small at five pounds nine and eleven, so you've not torn at all. Everything is still very much intact.'

Lisa was overjoyed to hear this news.

Billy seemed stunned at the sight of the two infants, but he looked at Dr Catlin and said, 'Thank you, we all thank you.'

Dr Catlin smiled. 'You are very welcome, Billy. The second twin was a little slow to come out, which is why I used the forceps. The marks on her forehead will disappear. I will see you soon, Lisa. You are in good hands now with Caroline. She'll look after the babies in the nursery and help you with breastfeeding, which you need to start right now.'

The doctor turned to Kate. 'Kate, all the usual post-delivery. I'm not sure where that light came from, maybe ask for the lighting in here to be checked. Flickering fluoro, maybe? So, ergometrine into Lisa's thigh, and the babies get their Vitamin K. Can you also check Lisa's uterus. I need it going hard and clamping down. Oh, and just check her BP. Make a note of everything on the charts.'

As Dr Catlin headed for the door, she suddenly turned. 'I have to say this,' she began, and they all looked at her. 'I have been an obstetrician for many years now and over the course of that time, true knots in the umbilical cord appear now and then. Fortunately, we had no complications. But,' Dr Catlin smiled, 'a true-knot baby means an amazing or charmed life. Perhaps an omen for your little girl. I'll see you soon, Lisa,' she said as she stepped through the doors.

TWO

HOMEWARD BOUND

July was a good month to give birth as there would be a good five months for the babies to adjust to the outback heat in readiness for the summer. Even though it had only been a few days, motherhood was every word Lisa could think of and more. It was overwhelming bringing two babies into the world with no prior training. Both scary and challenging, so she felt a whole gamut of emotions.

As they waited at the hospital to see Dr Catlin before discharge, Billy and Lisa longed for the smell of the outback and home. Their car was parked outside, and the baby capsules were ready for the journey to Woori.

Dr Catlin's consulting door opened, and the doctor beckoned to Lisa. 'Come in, you two. How are you and your bundles of joy?'

They followed her into the consult room and sat down, Lisa holding Jedda while Billy had Jesse.

'Well then, I have heard from Caroline that you are doing well breastfeeding. The babies are putting on weight and there are no problems.'

'Yes, Dr Catlin, but I'm a bit sore and have had a few belly cramps,' said Lisa.

'That would be expected, Lisa, after carrying around these two, and with a forceps delivery. The cramps are due to your uterus shrinking back to its regular size after pregnancy. They should subside in a few days. Your periods should return in a few months, some women are earlier, but if there are any issues, just call the rooms. Wait a good two months before having sexual relations. Just let your body heal.'

Billy reached out for Lisa's hand. It was plain to see this pair had a very special bond.

'Do you have any questions, Lisa? Billy?'

It was Billy who spoke. 'No, we all good, and we thank you again. We very happy.'

'Yes,' Dr Catlin laughed. 'So I can see.' The young man spoke in simple sentences, but he was no fool.

'Right then, you best be on your way. Lisa, make an appointment for six weeks' time. It's for a post-partum check-up. I will see you to the door.'

'Oh, there is one thing,' asked Lisa.

'Yes, what is it?' asked Dr Catlin.

'You said children born with a true knot have an amazing life.'

'Ah yes, I do remember. I told you that when I was leaving the birthing room, didn't I? Well, from my experience, even though true knots are uncommon, those who have had true-knot babies, well, those babies seem to have an amazing life, do amazing things. So, let's see if it rings true for your little girl. I do hope so, Lisa. But I wish that for all babies I bring into this world.'

On the drive back to Woori, pure joy filled the car. 'Oh, I can't wait to show them everything, Billy!' As they got further away from the hospital, Lisa rolled down the window, smelled the air and watched the kangaroos hopping in the distance. The emus looked up as their car sped over the red dust roads, some making an attempt to run towards the speeding car. Their long, gangly legs had always made Lisa laugh.

'I have missed this these past few days, and the open space, just the smells,' sighed Lisa.

Billy smiled as his hand reached for Lisa's. 'Me da same, my grasshopper. Hospitals, dey got da funny smell.'

Lisa laughed and said, 'I think their names suit the twins perfectly. Jesse means gift. Jesse Burnu. And Jedda means little wild goose. Do you remember when she was born, Billy, she cried. And she sounded just like a little duck! Jedda Zena Garrett.'

When they came to the first gate, Billy leaned over and softly kissed Lisa. 'Da first gate to Woori. We are home with da picaninnies.' The journey would be slightly longer as Billy was driving and also the gate-keeper. Lisa insisted on helping, but he wanted her to rest.

The last gate was in view and when Billy pulled up, they both let out a whoop.

'Home!' exclaimed Lisa. Billy leaned in to kiss her. 'Home. Ellimatta,' he said. 'Our home in my language.'

As they approached the big house, the dogs were barking, alerting Zena and Alan to their approaching car. They came down the back stairs, standing arm in arm, proudly waiting for the twins' arrival. Alan held a double bassinet.

'Hello, you two. We've been waiting excitedly,' said Zena, rushing to throw her arms around Lisa. The twins slept peacefully in their capsules. They'd had a big feed before leaving hospital.

'Let me give you a hand, Billy.' Alan helped Billy as he unstrapped the babies, placing them into the bassinet.

Alan stared down at the two identical babies. Both had beautiful brown skin and mops of jet-black hair. 'Incredible, Lisa, just incredible. What a pair of beauties. Does this mean I'm sort of like a grandfather?'

'Yes, my love, you're a sort of grandfather and I'm a sort of grandmother.' Zena laughed.

'Makes me so bloody old,' said Alan. 'But Aunty Zena and Uncle Alan are a mouthful, so what will they call us then?

'Plain old Poppy and Nan or just our own names will be fine,' said Zena. 'But they will make their own names up for us. Come on, I have some morning tea ready.'

When they entered the kitchen, the aroma of freshly baked bread was in the air and a plate of cookies was on the table. 'Let's sit and have a cuppa before you head up to Wooribilly,' said Zena.

'It's so nice to be home,' yawned Lisa. 'You don't get a lot of sleep in hospital, what with the noise and the door to your room opening and closing. I'm looking forward to my own bed, not that I'll probably get much sleep in it either. These two feed around the clock!' She gazed lovingly at her babies. 'They have slept most of the way home and are due for another feed.'

Zena nodded. 'Yes, nothing better than being in your own bed. You'll get better sleep at home, when you do get it. But if they don't settle, it's the motion of a car that makes them fall asleep. I remember my days nannying when I first got to London, waiting for a teaching post, and I'd do a quick drive around the block with restless babies. Remember that, because you will get those moments, so just get in the car and drive around the property.'

'Mother Nature never ceases to amaze me,' said Alan.

Billy leaned down to the bassinets. His face said it all. 'I am proud father.' Jedda's tiny finger curled around his own.

'You should be, son. Not one but two. I don't think you'll have time to do your work,' Alan jested.

'Sure will, boss,' replied Billy. 'Get no better worker than me.'

'I know that, Billy. But when do you think you'll forget about the word "boss".'

Billy laughed. 'Always thinking boss before thinking Alan.'

'I can't wait to see the twins talking and taking all this in. Life here at Woori will be a happy one and a big adventure for them,' said Zena.

Lisa remembered when she first arrived and how the place had given her such hope, peace and freedom.

'Yes, it will be,' Lisa replied softly. 'All that and more.'

After a quick bite, it was time to settle the twins into their new home. Alan shook Billy's hand. Billy flashed his big white smile as he helped Lisa to the car.

'I'll come up tomorrow. Rest now, Lisa, and let me know if you need a hand with anything. Oh, by the way, a bit of news from next door. I was chatting with Kate Walker.' Zena hesitated. 'Perhaps it can wait.'

'What news? I just have to know when you say something like that.' Lisa was intrigued. She had a soft spot for Kate Walker and her husband Dave. She had always felt sorry if she had caused Kate any hurt when the issues with their son Mitch had evolved. Kate had been deeply disgusted with her son's behaviour and the private investigator he had hired to find information on Lisa's past. It was a traumatic time, but it seemed so long ago now, and over the years they had made amends. She remembered the letter of apology he had written at the time, and then suddenly he'd had to marry Tess Dunphy due to getting her pregnant.

Zena paused. 'No, it can wait.'

'You are exasperating me, Aunty! Tell me before we head off.'

Zena relented. 'It's about babies, and babies being all around us at this time.'

Lisa looked puzzled. 'Babies?'

'Yes, as I said, I spoke to Kate, who was thrilled with the birth of the twins, but she mentioned that Tess is pregnant again. Just on ten weeks. Kate said it was miraculous Tess was pregnant again as Mitch is away for long periods and has as little to do with her as much as possible.'

Lisa smiled. 'That is lovely news. It was such a tragedy when they lost baby Tom to cot death. And then Tess fell pregnant so quickly with Polly. I just shudder when I think of finding your baby not breathing. I know I will be double-checking the twins in their cots all the time.'

'Thought you just might like to know,' Zena said.

Lisa nodded. 'I'm happy for them. It's a funny arrangement though. I could not understand conceiving a child in what seems a loveless marriage.'

'I hear you. Kate gets so fed up, yet Dave is adamant Mitch needs to make a go of it. Divorce is not a Walker thing. No bailing out.'

'It's sad, especially for the children.' Lisa gazed at her two babies. 'I grew up in a loveless household, and it was no picnic.' She climbed into the passenger's seat as Billy attended to the capsules.

'Indeed. Call me if you need any help. Somehow though, I think Billy will have it all under control.'

Billy lifted his hat in acknowledgement.

As they sat in the car, Alan leaned into the driver's side where Billy sat. 'Don't worry about work, Billy, just take the next few days off. There's nothing urgent. Shearing time is a good three months away. Perfect timing.'

'Thanks, boss. Alan.'

Zena waved until the car disappeared down the road, the red dust billowing behind them. 'How lucky we are, Alan, to have them all in our lives. The joy the babies will give to both of them and us. They are an absolute gift.'

'Yes, they are.' Alan smiled. 'I think she will be a great mother, fiercely protective, I'm sure.'

'Do you blame her, given what she went through as a child? Lisa reminds me of a farmer,' said Zena.

'What does that mean?' Alan drew Zena towards him.

'You'll understand this analogy.'

'Go on.' Alan looked bemused.

'Farmers get everything thrown at them: flood, drought, pests, stock disease, whatever, you name it. But it's only to make them stronger for the next thing. Everything was thrown at Lisa, yet we have watched her grow stronger. Her next thing is motherhood.'

Alan nodded and a smile crossed his face. 'Never a truer word, Zena.'

'Maybe I shouldn't have mentioned Tess being pregnant. Maybe I should have waited. I don't know, something just told me to let her know.

'Well, that young man made his own bed, so now he has to lie in it,' said Alan. 'But I can't understand if Mitchell's that unhappy, why doesn't he remove Tess from his life? And now she's pregnant again. What happened there? He could have divorced Tess and moved on after the baby Tom died. But she fell pregnant with Polly almost straight away.'

'Good Catholics, Alan, and I guess young men have their physical needs. You don't fall pregnant on your own,' added Zena.

'I hear some of the stories from Dave, and it's a bloody madhouse at Woodside. Miserable life if you ask me. A man has to make himself happy; for that matter, anyone does. Time is a thief, and life is too short to be in a miserable household.'

'It's the same for women, Alan,' said Zena. 'We're all in the same boat. We all just want to be happy and loved. A simple formula yet some never get it right.'

'Come on then, love of my life who makes me so happy,' said Alan, taking her hand. 'We've got work to do.'

◊

As Lisa and Billy lay in bed that night, it was their first chance for intimacy. Billy gently pressed his body to Lisa's, cuddling up to her. He had waited for her his whole life, and she was a part of him, but now their love was on a deep and existential level.

'My grasshopper, you now da mother of my picaninnies. Lisa, you touched my life in so many ways. Billy look at you and see da rest of my life, here in front of my eyes.' Billy kissed her tenderly, but not enough to arouse her. He knew she needed to heal first.

'I love you, Billy. I knew the first kiss with you was also for the rest of my life.' Lisa was so aware of the greatness this man breathed into her. She wanted him as much as he wanted her.

Lisa pondered for a moment. 'Do you think that flash of light...? Well, I don't know what to think. The flash of light in the delivery room, do you remember? You said the spirits were with us.'

Billy rolled on his side, propping his head into the palm of his hand. He gazed at Lisa as his finger traced her sleepy face. 'I told you in da hospital, da spirits dey were with us, Lisa. In da room. Always be with us, always be lookin' out for you, for da babies.'

She drifted off into a peaceful sleep, before getting up in a couple of hours for the next feed.

THREE

JESSE AND JEDDA

Ten years later

It was now 1985, and the shearers came and went, new faces were mixed with the old, and the Garrett twins proved themselves to be popular at Woori. Jesse, now a boisterous ten-year-old boy, looked just like his father, Billy, and was emphatic he wanted to be a shearer when he grew up. He would mimic the shearing process to howls of laughter, insisting on wearing the dark blue singlet Lisa had bought him so he could be just like the shearers. He would ride down with Billy, peering out from under his black hat, wanting to be part of the crew.

Seemingly older than his years and so like Billy in many ways, Jesse was more comfortable roaming around the outdoors and was respectful of Mother Nature. Lisa would often find lizards in his bed or other creatures he would catch, just so he could look after them. At times, Billy would take Jesse away on his own, much to Jedda's annoyance. Billy called this their special time. They would camp overnight, and Lisa knew Billy was preparing Jesse for his manhood rituals.

Jedda, also ten, was a little wild goose who managed to get into everything. Mischievous, head-strong and wilful, her thirst for knowledge and curiosity about anything and everything kept Lisa and Billy on their toes. She had a love of all animals, but particularly bird-life, and would try and imitate their bird calls or songs of the bush as she called them. Her favourite was the willy wagtail. Her jet-black hair had a slight curl, and her eyes were dark, like her father's. Jedda never walked. She ran as fast as her legs would carry her. The bonus in that regard was that she slept well, with Billy often carrying her to bed.

Binna's daughter, Ningali, and her partner Kev came to Woori for three seasons but had left outback New South Wales and were now in Queensland. Lisa missed them as they were so much a part of their family, with the fond memories of mother and daughter when she first came to Woori. She had laughed and danced with them as a teenager and could still feel and smell the cleansing and smoking ceremonies they did together. It had been a special time. Despite begging Ningali to stay, they left, always promising to be back. Their calls were infrequent but at least they kept in touch.

Lisa's father Des O'Connor and her brother Mark frequently visited the homestead in the school holidays. When they returned home, Lisa was always on the phone to them and sending photos of the children as they grew. The twins loved Des and Mark and were always excited when Lisa mentioned a visit. Des had insisted they call him Des. 'Plain old Des,' he called it, as Grandad made him feel ancient.

Despite her turbulent upbringing all those years ago in Fairfield, with her father and late mother, Lisa's relationship with Des had come a long way. He was now a kind father to her and a wonderful grandfather to Jesse and Jedda. He had been going downhill for the last twelve months but this past year, 1985, he was really unwell, battling prostate cancer. Lisa wanted to get down to the Southern Highlands sooner rather than later to see him.

Her father and brother had moved to Mittagong, Des's hometown, and had settled into a little weatherboard home on an acre of land. If Des felt the need to go fishing, Kiama was just over an hour's drive. Mark had settled into teaching French at the Fernhope Girls School. Des said it was very posh, but Mark absolutely loved it.

Mark had become obsessed with the French language and culture, studying at Alliance Française after leaving high school. He attained his diploma and was now accredited to teach French as a foreign language. He was so proficient it was difficult for even a French national to detect his Aussie accent. He described himself as a true Francophile. The twins adored their Uncle Mark, and it was hilarious when he tried to teach them French on his visits to Woori.

There was never a dull moment at the station. Between sheep, breeding stock horses, running the farm, and the boisterous twins, life was full and had never been better.

Zena and Alan's reputation for breeding stock horses was now renowned in the horse industry. They were producing high-performance working horses with quiet temperaments, intelligence and athletic ability. As a result, there was now a demand for their horses in Australia and overseas, which proved to be rewarding financially. It was a common interest for Lisa and her aunt as well.

Billy never stopped teaching the twins to horse ride. They were proficient and co-ordinated in the saddle from a young age. They looked so tiny when they first started riding, and Lisa was fearful they would fall off, but Billy ran alongside them as they rode their ponies at the tender age of three years. He enjoyed going bush with the twins, teaching them about the land, his country and people, bush tucker and survival. When they returned, excitement filled the air as they relayed their stories to their mother. Lisa elected to home school the children until they were ready for boarding school at secondary level, which Zena adored. Her old teaching skills quickly resurfaced, and every day she looked forward to teaching them something new, especially history and geography, while Jedda thrived on anything artistic. Jesse loved stories of travel, particularly around Australia and the vast outback. Zena would flop down in a chair, exhausted after every teaching effort, but the smile never left her face.

The twins would beg Billy for more and more Dreamtime stories and sat spellbound when the opportunity arose. It was important to Lisa and Billy that they learn about his culture, their culture. Jesse would try to repeat what Billy said when he spoke. Billy would repeatedly tell the twins that we are all just visitors to this time and place. He was so in tune with their needs, and both Lisa and Billy combined warmth and discipline, establishing secure emotional bonds that they hoped the twins could fall back on in the face of stress and adversity.

Lisa's mind would drift every now and then to her previous life, the stressors she faced and the horrors she had escaped, but she worked continually to repel the sadness and the memories that would now and then intrude. It was harder at night with the pervasive dreams, but she knew it would always be a battle with her demons. She would sometimes cry out in the night until Billy's warm body came to her side, his arms gently folding around her.

As Lisa now looked down at her sleeping children, she wondered if it had not been for her aunt and uncle, where would she be now? She would not have this life or these beautiful children. Lisa recalled a conversation with Dr Tyler, the psychiatrist she had seen so many times in her teenage years. A lot of girls that were sexually abused either turned to substance abuse or became very promiscuous, even turning to prostitution, self-harm and some even suicide. Zena and Alan had come into Lisa's life for a reason, their goodness aiding her physically, emotionally and spiritually. Zena had provided the nurturing she had so desperately needed to be able to move forward from the past and transform into the person she had now become.

It was a beautiful, crisp September morning, and Lisa wanted to ride Topi while the children were on their ponies. She loved September, as babies from the animal world were everywhere, lambs and foals were dropping, joeys were in pouches and baby kookaburras were trying to learn how to sing.

'Why don't you come with us, Billy? It's a perfect day and perfect temperature. In a few months, the flies will be horrid and it will be so hot. Do you have a lot on today?' Lisa asked as she slipped on her jeans. 'Your Jed needs a good run. We won't be riding them much longer as they're both getting on.'

Billy smiled. 'Not much on, grasshopper. Mebbe good idea. Tell a story down at da river.'

'I was hoping you would say yes. We can take turns with short sprints for the twins' horses. I don't want them galloping just yet. I know they have outgrown their own little ponies, but I don't want them thrown off at a fast gallop. The ponies will do for now and if they do fall off, it's not as far to the ground.'

Billy laughed. 'Dem kids, Lisa. Dey not gunna fall off. Got da grippo on da saddle. I teach dem good.'

Lisa laughed. 'Go on, you. Bring the horses around, and I'll pack a few sandwiches.'

As they headed to the river, it was an effort to restrain the twins, especially when Billy took off at a gallop. Lisa could see Jedda putting her heels into her pony, Teddy, to make him go faster.

'Jedda, stop kicking Teddy. He has short legs, and you are not ready to gallop, so please be patient. I will take your reins if you do that again.'

Billy slowed down as they caught up to him. 'Jedda, she wanna run with me.' He laughed, throwing his head back.

'Yes, and like I have told them, galloping is out of the question for now. It's a long trip to hospital for a broken bone. Are you listening to me, Jesse?' She scolded as he started to giggle.

'Yes, Mummy,' replied Jesse.

'Then what is so funny, Mr Giggly Pants?' As Lisa looked at Billy, she could see he was highly amused.

Jedda suddenly blurted out, 'Because, Mummy, you look funny when you try to be angry with us.'

Lisa looked to the sky and shook her head. 'What can I say now, Billy?' She started to laugh with them.

'Say nothing now.' He took Jesse's reins. 'Lisa, you do da same with Jedda. Take her reins. Come, we go slow now, we talk about da eagle and da bird sounds. River not far away. Remember what I said about da river?'

It was Jedda who answered. 'It's like an artery, and we die without it.'

Billy nodded. 'Da river, she like our arteries, inside our bodies and without da river, or our arteries, we stop.'

When they arrived at the river, Billy could hear the frogs. 'You hear da frogs, Jedda? He croaking all day. He da happy frog.'

Jesse giggled as Billy tried to imitate the sounds.

'What dat sound, Jesse? Da frog, he run away when he hear dat, my sounds,' laughed Billy. He knew already which story he would tell them. Lisa tethered Topi and the ponies then grabbed the sandwiches out of the dilly bag.

'Here you are, come and get some lunch.' Lisa spread a small blanket and lay down under the shade of the peppercorn trees.

'Come, I tell you about da greedy frog.' Billy patted a spot on the rug.

On the banks of the river, where so many beautiful memories were with Billy, Lisa now watched her husband tell his stories to their children. It would always bring back the stories that Binna had told her when she first came to Woori. Lisa inwardly sighed as a vision of her friend came to mind. *I miss you so much, Binna. You taught me well.*

Billy was a great storyteller, using his hands frequently. 'Dat big frog, he drink all da water from dis river. None for anybody else. He was da greedy frog and da biggest frog in da land. When da other animals come to drink, all gone. Da kangaroo, he very thirsty. Where dat water gone? Den dey look up and dey see da big fat frog. Kangaroo tell echidna, "We make him laugh so he spill all dat water out and den we drink." Echinda try, da wombat, even Mr Goanna. But da dizzy galah, dat bird, he crash into da big eucalypt and dis made da frog laugh until all da water came spilling out, filling up da river again.'

The children clapped and laughed hysterically. Jedda flung herself playfully at Billy, crashing into his chest. 'You are the big eucalyptus tree, Daddy.'

'And you are dat silly pink and grey galah dancing crazy in da sky,' he teased as he flipped her over. 'Come, we swim, and you have to try and catch me.' It was Billy's way of teaching the children to swim. He wanted no fear about water with his children. The twins were always up for a challenge and followed him like tadpoles, diving under the water, squealing when he threw them into the air and let them crash down into the water.

Zena had told Lisa about a couple who had lost their toddler a few years back when the child wandered off and fell into the dam. Alan said they sink like stones if they can't swim. From that day on, Lisa told Billy the twins had to understand water and its power.

'Dey gunna be like da fish, Lisa,' he simply replied. Never a truer word. Jesse could stay down longer than Jedda and then suddenly he would pop up, his little face beaming.

As they rode at an easy pace back from the river, Woori came into view, and they could see Zena outside in the garden. Lisa waved. 'Let's head across and say hello.'

Zena stood up as she saw the approaching figures. 'Good day for a ride. I must join you some time. I just got off the phone to Kate Walker, who has invited you, me and the children over for afternoon tea. She will be on her own with the two girls, Polly and Olivia. Dave and Mitch are at some big bull sale further north, and Tess wanted a break. She's gone to see her mother. Are you up for it?'

Lisa looked across at Billy, searching his eyes.

'Grasshopper, you make da choice.' But there was a look of concern on his face. He always worried about Polly, Mitch and Tess Walker's eldest daughter. He said he saw and felt something not right when he looked at the girl.

Zena continued. 'I think Kate is having a hard time over there. Polly is now fourteen and quite the handful. But that's teenagers. Kate's relationship with Tess is also fairly tumultuous, yet Kate has always been a gentle soul. Often when we have our heart-to-hearts, I can hear it in her voice, the sadness. I often wonder if it would have been better to get Polly in as a boarder when she turned twelve to stimulate her mind and meet new friends. But Tess wouldn't have a bar of it, and Polly refused to go. So, it was distance education. I just don't think School of the Air via the HF radio will enhance her mind as she hits those teenage years. Kate says she frequently avoids lessons, feigning sickness, and basically does everything and anything to miss lessons.'

Lisa nodded. 'Sad situation but afternoon tea sounds good. What time?'

'Wonderful,' replied Zena. 'Kate said around three, so I'll come down and get you.'

THREE

THE WALKERS

Although the Garrett and Walker children occasionally played, rode horses and had get-togethers at various times, especially during shearing season, always at the back of her mind was Lisa's fractured relationship with Mitch. Tess always eyed her suspiciously, but Mitch and Lisa both knew any feelings had long been buried. He had never put a foot wrong with her since she had been abducted all those years ago by the deranged shearer Jimmy, and in everyone's mind, the issues of the past were just that: in the past. Life moved on. But Lisa would sometimes wince at the memory of the hurt and embarrassment Mitch had caused her with his private investigator and disregard for her feelings and privacy. As Zena would say, 'You can forgive but you don't forget.'

Zena honked the horn just before three, and the children bolted for the door. 'Jedda, please try and keep clean!' Lisa followed, carrying Jedda's shoes as they all piled into the beloved blue Zephyr.

'Honestly, Aunty, she is so feral at times. My little wild goose. I can't get shoes on either of them. They're so like Billy in that way. He always said his feet were the best shoes God gave him.'

Zena nodded, 'Don't worry, Lisa. When Jedda steps on enough cathead weeds, she'll be asking for shoes!'

As they turned the slight bend in the road, the turn-off for Woodside appeared. The tree-lined eucalypt driveway was beautiful, and the scent of the lemon gums filled the morning air. They pulled up at the front gates, and Kate appeared on the porch. 'Welcome everyone,' she greeted.

Polly and Olivia were with her, and Lisa thought how Polly was becoming so strikingly similar to Tess with her flaming red hair, freckles and long legs. Olivia, or Livvy as everyone called her, was the same age as the twins but a few months younger and was very Nordic in appearance. She had Mitch's blonde hair and blue eyes.

Kate looked very tired and drawn. Her greying blonde hair was neatly pulled into a chignon at the base of her neck. She was as elegant as ever, and her usual warm and welcoming manner was ever present, but the living arrangements with them all under the one roof had clearly taken its toll. Kate had told Zena that the environment was very acrimonious with constant arguments, which was totally the opposite to Kate and Dave's nature. Living daily with such ongoing stress was damaging both physically and mentally. Lisa didn't know how Kate and Dave could stand it. And the poor girls, what must this be doing to them growing up in such a hostile household?

Polly had a look of defiance with her small mouth set hard, very similar to Tess. Olivia was happy to see her friends as she ran to greet them.

'Come in, come in, so lovely to see you. And look at these two, such energy,' said Kate as she hugged Lisa.

'Thanks for having us, Kate. It's so good to catch up as I know it's been a while. I'm sorry my urchins are barefoot. It was difficult to get shoes on them today.'

Kate laughed. 'No problem, Lisa. They are delightful. Full of energy. You would rather them that way than couch potatoes.'

Zena kissed Kate on the cheek and handed her a basket of scones.

'Let's go inside,' said Kate.

Polly managed a half smile, but her eyes were cold with a transfixing steady gaze, so it looked like she was sneering all the time. Lisa wondered if her behaviour at times was just due to her now being a teenager. There were days when she was quite pleasant and other times, like today, it seemed from her manner that she preferred they were not in her house.

Lisa felt a sudden ripple of unease go through her body. Binna would say it da bad spirit. *Yes, Binna, I feel this girl is a bad spirit. Something doesn't feel right. But maybe it's just my imagination. She is just a young girl after all.*

As soon as Kate opened the screen door, the twins hurtled through it. The long table was set beautifully, and the children's eyes were glued to the finely cut chicken sandwiches and the delicious-looking cakes before them.

'Jedda, Jesse, remember what I told you. Mind your manners and wait for Kate to serve you. Jesse, can you take your hat off, please.' Two sets of big brown eyes looked across at Lisa. *How can I ever get mad at these two?* An inner warmth spread to her heart.

Olivia always seemed fascinated with the twins. The three of them got on well and the fascination from Olivia was clearly returned. Lisa pondered the reason. Was it because the twins were dark? No doubt there would have been discussion amongst the Walkers about their heritage.

Olivia giggled. 'You two always look the same.' Her eyes went from Jedda and then to Jesse.

'Because we're twins, Livvy!' exclaimed Jedda. 'Jesse has told you that story before. We were in Mummy's belly together. Jesse was sleeping right next to me.'

'I came out first!' yelled Jesse.

'Jesse, shhh, softer voice, please. We are not in the backyard,' admonished Lisa.

They all laughed, but when Lisa looked across at Polly, she was almost scowling.

Lisa remembered Zena had told her years ago that there were mental issues or a psychiatric condition with Tess. She wondered if the young girl, Polly, had the same issues. She clearly didn't like the conversation the children were having. Kate had said Polly was becoming more sullen, often withdrawing, with impulsive mood changes. She was unpredictable and mercurial.

'Your skin is pretty,' said Olivia, looking directly at Jesse.

Jesse stopped eating and looked at his arm. 'We're brown. Mummy says sun-kissed. Daddy says we come from the red carpet of our land.' He leaned across the table, holding out his forearm for Olivia. She put her forearm next to Jesse's and giggled, noticing the vast difference in colour.

Polly snorted and pushed her plate away. Her eyes flashed. 'Can I leave the table?'

'Yes, of course, Polly,' said Kate, who looked a little embarrassed at her behaviour as she slinked away.

Lisa noticed she had not engaged in any conversation.

'Have you had enough now, you two?' asked Lisa. 'Do you want to go outside and play with Olivia? Is that okay, Kate? Sorry, I should have asked first.'

'No, that is perfectly alright. Sometimes you have to shoo them away from the table, especially with the sweeties, or they just keep eating until they make themselves sick.'

Kate turned to Olivia. 'Livvy, why don't you show Jesse and Jedda your new silky hens. Dave calls them fluff balls. Funny looking little things, but Livvy just adores them.'

'Yes, Nanny,' Olivia said excitedly, getting out of her seat.

Jesse scrambled after Olivia, followed by Jedda. The door slammed, and the three women were finally alone. It was good to sit and chat with Kate.

'My apologies about Polly. She has been so moody and cranky, but when I spoke to my GP, she mentioned that hormones do play a role in mood. The sex hormones, oestrogen, progesterone and testosterone, all affect teenagers. As the brain matures, the moodiness fades. Here's hoping!'

Zena felt sorry for her friend. 'No need to apologise.'

'Some days I fear there will be a murder in the house. It's like a battlefield. Mitch comes home but then goes and stays out for long periods of time. We don't know where he goes most of the time, but he's building up our sheep numbers, and we are now venturing into cattle. He frequently visits Queensland for stock, which has assisted us in good breeding, and of course, this is great in terms of monetary gain for Woodside. Keeps everyone in a job too. When drought comes, I feel terrible letting people go.'

'Breeding cattle?' queried Zena. 'That's interesting. What type?'

'We looked into what type of cattle best suited our weather and conditions. Mitch tinkered with the idea of Brahman only because they have a high tolerance to heat and sunlight, which you both know we get loads of, with also good resistance to ticks. But we ended up going with Herefords. They are great in cool climates and thrive in even harsher climates on every continent. You know we get our droughts out here, Zena, and we haven't had one for a few seasons now. Dave seems to think one is not far away. They are certainly predicting it.'

'I shudder at that thought, Kate. It's a worry, not having a lot of water, and hand-feeding stock is horribly expensive. We're lucky we have a bore. It also keeps the kids amused when they sit on the veranda and watch the wildlife come for a drink in the afternoon. Alan and I did that with Lisa many moons ago.'

'I still love it,' said Lisa, 'and the kids are fascinated with all the wildlife, especially at this time of year. All the roos and emus bring their babies, which is what makes this place so special. Nature surrounds us.'

Kate nodded and said, 'Dave is always worrying about water. He's building a new dam with much higher sides so we catch more rain, but that's a joke really, isn't it. Not much rain here, but rain is rain, and he wants every drop when it does fall.'

'It's interesting you're diversifying. I must tell Alan as he has often thought of doing something else other than sheep. But as you know, the stock horses we breed have been a great asset. That was our way of developing the farm and building more capital. We even had a query from Canada the other week. Ours are such good work horses.'

'Well done, Zena, and you too, Lisa. I know you have both worked hard with the breeding.'

Kate nodded. 'Yes, I think it's the way to go. We have also planted wheat in the far paddocks. It's basically dryland cropping but wheat is actually grown on more land area than any other food crop. Mitch did all the research. World trade in wheat is greater than for any other crops combined, so it's a good investment.'

'Wheat! Gosh, that really is diversifying, but you have so much more land than us,' said Zena, sipping her tea. 'You have to be patient when improving your livestock as it is a long process. You don't often see the results for up to two years when the offspring are on the ground. So, although we have good foals, it's the expense of keeping them for two to three years before a horse is sold!'

Kate nodded. 'That's the beauty of sheep, a quick return on your investment. But you could still do it, just on a smaller scale. We just didn't want to rely on sheep only. As you said, it is so expensive to hand feed them and then you sell them off during a drought, only to buy them back again.'

Lisa suddenly asked, 'How does Tess cope with Mitch's long absences, Kate?'

'I really don't think she minds, and to tell the truth, neither do I. It's much quieter when Mitch and Tess aren't under the same roof. All they do is fight when Mitch is home. I often hear objects thrown about, and Tess makes outlandish threats, like taking the girls away. Their fights are so intense, Dave said they could suck the oxygen out of a room.'

'Not good, Kate,' said Zena.

'No, it's not. We're lucky the house is big, and we have separate wings. Dave and I can get away from them, apart from the common areas. But Zena, as you well know, all you want to do is be near the grandkids and shield them from hostility. As you can see, Polly is a handful, very much like Tess, and I don't know what goes through her mind sometimes.'

Kate paused, as if deliberating what to reveal. She then said, 'And, Tess, well, she's not the best role model, which is why Dave and I try to keep the peace, so that the children can see some steadiness, for want of a better word. Polly can be so unpredictable, and Olivia is totally the opposite. Mitch tried in the past, but now he seems to have given up completely on making his marriage work. So, I can understand why Tess is so miserable and drinks. I do feel sorry for her.'

'It's hard being so isolated,' replied Zena. 'You have to have harmony and a good marriage or relationship out here. Otherwise, it would be miserable.'

Kate sighed. 'Polly seems to have this aura of anger about her. I can sense her anger or when I feel she is about to implode. But when parents are destructive and non-communicative, the collateral damage to kids can last a lifetime. I hope not, for Polly's sake. Olivia seems to be more well-adjusted and sweeter-natured, but I do worry about Polly's emotional state.'

'Maybe as she grows up, and particularly with secondary school, you will see a difference,' comforted Zena.

'Perhaps. We are trying to get her to accept the last two years of her education, from age sixteen to eighteen, at a private school. I fear she has missed out so much just doing long-distance education. But what a tragedy that this current family situation could ruin Polly for life. The girls are chalk and cheese, and I know we are all different. Olivia has such a gentle nature and a really special bond with Mitch, which Polly feels immensely. He was hardly home when Polly was born, and there has been a real lack of love for the girl. But it was a real shock to lose baby Tom. People handle grief so differently. Mitch just shut down and seemed to find solace in travelling to remote areas. And then Tess fell pregnant so quickly with Polly, but he didn't seem to want to get attached to the child. And then one night, years later, he had had too much to drink and well... things happen. But it brought Olivia to us.

'I try not to show favouritism, but it's difficult. It's like sweet and sour but from the same cup. The girls get on most of the time, but they also fight. All siblings do, I guess, but it has been worse the last twelve months. I'm sure Mitch would just like Tess to leave, but she won't go. She's onto a good thing here, financially. But Mitch gives Polly, or for that matter, Tess, absolutely no affection; actually, he hasn't from day one. He didn't want to marry Tess but she was pregnant and Dave insisted, but then tragically, we lost Tom.

'Cot death is so unexplained, and my God what a shock it would be,' said Zena.

Kate nodded. 'Dave and I have tried to make up for Mitch's lack of affection by showing Polly warmth and kindness, but it's like hitting a blank wall with her. She shows no interest in us and almost looks through us when we speak. She just shuts down. It's like there is nothing connecting.'

'That's not good, Kate. They are both his daughters,' Zena commented.

'I know. But the different relationship Mitch has with Olivia is so evident. He softens when he looks at Olivia, which is why he probably keeps Tess here. If Tess goes, so do the children, and he would be worried what environment Olivia would be raised in. He seems to have the attitude that Polly can fend for herself, which is ridiculous. Tess would certainly go back to live with her mother in that old house in Walgett on the outskirts of town. Nowhere else to go. Anyway, being a good Catholic, Dave won't hear of divorce, so this is our lot. I sometimes wonder if it would have been better just to support Tess financially in her own living arrangements, but I just couldn't bear the thought of what would happen to those girls.'

'I am so sorry to hear this. Children are such beautiful gifts to us. Billy and I never cease to be amazed by them,' said Lisa.

'It's not your fault, Lisa, but thank you for your kind words.' Kate paused. 'Sometimes I feel Mitch has never got over not having you.'

Lisa lowered her gaze and felt her ears burning. 'We did touch on that many moons ago, Kate, and it is long buried. We were young, and even Mitch apologised and said he did so many stupid things. I accepted his apology.'

Kate nodded absently. 'As you said, it was many moons ago. Mitch always got what he wanted, never lacked for anything, so you were the one that got away. He is, as we all are, responsible for his own actions as an adult. But I must say, maturity has been good for him. Although he fights terribly with Tess, he no longer has that ego, for want of a better word, like he could conquer the world and anyone in it.'

Lisa felt a wave of sadness for Kate. It would have been a perfect union in her eyes, but Lisa's heart only had room for Billy.

Zena nodded. 'The passage of time brings maturity. But you have two lovely grandchildren. I'm sure Polly will straighten herself out. She's only young, so perhaps it's a bit of a phase?'

'Thank you, my friend, I hope so. I would be lost without you, and heaven knows I have used you as a sounding board for many years now. As I said, we wanted to send Polly to a private school but she refuses to go. We are hoping to get her in there when she turns sixteen. I have looked at a few different schools, and they all seem to be pretty good. We may need to force her hand and send her there. God knows, they will be getting a handful.'

'But Polly would not be the first pupil that was a handful,' said Zena, placing her cup down. 'I am sure the teachers work very hard to turn some kids around if they initially arrive problematic. She just hasn't had a good role model with Tess.'

'What about you, Lisa? Have you given secondary education any thought?' queried Kate.

'Jedda wants to do anything and everything. She is such an avid reader and loves to sing. She does have a lovely natural voice. Jesse, on the other hand, wants to stay on the farm with Billy. He loves the outdoors. But to empower them with education and knowledge is what you would want for your children. Things are so different today when it comes to education.'

'Exactly, Lisa,' replied Kate. 'Education is so very important, but if they don't want to learn, what can you do?'

'What does Tess do all day when she's here?' asked Lisa, 'And for that matter, Polly? Are they interested in the land at all?'

'Tess is always on the phone, chatting. She does help with house-work but will just take off for a walk, and sometimes she'll ask one of the farm crew to saddle a horse. When she first came to Woodside, I have to admit, she really did try. I think she tried for Mitch, but then she stopped trying. After the birth of Polly, she learned to ride. She didn't have a bad seat on a horse but would never win a gold medal. We had an older guy here working, Will, one of the stockmen, but he's gone now. He was very patient with Tess, who seemed quite tak-en with him. But I tell you, watching her learn some days, he must have had the patience of a saint.'

Kate paused as if reflecting momentarily. 'Some days, I just see Tess drive off to return late in the day with shopping bags. Mitch bemoans how much money she spends. Other times, she'll be out for a week at her mother's place. She seems to like those lovey-dovey novels, you know, those Mills and Boon-type books. She always comes back with a bundle, and anything else she can find like that. So, she does read.'

'What about Polly?' asked Lisa, her curiosity aroused.

'Hmm, what can I say about Polly? As I said, I try to encourage her with different things around the house, whenever she comes out of her room. Like cooking or needlework or just the running of Woodside, but she gets this vacant look and goes back to her room. Often, I hear her talking as if she's in the family room or TV room. It's like a rambling, almost an incessant chatter. But she's on her own. I know Tess gives her those romance books to read as well, so not a lot of intellectual material. She seems to not want to learn or open her mind, feigns sickness or refuses to come out of her room when it's time for lessons. It really is exasperating. But what is awful is that sometimes Polly is deliberately cruel to Olivia. They do get along, as I said, but I feel like I always have to watch them together.'

Zena looked puzzled. 'Cruel. In what way is she cruel?'

'Oh, little things like pinching Olivia until she cries or pinning her down on the ground, slapping her really hard until she cries. It's like she enjoys watching suffering or pain, and she will pull Elly's ears, the little kelpie, until she yelps. We had to move Elly out with the farm crew. Livvy was so upset. She wanted Elly here today to show Jesse and Jedda. She misses playing with the dog.'

'And you say she's talking to herself?' asked Zena.

Lisa's brow furrowed as she looked across at Zena, concern clearly showing on her face as she looked out to the yard. She felt her protective instincts kick in. She could hear Billy's warning words about Polly.

'Yes, no one is there but Polly, yet she is having a conversation, and sometimes her voice is quite raised, as if she's arguing,' added Kate. 'When I do catch her talking, I interrupt, and say, "Who are you talking to, Polly?" But she'll just get up and walk away.'

'That is odd, and so awful. It's not natural behaviour for a fourteen year-year-old girl. Hormones or no,' said Zena.

'I know, I know. But Polly is not your average fourteen-year-old girl. I think because she shadows Tess it's like she's fourteen going on twenty! When I tell Tess about Polly's behaviour, she simply shrugs. Dave and I have sort of gotten used to how things are. But I have asked Tess to take Polly to see a doctor. She is so painfully thin, and of course there's all this unusual chatter I hear, but Tess becomes quite defensive and states there is nothing wrong with her girl. Polly was manageable up until the age of eight years, but now, it really has been six years of hell. Dave goes so red in the face I think he'll have a stroke. He's not one for confrontation, just bottles things up. He battles his blood pressure constantly, as do I.'

'What does Mitch say about all of this?' asked Lisa.

'When he is here, he focuses his attention on Olivia. Sadly, he will engage her in conversation but completely neglects Polly, who then gets jealous. Sometimes, when we're having dinner, Polly will suddenly throw down her fork or Tess will say something sarcastic, and it feels like the room is about to explode. Then Dave or I change the subject rapidly, like to the weather or sheep, so the focus is off Livvy. There is some rivalry between the two girls, but it comes from Polly. Sometimes, she just stomps off to her room. I have told Mitch to keep his comments or anger under control at the table, so we can all at least try to have a meal in peace. So, in a nutshell, he basically directs his attention to Olivia and tunes out the other two. But it gets under Tess's skin, and later, you can hear them arguing.'

'How very unpleasant, and you don't seem to get a break from it. Your nerves must be a mess,' said Zena.

Kate nodded, the weariness in her face showing. 'I'm terrified to leave, just for a break. Goodness knows what Tess or Polly would get up to, and I don't want to leave Olivia. Mind you, she does stand up to Tess.'

'I'm so lucky,' admitted Lisa. 'Zena takes the twins for a sleepover, which they just love, and it gives me a bit of a break, and of course, time with Billy without keeping one eye on them, or worse, them bursting into our bedroom in the morning.'

'That would never happen here,' said Kate solemnly. 'Love never entered into this union. Love never existed, nor will it ever make an appearance. Sometimes people thrown together grow together. Not in this case, I'm afraid. They sleep in separate bedrooms and have done so for a long time. I think Tess has her relationships, if you could call them that, in town, when she goes away to visit her mother in Walgett. I don't know what Mitch gets up to in terms of, well you know, his physical needs. He is still only young, thirty-three now.'

'What about music?' queried Zena. 'Do you think that would interest Polly? You know Alan and I don't play at the RSL anymore, but I could certainly try to teach her to play the piano. Jedda loves it when we get together for musical lessons. I'm happy to take them both on board. Polly may be reticent to muck up on me.'

At that moment, a piercing scream rang out from the backyard. Lisa had taught the children, as Alan and Zena had taught her, to only scream if you are in danger. Lisa knocked the chair over, moving so quickly, and was first down the back stairs.

Instant rage gripped her. Polly was straddled over Jedda, who was trying to push her off by flailing her fists, struggling to get up. Jesse was pulling at her Polly's hair. Olivia stood to the side crying.

'Get off my daughter!' Lisa commanded as she grabbed Polly and lifted her off Jedda.

The young teenage girl looked up at Lisa and sneered.

'Jedda, are you okay, my darling?' Lisa comforted as she helped her to her feet.

Jesse was about to have another go at Polly on the ground where she had sat down in a huff when Lisa grabbed his arm. 'Stop that, Jesse, that's enough.'

'She was trying to hurt Jedda, Mummy,' he wailed.

'It's alright now, just calm down,' said Lisa soothingly as the little boy wiped his face with his hands.

Polly spat on the ground as she got to her feet. 'I know who you lot are. You little black bastards, and I know who you are too.' She glared at Lisa. 'Boong lover. Stinking boong lover, that's what my mum says.'

Lisa felt the bile rise in her throat. What do you say to a teenage girl, hissing like a snake, ready to strike?

Kate and Zena watched, horrified, on the veranda.

'Polly, that's quite enough! Come inside and go to your room,' ordered Kate, who was clearly shaken and embarrassed.

The young girl stomped past the two women and slammed the back door.

Lisa went to Olivia, followed by Zena and Kate. 'Are you alright, Olivia?' asked Lisa.

'Yes, I was just very frightened. I didn't like what Polly was doing.' Her voice quivered with emotion. Lisa hugged her and reassured, 'Don't, be worrying now, Olivia, my Jedda is very tough.'

Kate took her youngest granddaughter's hand. 'Let's go inside, Livvy, and finish our cup of tea. Are you okay, Jedda? Jesse? I'm so sorry about Polly's behaviour towards you.' Kate's soothing voice washed over them.

'Yes, Mrs Kate, we're fine. But she better not hurt my Jedda again.' Jesse took Jedda's hand, following Kate and Zena back into the kitchen, with Lisa behind them.

As soon as they sat down, Kate broke down into tears. Zena put a comforting arm around her. 'It's all good, Kate, they're just kids,' Zena said. But in the back of her mind, she knew there was more to it. The spitefulness and venom they'd just witnessed from Polly, as well as the language, was not normal.

A tiny, soft voice suddenly broke the conversation. 'Is Nanny alright?' asked Olivia, watching Kate sob.

'Yes, Livvy, Nanny is alright.' Kate dabbed her eyes.

'Come to our place, Olivia, next time,' Jesse said innocently. 'We have lots of animals and no fighting. We can go swim in the river. Daddy says rivers are like our blood. Arteries. And my daddy has lots of stories.'

'We'll help clear, Kate, and then head off. Don't worry about what happened here today. It will go no further, and as Jesse said, come over. Might do you good to get out with Olivia. Polly is welcome too, but somehow after today, I think you will get a no-thanks from that one,' said Zena.

Kate nodded. 'That would be lovely.'

Lisa looked at Kate and wondered what life would have been like for her if Billy had never returned to Woori and she had warmed to Mitch and married him. So many what-ifs in life, with opening and closing doors.

Kate looked drained as they drove away. Zena glanced in the rear-view mirror, where she saw the twins sitting closely together. 'I can't say too much, Lisa, as the walls have ears, if you know what I mean, but there is no doubt in my mind that there are big issues in the older Walker girl's head. It's not normal, that sort of behaviour. I think it goes beyond even growing up with parents who despise each other.'

'Yes, I remember you said that Tess had some sort of psychiatric condition,' said Lisa. 'And Tess herself has always been somewhat spiteful. I never knew what Mitch saw in her.'

'You have a good memory, Lisa. Tess has bi-polar disorder if my memory serves me correctly. You will have to tell Billy what happened before the chatterboxes relay it. They will tell the story bigger than Ben Hur, not that it wasn't horrible.'

'Yes, of course. I would never hide anything from him, especially this, but boy, did I get angry when I saw what was happening to Jedda. All these feelings came rushing in and my first instinct was to protect.'

'All mothers would have the same reaction, Lisa. Just protecting your cubs.'

FIVE

THE MEN RETURN

Billy's brown eyes flashed with anger when Lisa told him what had happened at Woodside.

'Where are dey now?' asked Billy as he took off his hat, reaching for a glass of water.

'Both outside, they're okay. Jedda was just a little put out that Polly had her down on the ground and was pinching her, but she was giving her a run for her money. Those little fists didn't stop, and Jesse was having a good go at Polly. I had to stop him from pulling her hair.'

Billy shook his head, trying to visualise. 'Lisa, I don't really want dem here at Wooribilly. I said your decision, but I get bad feelings. Bad feelings about da girl Polly.'

Lisa came to him, and Billy put his arms around her, kissing the top of her forehead.

'Billy want to protect you, Lisa, always, and my picaninnies.'

'Yes, I know, Billy, as do I.'

'Mebbe girl not right. Not right behaviour. She have da cold eyes. Not right, Billy feel it.'

'Please, Billy, no more talk of this. She is a young adolescent growing up in a rather loveless home, between her parents, anyway.' But deep down, Lisa knew he was onto something. When Lisa had first met Polly, she had been unnerved at the girl's intense gaze. Calculating.

'Anyway, dinner is being served about five-ish at the big house. Zena and Kate had a very interesting conversation about diversifying on the farm, but I will let Zena and Alan explain.'

◊

'Sounds good,' said Alan as dinner got underway. 'Actually, Dave has mentioned a few things about cattle and growing wheat but as I understand it, he has set this up already. Seems to be working well. I said I would look into it myself, but I haven't got around to it. Certainly, if we did diversify here, we may have to look at getting someone to assist. Billy and I can't do everything, and Jesse is way too young at this time. Maybe Kev would like to help rather than trying to get work all over the place. What are your thoughts, Billy?'

'Oh,' cried Lisa, interjecting. 'That would be wonderful! I have missed Ningali so much, and the children would adore her and Kev. They were too young to remember them when they worked here.'

"Next time Kev or Ningali call, try and get a number where I can reach them. I doubt he will have a permanent phone number. No fixed abode, probably the back of the ute,' Alan laughed.

The vision of them sleeping in the back of Kev's bright yellow ute when they first met flashed through Lisa's mind.

'He'll probably use the public box again, if he can find one not broken. But he is due for a call, especially as shearing is not that far away. Kev knows we usually do it about the same time every year. If he is coming or not coming, he always calls. Be great to have him here.'

'Good, that's settled. Whoever picks up the phone to Kev, try and get a contact number,' said Zena.

Alan looked across at Lisa. 'Heard there was a bit of a scuffle out at Woodside today, kid, but I understand you got it under control quickly.'

Lisa smiled. He still used that terminology, kid, even though she was a mother now, and thirty.

'It was very unpleasant, Alan, but as you said, no harm done, and we all managed it quickly. But I was shocked at Polly's unprovoked behaviour, and poor Kate looked so embarrassed,' said Lisa.

Alan nodded. 'I hear Polly is getting to be a real handful. Dave lets me know what's happening, and he says he's happy when he clears out with Mitch and they get on the road to buy stock. Feels guilty leaving Kate behind though. It would be a horrible situation.'

'Tess had been diagnosed with a mental illness, bi-polar, as a young girl, probably in her teens if I can recall. Her mother told me many moons ago. She took her to see specialists then,' added Zena.

'Do you think Polly has the same diagnosis?' asked Lisa. 'Would it make someone be deliberately spiteful and hurtful, because that's what I saw today?'

'I hear what you say, Lisa. Don't forget, I was there,' said Zena. 'It's hard to say if Polly does have the same condition, only a professional could tell you that. Perhaps it is a genetic thing, passed down from Tess.'

'Anyway, I hope Polly grows out of that cruelty. I feel sorry for her but then again, I don't. I was so annoyed with her when I saw my little Jedda in trouble,' said Lisa, as she looked across to Billy.

◇

The following day, Dave and Mitch arrived home late in the afternoon. Dave looked exhausted as he came into the house, followed by Mitch. Kate knew she would have to tell them both what had happened. She was unsure how Mitch would react. He was losing his patience very quickly with Polly's behaviour worsening.

Kate took a deep breath as she wiped her hands on her apron. 'Welcome home, you two. How did you go, a successful two weeks?'

'It was productive,' said Dave as he kissed her on the cheek. 'Sorry I didn't call last night, but we got back to the motel way too late. Didn't want to disturb you.'

'So much driving, Mum,' said Mitch, removing his hat. 'Queensland is huge, but we got some great stock and a few good bulls that will be transported down shortly.'

'You look tired, Mitch.' Kate had watched time, stress and the harsh sun begin to remove his boyish good looks. 'Dinner will be ready shortly, so why don't you both hop in the shower.'

'Is Tess home, and where is my Olivia?' asked Mitch as a squeal of delight hit the air.

'Daddy!' The little girl ran towards her father.

'I've missed you, baby girl. Have you been behaving yourself?' Mitch swept her up into his arms.

'Tess is not back yet,' said Kate, noting the look of relief on Mitch's face. 'As I said, she took off some two days after you men left. She said she was staying with her mother.'

Olivia was planting kisses on Mitch's cheek, her arms tightly around his neck.

'Yes,' smiled Olivia. 'And Lisa and the twins came over for morning tea yesterday and we had a good time. And then they was fighting with Polly, and then Jesse tried to pull Polly off, but his mummy Lisa, she pulled Polly off Jedda, and Polly, she was very, very angry.'

'What the devil has gone on, Kate?' asked Dave.

'It was just morning tea with Lisa, Zena and the twins,' said Kate. 'Polly, well, what can I say, Polly decided to have a bit of a scuffle with Jedda, and Lisa broke it up. Anyway, it was all resolved, and Lisa said next time it's a visit to their home.'

All eyes moved to the little girl whose head was cradled into Mitch's shoulder. Olivia lifted her head.

'Yes, Daddy,' said Olivia, rubbing her eyes. 'I want to go and see Jesse's animals and lots of other things Jedda and Jesse want to show me.'

Mitch's heart softened as his little girl spoke. He felt inward turmoil as memories from the past surfaced. The feelings he had suppressed for so long. He had stuffed up, badly, and it had changed the course of his life.

Silence filled the room.

'Where's Polly?' asked Mitch, looking around for his eldest daughter.

'Mitch, I will explain later, after dinner. Suffice to say, it was just a scuffle between Polly and Jedda, which Lisa quickly stopped. Olivia wasn't involved. Now please, both of you, go and shower and I will have dinner ready shortly.'

Mitch took off down the hallway and came to Polly's door. He knocked and entered, Polly looking up from the floor as he strode into the room. She turned away and looked at the book in front of her. Her room was the usual mess, clothes strewn everywhere, a half-eaten sandwich on the floor, a stale smell filling the air.

'What happened yesterday, Polly?' Mitch asked, his voice tight.

Polly did not respond and lay on the ground with her back to Mitch.

The heat began to spread across Mitch's face. 'Polly! Please turn around when I'm talking to you.'

The girl slowly turned over and stared at her father. 'Not a great deal. Why?' Her mocking smile was the last thing he wanted to see right now. How had he fathered such a child? God, she was a brat.

'Don't lie to me, Polly. I know what happened!' Mitch responded evenly.

'Well,' said Polly, pulling a face. 'Your boong-loving friend and her black kids were here, so I thought I would play rough. That Jedda was such a smarty pants and never stopped talking. She gave me the shits.'

Mitch stepped back. Polly sounded just like her mother. It was as though Tess was speaking. He shook his head and closed the door. *How did I produce that?*

After dinner, Dave retired early, and soft snoring filled the bedroom. As Kate came out to say goodnight to Mitch, he sat staring at the television.

'Can't sleep?' asked Kate.

'No, Mum. I'll just sit here a while.' Resignation moved across his features. Kate noted the glass of whisky in his hand. He had begun to drink heavily after the tragic death of his first baby boy. She knew he drank to forget about his sadness and his situation.

Mitch exhaled deeply and looked at his mother. 'Life can be such a mess, Mum.'

Kate didn't know how to answer. His eyes were tired and full of sadness.

'I should never have married her.' Mitch hunched his shoulders and took another sip of whisky.

'Look, son, we cannot go on like this.' Kate's voice rose slightly as she continued. 'All I'm saying is that if you probably show Tess and Polly just a bit more attention, it may improve things. Just a suggestion, Mitch. Think about it. More bees are caught with honey. A few things to consider, for the benefit of your own children. Goodnight, son.'

Mitch sighed and closed his eyes. Love, frustration and sadness whirled in his mind. He had resigned himself to the fact that his life would always be like it was now.

SIX

OUT OF CONTROL

A florid orange hue came slipping through Mitch's bedroom as a new day began. He had been awake for some time and had run through his head so many times the mistakes he'd made in life. He cringed when he thought of the abuse that Lisa had suffered and how he had been so foolish to investigate and expose her past. He knew his mother was right. He did not want to make mistakes with his children. The fact that Polly was chattering away to herself was an indicator she needed professional help.

A transport truck pulled up late afternoon. Dave had invited Alan to come and see the new cattle. Mitch and the farm crew were unloading when Alan pulled up.

Alan looked at the stock admiringly. 'Nice cattle, Dave,' he commented as one by one they were loaded off the truck. 'The bulls are in good nick too.'

'Yeah, we did a lot of driving to get these. You think New South Wales is big, but when you get to Queensland's outback, that's another ball game. Anyhow, let's take a drive, and I'll show you the wheat crops,' said Dave as Alan hopped into the Land Rover. 'See you later, Mitch. We'll be out for a couple of hours.'

'Sure thing, Dad.' Mitch stood chatting to the transport driver then turned towards the sound of a car. In a swirl of red dust, he saw Kate's car approaching rapidly. His gut instinct told him something was not right. His first thought was of Olivia.

Kate's car came to a sudden halt, and Mitch leaned into the car window. 'What's the hurry, Mum?'

'I just took a call from Tess.'

Mitch winced. This would only be trouble. He so wished Tess would just disappear.

'What is it now?' He waited for the news.

'There's been an accident, not bad, but she hit a pole last night and the car is undriveable. She wants to come home.'

'An accident? Why was she out at night?' Mitch rolled his eyes. 'So, what am I supposed to do?'

'You need to go and pick her up,' said Kate as she watched her son stomp away, kick the dirt and then come back to the car.

His annoyance was clearly visible. 'I can see how frustrated you are. I don't know why she was driving at night. Who knows. But all she said is that she wants to come home. So, leave our crew to finish up here and go call her. Just let her know you're on your way.'

'I'm not her taxi, Mum.' Mitch stood with his arms across his chest, looking at the ground and waiting for his mind to make a decision. 'Okay, I'll go to the house and clean up, then go and get her,' he said, hopping onto his motorbike.

Kate watched her son roar off towards the house, the red dust billowing behind him.

◊

Tess was on her fourth beer by the time Mitch pulled up. The cul-de-sac looked deserted. The house to the left was abandoned with windows broken, obviously shattered by stones that had been thrown. There were no other houses, just vacant land. No wonder Mrs Dunphy got this dump cheap.

Mrs Dunphy had closed her haberdashery store a few years ago. He had not been to the house for many years and was dismayed at the exterior. Fences were falling down, and the garden was overgrown. The screen door mesh had holes, which the flies quickly found. He knew instantly, despite the turmoil at home with Tess, he had made the right decision. He would never let Tess leave and subject his girls to this shit hole. He would grin and bear it with Tess, although the grinning had long since gone.

As Mitch knocked on the front door, Tess's voice rang out. 'Come in, dearest husband. Mum hasn't seen you for ages. Isn't that right, Mum?' Her mocking laughter made his skin crawl.

Mitch stepped in and a look of disgust crossed his face. *My wife. Beer in one hand, cigarette in the other.*

'Hello, Mrs Dunphy.' It felt like he was stepping into a dark and odorous cave, a blend of tobacco and beer. Despondency dripped down the walls like melting ice.

'Mitch,' Mrs Dunphy's voice croaked.

He was taken aback at her appearance. She had always been on the rounder side, as his mother would say, but now she was grossly obese. It looked like she had not bathed for days, her clothing had food stains and her grey, unkempt hair hung down to her shoulders. She also looked well acquainted with a beer can.

Tess was leaning against the kitchen sink, her back pressing into it, almost steadying her.

'She's on the drink,' said Mrs Dunphy gleefully. 'Here's to you, Mitch.' She raised the beer can into the air.

'Yes, I can see that. What's new?' He just wanted to get out of there. 'You've obviously joined in too. Beer o'clock. Another frothy chops, Tess?'

Tess's eyes glowered at his remarks. She burped loudly. 'Yes, nothing like an icy cold beer and a fag. Can't smoke at Woodside now, can we? Everyone gets upset.' She took a deliberate long drag of the cigarette and blew the smoke up into the air.

Mitch took a deep breath. Patience. But he so wanted to just leave her there.

'Come on, get your bags, Tess, we're going. I have work to do. You can tell me what happened last night on the way home.' He tipped his hat to Mrs Dunphy as Tess moved to pick up her bags near the hallway.

'See you, Mum, and thanks for the visit. At least I got to have some fun,' she laughed.

Tess followed Mitch to the car. It was going to be a long ride home.

Mitch finally spoke. 'So, as I'm paying for the car repairs, would you like to tell me what happened?'

Tess had her feet up on the dashboard, her jaw working rapidly, chewing gum. She knew Mitch hated the smell of cigarette smoke.

'I went out, that's all, to see some friends, and on the way home I was sleepy. The next thing I knew, I hit a pole. Must have dozed off.'

Just my luck, Mitch thought. *Most people who hit a pole don't live to tell the tale.* But then he stopped himself. As much as he didn't like or respect Tess, she was still the mother of his children.

'You were pissed, weren't you? Well, next time you do this, you can pay for your own car repairs. You should not drink and drive, Tess!'

'How the hell am I supposed to pay for my own repairs? You have all the money, not me!'

'Yeah, and don't I know that! You've always got your hand out. Tess, when are you going to stop this behaviour?'

'Oh, stuff you. That's all you care about, Mitch. Money, money, money, and, oh yes, our little Livvy. You don't care about Polly or me. You don't come near either of us! You're the one who got me up the duff, now you have to support me! And do you think I don't know what you're up to? Ha!' Tess snorted.

Stony silence. Tess knew how to get Mitch rattled.

'Don't want to answer, cat got your tongue?' Tess scowled. 'You and your mother are trying to take my girls from me, aren't you?

Olivia already thinks Kate is more important than me. She prefers her company to mine!'

'Well, just for the record, Kate organised lunch with Lisa and her kids, and Polly messed that up by scrapping with one of the twins,' Mitch retorted.

'What are you talking about?'

'Next door, they had some sort of morning tea,' Mitch replied.

Tess started laughing. 'So, what are you telling me, Mitch?'

He rolled his eyes. 'Polly couldn't even behave. She started a fight, end of story, and stop chewing that damn gum.'

'Getting on your nerves, am I?' Tess harrumphed. 'Well, why don't you come near me? You want sex. I know you do. So do I. Happy to oblige there.'

'Now why would I come near you? You stink of cigarette smoke. And leave Olivia and my mother out of this!' said Mitch, the tension building.

'I can tell you, Mr Smart Arse, there are men that find me, well, attractive. Say I've got a hot bod. Kept myself in shape.' Tess pouted her lips and pushed her breasts up.

'Shut up, Tess. You were always the town bike. I just got saddled with the last ride.'

'Bastard! You are such a bastard, Mitch. Coming around when your balls ached. I'm telling you, Mr Walker, you're not as good in the sack as you think you are! The blokes are better in town. Why do you think I leave you and go there, whoring around as you put it. I do it just to put some excitement in my mundane life! At least the blokes tell me I'm beautiful and want more.'

Mitch glowered. 'That's just pork talk. Men just say that to get in-to your knickers. You're so dumb, you believe them.' He didn't fancy Tess anymore but he did not want to hear about her whoring around with other men.

'You know nothing, Mitch Walker. At least they can perform.'

'Shut up, Tess, for fuck's sake!' Mitch's hand slammed down on the steering wheel.

'Don't you think I know that you're getting your little bit of fluff on the side? I knew it from day one. When you wouldn't come near me. I knew you just had to be going somewhere to get it. You can't do without it. That's where we're the same. You can't go without it, and neither can I. I'm still young,' Tess yelled.

Mitch remained silent and knew what she had just said was right. He had not fancied Tess for so many years but was this going to be his life now. He had sought sex with different women over the years but he longed for a normal and loving relationship, to feel the closeness of a woman he loved.

'And you shouldn't hire blokes that aren't bad looking either. I've had a few.' Tess's laugh filled the car. 'That bloke, Will, the stockman who taught me and Polly to ride, he was bloody terrific. You all thought he was sooo patient teaching me. We had fun. I was sorry to see him go. So, they can't all be wrong.'

His mind grappled with the thought that his workers had been screwing his wife. *A damn laughing stock, I am.*

She watched his face twitch and knew it hit him right where she wanted it. She so enjoyed getting under his skin.

Mitch gritted his teeth. 'You had better not drag your arse home after these visits to your mother and tell me you're pregnant, Tess. I'm not going to raise anything that grows out of you, ever again. Ever!'

No more words were spoken on the drive home. An intense despair filled Mitch, but all he could think of was protecting his children from this woman. He would not allow Olivia or Polly to live in the rat hole he had just come from.

He looked across at Tess, whose head had lolled back, mouth open, snoring loudly. Mitch shuddered. *How do people spiral into such depravity? And God help me, how do I keep going without murdering her?*

SEVEN

A FATHER'S LOVE

Lisa stretched and welcomed the day. She was so happy. Her's and Billy's physical intimacy last night was sensual and powerful. They moved as one when making love, breathing in each other. Getting out of bed, she could hear everyone in the kitchen chattering. The clock on the bedside table said it was just before six. When Lisa had packed their bags last night, she was just as excited as the children. She looked forward to seeing her father and brother. No doubt the twins had stirred with the first light. Jedda had a particular fascination for the sunrise and its colours as the rays spilled into her room of a morning.

'It's the angels, Mummy, they come into my room,' she would say. Lisa wondered if the spirits surrounded her girl.

Lisa's hand reached up to the bush necklace Billy had given her so long ago, for her birthday, and smiled. The quartz stones Burnu had given her lay amongst her other necklaces. The tenderness and love Billy had given her had restored her faith from the moment she met him. He was so gentle and endlessly patient.

As she came into the kitchen, Billy was sitting with the twins, buttering toast. Lisa came up behind him and slipped her arms around his shoulders, kissing the side of his face.

The twins giggled. 'Kissing, kissing, always kissing,' sing-songed Jedda.

'That's because Mummy loves Daddy, so you have to kiss then,' said Jesse, making a kissing pout with his mouth.

'Yes, my darlings, Mummy does love Daddy, and when you grow up, you will also find someone to love,' Lisa said softly.

'I leave dem to you, my grasshopper.' Billy stood to leave.

The twins were always highly amused when he called her his grasshopper. He had told them the story behind the nickname, and Jesse would squat down on the ground watching the grasshoppers intently as they twitched their back legs. He would pick one up and show Jedda when he caught one.

Billy grabbed his black hat. 'Have to meet Alan. Careful on da roads. Call me when you get there. Say hello to Mark and Des.' He reached for Lisa and held her closely. He too, remembered last night. He looked deeply into her eyes and then his lips softly met hers, lingering, tasting her once again.

The twins watched intently. 'You'd best go then, before...' Lisa said mischievously.

Billy pulled back and smiled. He could so easily have swooped her up and taken her back to the bedroom.

'Be good, look after my grasshopper.' Billy glanced at the twins.

Lisa blew him a kiss. 'See you when we get back. Love you.'

Just before they left, Lisa dialled Des's number. 'Hi Dad, how are you? We're looking forward to seeing you and Mark.'

'Battling on, Lisa, that's all a bloke can do,' answered Des.

Lisa thought he sounded frail, his voice older in tone. 'The twins are so excited. I just thought we'd let you know that we're about to leave. Is there anything you want picked up? Fruit, bread, milk... anything?'

'Nah, it's all good. Mark has everything here.'

'Okay, then we shall see you in about eight hours, probably a bit more for toilet stops,' said Lisa, looking at the kitchen clock.

Des laughed. 'Okay, I shall expect you late afternoon.'

'Something like that, Dad. Make sure you have your ear plugs handy. They're getting to be a noisy handful, like chattering birds.'

'Can't wait, Lisa, look forward to it,' said Des as he hung up the phone.

Lisa arrived just after 5:00 p.m., the twins sleeping most of the way. As she pulled into the driveway, she looked at the pretty weatherboard cottage. The exterior was duck-egg blue and the window frames white. Des was obviously enjoying the garden with Mark's assistance. There were big, established trees everywhere. It was such a stark contrast to the house she'd grown up in. The old Fibro Majestic. Lisa was so glad her father had made the decision to move. Agnes's life insurance policy helped cover the purchase of the new home. It gave Lisa wry amusement. Alan said the old girl would be rolling over in her grave. Her death had given joy and a new lease of life for everyone.

When the engine stopped, Jesse was the first to wake, taking in his surroundings. Mark and Des had come outside upon hearing the car's engine.

'Hey, sis,' Mark said as he came to help her carry everything in.

'Hey, back.' She warmly hugged her brother.

'Hello, Uncle Mark,' shouted Jesse, trying to undo his seat belt. Mark leaned in and unbuckled both children. Jedda opened her eyes and yawned.

'You're a sleepy head, little wild goose, aren't you,' smiled Mark.

Lisa shook her head. 'Jedda was up early, but don't worry, she'll make up for it.'

The children ran towards Des and hugged him. 'Hello, Des,' yelled Jedda, now wide awake.

'Hello, little wild goose.' He looked at Jedda endearingly.

Lisa lightly kissed her father's cheek. The frailty of his voice on the phone matched his physical appearance. He was now completely grey, and his once-strong frame sagged.

As Mark led the way, the children raced inside. No sooner had they sat down when Jedda asked, 'Can we go outside and see your chooks?'

'Of course you can.'

'You have to come too,' said Jedda dragging at Des's arm.

'Jedda, Des may like to just sit a while,' cautioned Lisa, frowning.

'It's okay, I love to show them around.' Des slowly got to his feet.

The backyard was like a fairy garden to them. There were tall bird feeders, chooks, a cubby house, a swing from a large Camphor Laurel tree, winding paths through the gardens and a big veggie and orchard garden. Des happily pushed the twins one by one on the swing, until he could do no more, and then explained the veggie process and how things were grown. He plucked a carrot out from the dirt and held it up, saying food was from the dirt to the table.

Lisa turned her attention to her brother. 'How are things, Mark? Dad seems to be moving slower and he's lost a lot of weight.'

'Yes, he's really slowed down, and it's not good news. He saw a specialist a week ago, his usual urologist, and the cancer has spread to the liver and through his bones. It's an aggressive cancer, and there's nothing we can do now.' Mark's voice was heavy with sadness.

Lisa felt the tears well up. 'Nothing we can do?' Her voice faltered.

'I'm afraid not. It's a time thing now.' Mark caught his breath.

Lisa put her head in her hands and cried. 'Does he want me to know?'

'I'm sure he'll tell you in his own time, but for now, let's live in the moment and enjoy this week.'

Lisa wiped her eyes. 'Yes, you're absolutely right. I just think of all those wasted years, anger, hostility, alcohol, just so many things. And then I look at this. It's such... such a contrast.'

'I know, I lived there too, remember,' Mark said softly.

Lisa wiped her eyes and was all business. 'Okay, so what can I do, maybe help get dinner? Although those smells tell me you're well prepared.' She sniffed the air.

'Just a roast, Dad's favourite. I wonder how you feel about all of us catching a movie tomorrow. *E.T.* is playing at the Bowral cinema. I thought it would be great for all of us to be together and then have lunch somewhere, maybe even drive to Berrima, let them see the old jail.'

'Oh, that sounds fab, and I'm sure the kids would be delighted. I've read a few reviews about that movie. Creatures from outer space. Jesse will love that.' She changed the subject. 'How are you going at Fernhope?'

'It's wonderful, such a fabulous school, and they are so into making girls independent and achieving their dreams, while showing them the world in all its facets: art, literature, sport, you name it. It would be good for Jedda. She would thrive, and I could teach her French! I'm looking forward to giving you the guided tour if you're interested. I'm so glad I took a week off work. I really think you can do no better with that school for Jedda.'

'Sounds great. But I'll have to talk to Billy about education.' Lisa got up and looked out the back door. Des was sitting on a bench garden seat, a child either side. He was telling them a story and holding a potato. Perhaps a good Irish story about the potato famine?

'I'll put their bags in the bedroom and freshen up,' said Lisa.

As they sat around the table later, Lisa compared the easiness and love in the room to the home of her youth. Des drank in the vitality and energy of the twins, and Mark was highly animated when speaking French to them. Their attempts to sound the same were hilarious. It was a far cry from her childhood.

The night was drawing to a close, and the twins looked tired. 'It's just after nine. I'll put them to bed, make a quick call to Billy and be back.'

Jedda and Jesse kissed Des and Mark goodnight as they followed Lisa to their room. 'Goodnight, my sleeping angels.' She turned out the light and closed the door, leaving it slightly ajar.

Now for one more angel. Lisa stood in the hallway and dialled. Billy picked up almost immediately.

'Hello, darling, just checking in. We've finished dinner and it's not long for bed now. Best wishes from Mark and Des.'

'Grasshopper, da bed empty without you. Be safe, Billy misses you.'

'Me too, my darling, sweet dreams. I'll be home soon.'

Des looked up as Lisa came into the room. 'All good?'

'Yes, as I said, he was already in bed. Physical work is like a wonderful sleeping pill.'

Des nodded. 'Lisa.' He took her hand as she sat down. 'I know Mark has already probably told you, but my cancer has spread. It's very aggressive and has gone into the liver and my bones. The doctors tell me perhaps two to six months.'

'Oh my God, no.' The tears sprang to Lisa's eyes.

'It's okay, we all have our time, but our time in this world is limited. I am so happy that the past eight years have been perfect. How it should have been. I kick myself, really, for being such a fool earlier in my life.'

'Dad, please don't. I don't want to go back there. Remember what we said, we cannot change what's happened. Just try and go forward.'

Lisa looked across at Mark and saw him fighting tears.

'Anyway, I just wanted to tell you, as you live a good distance away and if anything happens to me, know that I am so truly sorry and that I love you.'

'Oh, Dad.' Lisa's tears turned into heaving sobs, her head dropping between her hands. The heaviness of his impending death had entered her heart, tearing it a little.

Mark went to her side. 'It's alright, Lisa. Dad wanted to tell you so we could have this special week together.'

Lisa wiped her eyes. 'Sorry, Dad, I knew you were sick, but this is just a shock.'

Des stood up and came to her. 'Lisa, my beautiful daughter, and I say that proudly. After all the mistakes I've made, life is still a wonderful thing, and my life has been enriched by you, Mark, Billy and the twins. When I'm gone, please don't be sad. Just think of me fondly.'

Des kissed her forehead. 'I'll say goodnight now. I look forward to what Mark has planned for tomorrow. The movie sounds good as do the few other things on the itinerary this week.'

When he left the room Mark and Lisa held each other. 'It's okay, sis, don't cry. Be strong now, even though it's a shock. But he's a happy man. Come on, time for bed. It's going to be a big week.'

When Lisa pulled the covers over her, she ached for Billy as she buried her head in the pillow. Death was so final. She wanted to keep her father longer on this earth. She had only just found him.

◊

As they entered the cinema the following day, the twins carried all the treats they wanted, from huge paper cups of buttered popcorn to choc tops. They looked like any other family, just out enjoying a movie, but Lisa's heart was heavy. This may be the last time they were all together.

They visited the Berrima Jail and were fascinated by the cells where prisoners were kept. Des took them to Lake Alexandra Reserve and the beautiful waterfalls in the highlands. Everyone could not believe how much water surrounded them, but the highlight was the trip to Kangaroo Valley, a neighbouring suburb, and the kayaks they hired to paddle down the river. Jesse and Jedda now wanted one for the river at Woori.

The following day, Mark arranged to take Lisa and Jedda to Fernhope. 'Do you want to come, Des?' asked Mark.

'No, you lot have worn me out, and I'm happy to take it easy today with Jesse,' replied Des.

Lisa felt so guilty leaving him. 'Look after Des, won't you, Jesse. We won't be long, maybe a couple of hours.'

'We'll be fine,' reassured Des.

'I can look after Des. You don't worry, Mummy,' Jesse said proudly.

Driving into Fernhope, it was so impressive. Lisa loved that their motto was to make a meaningful contribution to the world. As they wandered the grounds, Lisa looked at all the young students and couldn't wait for Jedda to socialise, learn and grow.

'What do you think, Jedda?' asked Lisa.

'It's so big with so many girls, Mummy. I'll make lots of friends.'

'They have a rich culture of musical excellence, Lisa. They have practice rooms and rooms for rehearsal and performance. I know you said Jedda loves to sing, but they also teach the girls how to play instruments from orchestral to contemporary.'

'Sounds wonderful, and Jedda has a lovely natural voice. Aunty practices with her, which has been great.'

'They really seem to support the development of a girl's character to embrace challenges, physically, mentally and spiritually. I think she would do well here, Lisa.'

As they drove home, Lisa couldn't wait to tell Billy what a fabulous place this was for an education. 'What do you think, Jedda?' Is this something you would like to try? It means leaving us, but then you would be home for holidays.'

'I think I would really like it, even though I would miss home.'

'And you can see Uncle Mark every day if he's there. It's his school, Jedda, so it's lucky that you will have your uncle close by.'

Jedda nodded her head vigorously.

'Great,' said Lisa. 'All sorted. Now for Jesse. I want my children to have the education I never had, Mark, and to be nurtured along the way by these wonderful mentors, and one of them just happens to be my brother!'

Mark grinned. 'You could try Orange Ag for Jesse. They do wonders with boys from a rural background.'

'I'll look into it, but I just know Jesse will be so stubborn if I try to send him away. He is a mini-Billy now and just wants to emulate his father. But perhaps if I do the same with Jesse, that is, take him to the school, he may have a change of heart.'

'Great idea, and take Billy too, even Alan and Zena. It may make him feel more comfortable if you are all with him.'

A few days later they were packing to head back to Woori. As Mark and Des carried their bags to the car, Lisa felt great sorrow. Would this be the last time she would see her father on this earth?

'Goodbye, Dad. I love you. I'll talk to you soon.' She kissed him on the cheek and held him tightly. 'Bro, give me a hug.' As she leaned into Mark, she whispered, 'Please look after him and call me if anything goes wrong. I'll be down in a flash.'

To her children, she said, 'Okay, you two, time to hit the road,' The twins rushed to give butterfly kisses to Des and Mark and then scooted into the back seat.

Lisa honked the horn as she reversed, and her heart felt like it was shattering into a thousand pieces as they waved goodbye. *Keep it together, Lisa.* She felt like she would open up any moment. *Hold back your tears.*

When they hit the road, Lisa remembered what Billy said about death. A person's soul or spirit continues on after our physical form has passed through death. *Goodbye, Dad. I hope next time your soul will be restored and your next life peaceful.*

EIGHT

EMU IN THE SKY

Lisa had wanted to stay longer with her father but it wasn't school holidays. She was insistent that the twins never miss School of the Air and she worried about Billy. Not that he couldn't cope on his own, it was just that she wanted to be with him. Always. Every day apart was a day she could never get back.

By the time they got back to Woori, it was just on nightfall. She had stopped at Bathurst for lunch and then kept going. She wanted to get through all the gates before dark. The feral pigs were always about when the sun went down, and the big boars were a worry as they were increasing in numbers. They were dangerous and aggressive, and Alan had repeatedly told Lisa they would not hesitate to attack. She took a deep breath, scanned the area before getting out and steadily opened each gate.

When she came through the last gate, she was relieved when she saw all the lights on. Billy.

'Wake up, you two, we're home,' she roused, feeling her own exhaustion creeping in. Billy was already walking towards the car as she pulled up at the gate to the house.

'Grasshopper.'

Lisa hugged him warmly.

'All good?' he asked as his children yawned and rubbed their eyes. Billy opened the back door and began to unbuckle their belts.

'All good, just tired, but Dad is not well, not well at all. I may have to go back down there and in a hurry.'

'Why?' asked Billy.

Lisa's bottom lip trembled. 'The cancer has spread and the doctors give him two to six months.'

He took her into his arms and just held her. He could feel her heart beating rapidly.

'Come in, you tired, Lisa, and so are dey. Come, you two,' said Billy, watching them as they clambered out. 'Follow Mummy, I bring da bags.'

After the twins were in bed, she made her way to her room and closed the bedroom door. Billy was waiting for her. Lisa came towards him. 'Lift your arms,' he whispered as he gently pulled off her T-shirt. He traced kisses down to her breasts. Lisa unzipped her jeans and stepped out of them. Billy did the same and then he picked her up and carried her to the shower. They stood under the steam, the water trickling over their bodies as Billy sponged Lisa's body.

He breathed into her ear, 'Billy take some pain away.' He took his time, moving the soapy sponge over every part of her body until Lisa felt the tension slide out of her.

As they lay in bed, Billy traced his fingers over her body. His voice was low and husky, and Lisa closed her eyes, listening to him.

'Lisa and Billy, dey young lovers who played down at da river banks. In dat river, a spirit lived. He watch dem lovers. He too fell in love with Lisa, and he wanted her for himself. He cast da spell and turned her into da flower of da river. Billy so sad, he cry and look for his Lisa every day down by da river. The spirit saw Billy so sad and turned him into da bulrush so dey close together. When da wind blows da bullrush, it hold hands with da river flower. Lisa and Billy always together.' By the time he had finished, she was sleeping peacefully.

When Lisa woke the next morning, the house was silent, and Billy was gone. She had slept so well, and the twins were still asleep. Lisa threw on her dressing gown and padded out to the kitchen, grabbing the jug for her first cup of tea. It was good to be home as she sat on the veranda and looked across the vast plains.

In the distance was that familiar figure. Black hat, black horse, galloping towards the house, the red dust billowing behind. Lisa's heart skipped a beat. *My Billy.* He seemed to be carrying something in a little hessian bag, and a big grin spread across his face as he pulled up and swung his legs off Jed.

'Billy got da present.' He held up the bag, the object inside clearly struggling to get out.

'Yes, I can see that, but what is it?' asked Lisa, somewhat apprehensive. 'Please tell me it's not a baby snake.'

'It da baby emu. Dey gonna love this.'

'A baby emu? Billy where did you find it? The twins are still asleep. I'll go wake them. But where did the baby emu come from and where are you going to keep it?'

'Grasshopper, you gotta lot of questions.' Billy put the bag gently down and disappeared, returning a short time later carrying a large, old wire crate.

'Jesse is just splashing his face,' said Lisa, reappearing. 'Oh, that's perfect,' she said, looking at the crate. 'But little emus turn into big emus, so the bird will get way too big for that crate, Billy. You know they get to about six feet.' Billy lifted the struggling baby emu out of the sack and placed it in the cage.

'His mother, she just lay down dead, mebbe snake. But she go to the sky now.'

'They are so cute,' said Lisa, looking at the little brown- and white-striped chick, its fluffy head ducking in and out of the bars. She loved the emus and remembered when she first came to Woori it was fascinating to watch them chase the car. Her thoughts suddenly drifted to Binna. The special ceremony, just the two of them, when Binna showed her some glass stones. Emu eyes, she called sky charms. Lisa could see the memory so clearly as she sat with the old lady. *Powerful medicine. Good for da storms in your life.*

When Jesse appeared on the veranda, he squealed with excitement, jumping up and down. A tiny baby emu chick sat in the crate, looking up at Jesse as he poked his fingers through the wire, gently pecking them, much to his delight. Jedda came out shortly after and gasped when she saw what was in the cage.

'It's a baby, Mummy. I want to hold it. She's so fluffy.' Jedda squatted, looking enamoured at the baby chick who cheeped and chirped, making the twins giggle.

'How do we know if it's a boy or a girl chick?' queried Lisa.

'Have to wait, Lisa. Mebbe in twelve months. Da girls, dey make a different noise. Da boys have different feather pattern. Like da bullseye. Da girls speckly. But dem girls dey chase da boys in mating season.'

'What's mating season?' asked Jedda.

'Now you've opened a can of worms, Billy,' Lisa laughed. 'May be time to have a little talk to them.'

Billy squatted down with twins. 'I think dis one maybe a boy. He have da bullseye, see look here.' He put his finger through the wire cage and scratched the chick's head. 'Da boys tamer than da girls and emus likem da water. Billy have to make da bath for him.'

'A bath?' asked Jedda, shrieking excitedly.

'Yeah, da emus love da water, like you and me. Dey good swimmers, see dem in da rivers. Lucky we still got dis big bird. My mob tell me about the Great Emu War. Emus killed all the time.'

'Oh God, why would anyone want to kill an emu?' asked Lisa.

'Da emus destroy da crops, long time ago. Government get angry as emus eating all da wheat. So dey get da soldiers dey hired to come and shoot da emu. Many birds. Bring in da machine guns. Dey kill mebbe hundred emus a week and lotsa emus get injured. Leave dem to die. Called Great Emu War.'

'That makes me so sad. What will we feed this little chick?' asked Lisa.

'Get da dog kibble, some corn, dey like fruit too.' Billy scratched his chin trying to remember. 'Yah and da grapes and pineapple.'

'Great, I'll get something together then,' said Lisa. 'Maybe he can stay in this cage for a few days, but the Chook Hilton is so big that he can live there.'

Billy grinned. 'Good idea, grasshopper.' Lisa had asked for the chicken run to be built on the larger side. She didn't like chickens being in tight spaces and wanted them to roam, letting them out to scratch around in the dirt. Another advantage to not having a dog inside the compound; otherwise, there would be only the remnants of chooks.

He turned to his boy. 'Jesse,' said Billy, taking his hand. 'Da Aboriginal emu tracks very magical and protective.' He drew the tracks in the dirt. 'He be your talisman. Emu totem meaning have deep and powerful spiritual guidance. Dey the second largest bird in da whole world. Run fast. Fast as a car. Mebbe 48–50 kilometres on da flat road.

'What's a talisman, Daddy?' asked Jesse.

'Mmm, like a stone or mebbe a ring, but you have da emu as talisman. Dat talisman have magic powers and bring good luck. Strengthen Jesse's powers. I show you da emu in da sky tonight,' said Billy.

Jedda poked Jesse. 'There's no emu in the sky.'

'There is.' Lisa smiled, coming to stand next to Billy. 'Daddy showed me one night, so we will point the emu out in the night sky. You already know the Southern Cross, so we'll add this to your astronomy lesson. The emu in the sky is very close to the Southern Cross.'

'What shall we call him?' asked Jesse.

Lisa pondered and looked at Billy. 'Well, emu spelled backwards is Ume.'

Jedda shrieked, 'Ume! Ume!'

Da mob from Yuwaalaraay nations call da bird Dhinawan. Mean Emu. I'm a Dhinawan,' added Billy.

Jedda giggled. 'You're not an emu!'

'No, but da Dhinawan he always take the role of da father, mother, teacher and provider. Dat's me.' Billy grinned.

Later that day, after dinner, the twins followed Lisa and Billy out into the yard. Lisa lay a rug down on the ground and they lay on their backs looking at the stars. 'Mebbe hard to see. Best time is June, your birth month,' Billy explained, looking at the twins.

'That's soon,' said Jedda.

'April, May, she chasing her mate. Den early June/July is da laying season and in da night sky a huge dark shape in da form of da emu appears. I show you. You can see da head just under da Southern Cross and da body throughout Milky Way. This is da sign in da night sky to tell my peoples and all da mobs it's time to go collect da emu eggs for food. We don't take all da eggs, just a few. Gotta leave some for da next generation.'

Lisa smiled. 'Story time. Come. You can't be chattering or you'll miss it.'

Billy pointed to the sky. 'Da sun, moon, da stars and all da planets are all animals and things from here, down here that once were amongst us. So, dat is da Milky Way and dat Southern Cross.' He pointed to the left. 'So, you go to da left side of our Southern Cross and you see a dark oval shape. Dat head of emu with her beak pointing downwards. You see da neck, it stretches out, and da body and legs stretch across da skies.'

'I think I see it, Daddy,' yelled Jedda.

'Me too,' said Jesse, his eyes fixated on the starry sky.

'And now, I tell a story and then to bed. It's da story about a blind man and da emu.'

Lisa lay next to Billy as she cradled her daughter, while Jesse snuggled against his father. *Does it get any better?* she thought.

'Da blind man live in his camp in da bush with his wife. He send her out every day to collect da emu eggs. She try very hard to please him but blind man always complain. He say eggs too small and get angry. One day, she go out looking for eggs and came across da tracks of a very big emu. She thought da big bird lay da big eggs, so she follow da tracks. She find a big bird on da nest, so she wanted big eggs. She throw da stones at da emu but dat bird, he not scared and he attack her and kill her. Her husband, he now very hungry so he try to find her but along da way he find berries from da bushes. He ate da berries and dey make him see again, so he pick up his spear and found her body at da emu nest. He spear da emu and its spirit go into the Milky Way. Dat emu in da sky.'

'Can we hear some more, Daddy?' asked Jesse.

'Time for bed,' interrupted Lisa. 'But I want to catch a bit more of this spectacular show.' She looked up at the stars.

'I take dem,' said Billy. 'Come on you two, and we check on Mr Ume.'

When Billy returned, Lisa was curled up on her side. 'All good?' she asked as Billy lay down next to her.

'Twins and Ume asleep.' He reached out for her. 'Are you sure, absolutely sure?' Lisa began to unbutton his shirt. Billy's skin glistened in the dark as the desire and need for each other enveloped them.

'You are so beautiful, husband of mine.' Lisa's hands speared through the thickness of his thick dark hair, feeling his arousal as her legs wrapped around him. So deeply in love, their bodies entwined under a canopy of stars.

'Billy want to kiss every soft place of you,' he whispered as they made love in the darkness.

NINE

UME

The little emu chick was moved to the Chook Hilton, with high fences and a long run. Ume kept them all amused, and he grew quickly, his chirping and cheeping keeping them awake. Lisa was glad she had asked for the initial chook shed to be built on the larger side. It was serving Ume well. Billy and Alan had dragged an old cement tub into the run and filled it with water. The chick constantly played in the water.

Jesse was drawn to the creatures of nature. Ume would roam free and wander around the compound through the day, scratching in the dirt and occasionally chasing the children. Lisa was sure Zena could hear their raucous squealing all the way down to the big house. He was very tame, extremely inquisitive and would come up the back stairs to look through the screen door. For now, he was the family pet and followed Jesse everywhere. When Lisa looked into Ume's eyes, Lisa could hear Binna chanting, 'Da sky charms.'

Six weeks had passed since the eventful day at Woodside. Lisa wondered when Olivia would want to come over. Children never forget anything and was in no doubt that she would be reminding Kate, just like Jesse and Jedda. 'When can we go to Olivia's place? When can Olivia come here?' they continually asked.

After School of the Air one morning, they went up to see Zena, who had lunch prepared. 'Come in, it's just salad sandwiches,' said Zena as everyone sat down. 'Had a call from Kate about an hour ago.'

'Let me guess. Olivia has been asking when she can come here?'

'Yes,' Zena affirmed. 'Just wanted to run it by you before I make any suggestions to Kate.'

Lisa looked at the twins. 'Olivia wants to come over to Woori.'

They both stopped eating and looked at each other, almost in unison. 'Umm, just Olivia, not Polly,' said Jedda, pouting.

Lisa felt the same. 'Well, darling, we have to be fair, and we said that, remember? Anyway, I doubt that Polly would want to come after what happened last time.'

Jedda scrunched up her face.

'Right then, Aunty, I'll leave it to you. Any afternoon is fine, I guess. But their schoolwork, housework and chores all have to be done,' said Lisa, looking apprehensively at the twins.

'I agree, though I doubt that Polly will want to come. I'll call Kate and let you know when they can come over.'

Later that afternoon, Lisa had lunged a few stock horses and checked on the pregnant mares. She was excited about the new foals that would soon be born. As she went inside and changed, ready for dinner, the phone rang, and a chill went through her body. Lisa knew it would be her aunt. *Please just let it be Olivia and Kate.*

'Hello,' answered Lisa.

'Sweetheart, it's all good,' said Zena. 'Just Olivia and Kate. I have suggested afternoon tea tomorrow or the day after. What do you think?'

'Let's make it the day after. So, Thursday it'll be, about three-ish. Please tell Kate I'll make a slice as she did the last one.'

'Splendid, and please don't worry. I'll be there too and it's just a short visit to see how they go. But you know, with the three of them, it will be smooth sailing.'

Over dinner Lisa re-emphasised, 'Polly will not be here, Billy, so it's just me, Zena and Kate, and of course, Olivia.'

'I'm so happy,' said Jesse. 'When are they coming?'

'Yes, when are they coming? Wait till Livvy sees Ume,' laughed Jedda.

'One more sleep, that's tonight, and then the following day, Thursday, they will come,' Lisa said.

On Thursday, the twins became more active as the morning turned to afternoon. Lisa looked at the kitchen clock. 2:45 p.m. The twins ran up and down the front stairs, searching for cars in the distance. They stood looking through the cyclone wire with Ume next to them, when Jesse let out a hoot. 'Mummy, I can see a car coming.' They were like pogo sticks, hanging onto the wire and jumping up and down. Ume took off from their racket, flapping his wings, and sought comfort in the compost heap, scratching around.

As the car pulled up, Olivia was in the back seat and wound the window down. 'Hello, Jesse.' She waved.

'Coooeeeee,' Jesse yelled.

Kate and Zena waved as Lisa came down the stairs. She breathed a sigh of relief. No sign of Polly. It was going to be a good afternoon.

Jesse rushed to Olivia's passenger door when the main gate opened. 'I'm just trying to get my seatbelt undone,' she said as she wriggled.

'Do you want me to do it?' asked Kate.

'No, I can do that, my daddy showed me,' said Jesse proudly as he opened her seat belt and Olivia slid out. Jesse was so excited he put his arm around her.

'Olivia!' Jesse exclaimed, 'I can show you our Ume,' he said proudly.

'Ume, what's an Ume?' Oliva asked.

Kate looked at Zena quizzically.

'You'll see,' laughed Zena. 'He is close to about three feet now and hairy and starting to grow his stripes out.

'Sounds interesting,' said Kate, looking puzzled.

'Lisa, you have this lovely way about you with children. Are you stopping at two?' queried Kate.

'Umm,' Lisa looked embarrassed.

'Oh dear, I think I have embarrassed you. I am so sorry, dear.'

'No, it's alright, really. I have had this conversation with Zena. I would love to have more, Kate, but nothing seems to eventuate. It's like my body says no more. Billy and I did go into Walgett and have tests. There's no physical reason.'

'Well, you are only still young. I'm sure one day it will happen,' said Kate awkwardly.

'I hope so. I would love to have a house full of children, and so would Billy.'

'But,' said Zena, 'it's not uncommon to hear of people trying to conceive and then seemingly put it to one side, only to fall pregnant without trying too hard. In any event, we have IVF now, and the first baby was born by that method in 1978. They are making advances all the time, so it's something we could investigate.'

'Who knows. What will be, will be,' said Lisa. 'As long as I have two healthy children and a man who loves me, and all this, I could not want for more.'

'True, Lisa, so true,' replied Kate wistfully. It was almost as if she was thinking if only Mitch hadn't of buggered it up, what a beautiful girl she would have had as a daughter-in-law.

There were squeals of laughter coming from outside.

'Let's go see what they are up to,' said Zena.

As they entered the garden, Olivia stood next to Jesse as the baby chick emu was pecking at the food from his hand. Every time Olivia held out her hand, she squealed with delight, a giddying laugh coming all the way up from her boots.

'Oh, it is wonderful to see Livvy laugh like that. It truly warms my heart. So, this is Ume. My goodness,' said Kate.

'Yes, that's our Ume. Emu spelled backwards. He keeps everyone amused,' replied Zena.

The children ran around, and they were quickly followed by the bird. 'Fascinating,' said Kate, staring in almost disbelief.

'It goes on all day if you let them. Ume is still only a baby and so curious, like all emus. We are just waiting until he is fully grown and then we'll release him. He'll probably stay around the compound but once they get attached to you, emus think you are their mate. So, it's highly unlikely he will look for a female now. But then, the female emus are aggressive when mating, and chase the males, so they may chase poor Ume. But he has a good two to three years before becoming sexually active.'

Olivia ran up to Kate, breathless from laughing. Her pink dress was filthy, the pink ribbon in her hair long gone, but clearly, she was having a ball. 'Ume is chasing me, Nanny, the big bird.' She clung to Kate's dress.

The afternoon went quickly. It was great fun for the children and the conversation flowed for the three women.

Kate looked at her watch. 'We have to go now, Olivia.'

'No, I want to stay with Jesse and Jedda and Ume,' her little voice pleaded.

'Olivia, you can come back another time. We said we would do that.' Kate tried to pacify her.

Olivia started to cry, and it was Jesse who came to comfort her. He suddenly ran off and then returned with a small yellow daisy.

'Livvy, please don't cry,' said Jesse. Jedda joined him. 'Yes, Olivia, we had fun.' They all looked up as Ume picked his way towards them, his long neck reaching out to the flower.

Olivia squealed. 'He wants to eat it!'

Jesse tried to shoo him away, but his head bobbed up and down, trying to see the flower.

'Yes, no more tears Olivia. We'll see you soon,' assured Lisa.

They all stood waving until the car was out of sight.

'Olivia is a lovely girl. So very different to Polly,' said Lisa.

'Indeed,' said Zena. 'Kate has tried her best with both girls and has done a great job considering what she has to put up with.'

◊

79

Over dinner, at Woodside, Olivia still bubbled. Her enthusiasm was infectious, and she told the story of Ume and how he had chased them. Mitch smiled. He had never seen his little girl so happy.

'What is Ume, a dog or something?' asked Dave.

'It's an emu. They've got an emu!' Olivia exclaimed. 'He liked my daisy and wanted to eat it. Jesse picked it for me.'

'An emu?' queried Mitch.

'Yes, it's an emu chick. Billy found it and brought it home,' replied Kate.

Mitch suddenly made an explosive guffaw. 'An emu chick as a pet! Bloody hilarious.'

'Language, please,' said Kate, although she did find it quietly humorous as well.

Polly caught her mother's gaze and her lips pressed into a hard line. There was no room in her heart for anything but jealousy as she looked across the table at the perfect princess, Olivia. The favourite. Her jealousy morphed into hatred as she saw how happy her sister was.

Polly suddenly interjected, curiosity creeping in. 'When is the next visit then?'

'Yes, when is the next visit?' asked Tess, resentment tinging her voice.

Kate shivered. Why would Polly suddenly be interested? No doubt Olivia and their chatter about the day had aroused her curiosity.

'You know, I'm not sure,' said Kate, hesitation in her voice.

'Well, I want to go,' said Polly, almost demanding. 'You asked me the other day. I said no, but it sounds fun, and I can change my mind.'

'Err, yes of course, Polly. I'll let you know,' replied Kate, her gut suddenly churning.

After dinner, when Olivia had happily regaled everyone with the day's visit to Woori, Tess went to Polly's room. 'You get across the next time they go.'

'Yeah, sure,' sneered Polly. 'Olivia makes it all sound so good. Miss Princess. I nearly told her to shut up tonight. Nobody else could get a word in.'

A few weeks passed and then Olivia began to ask for another visit. Dave and Mitch kept her busy riding and learning about the farm. Olivia loved it and had a natural instinct for the land, even at her young age.

'Daddy, when can I go see Jesse, Jedda and Ume?' Her big blue eyes looked up at Mitch as they saddled up for a ride.

'Not sure, baby girl. But I can find out for you.' It only appeased Olivia momentarily, as the following day, she again asked. Her persistence finally made Kate make the call. Olivia sat at her feet while she dialled the number, hanging on every word.

'Wonderful, Zena, we will see you Friday.' She looked down at the smiling girl. 'I will see if Polly is interested. If I don't ask, then it would cause a lot of friction, but I'm sure it will be the same response as last time.' Even though Polly had asked to come, she thought when the time came, she would say no. It had been just plain curiosity.

As they all sat down for dinner, Kate said, 'We're heading to Woori this Friday.'

'Yes, I'm so happy,' Olivia blurted and clapped her hands.

'Of course, that invite has been extended to you, Polly,' said Kate, almost choking on the words.

Polly sat chewing her food, the same mouthful over and over again. Tess was enjoying the moment. She could see Mitch simmering inside. Polly annoyed him with the way she chewed her food.

'Polly, please swallow your food. You eat like a cow chewing on its cud,' Mitch said.

Olivia started to giggle.

'Um, yes, I want to go,' said Polly. 'I want to see what's so much fun there with that emu.'

'Yes of course, Polly. But you do know there can be no repeat of what occurred here. I will be there with Zena and Lisa. Do I make myself clear?'

Polly made no response but played with her food on the plate.

It was Dave who spoke. 'Polly, did you hear what your grandmother asked of you?'

Again, no response. Suddenly Dave thumped the table. 'Polly!' It was such a shock to everyone.

'Yes, I heard,' she replied sarcastically.

'Alright then,' said Dave. 'You heard what Nanny said, so none of your nonsense if you do go over there.'

'I second that, Dad,' said Mitch as he eyeballed Polly. 'You will cause no trouble, Polly.'

Olivia was counting down the sleeps. Kate had nervously spoken to Lisa and Zena. They agreed to let Polly come, especially after Kate said Dave and Mitch had laid down the rules.

Friday soon came around. Kate looked at her watch. 'Finished school, darling?'

'Yes, all done, Nanny,' said Olivia.

'Okay, get yourself ready while I see what Polly is up to.'

Kate went to Polly's room. 'Polly,' she said, knocking on her door. 'We'll be leaving in about half an hour.'

No reply. *I hope she's changed her mind.* The room was mysteriously quiet when usually there was always the radio playing. *I'll just keep moving.*

'Right, Miss Olivia,' she said as she marched the little girl to her room. 'No pretty pink dresses for you. Shorts and a T-shirt. Get as dirty as you like today.'

Olivia giggled. 'I like that. I like getting dirty with Jesse and Jedda.'

'Yes, so I saw. Come on, we don't want to be late. I have some fruit cake to take up there.'

As they came into the kitchen, Polly stood waiting. There was no indication that she was excited. Nothing. Just a total blankness.

'Oh, Polly, I didn't hear you out and about. I thought you were still in your room.'

'I'm ready,' Polly said dryly.

'So, I can see. I did knock on your door.'

'Well, I wasn't there, was I?' Polly smirked.

'I'll just grab my car keys and the fruit cake,' said Kate. *I don't feel good about this. Her manner says it all. She's in one of her moods.* Her anxiety suddenly kicked in.

◊

Zena had wanted to head down there to join Lisa before their arrival. They both wanted to be prepared for Polly.

Lisa scratched her arms as they stood at the front door. 'Haven't seen you do that in years, love. It will be okay. We just won't let them, rather Polly, out of our sight. It's not a good thing to say, but I just don't trust the girl. Hopefully, she may be bored and never come again.'

Lisa exhaled. 'I don't trust her either. I always feel unsettled around her. Maybe she's going through a phase. But there is such an aura of cruelty and anger about her. I don't know, but Billy feels the same.'

'Well, Polly hasn't had a good start to life, but I'm not making excuses for her behaviour. It goes way back, perhaps when she was born even. Mitch was so grief-stricken, as was everybody else when they found Tom dead in his cot. Mitch tried desperately to resuscitate him. After the funeral, he basically took off and didn't come home for, from memory, about a month. He was drinking heavily and then of course, we know when he did come home, as Tess was then suddenly pregnant. After Polly was born, he just seemed to abandon both of them. Mother and baby. Sadly, I think he still had unresolved feelings of guilt at Tom's death, and grief.'

'I think I would come close to losing my mind if that situation ever happened to me, Aunty,'

'The mother is the child's first teacher. Polly just copies Tess and because Mitch seemed to have nothing to do with either, Polly has had a very close relationship with Tess. Kate has always been there for both girls, but she just does not understand why they are so different in nature.'

Lisa nodded. 'My children are so different... but good different.'

'Indeed, Lisa. God knows Kate has tried with Polly, but there is just constant rejection from the girl. Mind you, Kate said some days she can be like an angel and then her mood will suddenly change. Maybe it is, as you say, anger. She takes it out on Kate, the grandmother, as she cannot get to Mitch. Anyway, just remember, we go where Polly goes. Let's not get distracted. Keep an eye on her. Here they are now.' They both watched the car in the distance pull up at the main entrance. Jesse and Jedda stood at the gate, but unlike before, Jesse peered intensely at the occupants of the car.

'Polly! Mummy said she might come,' he whispered to Jedda, who moved closer to her brother.

Jedda put her hands on her hips and looked at Jesse. 'Mummy says we have to be good, and that Polly, she is supposed to be good too. I don't like that one. She's not going to get me on the ground again. Nope.'

Polly looked at the twins as she got out of the car. She saw Zena standing on the porch with Lisa and frowned.

Jesse opened the gate. Olivia already ran out past Polly, straight to Jesse and Jedda, who all hugged. Polly's face was surly as she followed Kate, her head down.

'Hi, Polly,' said Lisa, trying to make her feel welcome as they all stepped inside. Again, there was that sly smile as Polly purveyed their home and surroundings. There was no escaping the feeling of apprehension that had taken over the room. Once again, Polly made no effort to join the conversation.

Jedda, Jesse and Olivia sat chatting to themselves. Jedda would occasionally lock eyes with Polly. She stared at Polly's mouth, which jerked spasmodically, as if trying to say something.

'Can I see the baby emu?' Polly suddenly asked. Silence. You could hear a pin drop.

Kate's mouth went dry. Polly had never taken the slightest interest in any animal, apart from her early stages of learning to ride.

Lisa looked at Zena, her heart began to beat rapidly, and she could feel her muscles tensing. *Stay calm, Lisa.*

'That's my Ume,' Jedda suddenly shouted across the table.

'Yes, we know that Jedda,' said Zena quietly. She turned to Polly. 'Of course, we were going to head outside after we finish here.'

Zena could see Kate was on edge. It wasn't the same as the last visit. They were all relaxed when last together. How could a fourteen-year-old girl generate such anxiety and uneasiness?

'Let's go, Jesse,' said Lisa. 'You lead the way.'

Olivia chased Jesse and Jedda through the garden as they made their way to the chook pen. The little emu chick was flicking water from the cement bath and turned as the excited children ran towards him.

'Let Ume out, Jesse,' Olivia squealed.

Jesse unlocked the gate and the little chick chirped and cheeped and ran towards him. Jesse reached into his pocket and pulled out some corn, laying his open palm flat for the chick to pick at.

His long neck lifted and bobbed about, pecking at Jesse's hair. 'The Aboriginal people say the emu gets his long neck by always stretching up to tall trees to get food.'

Olivia giggled at Jesse's explanation. 'I like your stories, Jesse.'

'Yes, and my Mummy says their eyes are magical, and Ume has two sets of eyelids,' added Jedda. 'One for blinking and one to keep out the dust.'

Polly seethed and her expression hardened. The voices in her head had returned and were getting louder. She walked behind Kate and Zena, watching Lisa who was just ahead and moving towards the giggling children.

'Here.' She pointed to a garden seat. 'Let's sit and watch for a bit,' said Lisa, trying to calm her nerves.

Polly walked towards the three children who had gathered around Ume, squealing as the bird pecked at their clothes.

Ume was nearly as tall as Polly, and the bird picked his way towards her. He raised his head to look at the girl, and then suddenly, Polly waved her hands at him.

Sensing the girl's fear, Lisa called out, 'It's okay, Polly. Ume is very docile. He's just very curious and playful. He's only being friendly.'

Ume suddenly fluffed up his feathers and hissed at her.

'Aaaaggh, I don't like it,' shrieked Polly. 'Get it away from me.' She began to step back and then suddenly tripped over, falling to the ground. Ume's long neck followed her and began pecking at her legs.

Polly lashed out with her legs kicking at the bird. 'Get it away!' she screamed.

'It's alright, Polly,' said Lisa, dashing across to her aid. Zena and Kate were on their feet.

'Ume is just curious.' The three children came running up to Lisa, trying to assist the distraught girl to her feet.

'Here, Polly.' Lisa extended her hand. 'It's okay, truly. Come, let me help you up.'

'I don't need your help, just get it away,' replied Polly as she got to her feet.

Ume clucked at Jesse, who put his hand in his pocket, wiggling his fingers inside as if he had more food. The chick turned and followed him around the garden.

'It's okay,' said Lisa. 'Polly just got a fright.' The three women sat down again to talk, and the children disappeared momentarily.

Polly had wandered off around the side of the house. She heard a cheeping and turned around. Ume was suddenly behind her. The voices crashed into her head. *The devil, it's the devil. Kill the devil!*

Polly screamed loudly. 'Get lost, bird, get away. Get away!'

'What was that?' said Zena.

'Oh my God, where's Polly?' Kate shivered, her throat tightening in fear.

Lisa was already on her feet and running in the direction of Polly's voice.

Ume came closer to Polly, his curiosity ever-present.

Polly leaned down and picked up a large wooden tomato stake, and as Ume extended his neck towards her, she suddenly swung with all her force, striking the bird in the head. Ume wobbled and then fell to the ground.

Polly smiled at the writhing creature. She raised the tomato stake and brought it down again and again, smashing its skull. The little bird's eyes closed and blood spilled to the ground like a splattering of rain.

'I told you to get lost, stupid bird.' She threw the bloodied stake to the ground.

Lisa came careening around the corner. 'Polly, what have you done!' Lisa shrieked. 'Ume, Ume!' Gut-wrenching sobs tore through her chest. Her fingers stroked the little bird's feathers as it lay motionless on the ground, blood seeping from its mouth and head.

The twins had seen Lisa suddenly dash to the other side of the house near the rose garden. Jesse knew something was wrong and ran with Jedda and Olivia towards Polly's scream. Zena and Kate were shortly behind.

As they came around the corner, Zena's heart began to beat wildly. Lisa was kneeling over something and the picture was clear as the feathered creature came into view. She drew in a sharp intake of breath, just knowing Ume was dead.

Jesse looked at the dead bird and howled. A great sob escaped from his mouth, and he covered his face with shaking hands, torrents of grief coursing down his face. Lisa came to him and put her arms around him.

Jedda became red in the face and suddenly lunged at Polly, beating her stomach with her fists. Zena pulled her away as the sound of her wailing echoed through the garden. Kate screamed, 'Polly, what did you do!' Then she reached for Olivia, tears running down her cheeks.

Lisa's face, distorted with rage and sorrow, looked at Polly. Her voice was almost guttural. 'What have you done, Polly! Get out of my house. Now!'

Kate was devastated as she picked up Olivia and carried her to the car. Whimpers escaped Olivia's lips as the sorrow of what had just occurred seared through her little heart. Polly did not speak, merely followed.

As she got into the car, Polly turned to look at the scene. The two children sobbed inconsolably into Lisa's arms. She smiled with the feeling of power. *The voices are happy.*

◇

That afternoon, Billy placed a sheet over the Ume and proceeded to dig a hole for the bird under a big peppercorn tree. Alan had brought over the tractor to dig a large hole. He helped roll the bird onto the sheet with Billy and they then took an end, carrying the corpse to the grave. Jesse and Jedda had picked flowers from the garden, and Zena had a plate of food. They opened the sheet, and the children placed the flowers and the food for Ume's trip to the stars. Lisa held a quartz stone that Burnu had given her so many moons ago. She gently kissed the stone and placed it on the sheet.

Billy looked at his children who huddled around Lisa, the weight of their grief stinging his heart. 'Ume, he travel to da night sky and live near da Milky Way,' said Billy as he pointed to the sky. He knew the twins would look every night for Ume as he began to shovel the dirt over the body. He couldn't understand what kind of child could do that to an innocent baby animal. He sensed a dark storm brewing, and danger.

PART TWO

DARKNESS COMES

TEN

GRIEF DESCENDS

Kate was distraught as she drove home to Woodside. Polly had not spoken a word in the back seat. Her eyes were emotionless. Olivia sat next to Polly, sobbing. Grief travelled with them, thickening the air.

By the time they reached the homestead, Kate, who was normally very composed, was on the verge of exploding. Her face was contorted with anger as the veins in her neck bulged and the feelings of devastation in her heart consumed her. She felt uncontrollable rage for what she had just witnessed. The deliberate battering and slaughter of an animal by a young girl. This was no ordinary child. Her deepest feelings were confirmed: Something was not right with her oldest granddaughter.

When Kate got out of the car, she looked to the heavens, wringing her hands. This was followed by a flood of words. 'Get out. For God's sake, get out of the car, Polly. You need help. What you just did, it's inhuman!'

Polly glared at her grandmother then ran towards the house, feeling no remorse for her actions. The only sound heard was the laughter of the kookaburras.

Tess heard the commotion and came to the screen door that led down the back stairs. Seeing Polly approaching, she asked, 'What's happened? Where are Olivia and Kate?'

'They're out there at the car,' Polly mumbled. 'Nan was screaming at me. I killed the stupid bird.'

'What bird, Polly? What are you talking about?'

'Ume, stupid Ume. The devil bird. The voices told me to kill it. It wouldn't leave me alone. He was trying to peck at me, so I hit it with a tomato stake.'

Tess was momentarily stunned and watched as Polly went to her room. God, what happened over there? Even she was shocked by her daughter's admission. What on earth had she done?

She gathered her thoughts and went outside to Kate's car. It was a pitiful sight. She had never seen Kate lose control and was shocked to see her sitting in the dirt holding Olivia tightly.

As Tess walked towards them, Kate looked up. 'What the devil is going on inside Polly's head?' she seethed.

Tess was going to offer some sympathy, but she quickly withdrew any condolences. 'What happened over there, Kate?' asked Tess. 'Polly just told me about a bird trying to attack her or something?'

'She killed their pet emu. It was vile. Polly battered it, Tess! Your daughter, our granddaughter. She needs help. You must be able to see that. It's not normal what Polly did!'

'Olivia, come with me please.' Tess extended her hand.

The little girl buried her head further into Kate's shoulder, ignoring her mother.

Tess's eyes narrowed. 'Fine. Have it your way.' She stormed off.

Kate took Olivia's hand and they went inside and down to Kate's bedroom. 'We'll just wash up. Can you do that for me, Livvy, and I will get some clean clothes for you.'

As Kate headed down to Olivia's room, she could hear Tess inside Polly's room. Kate didn't bother to knock but opened the door and stood defiantly looking at them, the anger and sorrow still flashing in her eyes. 'You and Mitch will take Polly to see a psychiatrist, Tess, and the sooner the better. If you don't, then we will use every resource we have, money, whatever it takes, to remove both girls from your custody and get Polly the help she so desperately requires. I don't care what you do with yourself, Tess, but as a mother, you will get control of Polly. This is not normal behaviour for a fourteen-year-old girl. You must get help immediately. Do you hear me! She killed an innocent baby animal!'

Tess's nostrils flared. 'Oh, for God's sake, back off. I will handle this!'

Polly pursed her lips as her eyes rolled to the ceiling. Kate slammed the door, her heart breaking.

When Dave and Mitch came home, there was no familiar cooking smell, no music, and the house was deathly quiet. 'Something is wrong here, Mitch, my gut feeling is telling me so.' Dave removed his hat and went to look for Kate.

'Yeah, Dad, something is definitely up. I'll grab us some beers.' His eyes followed his father.

The bedroom door was ajar and Kate lay on the bed with Olivia. It was not like Kate to be lying down at this hour of the day. 'Kate. Are you alright? Olivia, are you okay?' asked Dave, coming to her side.

Kate's eyes fluttered open, and he could tell they were red and puffy from crying. She looked across at Olivia who slept soundly.

Kate spoke softly putting her finger to her lips. 'I don't want to wake her. Where's Mitch?'

Dave lowered his voice. 'Outside, grabbing a cold beer. What's happened?'

'I will tell both of you.' Kate swung her legs over the bed, Dave following her down the hallway to the kitchen.

'Mum, you look awful.' Mitch moved over to her in concern.

'You'd best both sit down while I tell you this. It's really bad, and I don't want either of you to react and wake Olivia. Suffice to say, I have already given Tess an ultimatum.'

'React to what, Mum?' Mitch's voice thickened.

When Kate had finished telling them of the events that occurred, a numbness crept through Mitch's body. What sort of girl could commit such a violent act? He was horrified.

'Now, I don't want any more drama, no more yelling. I told Tess I want a psychiatrist to see Polly. Something is dreadfully wrong with the girl. Otherwise, if she does not heed my advice, I said we would use everything, whatever it takes to prove Tess an unfit mother if need be. We have to remove Olivia and Polly from Tess if she does not start taking control of Polly. Mitch, Polly is also your daughter. You need to act on this swiftly. You and Tess need take that girl to see someone.'

'I agree. The girl is not right, and that's not rocket science,' added Dave grimly. 'Something needs to be done about our granddaughter. I know she's always been sullen and withdrawn, and so bloody moody of late, but I could never have predicted she'd do this. It's bad news, very bad news.'

Mitch pondered what his parents had just said. 'I'll make some calls tomorrow, Mum. I'm so sorry this has happened. I don't know how you can prove Tess is an unfit mother. Sure, she drinks, and I know she has her men friends in town, but these were Polly's actions today, not Tess's.'

Dave shook his head. 'The Family Court is pretty tough, Mitch, and the judges have a tendency to lean towards the mother, even if Tess drinks and is promiscuous. Is that grounds for an unfit mother? The newspapers are always reporting the fathers are hard done-by in the courts. If you open this can of worms up, we may lose. We need to think this over carefully. Seeking professional help and treatment first is the best step.'

Mitch winced. 'God forbid Olivia or Polly going with Tess. I would never let her take them to that rat's nest in Walgett with Mrs Dunphy. It was horrible when I went there, the state of the place. I don't know why she has deteriorated so badly.'

'Perhaps it's early dementia, Mitch. I don't know. Mrs Dunphy was always eccentric in her ways but really, a dear old soul with a good heart. For now, can we just let things settle? It's been the most dreadful day. As I have said before, we cannot continue the way we have. I often wonder if we are to blame.'

Mitch crossed his arms across his chest. 'What do you mean, Mum? We've given Tess everything, and the girls. Why would we be to blame?'

'It's a loveless marriage, Mitch. Maybe all of what has happened has evolved because of that. But you either include Polly and Tess in your life and try and improve the situation, or you can move out and find your own place. But Dave and I just cannot live this way anymore. I can't even bear to look at Polly. My own granddaughter!'

A thousand thoughts went through Mitch's mind. *In a house alone with Tess and Polly, who would look out for Olivia while I'm at work and away?* It would be like leaving her to the wolves.

Olivia woke screaming in her sleep that night and when Tess went to console her, she only wanted Nanny. The little girl slept with Kate and Dave for the next two nights.

Kate called Zena a few days later and as she dialled the number, her heart was in her mouth. She hoped she still had a friend.

'Hello, Zena, it's Kate. Have I got you at a good time?' she asked nervously.

'Yes, I'm just inside doing a few things.'

'I am calling to apologise and—'

Zena cut her off. 'Kate, there's no need for you to apologise, but thank you. It was a horrible day, and the twins are still getting over it. Billy has gone bush with Jesse and we're not sure when he will be back. Lisa said probably when his spirit has healed. Jesse really was inconsolable and of course, Lisa has Jedda. What can I say? It certainly wasn't your fault, but we didn't stick to the plan of not letting Polly out of our sight. It all happened so quickly. I hope her parents are taking her in for psychiatric help.'

There was a long sigh. 'Yes, Mitch and Tess will seek help. I run that dreadful day through my head so many times, Zena. I want you

95

to pass on my dearest condolences to Lisa and the children. I just don't know what else to say.'

'It's a time thing, Kate. They will eventually get over it, but they won't forget.'

'Yes, I agree. As I said, I have told Tess and Mitch they have to take Polly to see a psychiatrist. Between her chattering loudly to herself in the room and then telling us that the emu was talking to her, and that it was evil, it is all just madness,' said Kate.

'Lisa doesn't blame you, Kate. You didn't kill the bird. Anyway, we'll catch up when this blows over. Best to let things just settle. How is Olivia?'

'She was the same. Nightmares. But she is much better now. Mitch has been taking her out with him, which she just loves. We gave her a few days off school as well. She's a real bushy, like a sponge when it comes to learning about the land, and getting out with Mitch, well, it has been quite restorative for her.'

'Don't be hard on yourself, Kate. I'll let you know if and when it's okay for Olivia to head across again. But Polly is not welcome at this stage. They have all been friends over the years as they have grown up, and kids always have their spats and arguments, but what happened with the killing of that emu could have been a matter for the police.'

'I know, Zena. Thank you. Take care and please pass on my regards to Lisa and the children. If there is anything I can do, just let me know.'

◊

Mitch looked up as he chatted to Olivia in the booth by the large window, waiting for their order at the milk bar in Walgett. His heart skipped a beat. Lisa.

Jedda saw them and waved, trying to drag Lisa. 'Mummy, come on, it's Olivia.' She broke free and ran towards where they were sitting.

'Hi Olivia, Jesse and me have missed you. We're here for a milkshake.' Her little face beamed.

Mitch stood up slowly. 'Hi Lisa, Jedda. Won't you join us?' Lisa looked at the man who had caused her pain many moons ago. Tiny facial lines had now appeared, but he was tanned and his blue eyes just as piercing. He was still a handsome man, and she recalled at one stage how she'd found Mitch to be charming, so much so such that she had developed feelings for him back then. Lisa wondered what her path would have been if it had not been for Billy. A flood of old memories quickly spun through her mind. Mitch digging into her past life, the sexual abuse she incurred and of course, the day at the river when he had lunged at her while telling her about the private investigator. *Shake it off, Lisa. It was a long time ago.*

'Thanks, Mitch, that would be lovely.'

Olivia wriggled closer to her father as they moved around the booth to make room. Jedda slid in next to Olivia as Mitch signalled the waitress.

'We've just ordered hamburgers and chips with two chocolate milkshakes. Do you know what you want, Lisa?'

'Oh, can we have the same?' said Jedda pleadingly.

'Yes, of course we can. We'll have the same, please,' she said calmly as the waitress scribbled on her note pad.

'I'm so terribly sorry for what happened with the emu. It's one of the reasons we are here today. Time out. And we're taking Polly to see a professional about her behaviour.'

'I think that's a great idea, Mitch. It was very traumatic,' replied Lisa.

'Olivia does love coming across to Woori, so I hope that doesn't stop. It's great for kids to have mates, and they all got on reasonably well before this,' added Mitch.

'I agree,' said Lisa. 'We are so isolated and for the time being, there is no reason to stop Olivia visiting. Jesse and Jedda adore her. But until Polly gets the help and treatment she needs, well, you know what I'm trying to say. You would understand our feelings currently regarding Polly.'

'You're not alone there. She's been a handful from day one. I don't know how Mum has managed. They say kids are all in the genes. I think Livvy here is a throwback to Kate, but Polly.' Mitch let out a sigh. 'Well, she has my height already, tall lanky thing, but she's straight out of the Dunphy gene pool. We thought she was just contrary and sullen at first, and I know all kids have different personalities, but after what happened at Woori, we're now aware it's much more than that.'

Lisa noted the tension creep into his voice before Mitch changed the subject. 'Are you looking forward to the shearers coming out? We had a lot of fun last year as they were a great bunch of blokes. Some were a handful, but they were good workers. So, no complaints. Dad was very happy.'

'Yes, it's always fun. The place comes alive. Alan is already getting things underway. We may need more help with running the place as he is quite keen to do what you're doing. Some new stock, cattle, arrive next week, and he wants to grow wheat as well, probably after shearing.'

'I could give you a hand,' offered Mitch.

'Oh no, we'll be fine. Alan has his eye on a bloke called Kev. He worked with us a few years back. But thank you, Mitch.'

Mitch watched Jedda talking to Olivia.

'She's very sharp, Lisa,' said Mitch.

'That she is. Jedda is our true-knot baby.'

'What does that mean?' he asked curiously. 'Something Aboriginal?'

'No,' Lisa laughed. 'There was a knot in the umbilical cord when she was born. Just a small knot. Sometimes the baby moves around inside the womb, and they become entangled in the cord, which can have disastrous consequences. But I had two babies, so not much room to move. The doctor mentioned that true knots have an amazing life. So, here's hoping.

'Interesting,' said Mitch.

'Yes, I know. It sounds odd, but I just have a feeling Jedda will be famous.' Lisa placed an arm around her daughter.

'Anyway, we better be moving. Jedda wants to pick out something for Zena, and I want to do a bit of shopping as well.' She searched around in her bag for her purse.

'No, I'll get this, Lisa. It's all good.'

'Thanks so much, Mitch. Lovely to see you, and of course Livvy. Good luck with Polly.' She really did wish him the best and hoped that a professional could help with his oldest daughter.

As soon as the homestead came into view, Lisa saw Jed in the resting paddock not far from the house. Her heart leaped. 'Jedda, they're home!' Lisa's foot hit the accelerator.

She pulled up and leaped out of the car, quickly followed by Jedda. 'Billy, Jesse, where are you?'

'Grasshopper, over here,' replied Billy.

'Quick, Jedda, they must be around the other side of those paddocks.'

Lisa walked swiftly to Billy then he swept her up in his arms. 'My beautiful man, I have missed you.' Lisa breathed in his sweet and familiar smell.

Jedda tugged at Billy's legs. 'My girls,' he grinned, his white teeth dazzling.

'Are you both okay?' She looked at Jesse.

Billy stroked her hair as he looked into her eyes. 'We both good. Bin near da spirit, Rainbow Serpent. He create da universe and da dry gullies in da tracks he made, looking for a resting place. Jesse and me, we find da good resting place. Make Jesse heal, find da strength again.'

As Billy kissed Lisa that night, his lips felt so soft, so effortlessly sweet as she let him roam her body. She was desperate to have him, the heat and desire for him never fading, and his absence brought those feelings to the fore. As he kissed her again, this time stronger, her heart beat rapidly, drinking in the pleasure he gave her, a noise deep in his throat, raw and animal, demanding more. As his growl reverberated in his chest, his body in hers, she groaned his name and they both shattered.

ELEVEN

A TROUBLING DIAGNOSIS

When Mitch arrived home after taking Olivia to the café, he found his mother on the veranda reading. 'Hey, Mum,' he said as he and Olivia sat down and joined her.

'Have a good time?' she queried, folding her newspaper.

'Yeah, ran into Lisa and Jedda, and they joined us. Mentioned the bird incident briefly. I told her we were getting professional help for Polly, which she seemed pleased about.'

Kate smiled. 'That was good you let her know, son.'

'She's just such a gorgeous person, Mum, inside and out. Shame I behaved like a total idiot all those years ago, but I was just a spoiled big boofhead, really. I didn't mean her any harm. I just wasn't used to not getting everything I wanted, when I wanted, and I crossed the line.'

'Water under the bridge now, Mitch.'

'Anyway, she's happy for Olivia to still go around there and see her friends, but not Polly at this stage.'

'Understandable, and really, for Olivia's sake, that family could be a very stable influence in her life.'

'I hear you, Mum, more than you know. If I had listened, I probably wouldn't be living the life I am now. Speaking of Polly and for that matter Tess, where are they?'

'They both took off not long after you. Tess's mother is not well and they admitted her to Dubbo Hospital by ambulance. Found her wandering the street, mumbling, incoherent and apparently in a terrible physical state.'

Mitch grunted. 'Madness, old age or dementia? I feel sorry for the old girl.'

'I think you may be right. Mrs Dunphy was a kind old soul, but we all know that Tess was diagnosed with bi-polar disorder. I don't know why she's not on any medication. She's so up and down. I remember that night at your nineteenth birthday party when Tess made a spectacle of herself. It was her mother who got her under control and took her home.'

Mitch just nodded in agreement and wondered for the thousandth time why he'd chosen to bed Tess all those years ago, knowing she also had a mental illness. God, he had been so reckless and stupid in his youth, with both Lisa and Tess.

◊

It was dark when Tess pulled into the driveway at Woodside. 'Home sweet home, Polly. I'm glad we got to say goodbye to the old girl. I know she wasn't the best mother to me or grandmother to you, but she'd had a shit life. She worked so hard all her life and always thought I would get it good because I married Mr Moneybags. Never more untrue. Come on, let's put on our happy faces.'

Mitch had opened a cold beer and was sitting with Dave in the kitchen talking about the pending shearing crew. Kate sat quietly reading to Olivia when they heard the car pull up.

'That'll be them,' said Kate. She handed the book to Olivia. 'Livvy, you keep reading. I'll just see if Mummy is okay.' Kate got up to greet her daughter-in-law.

Tess's expression was weary and haggard as she came inside.

'Tess, how is your mother?' Kate's voice was full of concern.

Tess's mouth twitched as if trying to find words. A gloomy silence filled the air. Suddenly, she seemed so fragile. Polly stood motionless, with restless eyes.

'The old girl snuffed it, just after 2 p.m. this arvo. She had collapsed on the street when they found her. Heart attack.'

'Oh, Tess, I'm so sorry to hear this news, what can I... we do?' The shock was evident in Kate's voice.

'Nothing. Polly and I will sort it, won't we, Polly?'

The girl nodded.

'At least we got there in time to hold her hand, and I told her she'd done a good job. Last time I was at her house, she must have known something.'

'Why is that?' asked Kate.

'She gave me this envelope and said to read it after she had died. It was only a few lines. I put it in my top drawer. When the ambulance called, I just thought to grab it and I read it at the hospital.'

'I'm sorry, Tess,' said Mitch suddenly.

Tess was taken aback. He had never offered her a kind word in all the time she knew him. She cleared her throat and looked at him, her shoulders slumped as the tired words stumbled out of her mouth. Even though he had offered condolences, his eyes still looked disinterested. Tess could smell his insincerity. 'Buy her a coffin then, Mitch,' she said sarcastically.

'Sure, Tess, sure,' said Mitch.

'When is the funeral?' asked Dave.

'Dunno. Her body was taken to the funeral place. They will let me know, and I have to make the arrangements.' Tess still clutched the small white envelope.

'Would you like a cup of tea? Do you and Polly feel like dinner?' queried Kate.

'No, we had something at the hospital, and are just tired now. Going to hit the sack, aren't we Pol.' Tess could hardly wait to get to her room. She needed a Jack Daniels desperately.

Polly nodded as Tess took her hand and left them all standing in the kitchen.

After dinner, Kate made two hot chocolates and went to Tess's room. She placed one cup on the hall stand just nearby and knocked softly.

'Come in,' Tess answered.

'I just thought I'd see if you're okay. We can all have our differences with our mothers, but at the end of the day, they are still our mothers.' Kate handed her the hot chocolate and placed the other one on Tess's dresser. She saw the empty spirit glass.

'This is for Polly. I didn't want to disturb her. If you need anything else, I'm happy to talk or help with the funeral arrangements. Anything really. We all know that death is so final.'

'We didn't have a good relationship, that's for sure. Mum was a bit eccentric, some thought a bit bonkers, but people liked her. She had a kind heart and was a single mum who worked hard in that haberdashery store. I was a shit sometimes. I know I caused her some grief. Do you wanna know what's in the letter? I'll read it to you.'

'No, that's not necessary. These things are private, Tess.'

Tess was on her knees on the bed, wanting to read it anyway. 'It says, "Dear Tess, by the time you read this letter, I will be dead, pushing up daisies as they say. I want a simple funeral. Don't want to be buried. I don't want any visitors. Burn me and scatter me to the winds."'

Tess put the letter down. 'Pretty simple, Kate.' She threw the letter on the bed.

'I think, Tess, it is a letter full of sadness.' Kate gave her daughter-in-law's shoulder a squeeze before she turned and left the room.

◊

Mrs Dunphy was cremated one week later. Tess scattered her ashes through the streets of Walgett where she'd spent most of her life and then stayed in her mother's house for the next week. The front door, however, was like a revolving door and most nights she was at the pub. Tess liked men and she liked a drink, and there was no shortage of men who wanted sex and a good time.

After cleaning out the majority of her mother's contents, Tess threw her things in the car to head back to Woodside. Polly's first appointment with the psychiatrist was tomorrow. The drive home was quiet as Tess pondered what the session would reveal.

Tess had left Walgett late afternoon, hoping by the time she arrived that no one was up. She didn't want any conversation. Her head hurt and she was hung over as she hit the main highway.

She lit up a cigarette and said to herself, 'I'm gonna keep the old joint for a while. Somewhere to stay when I come into town. Ha, it'll be like a holiday. My own little holiday house.' Tess laughed loudly at her own joke.

Tess tossed and turned that night. What would the shrink find wrong with Polly? What questions would she ask? Would Tess be blamed for Polly's behaviour? Tess hated Woodside but grimaced at the thought of permanently living in her mother's home.

After a fitful sleep, the morning light filtered into Tess's room. She had left the curtains open so she would be woken by the sun. Her mouth was dry from the Jack Daniels she had consumed in her room.

She headed to Polly's room. 'Get up, Polly,' said Tess, shaking the sleepy girl. 'Your appointment with the psych is today. Get a move on or we'll be late. I'm getting some breakfast. Have a shower and I'll bring you in some toast.'

Polly opened one eye and looked at her mother. 'I don't want to go.'

'You've got no choice now. You shouldn't have killed that bloody emu. We wouldn't be in this shit if you hadn't.'

They drove without speaking, the radio blaring and Tess chewing gum. As they saw the sign to Walgett, Tess finally spoke. 'I dunno what this psych is going to say or do, Polly, but as I told you, we just have to comply and go along with everything, you hear me. I'm not getting tossed out of Woodside because of you. I remember years ago that Mum took me to see someone. Maybe I was about your age. They told us I had a thing called bi-polar. I get excited and then so bloody tired. But the depression is the worst. I feel so flat at times and then I get restless. They tried to put me on medication, but I stopped taking it. I don't need it. I don't want it. Made me sick with vomiting and diarrhoea, and I was more confused than ever! Shit medications.'

Polly looked out the window. 'What will the psych do about the voices? They will get angry with me, very angry, I just know it.'

'I dunno, she's the shrink,' said Tess. 'What are these voices that you keep banging on about?' She didn't want to admit it but even she was concerned about the voices.

Polly shrugged. 'They just start chattering in my head and get louder and louder. Sometimes I try to hide in the wardrobe, but they always find me.'

Inside Tess shuddered. She had never heard voices. Something needed to be done for Polly. 'Right, here we are. This is the medical centre. Let's see what the psych can do to help you.' Tess pulled into the car park. She took out the referral letter. 'Dr Rebekah Adams. Let's go.'

Polly sat motionless in the car.

'Polly, get out, will you. You'd think you were like a lamb to the slaughter. It's just talking and stuff.'

They sat in the waiting room until Polly's name was called, then walked towards a woman of about thirty-five, attractive in a hand-some way, with red-rimmed glasses, bright red lipstick and dark hair neatly cut into a shoulder-length bob.

'Hello Polly, Mrs Walker, please come in.' Dr Adams greeted them warmly and her soothing voice immediately put Tess at ease.

Tess glanced around the room, which was devoid of any pictures on the walls. It was very sterile but professional with a desk, two chairs and a small lounge. Another door just to the right of the psychiatrist's desk led out to a back area.

'I have read a bit about your background, Polly. The general practitioner has obviously taken a comprehensive history from you, Mrs Walker.'

'Yes, that's right,' said Tess. 'My girl says she hears voices, people talking to her that aren't there. Tell her, Polly.'

'Is that correct, Polly?' Dr Adams asked gently.

'Yes,' said Polly, nodding slowly.

'And what do the voices tell you or say?'

'They tell me to do things. Like the other day. This stupid emu bird was following me so I hit it. The voices told me to. They said it was evil.'

Dr Adams face showed concern as she looked at Tess. 'How long has she been like this, Mrs Walker?'

'It's just started. She's always been a bit withdrawn, but I hear her having conversations quite often now. Like she's talking to herself or arguing with herself. She doesn't like to come out of her room and just picks at her food. Sometimes she will smile for no apparent reason or just shriek.'

'Are there any relatives, cousins, any family history of mental illness, Tess, that you can recall?'

Tess paused. 'I was diagnosed with bi-polar when I was about seventeen years old.'

'Are you on any medications, Mrs Walker?'

'No. I tried them, tried a few, but they made me sick. I was just telling Polly on the way here.'

Dr Adams continued writing notes. 'Anybody else?'

'No,' Tess replied quickly.

'May I ask if it is a happy family home? I only ask this as sometimes stress and volatility can cause a great deal of issues for young children and adolescents.'

Tess hesitated, and Polly's eyes darted down to the floor. Dr Adams knew instinctively that there were problems at home.

'Um, not really. My husband, err Polly's father, he doesn't really give us a lot of his time. He's always away,' said Tess.

'Any other siblings?'

'Yeah, Olivia, she's our youngest daughter,' added Tess.

'She gets all the attention! All of it! From everyone!' Polly suddenly blurted out.

Dr Adams made a note in her records. 'So, Polly, tell me about the voices.'

Polly tilted her head to the side, playing with a hair strand, winding it around her finger, and began to explain what they tell her to do. 'The voices are powerful, and they know all about me. Sometimes I try to hide, like in my closet, but they always find me. I'm sure that sometimes, the voice comes from God or his angels. But I know they can read my mind. And, they are plotting to kill me sometimes!'

'What else, Polly?' asked Dr Adams, stunned by the ferocity in the young girl's voice.

'They tell me to damage and harm things. Harm things that people love. Harm people. They get real nasty. Sometimes I don't want to get out of bed. I try to shut them out and put my hands over my ears, but they just get inside.'

'Do you talk to them, Polly?'

'Yes, all the time. We argue a lot. They want me to hurt people.'

'And how do you feel about that, Polly, hurting people or hurting things you or they love?' asked Dr Adams.

Polly shrugged her shoulders and looked at the ceiling, avoiding eye contact. 'Umm,' she said as her fingers fidgeted with her dress, 'I'm not sure. It's like I have storms in my head. They told me to kill the emu bird. Sometimes I just want to scream and break things. Because they, these voices, they won't shut up. And they get angry if I don't answer.'

Dr Adams looked across to Tess, showing her concern.

'The stupid emu bird, he wouldn't leave me alone. Chirp, chirp, chirp. It made the other kids cry when they saw it dead. That made the voices happy. Happy, happy.'

'Dead? Do you mean you killed the bird, Polly?' Dr Adams looked at the girl, astounded, and her eyes once again went to Tess. Polly appeared to have no judgement or remorse about the fact that she had killed a living creature. She appeared expressionless. A classic symptom of schizophrenia: flat-affect and inappropriate reactions.

'Were you frightened of the bird, Polly?'

'Yeah, a little, but the voices told me what to do.'

'How do you spend most of your time?' asked Dr Adams.

'A bit of School of the Air, when I feel like it. Listening to music, watching TV in my room, reading Mum's books, and Mum spends lots of time with me. Sometimes we go shopping and sometimes we go to Granny's house. But we can't anymore, because the old girl just snuffed it.'

Dr Adams noticed the complete lack of emotion as the girl talked about her grandmother's death. And although she was only fourteen years old, the girl seemed much older, not only because of her height, but because she was also parroting someone's speech. The old girl snuffed it.

Dr Adams continued writing. There was no doubt in her mind that the adolescent girl copied someone close to her. She glanced at Tess and wished the father had also come to this appointment so she could gauge his character. Was the adolescent girl sitting before her an almost a mirror image of the mother?

'Mrs Walker, Polly, I have seen a few cases like yours over the years. I believe you may be suffering from a diagnosis called schizophrenia. You may not fully understand this, but it is the reason why you are hearing the voices. It affects your behaviour and your emotions, as well as your motivation to do things.'

Tess took Polly's hand and nodded.

'I will need you to take the medications I prescribe and see you on a regular basis until things improve. It would be beneficial if Polly's father also attends a few of these appointments. Do you both understand?'

'Yes, I err, yes we do,' said Tess, looking at Polly as she drew a deep breath.

The session continued for about an hour, and then finally Dr Adams looked at her watch.

'Our session has drawn to a close, and I thank you, Polly, for describing your feelings today. I know this can be a very difficult and frightening thing. Would you mind if I spoke to your mother alone? You can wait outside in reception. Gail, my secretary, is there if you need anything. She will look after you.'

'Go on, Polly,' said Tess. 'I've gotta have a quiet word with the good doc here. I won't be long, so just wait for me out there.'

Polly was wooden in her movements as she slowly got to her feet and then slouched out the room.

Dr Adams opened the door to her consulting room. 'Gail, can you just help Polly if she needs anything. I will be with her mother.'

When the door closed, Dr Adams sat back down facing Tess, who sat with her arms rigidly folded across her chest.

'Mrs Walker, as I said, it is clear to me that Polly may be suffering from early signs of adolescent schizophrenia. The child will often display thought disorder, delusions and sometimes paranoia and hallucinations. The youngest I have seen was a nine-year-old boy who lived with his mother. She also had it and was very unwell. Other possibilities than schizophrenia would include severe trauma and abuse, resulting in behavioural disturbance and dissociative symptoms, but I really feel we are seeing early signs of schizophrenia.

'In the interim, Polly needs supervision and monitoring. It will be challenging. She may have a fear of other animals, but certainly Polly was fearful when the emu was pecking around at her. So, she would be highly distressed at the animal approaching her and feel out of control.

Tess looked bewildered. 'Why so young? I mean... why...?'

'As I said, my youngest case was a boy aged nine years. He had his head covered at all times as he believed the rays of the sun were stealing his thoughts and trying to control his mind. He did need hospitalisation.

'What will settle her is anti-psychotic medication. It's very effective in helping people deal with voices. About 70–80% of patients improve on this. What concerns me is the killing of an animal with seemingly no remorse. This behaviour can be quite dangerous, not only to herself but to others. You need to make sure Polly stays on her medication and if she does not improve, we may have to look at scheduling her for treatment.'

Tess shifted in her seat. 'What's scheduling?'

'As a psychiatrist, I would recommend that she be institutionalised or scheduled, as we call it, to ensure Polly's safety and the safety of others.'

'Institutionalised! Taken away!' Tess was alarmed. She didn't realise it was this bad.

'Yes, that can happen. She has killed an animal. This could easily have been a matter for the police.'

Dr Adams started writing a script and then tore it off the pad. She opened a drawer and reached for some pamphlets.

'We will try Polly on this medication at the recommended dosage. These are pamphlets about schizophrenia and support groups. It usually takes about a week for the medication to have some effect and we may have to reduce or increase the dosage. I would suggest also, once Polly has had some benefits from this medication, that you try and bring in other stimuli.'

'Stimuli? Like what?'

'Perhaps riding, as you live on a property, socialising, a hobby of some sorts, something she enjoys, anything outdoorsy. Try and get Polly interested in physical activity and out of her room. All this is stimulus to an adolescent girl's mind. It appears from our discussions today that Polly spends a lot of time in her room, listening to her radio and watching TV. Try to avoid letting her skip school as this is also another interaction with someone else, a teacher, whom I'm sure has her best interests at heart. She does need education, Tess. Why didn't she commence schooling as a boarder? The country kids usually do this when they hit twelve years of age.'

Tess paused. 'I wanted Polly with me, and Polly also refused to go. Put on quite a performance.'

'That's a real shame, Mrs Walker. Initially, boarding school and leaving the family home can be upsetting, but they then thrive. As I said, start the medication and then try and get Polly to do more things. You and her father are her guides and her mentors on the road of life. Young children need good role models.'

'Are you meaning to say I'm not a good role model? Is that what you're saying?' said Tess, becoming quite defensive, her jaw set in defiance.

Dr Adams knew she had hit a raw nerve. 'No, not at all, Mrs Walker, just emphasising how important your role is. I would remove the TV and the radio as schizophrenic people think the voices are coming from either of those two. Make Polly watch TV in the family room. Is there a common room for family or something you can all join in together? And what about her younger sister, can you make an attempt to bring them closer? Clearly, Polly thinks there is favouritism. I suggest talking to your husband, or better yet, bring him to the next appointment. He is also welcome to come and see me to discuss Polly.'

Tess's nervous laughter bubbled up. 'That's a joke. If only you knew our house.'

'Well, the situation is this, Mrs Walker: You have to make an effort. You have no choice. Although the actual cause of schizophrenia is not fully understood, genetic and environmental factors play a part. Battering animals to death or wanting to harm people is very serious. As I said, she could be committed for this. I haven't seen her daily routine, but I have no doubt she exhibits disordered thinking and behaviour, as well as a lack of motivation to do anything.

'Well, yeah,' said Tess slowly. 'But up until the last maybe six months, she has been okay. She always had friends on the property next door and the usual sisterly squabbles, but nothing like this!'

'Unless we get this under control, those symptoms will continue and magnify as she gets older. The medication I have prescribed will help, but it is also up to you and your husband. Polly has to stay on this or she will be at significant risk of a relapse, and I don't want her harming anything or anyone else. The worst-case scenario is if she were to harm a person. She will then be institutionalised and there's also the possibility of being charged by the police, depending on the severity of harm.'

Tess's mind went into overdrive.

'Here, this is my business card. Please keep it and if you are having problems, just give my rooms a call. I want to see Polly in one week's time and we will need regular sessions until she is stable. I would recommend weekly for the first month and see how she progresses. Please call me at any time if you have concerns once she starts taking the medication. If there are any side effects from the medication or you are worried about anything, call the after-hours number on this card.'

Tess looked dumbfounded. She knew something was wrong with Polly, but now it was confirmed and more serious than she had thought.

'Come, let's go see Polly.' Dr Adams opened the door.

'Thank you, Polly, for waiting,' said the psychiatrist. 'I have given your mother a script that will stop those voices, so please comply with this medication. I know the voices can be scary, but they will settle if you keep on this medication. I have chatted to your mother, and you are both going to try to do activities together and with your family, especially those which do not involve staying in your room. You'll feel a lot better, Polly. I have asked your mother to bring you for regular sessions. My receptionist Gail will sort out appointment times for you.'

Dr Adams wondered if anything she had just said registered. The lack of light behind the girl's eyes was concerning.

'Yeah,' Polly drolly replied.

'See you in a week then, Doc,' muttered Tess.

'Goodbye, Polly. I'll see you soon.' Dr Adams inhaled deeply. It would be a challenge over the ensuing months. The young girl was clearly disturbed, and she may need hospitalisation at some stage.

As Tess got on the road after filling the prescription, she wondered whether to tell Mitch their daughter had a psychiatric illness that was so serious she could be involuntarily hospitalised. She knew she could not keep it from him and he would need to be told. She had a gut feeling he would react badly.

It was on dark when they arrived home. Kate was busy getting dinner while Olivia sat reading. Mitch and Dave were chatting.

'Hello, Tess. Polly. You're just in time for dinner. How did you go?' queried Kate.

Tess's mouth tightened. 'Polly got some pills, and we have to see the psych weekly for counselling. The pills will help calm Polly down.'

'What medication is that?' asked Kate.

'Just calming stuff,' shrugged Tess. 'And we have to do things as a family. You know, like going out, doing outdoors stuff, riding. Get Polly interested in life. The doc said it could be environmental factors, you know, causing her to act out.' Tess shot Mitch an accusing glance.

'What does that mean?' asked Mitch.

'Her surroundings may be causing problems with her head,' Tess admitted.

'Sounds like rubbish to me, more of your rubbish, Tess,' said Mitch.

Tess continued. 'I have to take the TV out of her room and the radio too. Can you help me, Mitch?'

Mitch looked closely at Tess. Was she telling the truth? His gut feeling said no. *She's lying.* He knew their homelife and marriage wasn't great, but he was sure Polly had more of a problem than this.

As Tess and Polly left the room, Mitch said, 'She's lying, Mum, I just know it.'

'Mitch, calm down. It's alright, Olivia,' said Kate, trying to soothe the confused girl who was listening. 'Why don't you go wash up.'

Kate waited until Olivia was out of earshot. 'I told you before, only a few weeks back, that it would be in all of our best interests to try and include both of them in everything. Maybe we are at fault. I would hate to think her behaviour the last few years is due to anything we have done or, that we are partly to blame. Children are the innocents in this mess. But I have never heard the term environmental factors.'

'She's lying, Mum. I'm going to call the doctor and find out myself.' Mitch was adamant. 'I've tried, but honestly, I rue the day I took her to bed. The only good thing to come out of our relationship is Olivia. I'll call the doctor and find out exactly what went on in that appointment. Polly killed an innocent animal. That's not because of the radio or TV or her homelife. Something is wrong with her.'

'I agree, Mitchell, but we are all going to try. That's all I'll say at this point.' Kate gritted her teeth. 'Now, please make an effort, and if that fails, and it's not going to be easy road, then at least you, or we, can say that we tried.'

As Kate finished her sentence, Tess suddenly appeared looking apprehensive.

'Hi Tess, we were just discussing how we could help Polly.'

'Umm, I'm sorry. I haven't been truthful. I guess I'm in shock and I just don't know how to handle this.'

'Handle what?' asked Kate, concerned. 'What have you been untruthful about? Please sit down, Tess.' All eyes were on Tess as she sat down.

'Polly does need counselling and she also needs to keep on medication, perhaps lifelong, but Dr Adams, the psychiatrist, seems to think she has adolescent schizophrenia.'

Mitch's eyes widened. There really was something mentally wrong with his daughter.

Kate reached across to take Tess's hands. 'Right, so now we know there are reasons for her actions. I'm so glad you told us, Tess. We can all work together to help Polly.'

It was then Tess lost control, sobbing heavily in Kate's arms.

TWELVE

CHANGING OF THE GUARD

Zena was with Jedda for another singing lesson. 'You have a lovely voice, Jedda, like a songbird. I'll have to pick out some interesting songs for you. Music is so soothing, and you can be as upbeat as you want or play something soft like the night.'

Jedda smiled. 'I want to sing, Nanny. I always sing. It makes me feel good.'

'Me too, Jedda,' smiled Zena.

Lisa came to pick up her daughter just towards evening.

'How did she go?'

'She's a natural. Jedda has a lovely voice. It's a pleasure to teach her and use my musical skills. She breezed through the first lesson, and she seems to have a natural ear for playing the piano. If her voice doesn't change, I would think she is a soprano.'

'Which means?' asked Lisa.

'Well, if we can develop her voice, sopranos can sing one or more octaves above a high C. Basically, it's based on the singer's vocal range and timbre of their voice. Lots of classical and operatic voices are sopranos. When she's older, we should go to the Opera House in Sydney to see something like *La Boheme*. It would be a real motivation for her to see what practice does and where she could end up.

Pie in the sky at this stage but you never know. Jedda may find that particular opera amusing when she's older. It's set in Paris and is about the Bohemian lifestyle of a poor seamstress and her artist friends. I think we would all enjoy it. I loved going to the opera.'

Lisa smiled. 'Sounds good and I would love to show her around Sydney when she's older. She would be fascinated at the sheer difference. Big city to the bush. But I don't know where she gets the voice from. I'm a hopeless singer.'

The phone rang and Zena went to answer it. 'Just excuse me,' she said as she darted away.

'Oh, Kev!' Zena exclaimed. 'Lovely to hear from you. Yes, we were only talking about you the other day. We wondered when you would call. Alan will be so excited. Everyone will be. Look, is there a permanent number? Alan needs to talk to you about staying on and perhaps doing a bit more around Woori. You two must surely be getting sick of shuffling from post to post.'

Lisa looked down at Jedda. 'Aunty is talking to a very special person. You'll meet him. Kev is his name, and Ningali is his partner. They both were here a few years back, but you and Jesse were so young you would probably not remember them.'

Zena continued. 'Oh, okay, still using the phone boxes.' She laughed. 'Are you able to call tomorrow night? Say about seven? Alan will be in by then.'

Lisa poked her head around the hallway, and Zena looked up, giving her the thumbs up.

'Wonderful, Kev. We'll look forward to seeing you when you both get here, and I'll tell Alan you will call tomorrow night. Give our regards to Ningali.'

Zena hung up the phone. 'They're coming, Lisa! He seems very keen on the idea of permanency here. Like all of us, they aren't getting any younger.'

'That's great news! Wait till I tell Billy. Come on, little songbird, we need to get dinner ready.'

Lisa kissed Zena goodbye and took off with Jedda. 'I'm so excited, Jedda. Wait till you meet Ningali. She is wonderful, just wonderful, and she has loads and loads of magical stories, just like Daddy.'

As Lisa headed home, she thought of Binna and Ningali and how they had entered her world at a time when she'd needed it most. She could see them both so clearly under their humpy, remembering Binna's wise words and the smell of the fires from the cleansing ceremonies. Lisa sniffed the air; it was a heady and warm fragrance she could still recall that brought comfort.

When she told Billy that evening, the grin never left his face.

◊

The next day, Alan came in for lunch. He picked up the note from Zena on the kitchen table. 'Up at Lisa's for School of the Air.'

As he sat down to a cold corn beef sandwich, the phone rang. 'G'day, Alan.' The male voice sounded hesitant to speak. 'Err, you don't know me, my name is Brian. Brian Pettigrew. Jack's younger brother.'

'Oh yes, mate,' said Alan, as he felt a strange feeling come over him, the muscles twitching in his face. A relative calling on behalf of someone always meant bad news.

'Alan, this is a sorry call I have to make.' The voice faltered and Alan gave him space to continue.

'My brother Jack, he has been your overseer at shearing time for some years now.'

'That's correct, Brian, never a better bloke. I was expecting a call soon from him, well, I hope.'

'That's why I'm calling. I've got sad news. Jack, he was killed two months ago. I'm just getting round to telling people and settling his affairs.' The sadness spilled out in his voice.

The shock dislocated Alan's mind and body momentarily. He felt his legs wanted to buckle as a thousand visions of the big, gregarious man flashed before him.

'What! How Brian? Jack was larger than life and much loved.'

'Yeah, he was loved by everyone. He... he was stabbed. Working up in the Territory, he went to break up a fight when the fellow pulled a knife and pierced his heart. Jack was getting slower, like all of us. These young blokes all carry knives. The police got him, but we don't have Jack anymore. I'm just going through his black book, as he liked to call it, ringing people.'

Alan was bereft with grief, and his words came slowly. 'What a tragic loss, but that was typical Jack trying to do good. Look, mate, take care. I don't know what else to say. He was a top bloke.'

'Don't I know that.' The voice finally broke. 'Bye, Alan. I'm sorry to be the bearer of such bad news.' The line went dead.

Alan sat down. He did not know which was worse: the pain he felt in his heart or the profound sense of loss that he would never shake the hand of the big man again.

When Zena pulled up, she thought it odd for Alan to be home early afternoon. She looked into the cabin of the ute. Nothing unusual and no blood. She exhaled a sigh of relief.

'Coooeee... it's me. Where are you? Got an early mark today?'

'Here, sweetheart, in the study.' His voice was sombre, and Zena had an uneasy feeling as she walked towards the room.

Alan's face said it all. 'What on earth is it, darling? Your face is ashen.'

'Sit down, it's sad news,' said Alan as Zena eased into the leather chair.

'It's Jack. I just took a call from his brother, Brian. Jack was killed two months ago. Working up in the Territory. Tried to break up a fight, and the bloke stabbed him.'

Zena stared at Alan in bewilderment, deeply shocked. She shook her head from side to side, as if trying to block out the dreadful image that swam before her eyes. 'Oh no, Alan, this is dreadful news.' The tears coursed down her face. 'Jack's gone?' She wiped her face with the back of her hands, overcome with sorrow. 'It's just so unbelievable.'

The only sound was Zena's gentle sobbing as Alan held her close. It was if the knife had been stabbed into their own hearts.

◊

The following morning, Zena phoned Lisa. 'Morning,' Zena greeted when Lisa picked up. She could hear the twins playing in the background. 'I'll be brief, Lisa, as it's hard to speak.'

'Aunty, what's wrong? I can hear it in your voice. What's happened?'

'It's Jack. He... he's dead.'

Lisa gasped and cried out in despair. 'Dead! No, no! What! My big Jack, dead?' She began to weep. 'How, what...?'

'Tragically killed in a fight, trying to break it up. Alan got the news yesterday. Jack's brother called. I can't speak any longer, Lisa. It really has hit us hard, particularly Alan. Come up for dinner tonight and we'll have a drink for our friend. Say about five-ish.'

'Okay, we'll see you then.' Lisa's shoulders sagged as she put the phone down. She recalled the big hands, the beaming smile and Jack's wonderful and warm reassuring ways. He was such a kind man and had a great understanding of people and life. A bush legend. Gone. Life could suddenly be snatched away. Her thoughts abruptly visualised the day in the laundry at the Parramatta Girls Home when her friend Julie had been killed. Lisa closed her eyes and felt the pain as she wiped the tears with the back of her hand.

When she came back into the kitchen, Jedda spoke. 'Mummy, why are you crying?'

When Lisa sat down, Jedda and Jesse came to her side and put their arms around her. 'My beautiful babies.' She kissed the top of their heads. 'A friend of ours has died. Jack, you remember big Jack.'

Jedda's face crumpled.

'He's the big, big man who always made us laugh,' added Jesse.

'Yes, he did. He always made us laugh. After I first came here to Woori, Jack became a good friend over the years.' It was a teary discussion.

'So, we will wait for Daddy to come home and then we are going to Nanny and Pop's to celebrate Jack's life and that we were glad to have known him.'

'Did he get buried like Ume?' asked Jedda.

'Yes, my darling, just like Ume.'

Billy already knew when he arrived home.

'You know?' whispered Lisa.

'Yes, my grasshopper, Alan told me.' A hushed tone wedged itself between his words. 'My mate Jack, he with da spirits now. He go to da Land of da Dead. Sky-World.'

The decision was made that evening as they raised their glasses to Jack. They were so close to shearing now that Billy would move into Jack's role. Although he had no skills at supervising staff, Alan would be there to help, and with Kev arriving in a matter of weeks, they hoped everything would be under control.

Cookie had written a short note, as did old Ned, to say they would be along for one more season. Alan had placed an ad in the local newspaper for shearers due to some of his usual crew dropping out. Some of the younger shearers were different to the old guard, and he wondered how they would react under Billy's rule. He just wasn't sure who would be available. Jack had always rounded up a crew that were ready to go. He would turn up and everything went like clockwork. Alan now had to run an ad, something he had never done before.

THIRTEEN

RIVER RIDE

Over the ensuing weeks, Kate noted a marked improvement in Polly's behaviour, as did Mitch and Dave. Her eyes were clearer and more focused, and Kate no longer heard her chattering to herself. Whether it was the medication, or the intervention of the psychiatrist, probably both, sanity finally prevailed at Woodside. Polly seemed to be adapting once again to the rhythm of rural life. Olivia began to interact more with her sister. There were a few ups and downs, a few dummy spits, but it was so opposite to the situation previously. They were on track again. Dave said it was a bloody miracle.

Since Mitch had moved the TV and radio from her room, Polly was interacting more in the family room. She was scheduled to see Dr Adams in another week's time and wanted to continue seeing her.

Mitch reluctantly agreed to Tess and Polly being given the daily chore of riding the boundaries of the property to check the fencing for holes and all the water stations for the sheep. It made them both get out of bed. Kate continually said everyone needs a reason and purpose to get out of their bed.

Tess hoped Mitch would acknowledge their contribution, even though it was only minor. She hated him, but she also loved him.

Always in the back of her mind, she knew she was never good enough in Kate's eyes for her son. She was so desperate to please him and to gain his attention.

It was a beautiful morning as they rode in a westerly direction. A good, hard ride of about two hours, there and back and under the searing rays of the sun.

'Hey, Polly, we're done here, so how about we head to the river and have a swim. What do you think? Zena has always said it's a good ride and you end up having a swim afterwards.'

'Yeah, that would be great. I've got no swimmers though, Mum.'

'Who cares, it's just us. Come on, we'll see what Madam Zena is on about. She always said the ride to the river and a swim was invigorating or some shit like that.' They cantered on and as they came closer, they could see a big black horse tethered to a tree.

'Hold on, we've got company,' said Tess.

Billy had heard the horse hooves thundering on the road and started to swim back closer to shore. The Walker females were upon him as he stood waist deep.

Tess's eyes widened. Sheer masculine beauty stood before her. Raw sex appeal. The chocolate skin and musculature. 'My, my, what have we got here?'

'You stay back, don't want no trouble.' Billy started to wade towards the banks of the river, very aware he was totally naked.

'Well, I don't want to give you any trouble, but I sure as hell wish you would give me a bit of trouble,' said Tess, grinning.

Billy didn't acknowledge her but made his way towards Jed.

Tess licked her lips. No wonder Mitch lost out. This man was magnificent. Lucky Lisa. She got everything. Lust filled Tess's mind.

Over the years, she had always envisioned what Billy looked like naked and now she had the complete picture. Her sexual urges kicked in. *God, I need sex.*

'Mum, let's go,' stammered Polly. She had seen that look on her mother's face before.

'Sure, Pol, but I want to see a little bit more of that.' Tess's eyes feasted on Billy as he quickly finished dressing. Her body ached for some male attention. She had not been into town for a couple of months, and Mitch was a dead loss in the sack.

Billy tipped his black hat and began to make his way past the two women. He spurred Jed on. He didn't like the look of either of them. Flaming red hair. Red devils.

When Billy told Lisa, she expressed concern. Billy kissed her forehead. 'Grasshopper, Billy sees all.'

Later that evening, Lisa discussed Olivia's request to come to Woori with Billy. 'Olivia wants to see Jesse and Jedda, and it has been a while. Jesse wants her to have a sleepover. They talk on the phone constantly. Do you think it's okay?'

'Dat alright, da little one on her own.'

'Okay, I'll let Kate know. Maybe this weekend. I'll find out and see what suits.'

The following day, Lisa made the call to Kate. 'Yes, Lisa, Livvy will be so excited and of course she can stay overnight.'

'How are things over there? Are you getting ready for the shearing crew to arrive?' asked Lisa.

'Things are set to go. Dave always has it under control. How about you?' queried Kate.

'We do, Kate. But our overseer, Jack, who has been with Alan for a long time, was tragically killed two months ago. So we're slightly unprepared as Jack would have a crew organised and they would simply turn up a few days after him. But Alan has it under control. We'll see a few new faces, and we put an ad in the newspaper.'

'I was sorry to hear of that news. Zena told me that Jack had died. A very good person and no doubt sadly missed by all who knew him. But life goes on, Lisa, and we have to change and adapt. Always happy to send some of our crew. Who will be the overseer then?'

'Billy. He'll be looking after things with Alan.'

There was a short silence. 'Billy? Is that a good thing? I mean, he has had no prior experience. Sorry, Lisa, I don't mean to sound rude, but shearers need a tough hand. Some of them can be quite difficult. Salt of the earth types, rough and ready. I think you know what I'm trying to say.'

'No, it's okay. Alan is confident, we all are.'

'Very good, you know your own lot. I'll drop Livvy off Saturday morning at about ten.'

Lisa wondered if she made reference to Billy because of the colour of his skin.

When the weekend came around, Olivia was pleased to be with her friends again. When Billy came home, Olivia ran to him. 'Billy,' she squealed as he picked her up and whirled her through the air.

'Hey, Lisa, looks like dis lot bin having some fun?'

Lisa smiled. 'They sure have. I was about to go and check the broodmares. Let's all go.'

Once they reached the paddocks, Billy ran his hands over the mares. 'Always be kind to creatures, dey know da goodness.' The mares nuzzled against Billy and softly whinnied.

'Lisa, she bin lunging them proper good. Look strong and healthy. Good babies, Jesse. Not far now, mebbe another week.'

'Can we watch?' asked Jedda.

'If she have da babies in a time you ain't sleeping, sure. But you know, da girls have dem usually very early morning. Sun not up. Neither are you.'

'Why?' asked Olivia.

'So she sees her baby is up and walking. Can't lie on da ground in da sunrise or da crows come, pick dem eyes out.'

Olivia gasped and touched her eyes. 'They eat their eyes?'

'Yep, true talk. So dey have da babies when no one around. Still dark. Make sense?' asked Billy.

They all nodded.

'Do you have a story, Billy?' asked Olivia. 'Your stories are like magic.'

'Now... or we wait?' smiled Billy.

'Now, Now!' they almost chanted in unison. Billy sat down with Lisa on a bale of hay with the children at his feet. The only sound was the crows and parrots with a soft breeze whispering through the eucalyptus tree they sat under.

'I tell you about da little green frogs, when dey came into da world. One morning in dat shallow pond, all da little tadpoles, dey swimming around and one cheeky one, he jumped too high and landed on da river bank. He didn't move. Da animals and birds try to wake him but he just lay on da ground. A wombat come and say dat tadpole, he lose his breath. All da animals believed da spirits had done this, so dey call a meeting under a big gum tree. Just like we do now.'

Olivia sat spellbound, her mouth half open. Jesse held her hand.

'Then what happened next?' asked wide-eyed Jedda.

'When dey all talk talk at da gum tree, da spirits, dey come and take da little tadpole high up into da sky. Da wombat say because da powerful spirits can change him to something else. All da animals listened and say someone should go into da sky and see what happened. All da tadpoles do one big wiggle and find a pond in da big sky waiting for spring. Den da first warm day come and all da frogs start to hatch. Den all da colours of da frogs appeared in da sky. Red ones, green ones, brown ones, dey all ready to start a whole new adventure and explore da land. So, dem spirits dey give da tadpoles a beautiful shape and colour and dey can jump and swim. So da spirits say, all dem old animals say dis how it must always be. When you see dat tadpole in da river or pond or da billabong, he waiting to turn into da frog. Special frog and dey all happy. You hear dem sing sing all day long.'

'Oh,' exclaimed Olivia. 'Whenever I see a tadpole, I'll know she is waiting to turn into a bright green frog!'

'Or a brown one!' replied Jedda.

'Come, Billy hungry.' He half squatted and Jedda leaped onto his back, carrying her as the other two walked hand in hand.

'Lovely story, Billy,' said Lisa as she took his hand. The house was noisier than ever. The chatter and laughter never stopped. It was only tiredness that ceased the children's tongues. They had fallen asleep on the piled-up cushions on the floor. Billy carried them all to bed.

'I think our Jesse is smitten, Billy,' said Lisa. 'Puppy love.'

'See it today, when I tell dem my story. My Jesse he hang on tight to Livvy's hand. Come, grasshopper, I tell you a story,' said Billy.

'Now what story would that be?' Lisa asked cheekily.

'About da girl who take my heart.' Billy swooped her up and carried her to the bedroom.

FOURTEEN

A MONSTER COMETH

It was a Sunday afternoon as they sat on the veranda at Woodside. 'I'm getting another beer. Want one, Dad?'

'Yeah, I'll go another round. How about you, Kate, would you like something?' asked Dave.

'What a good idea. A gin and tonic will do nicely.'

When Mitch got to the kitchen, Tess and Polly were coming up the back stairs.

'Hi, Mitch,' Tess broke the ice. 'We just hosed the horses down. Polly has made a note of the gaps we saw in some paddocks. Give your dad the note, Pol.'

Polly reached into her top pocket and pulled out a small note pad, ripping the top sheet off. 'Here Dad, it's all written down.'

'Thanks, Polly,' Mitch mumbled.

'Having a few drinks, are we?' Tess queried.

'Yeah.' Mitch reached into the fridge.

'Well, I hope it's okay to join you?' queried Tess.

'Sure, Tess.' Mitch grabbed the drinks and headed outside.

'We'll be right with you,' said Tess, reaching for a beer. 'Get yourself a soft drink or something Polly.'

They headed out to the veranda and sat down on the sofas.

Once she'd finished her drink, Kate said, 'Look, I think I had best get dinner ready. Not far off everyone, so twenty minutes is all you have. Come on, Dave. Livvy, you can help me too, please.'

Tess looked across to Polly. 'You best go shower and clean up too. I'll just finish my beer with Dad.'

'It's nice sitting here with you, Mitch. Do you want another beer?' asked Tess as she took another guzzle.

He was about to say no, but he was enjoying the beer and the first two hardly touched the sides. 'Yeah, why not,' he said, about to get up.

'No, you stay, I'll go get them.' Tess was clearly relishing the opportunity to sit and drink with him. He'd never done this before. Maybe he was turning and finally appreciative of what she was doing with Polly.

Mitch leaned back wearily into the big couches and closed his eyes.

His eyes fluttered open when Tess sat back down.

'Here you go.' Tess passed the beer. He regretted instantly going another round and didn't want to make small talk with her anymore.

Mitch flicked the ring top and drank, too quickly. Tess laughed. 'Boy, you were thirsty. There's not much of that one left.'

'I need to wash up,' Mitch said. 'I'll see you inside.'

Tess sipped on the can. She longed to have him inside her again, and her memory never faded from the times he had entered her body.

Dave opened a couple of bottles of red over dinner and the warmth of that red juice oozed through Tess's veins. Her appetite for Mitch only increased the more she drank.

As Tess lay in bed that night, she listened to his footsteps coming up the hallway. She was so willing to make do with the tiniest crumb from him, smelling him, touching him. She flung her legs over the bed and headed to his room.

The light was off as she opened the door and moved towards him. 'Tess, what are you doing?' He let out a tired breath. She dropped her robe to the floor. She still looked good naked, and he felt his arousal running wild through his body. Tess moved closer and slowly pulled the covers back. She smiled at the sight of his erection and crawled in.

He wanted to push her away but he groaned with pleasure as her mouth roamed his body.

'That's it, baby,' Tess cooed. 'It's not healthy for a man stifling his ejaculations.' She moved tighter against him, hooking one leg over his hip, and mounted him.

'That feels so good.' Tess clasped him hungrily as Mitch moaned uncontrollably, moving with her, pushing deeper and deeper inside her body with raw force. She was so hungry for him. He was beyond stopping, and Tess could feel his throbbing contractions as she drove him to a powerful ejaculation. A deep, guttural sound tore from his throat then he suddenly exploded, a shattering burst of rapture.

As they lay next to each other in the moments afterwards, Mitch spoke up. 'Can you go back to your own room, Tess? I'm exhausted and I need a good night's sleep.'

Tess suddenly reached out and smacked Mitch's face so hard her palm stung with the impact. 'As if it's so bloody hard to sleep together like husband and wife!' She was so furious, she stomped out.

When she woke the next morning, her only feeling was anger. She began to pack her bag. She needed to get out of there and find some real men. Sex was on her mind. It was always a game, a game she enjoyed. She showered and dressed and went to Polly's room.

'Hey Pol,' Tess said as she entered the room.

Polly sat up, rubbing her eyes.

'I need to get away for a few days. I'll be back to take you to your next appointment. Make sure you take your meds and do your chores. You do a great job, and everyone here knows it.'

'Why can't I come? Please take me with you,' pleaded Polly.

'Because I have things to do... and besides, I don't want you getting out of your rhythm. School, chores and stuff.'

Tess bent to kiss Polly on the cheek, but the girl turned her face away. 'Alright, have it your way, but just take your medication, promise me. I'll call you, Pol, be good now.'

Polly remained silent and then heard the door close.

As Tess came into the kitchen, everyone was there except Olivia. Mitch saw her bag. 'Going somewhere?'

Tess's eyes flashed with contempt. 'As if you care! I'm doing a few things in town, Kate. Can you keep an eye on Polly?'

''Sure, Tess, no problem,' she said as they watched her bolt down the back stairs, slamming the door behind her.

'Good Lord, what was that all about?' asked Dave.

Kate shook her head. 'Something to do with the shouting we heard last night, no doubt. Arguing, Mitch?'

'It was nothing, just nothing.'

'Nothing? Then what is that bluish tinge under your eye?' queried Kate.

'Mum, I said it was nothing. Leave it alone,' his tone now one of extreme annoyance.

◊

By the time she hit Walgett, Tess was dying for a drink and to feel the excitement of a man who wanted her. She always had a feeling of power when she controlled the bedroom.

When she opened the door to her mother's house, she pulled a face. It smelled bad. Tess opened all the windows with fly screens and then poured herself a drink. It was early evening when she hopped under the shower and put on a red dress with flat sandals. She peered at herself in the mirror as she applied bright red lipstick, puckering her mouth. 'Not bad at all, Tess, not bad at all.' She fluffed up her red hair, sprayed some perfume on and walked towards the pub in Walgett.

The bar was filling with local men who knew her, passers-by, truckies, council workers and shearers. No vanilla sex here, she wanted it rough and hard. She slid up onto a bar stool and it wasn't long before Johnny, a previous acquaintance, sidled up next to her. As he did so, a big man with menacing eyes watched her intently from a corner in the bar. He had known this type of female, a prick-teaser who wanted sex. He could give it to her. He'd known lots of women like her. She played a good game. His big hands clenched in and out. He would get his turn with the redhead.

'How you going, Tess, back in town, are ya?' Johnny's eyes wandered over her body.

'Yeah, Johnny, out for a bit?' He was well hung and could go all night. He would do, but for now she would enjoy the teasing.

'Buy you a drink?'

'Sure, Johnny, a double Jack Daniels and Coke. You should remember that,' Tess purred.

Two hours passed and a few other men had joined them. Tess could tell they were all ripe for it. No too much action in Walgett. The alcohol had made her feel sexy, and she was ready.

'I'm heading home now Johnny.' Tess grabbed her purse and keys.

'Want some company?' His voice was slightly husky with anticipation.

'Sure, let's go.'

When they walked towards Tess's house, they were not aware of the big man following in the shadows. He turned and left when Tess arrived at the shabby cottage. He smiled. *I know where you live now, you dirty little fuckbird.*

When she woke the next morning, her throat was parched and dry. There was no one in the bed but her. She was sore and felt bruised all over, but what she could remember made her smile. Definitely not vanilla sex.

Tess stretched and her hand came up to her pulsing head. She reached for the pills in her handbag to dull the ache and took a deep breath in then exhaled, her bloodshot eyes scanning the room. *Think*

I'll just stay right here, she thought as she peered at the cobwebs in the corners. Watch some TV and call Polly.

It was early afternoon when Tess dialled Woodside. She knew Polly would not pick up. She never did. Kate answered so she asked her to let Polly know she'd be back soon to take her to the next psych appointment.

When Kate put the phone down, she shook her head. Tess's sudden departure was undoubtedly to do with Mitch and the arguing she'd heard. *Damn. Just when things were a whole lot better.*

The phone rang again at Tess's mother's place, the bells seeming so loud. 'Alright, alright, I'm coming.' Tess shuffled down the hallway.

'Hello,' her gravelly voice answered.

'Tess, it's Kate, sorry to bother you. I know you wanted some time out, but I think Polly is missing you. She's having those conversations again. I heard her this morning, and now she's missing. Probably riding, and I may just be panicking.'

There was silence as Tess took a deep sigh and held the phone to her chest. 'Alright, I'll head home. See you late this afternoon.'

'Thank you, Tess. I just don't want the situation to get out of hand. She has been so settled of late.'

'That's okay. See you soon.' She leaned against the wall and then slowly slid down. She started to sob, her head on her knees, and felt a stabbing pain in her heart. She wanted to scream. What had she done in her life to deserve a husband who didn't love her and a daughter who was mentally ill?

FIFTEEN

THE NEW DAM

Kate had begun to panic when she'd noticed the change in Polly's behaviour. When Mitch came into the house at lunch time, he quickly dialled the number on Dr Adams's business card. Gail, her secretary, rearranged a few patients, and Mitch was fitted in urgently with Polly. They arrived at the doctor's rooms just before 2:00 p.m.

Dr Adams opened her consulting door and called them in. 'Hello, Polly, and you must be Mitch, her father,' she greeted as she extended her hand. 'I've looked forward to meeting and chatting with you.'

Mitch was taken aback slightly. He didn't know what to expect. In his mind he had perhaps envisioned someone older, but she was slim and attractive, and her blue eyes spoke of softness. He relaxed and explained the slight downturn in Polly's behaviour.

'So, tell me. What has been happening, Polly?'

Polly began flicking her fingers unconsciously. 'Umm, I heard the voices talking to me again. They've been quiet for some time but suddenly they were there, in my room with me.'

'And are they giving you commands, Polly, like before, to harm you or other people?'

'No, not really, it's more like hearing my name called and then the sound of rats scratching behind my ears. I went to the barns to see if I could find a rat's nest to destroy them. Another voice told me to hold my face under the water in the sink, like to drown me.'

Mitch looked down at his hands and closed his eyes. It was painful to hear.

'Have you been taking your medication consistently, Polly?'

She paused and shook her head. 'No, Mum went away and I sort of went off them for a few days. Then the voices just came on so quickly.'

'We have discussed before the importance of maintaining your daily medication regime. If you don't keep taking the tablets I prescribed consistently, Polly, these are the things that can happen.'

Polly shrugged. 'I'm sorry. I guess I just missed Mum.'

'Alright, let's begin one of our CBT therapies and practice reducing the emotional distress when your mother goes away.'

'Um, what's CBT?' queried Mitch

'Sorry, Mitch. It is Cognitive Behavioural Therapy. It's used in conjunction with medication to help reduce the stress of hearing voices or when experiencing emotional distress. We came up with humming or singing the song Happy Birthday to override the voices.'

'Sounds... weird, but I'll leave that to the experts,' said Mitch, sceptical that singing Happy Birthday could assist with mental disorders.

Dr Adams smiled at Mitch, feeling his lack of understanding. 'Just give me an hour, Mitch.'

'Sure, I'll be back in an hour then.'

On the drive home, Polly seemed more settled. She was not as restless.

'How are you feeling, Pol?' He genuinely wanted to know. He felt for his daughter being afflicted with such a terrible diagnosis.

'I like talking to her, Dad. She helps me. I like seeing her.'

That's good Pol, I liked her too. Nice lady. Now, when we get home, we'll all make sure you take your medication consistently, and at the same time each day. It's important for your mental wellbeing, and you've been doing so much better on it.' He reached over and squeezed her hand, feeling closer to his eldest daughter than he'd felt in a long time. Mitch resolved to make more of an effort with her in future.

◊

Alan wanted to see the Woodside's new dam. There was talk of legislating the size of dams and how they were constructed. He wanted to build a bigger dam himself and was interested to see what Dave Walker had done with his, so headed out there with Billy.

Cripes, Dave wasn't kidding. The dam was huge. What a great spot though, with a few peppercorn trees scattered about, good shade for stock. Sides were steep, and the angle of the road leading down to it meant that all rain would flow down into the dam.

'Head water catchment, so crucial out here, Billy. We could do this at Woori.'

'Good swimming hole,' said Billy.

'Dave is ahead of the bureaucrats as usual. Another reason why I wanted to take a look. I don't need government officials telling me what to do in my own backyard. Let's head back.'

As they headed to the Ute, a bike was travelling towards the dam, the red dust billowing around them. '

'What the devil is that contraption?' said Alan.

'Not two wheels,' Billy replied.

'Yep, can see that. It's Dave with Olivia.'

Dave waved and pulled up at the gates as Alan and Billy met him and the laughing girl. 'Billy!' she squealed as she jumped off the bike and ran into his arms.

'So, what is this machinery, Dave? It's a beauty!' said Alan.

'It's a 4-wheeler for the farm. Suzuki are making them. Called a Quadrunner. Five forward speeds and reverse. Picked it up a week ago in Walgett. Livvy loves getting on the back behind me.'

'I love it, wait till Jesse and Jedda see it,' Olivia shouted, her arms entangled around Billy's neck.

'You've got to get one, Alan. Someone had a bit of nous when making this.' Dave pointed to his head. 'Just got to be careful you don't roll or flip them.'

Alan looked at Billy. 'What do you think? Better than horses?'

Billy shook his head. 'No way. Horses not gonna roll or flip.'

'Yeah, right,' Alan laughed, 'but they can certainly flip you when they want. You had best get Jesse and Jedda used to driving. I'm sure they'll be fighting over who gets to drive this thing. I'm off to Walgett to get one.'

'What did you think of the dam, Alan?' asked Dave.

'Perfect position, mate, in terms of water catchment, and not a bad swimming hole. Well done,' said Alan admiringly.

'Yeah, instead of heading to the river on those hot days, a splash out here won't do you any harm,' said Dave. 'It's just those government twits thinking they can tell me how to construct a dam if that legislation goes through.'

'Yeah, mate. I just told Billy that we need to do the same before the rules change,' added Alan.

'My kids love dat. Dey like tadpoles in the river. Teach dem from da young age. Good swimmers,' added Billy.

'Well, perhaps they can get Livvy to swim. She doesn't like the water, Billy, but if she is out here on her own, it's now imperative to learn to swim. Anyway, do you want to have a bit of a bash on this thing before you buy?' asked Dave.

'Good idea. Come on, Billy, hop on, take it for a spin, if Olivia can let you go,' said Alan as Billy gently lowered Olivia to the ground.

'Please, can I come, Billy?' Her blue eyes gazed up at him.

Alan looked at Dave. 'Sure, no harm, just take it easy, Billy, it's a bit clunky on the turn. The steering is a bit heavy and just remember, like all bikes, there's no safety.'

Olivia scrambled on the back with Billy and wrapped her arms tightly around his waist. *What a contrast*, Alan thought. *The chocolate-skinned young man and the tiny blonde girl.*

Billy slowly headed away from the dam and then cranked up the quad a bit faster. 'Hang on, Livvy,' he said as she giggled and clung even harder.

'She's got a soft spot for your Billy, Alan,' said Dave. 'Never stops talking about him and his stories, or your twins.'

'Yeah, Dave, know what you mean. He has this charisma with animals, kids. Zena says he is shamanic.'

'What's that? Some new hippy talk,' Dave scoffed.

'Nope. He just seems to tap into the power of Mother Earth. Indigenous people care for everything, people, plants, animals, you name it. So, having known Billy now for as long as I have, I think it's never a more apt description. Like his old man Burnu. He was the same.'

'How did you go with the ad in the paper for crew?' queried Dave.

'I was going to raise that with you. Left our run too late, so the ad was really necessary. Most of the shearers have picked up work already, no doubt at various properties around New South Wales as well as Queensland. Poor old Jack's demise put a spanner in the works somewhat. He was always beavering away in the background, contacting old and new crew. He also seemed to pick a bunch that got on. God rest his soul.'

'Shame, Alan, good bloke, but as I said, our boys can give you a hand. Happy to help. It will be all action stations in about four days' time. We should have a mutual get-together, so your crew know our crew, if they'll be working together. You know what I mean.'

'Great idea. I'll let Zena know.'

'Yeah, and we can set up the BBQ at Woodside. The crew can get pissed for the night as they usually do, and then into it.'

As Billy and Olivia approached, they didn't know who had the biggest grin.

'Bit of fun?' said a bemused Alan.

'Good machine, Alan.' Billy swung his legs off the quad.

'Dave was just saying that the twins are welcome to come here swimming. Might be quicker than heading out to the river. We'll get going now, but thanks, Dave, for everything. I'll let Zena know about the season and having the get-together here.'

SIXTEEN

GOOD FRIENDS RETURN

It was late in the afternoon when they heard the engine at the last entrance gate to Woori. Jedda looked up when she heard the noise and imitated the sound, 'vroom, vroom, vroom' and then proceeded to run madly around the yard. Jesse was amused, and they both looked at the bright red ute heading towards the main house.

'Who is that, I wonder?' asked Jedda.

'He's got the flash car. I want one when I grow up,' added Jesse. 'Come on, let's tell Mummy.'

They raced inside. Jedda was yelling at the top of her voice. She knew this bright red car was connected to the visitors who were coming. 'Mummy, a bright red car that makes loud noises went up to the big house.'

'Yes, children, I heard. Come on, let's go.' She grabbed the keys, excitement in her voice. She knew it was Kev and Ningali.

As she drove towards Woori, she saw those unmistakable long, thin legs standing next to the ute in the distance. 'Look, look, it's Ningali. It's my friend Ningali!'

Ningali looked at the approaching car and squealed, 'Lisa, my picaninny,' then began waving madly, running towards her and the children.

Kev came down the back stairs with Alan and Zena as Lisa reached Ningali, hugging her madly. Tears flowed down their faces as the twins watched curiously.

'Why is Mummy crying?' asked Jesse.

'Oh Jesse, come here. Jedda, they are happy tears for my friend.'

'Well watta we got here now? Dem two picaninnies, dey all grown,' said Ningali.

'This is Ningali, the special lady I told you about,' said Lisa, wiping her eyes.

'I'm Jedda.' The little girl stepped forward, extending her hand. 'We've heard all about you.'

'She got Billy's eyes, dis little beauty. And dis one, you gotta to be dat Jesse.' She inspected the small boy who couldn't stop staring.

Jesse grinned. 'I like your car, it's flash.'

Ningali chuckled. 'Yeah, my Kev, he gotta have da flash car. Where dat Billy?' Ningali chuckled.

'He's with the cows,' Jesse replied quickly.

'Da cows? I thought we got da sheep here?' said Ningali.

'We have both now, which is why we need your help, you and Kev. But I will leave that Alan and Billy to explain,' said Lisa.

Alan and Zena watched on with Kev, amusement crossing their faces as the twins chatted to Ningali, when a cough came out from underneath the canopy of the ute.

Jedda's eyes widened. 'Who's there... under that top?'

'Haaaaa. Dat top secret. We put da canopy over da back, so my friend, she don't get burnt too much. She bin sleepin'. She like da sleep,' said Ningali.

'Burnt,' blurted Jedda. 'But you're already black, so how do you get burnt?'

'Jedda,' cautioned Lisa, 'That will be enough.'

'But Mummy.' Jedda came to the back of the canopy and lifted up the canvas. She gasped.

'There's a large black lady in here!'

'Yep, she my friend. We got to help Mum Shirl out, she kinda a big lady, but she got da good heart. You see for yourself,' chuckled Ningali.

'Nice ute, Kev,' said Alan.

'Yeah, she the 1982 WB ute. Got to get me some black flames up da side, like da old yellow one.'

Alan laughed. 'Yeah, I remember that big old canary.'

'So, who have we got in the back then?' asked Zena.

'Everybody, meet my friend Mum Shirl. She gotta lot of stories,' said Ningali as she began to unlace the tarp that covered the top canopy. As she pulled the canvas off, sitting underneath the canopy was quite a large lady, her black face covered with red dust. When she smiled, she had very few teeth remaining, and as she laughed, her whole body rocked and jiggled.

'I Mum Shirl,' she greeted, as her eyes swept over the small gathering of curious spectators who stood at the back of the ute.

'Let me give you a hand,' said Lisa.

'Here, Lisa, I'll help too.' Zena came to her aid. She looked at the woman covered in red dust and smiled. Her dark wiry hair had one white streak at the front.

'Mum Shirl, I'm Zena and this is Lisa. Welcome to Woori.' Zena couldn't help but think she looked like a plump purple fig, and from every branch of the tree from which she had grown, there would be a story.

'Mum Shirl, slide your backside towards us,' commanded Ningali.

The elderly lady began to wiggle her bottom towards them as she extended her arms. The twins thought it hilarious, giggling loudly, not at her size, just how awkward it looked.

As she got to the end of the tray of the ute, they heaved and pulled her out. 'We gotta put Mum Shirl here, 'cause she don't fit in da front. She da big lady, mebbe not too quick on da feet but she plenty strong. Like da bloke. Mum Shirl, she can carry anything and once she grab you, she got da big grip. Strong hands and da strong legs. Never let ya go,' giggled Ningali.

Mum Shirl steadied her feet on the ground and dusted her dress, which had seen better days. She had a twinkle in her eye, and the twins were curious to know more about her.

'Got your hands full, Kev, old mate,' Alan muttered.

'Yeah, brudder, da girls, dey keep me in line, proper true,' replied Kev.

'Well, you're the first to arrive, so where do you want to stay? Shearers quarters? But if you stay permanently, which we want you to do, we can build a small place for you and Ningali. Just a few creature comforts instead of being in the back of the ute.'

'Yeah boss, I do da talk talk with Ningali, but for now, we got da tents. Happy sleeping dat way. Mum Shirl, she got her own tent. She snores, wake da spirits.'

With that, everyone broke out laughing. 'Hey, you Kev, you dat cheeky bugger,' said Mum Shirl shaking her finger at Kev. 'You got da snore bug too, ya know.' Her whole body shook in joviality.

'Mum Shirl, you have a bit of a quick tongue, so you'll fit in nicely here,' smiled Zena, delighting in the light-heartedness of the situation.

'We'll leave you to it then, Kev. You know where the shearing sheds are and the men's quarters. Just show the ladies where they can wash, and everyone here at six for dinner.'

'I get in da back,' said Ningali. 'Mum Shirl, you get in da front.' They all watched as she waddled and heaved herself into the front seat, filling the cabin.

'See you in a bit, Kev,' said Alan leaning into the window. 'Let me know if you need anything. Zena has taken food down to the kitchen, so help yourselves. Lisa took up three stock horses as well yesterday, so pick which one you want, mate. They'll be around in the yards behind the shearing shed.'

They all watched the bright red ute head to familiar ground.

'Well, I'm sure we'll find out Mum Shirl's background. What a character,' said Zena bemused.

◊

When Kev and Ningali got to the sheds, they knew they had made the right decision. It felt like home.

'We stay, Ningali?'

'Yeah, we stay.' A big smile lit up her face.

He pitched their tents well away from the shearer's sleeping quarters, and they began to get ready for dinner. Kev sat waiting on the tree stump outside the men's quarters where he had sat so long ago with Jack. In the distance, he saw a big black horse heading towards him. He grinned broadly like his smile would crack open his face. He took off his hat and waved madly. Billy did the same.

'Hey friend, my brudder, Billy, how ya bin?' said Kev as Billy dismounted. They gave each other a bear hug, Kev affectionately slapping Billy on the back.

'Good to see you, Kev. Me and Lisa, we miss you,' said Billy, stepping back. 'Lookin' good, mate. Ningali, she bin looking after you.'

'Sure has, she in da shower with Mum Shirl. We gonna stay, Billy, no more bunkin' down anywhere. Got to find me a stable place, not getting' any younger.'

A look of relief came over Billy's face. He had longed to hear those words. 'Makes Billy happy,' he beamed.

Ningali suddenly appeared and squealed when she saw Billy. She rushed towards him. 'Billy, Billy, you getting da more handsome, dat Lisa, she da lucky girl.' She giggled girlishly and Billy didn't know where to look until he saw the large dark lady step out from the sheds.

Ningali started to cackle. She was so used to that reaction. 'Mum Shirl, you come come. Here Mr Billy. Dat bloke we always mention. Lisa's husband.'

The old lady grinned and waddled towards them. 'G'day, young fella, Me Mum Shirl, and you be Billy.' She stood with her hands on her hips. 'You got da good looks orright. You da good looker.'

'Mum Shirl, she stayin' with us. We travel together now,' said Kev. 'Mum Shirl, she come with da husband from Darwin, Larrakia people, but dey travel to Queensland, and we meet dem on a property up there. But he no good. Always beat Mum Shirl. Dat fella no good, he da bad ringer, on da grog and fighting, and one day he just take off. Boss owner want to get rid of her but we say she with us and he get real angry. He say don't want no baggage. So we pack up and go, head here.'

Billy looked at the old lady and immediately felt a softness. He spoke the words gently, 'You happy here, you have place to stay, always. Me got to get back, dinner soon.' He mounted Jed, tipped his hat and turned his head for home, the hooves thundering along the dusty road.

'Dat man special. He got da kind eye,' said Mum Shirl. 'He got da spirits around him. I feels it.' She waved her hands above her head, gesturing to the sky.

Ningali nodded. Everyone knew Billy operated on a higher plane of existence. Like his father Burnu, he had the ability to manipulate the unseen through energies, spirits, spells and dreamwork. He tapped into his land, the environment, and such shamans could transmit messages over long distances. His connection with the spiritual ancestors was deep.

As they loaded into Kev's ute, Mum Shirl spoke. 'You sure dis proper true... Black people, dey eatin' with da whitefellas?'

Kev and Ningali laughed. 'Proper true, things different here.'

◊

Zena cringed when she saw the dress Mum Shirl had on. It had seen better days. Alan could see her mind ticking over at the dinner table.

'So, tomorrow, Kev, we'll take you out to see the new cattle and then I'm heading into town to buy a 4-wheel bike, called a Quadrunner. Dave next door has one, and it's a beauty. Billy took it for a run.'

Billy nodded. 'Yeah, good bike, seem steady, better dan two wheels, but stiff in da steering.'

'You boys can come with me if you like,' added Alan.

'Sound good,' said Kev.

'Big Jack died recently, Kev, so I have Billy organising the crew this year. Are you happy to give him a hand?'

'Sure thing, boss, but what happened to dat Jack? He da top bloke, bring me here to Woori.'

'Yeah, and don't I owe him for that one. He was trying to break up a fight and one of the idiots pulled a knife.'

'Sorry business,' replied Kev as sadness came into his eyes. He smiled grimly and there was a momentary silence. Alan knew they would not speak Jack's name again.

'So, between you and Billy, you blokes will have to step up, and I'll be right there with you. Dave from next door is giving us a hand as well.'

'Gotta be careful now, boss, with da young fellas.' said Kev. 'Since da mob got equal rights, da young fellas, dey get da grog. When we was young, didn't get no bloody drinking. Dey think dey tough and have to drink, but den those blokes dey fight, causem heaps of trouble. Seen it on nearly all da properties, and now da buggers drinkin in da whitefellas' pubs. Proper bad.'

'Be fine,' said Billy. 'We always do good work and keep da trouble away. Jesse, he want to help too, so we teach him about da shearing and what important at dat time.'

'Got no problem with that, Billy, and if he turns out like you, I'm a happy man. Got to learn about cattle and wheat as well now,' said Alan.

'I bin telling Mum Shirl about our parties, especially when we start. Tell her dat dey lotta fun. Me love to dance. We gunna have dat soon, Zena?' queried Ningali.

'Yes, we are, but a slight change. Instead of here, we're all heading to Woodside. Because Jack died suddenly, we didn't have him in the background confirming who was coming, so we left our run for crew to the last minute. Alan even put an ad in the paper, but everything sorts itself. Dave, from Woodside, will give us a hand and we will probably have some of his crew. That's the reason why we are having it together, so everyone knows each other.'

Ningali pondered, 'But dat means...' And then she stopped.

'Means what Ningali?' asked Zena.

'Dat big white rooster, he caused da trouble. Lotta trouble,' replied Ningali.

Mum Shirl saw Billy's face change. He had suddenly gone from relaxed and happy to a look of tension.

'White rooster? You gotta big rooster here?' queried Mum Shirl.

'No, not that type of rooster,' said Lisa smiling. 'There has been no trouble, Ningali. Everything happened a long time ago, it's all good, and he has his own family now.'

An awkward silence filled the room until Jedda spoke. 'Are you Dolly Dimples?' she asked. 'Are you the lady from the circus?'

'Circus. Who dat? I don't know dat lady. I'm Mum Shirl.' She opened her squinty eyes and smiled widely.

'Let's change the subject, Jedda, please,' said Lisa. She had overheard Alan telling Lisa about Dolly Dimples from the circus, a rather rotund lady.

'Mum Shirl, she know lotta stories too, Jedda,' said Ningali. 'You and Jesse, come to da tent, and Mum Shirl, she make da big magic.'

'Yeah, make da stories for da picaninnies, big maaaaaagic.' Mum Shirl waved her hands. Jedda and Jesse looked at each other with great enthusiasm and eagerness.

'Well, just before we all say goodnight, Jedda and I have been practising, and she would like to sing a song for you,' said Zena.

'Ahh, da baby, she sing like da bird?' said Ningali.

'Come on, this way.' Zena opened up the concertina doors to the music room.

'We have been looking at some of my favourite songs, and Jedda loves this one. It's from a very popular movie, The Sound of Music, and when she sings it, she says it makes her feel extra happy, not to mention she has watched the DVD so many times.'

Jedda showed no sign of nerves as Zena began to play the piano. Her voice was pure and pitch perfect. Mum Shirl stared intently at the girl.

When Jedda finished, Billy went to her and kissed the top of her forehead. 'You my special little bird, my little wild goose.'

'Dat baby, she gotta gift orright,' said Mum Shirl, beaming. 'You come sing me for anytime.'

'Alan, I think we will join you when you go into Walgett,' said Zena. 'I'll contact the music teacher there. Her name is Lydia Upjohn. Certainly, I cannot teach the technical usage of a voice, but I do know one thing: Jedda sings with ease and could certainly be soprano if her voice doesn't change.'

SEVENTEEN

OLD HABITS DIE HARD

It was a Saturday morning, and Alan was up early. He wanted to get into Walgett and get the 4-wheeler Quadrunner. Dave said there were a few there in stock. It would be an asset on the farm. Billy and Kev were along for the drive as was Zena with Mum Shirl and Ningali.

It was a cheerful trip as they drove to Walgett. Ningali relayed some of their stories, ably assisted by Kev with Mum Shirl interjecting.

After buying the Quadrunner, Alan said to the men, 'What about lunch in town? The Thirsty Dog always has good pub grub. My shout.'

Kev's eyes widened. 'You mean we gunna sit with dem whitefellas out in the open? Gunna drink a beer? Dey gunna look at us and say dem blokes bad with da drink. Got no bloody control, see!' Kev said anxiously.

'It's okay, Kev, calm down, you'll be with me and Zena, and things have changed. You blokes have equal rights now.'

Kev stood stock still. 'Don't want no trouble, boss.'

'Mate, I said you have equal rights. You're with me, and Zena will be joining us soon. Now calm down and just stick by me. Flash those choppers, that would make any bloke smile.'

When they walked into the pub and headed towards the bar, heads slowly turned. Alan tipped his hat. 'Gentlemen.' He looked around the room. A big, burly barman named Owen, whose belly had seen too many beers, nodded and came to take Alan's order. He had seen Alan come in before and knew he was a local. It was odd to see him bring in two Aboriginal men though, but he had no grief with that. When he looked around the room, he could see some of the patrons disagreed.

'What'll it be, chaps?' asked Owen.

'Mate, three schooners of Tooheys will help wash the dust down.' Alan put his money on the bar.

'Sure will.' Owen poured the beers.

'Owen, my wife is on her way here, due any minute now. She'll have two other women with her. I would appreciate it if you could send her outside. We'll be under the terrace out the back. Oh, and what she orders, I'll pay for on my way out.'

'No problem,' said Owen as he wiped the bar over, oblivious to the stares and muttering.

As Alan crossed the room to the outdoor seating area, he knew that although the rights for Indigenous people had been granted, some would never accept it. Tension brewed just under the surface and crackled in the air, ready to erupt. If he felt it, the men would too.

'Let's sit and enjoy this beer,' said Alan as he drew up a seat. Kev sat upright, and Alan sensed his tension.

'Kev, relax mate. Enjoy your beer. If anyone says anything, I give you full permission to bite them. With those choppers, you could do some serious damage.'

Kev's eyes widened and he looked at Alan. 'Bite em, boss?'

'Yeah, bite em good.' Alan tried to copy the way Kev spoke, smothering a burst of laughter.

Billy and Kev began to laugh and then the three of them couldn't stop.

The day became even stranger for the patrons of The Thirsty Dog when an elegant white woman stepped into the pub shortly after Alan with two black women, one quite large, who appeared to have difficulty mobilising. The other was tall with a shock of wiry white hair. Owen, the barman, knew instantly who this was.

Zena smiled as she walked towards the bar. 'May I please have three lemon squashes, tall glasses with ice.'

'Sure, and your husband said to let you know he's just outside on the terrace. He's paying.'

Zena looked to see where they were and then turned back to face the barman. 'Thank you. Ningali, I'll take Mum Shirl's glass. Just follow me, ladies.' Ningali hooked her arm under Mum Shirl's, and they headed to an outdoor area. All eyes in the room followed them.

'Hello, there you are,' said Alan as the women sat down.

Ningali giggled. 'Dis strange orright, boss. Not bin sittin' in a white fella's pub before.'

'Me neither,' said Mum Shirl. 'Dat bloody strange to me. Drinkin' with dem while folks.'

'Always a first time for everything,' said Zena with a bemused smile.

'Did you get the same feeling as we did when you came in?' asked Alan.

'Yes of course, but I'm always ready, you know that. As I said when the legislation changed, things will move slowly.' Zena sipped on her squash.

'How was the bike, Billy?' asked Zena.

'Good. Bit stiff with da steering. Me and Kev had fun. Alan bought it.'

'Oh, well done,' said Zena.

'The bike was better than the salesman though,' added Alan. 'Sweaty palms, and I'm sure he sits down to pee!'

There was silence and suppressed giggles but when Alan started to laugh, Zena couldn't help it and then they all joined in.

Alan was amused as he watched his wife wipe the tears of laughter away. 'Really, Alan, sits down to pee!'

'Right, time to hit the frog and toad,' said Alan. 'I'll fix up the barman on the way through.'

As they all entered the bar area, a voice yelled out, 'No fucken blacks.'

Alan looked in the direction of the voice. Four men at a table sat staring at them. Their faces said it all, hardened and weathered, grimy from years of working hard on the land. He thought they looked like old ringers or shearers, pushing mid-50s. Blue singlets and shorts. Zena hated the singlets. Wife-beater shirts, she called them.

'Got a problem, anyone?' asked Alan, confronting the group as his eyes glanced around the room. 'Well, if you have the need to say that comment, then you should have the guts to stand up. Show your face.'

'Alan, come on, we don't want any problems, not now.' Zena grabbed his arm.

Alan paid the barman and as they began to leave, a chair's legs squeaked across the floorboards and a big redhaired man stood up, his belly protruding over his shorts. His face was heavily lined and his complexion ruddy, years from sun exposure in the harsh summers. He could barely stifle a disgusted snort.

'Me. I said it, and I'll say it again. No fucken darkies. They drink at The Royal, the pub around the corner.' He raised his pointed finger at Alan. Owen had moved swiftly from behind the bar.

'Sit down, Fred. There'll be none of that here,' said Owen as he stood next to Alan.

Billy stood with Kev a metre away from Alan, and he didn't flinch as his hands curled into tight fists. 'You heard dat man. Me, my brothers, my sisters, got da same right. You be quiet now.'

The big redhaired man growled at Billy. 'Fucken cheeky darkie, this one. Gonna knock some sense into you!' He suddenly lunged at Billy in one powerful swoop, swinging high at Billy's face. But as Billy ducked, he pushed Fred, who lost his balance and crashed into the table he'd been seated at. He landed like a side of beef, his body ploughing into the glasses as they smashed on the floor.

Zena screamed, seeing visions of Jack in a bar somewhere doing exactly the same, but losing his life. 'Ningali, move, get Mum Shirl away. Move to the door,' she ordered, the blood draining from her face.

As Fred lay on the floor, he looked up at Billy. 'I see you on the road, my friend, you better be prepared. I'll give you the floggin you so bloody deserve. Small town. We'll cross paths one day.'

Billy's anger retreated as he regained his control, but his eyes remained fierce and his mouth set.

'Get out, Fred!' roared Owen as he took a step towards him. 'And find another drinking hole. I don't want to see your face in here again.'

Fred got to his feet slowly, the anger flashing in his eyes, his gaze fixed on Billy as he swept past them, glancing over his shoulder as he left the hotel, followed by his mates.

'Sorry, everyone. He's a bit fiery, our Fred, but I didn't expect that reaction,' said Owen, apologising.

'We thank you for your apology, but fiery is not the word I would have used. Ignorant would be more appropriate. Good day. Come on, let's make our way home,' said Zena as she ushered the ladies to the door.

EIGHTEEN

DEATH COMES CALLING

Mark called early the following morning. The medical news was bad. Des had taken a turn for the worse, and his condition was deteriorating rapidly. He was transported to Bowral District Hospital. Des was terminally ill and would need palliative health care.

'Oh no,' said Lisa, the tears welling in her eyes. 'I'll pack quickly. What are they going to do now for him?'

'They'll make sure he's comfortable and reduce his pain and suffering. They'll also look after his emotional and spiritual needs so that his last days are spent with dignity. Dad has talked a lot about spirituality lately.'

Lisa sighed deeply. 'Billy says there's an afterlife and that death is the destruction of the body but not the spirit, which returns to its source. Dad will go to the Sky-World. Souls go there but then you are reborn, you die and you are born again.'

'I hope so, Lisa, and I hope he comes back to a better life,' said Mark sadly. 'Can you let Zena know too? She obviously may want to come with you. He is her brother. I don't want to repeat this again.'

'Yes, of course. But I'm sure he'll come back to a better life, Mark. Death is seen as a rebirth from your previous life, so he will be reborn again. It sounds spooky, but it's also a comforting thought,' said Lisa.

'When do you think you'll be down?' queried Mark.

Lisa looked at her watch and exhaled loudly. 'Late afternoon or early evening. We have the shearers welcome do next week, but Zena and Kate have that under control. I'll get organised now. Zena will want to come. Like me, her better years with Des were sadly after Mum passed. I won't bring the twins down. Billy can manage, but luckily Ningali and Mum Shirl are here and can help. I don't want to interrupt his routine or cause him any extra stress at this time. He'll be supervising this year, so he has a lot on his plate. Thanks for calling to let me know. I'll see you soon.'

As Lisa hung up the phone, her hands shook. The memories of her childhood came flooding back. It was many moons ago, but the pain still rested in her heart. Her dad was so different now. Could a person you're married to change your personality completely, or was it the alcohol? He had said many times over the years that he had drunk to mask his own sadness at being with Agnes.

Lisa called out to the twins who were playing outside. 'Jedda, Jesse, come in quickly.' She stood at the back door and heard Jesse's voice.

'Coming, Mummy.' The two children raced each other to the house.

'Hello, my darlings, please sit down. Mummy has some sad news,' said Lisa hesitantly.

Their eyes widened as they hopped up onto the kitchen chairs.

'Mummy's been crying,' said Jedda as she scanned Lisa's face.

'Yes, Jedda. Uncle Mark called this morning and Des has been taken to hospital. He is not well, and we don't expect him to live much longer.' Lisa's voice was beginning to crack.

Jedda's face crumbled and her bottom lip trembled. 'Does he go to the Sky-World, Mummy?'

'Yes, my darling. He will come back again,' Lisa said softly.

'So will he visit us? How will we know it's him?' queried Jesse, sadness crossing his small features.

Lisa paused. 'I'm sure we will know, somehow. What I want you to do now is quickly write a little note for Des to say goodbye. It doesn't have to be long, but he will take great comfort reading what you write. I will go and pack a bag. Can you both do this for me?'

The children nodded in unison as fear and tears began to develop. 'Don't cry, be brave. Des would want you to be happy. But we will wish him well on his next journey.' Lisa ripped two pages from a note pad on the kitchen bench and handed them a pen, barely able to contain her own tears.

'Now, I won't be long. I just have to call Nan and let her know, and then I have to find Daddy.'

When Lisa got to her bedroom, she sat down and broke into deep, heaving sobs, which shook her whole body in the stillness of the room. She squeezed her eyes tightly and wiped the tears as she dialled.

'Aunty, Des is... he's been taken to hospital. It's his final time.' The tears choked her next sentence.

'Oh my God! Lisa, I'll be down in twenty minutes. I'll pack my bag. Take a deep breath. We knew this was coming. Are you leaving the children with Billy?'

'Yes, but he will have Ningali and Mum Shirl to watch over them. They'll be fine. They're writing a letter to Des now. I'll head down to the shearing sheds and have a quiet word with Ningali. Does Alan know where Billy would be?'

'Good question, hun,' replied Zena. 'I'm pretty sure he is up supervising with Alan and Kev about where that new dam is going to be. Do you want me to see if they're up there before I head down?'

'Yes, Aunty, that would be a help,' said Lisa, struggling for words.

By the time Zena arrived, Lisa was sitting with the children, Ningali and Mum Shirl.

They all looked outside when they heard the roar of Billy's motorbike pull up, followed by Alan and Kev in the old ute. Billy quickly came to Lisa. She stood to meet his embrace.

'Grasshopper,' he whispered into her ear as she leaned into his shoulder. She wanted to bury herself there and for the pain in her heart to go away.

'Are you okay, kid? Silly question, I know,' Alan said

'I'm fine, Alan, thank you for asking,' Lisa croaked, wiping her tears. 'It's just the shock.'

Lisa kissed Billy softly on the cheek and went to Zena. They embraced, and Zena stroked Lisa's hair.

'It's alright, Lisa. His time has come. We need to get on the road. Are you ready?'

Lisa nodded. ''Ningali, Mum Shirl, I have shown you where everything is.'

'You don't worry none, Lisa,' said Mum Shirl. 'Me and Ningali, we look after the piccaninnies proper good. Ain't dat right?' She looked at the twins who held crumpled bits of paper.

Lisa squatted down as the twins cuddled up to her. 'Are these the letters for Des?'

Jedda nodded as she rubbed her eyes. 'It's alright, my darling little goose, Mum Shirl and Ningali are here, and I will call you tonight. I'll give these to Des to read. It will make him very happy.'

'Right then, we best be on our way, Lisa. I have the Land Rover. I don't trust the old Zephyr for long distances anymore.' Zena opened the driver's door.

Lisa kissed the twins and Billy and then followed Zena. The trip to the highlands would be a long, sad one.

By evening, the signs to Mittagong came into view, and Lisa was relieved when they finally pulled into the driveway of Des's cottage. Mark came to greet them, and Lisa could tell by his eyes he had also taken it hard. They hugged. No words were spoken. It was if they read each other's thoughts.

'Aunt Zena,' said Mark as he pulled away from Lisa. He suddenly couldn't speak as he choked back a sob.

'Come on, let's go inside,' said Zena, giving him a hug. She grabbed their bags.

'Good idea,' said Lisa trying to gather up some courage.

As the three of them sat at the kitchen table, heaviness filled the air.

'When did he go downhill?' asked Lisa.

'He hadn't been well for days. Not eating but sleeping lots and then he said to me the pain was getting to be unbearable and that he wanted to go to hospital. He just wanted to hang on and stay here for as long as possible. I should have known, especially as he couldn't eat. It was early evening when I took him to Bowral Hospital yesterday, and after talking to the doctors and getting him settled, it was about ten-ish. I didn't want to bother you, which is why I called early the next morning.'

Lisa nodded and let out a loud sigh.

'A wounded heart will heal, with time,' said Zena. 'That's a given, and the good memories and love are sealed inside. I know he used to be a different man to the one he is now, but that's life. We all make mistakes and we all make our choices.'

'There are a thousand thoughts in my mind right now. I can't adequately describe the intensity of what I'm feeling at the moment. It was different with Agnes. I just felt this profound sadness of what could have been and of course, there were no goodbyes. Not that Agnes would ever want to speak to me, but I'll never know. But with Des, it's just been so different since Agnes's funeral, such a normal relationship. He opened up and showed sympathy, all the things I wanted for so long. There were so many other things I have wanted to say and now he'll die before I get the chance.'

'I'm sure he knows in his own heart. It's been good for him too, Lisa, being able to have a normal relationship with you and your family,' said Zena.

'I guess what I've experienced these past years with him is how it should always have been and now we have to say goodbye, which will be so very hard.'

'Saying goodbye is always hard, particularly as death is so final,' Zena said gently. 'But these last years you have both created memories, much better ones, and these ones will replace the old.'

'I have love, anger and sadness all whirling together,' said Lisa as she met Mark's gaze.

'Grief and love are conjoined. I don't think you get one without the other,' said Mark solemnly.

'So, what happens next?' sighed Lisa.

'The doctor said perhaps two to three days. He's on morphine now, and they basically up the dose and then...'

'Then what?' The sadness and confusion swept over Lisa's face.

Mark looked at Zena and took a deep breath, unable to speak.

'They basically, the body, it just shuts down, Lisa, and they drift off to their next journey,' said Zena.

Mark was glad Zena spoke as he could not find the words.

'Then we have to go to the hospital now!' Lisa sounded desperate.

Mark looked at his grief-stricken sister. 'He would be asleep now, so I recommend we go first thing tomorrow morning. He's in a terminally ill ward and there is a lot of care, toileting and other things the nurses have to do.'

'Yes, I agree, Mark. Let's all have an early night. This is my brother and your father.' The heaviness of loss was spreading in her heart. 'It will be a rough day tomorrow.'

As Lisa lay in the darkness, alone in the magnitude of her grief, she wanted to curl up in a ball and hide somewhere. She prayed for lucid time with her father. She would call home after visiting Des tomorrow. She didn't want Billy or the children to hear the sadness in her voice.

The following day when they arrived at the hospital, Lisa shivered. 'I'm frightened, Aunty.'

Zena held Lisa's hand as they followed Mark to the ward. The silence was deafening, and Lisa's eyes scanned the bedrooms they
passed, watching the nurses go about their care of the dying. When
they got to Des's room, Lisa was shocked by his appearance. Zena
took a sharp intake of breath. Des had lost so much weight.

A nurse looked up as they entered the room. 'How is he?' asked
Mark.

'Hi, I'm Jenny. Des had a bad night, and he's semi-comatose.' She
moistened his mouth with a sponge. 'I have just given him another
shot of morphine, but I'm inserting a canula soon so he will be on
continuous subcutaneous infusion over twenty-four hours. We administer a dose hourly. You can keep moistening his lips with this
sponge if you like.'

'What are all these cords?' asked Lisa.

'This is a pulse oximetry monitor where we record his oxygen levels along with his pulse and heart rate. This is a 5-lead ECG, which
gives us an accurate reading of your father's heart rate. We can pick
up a lot of patterns and change of rhythms, which is common in
someone deteriorating. The tubes in his nose are to assist with feeding,' replied Jenny.

They all watched as Jenny left the room, no doubt the next patient needed care. Lisa could only admire these nurses who were
present at both the beginning and the end of life. Death was an inevi-
table phenomenon that affected every human being yet to face it
every day, required special skills. She wondered if a special spirit
guided the care workers.

Zena dipped the sponge into the small water container and gently
dabbed her brother's lips.

Mark cleared his throat. 'They asked me did I want this, Lisa, you
know, all the leads that you see, and I said yes. Some people don't
want their loved ones hooked up to anything, but I just wanted to
know what was going on. Subcutaneous infusion means the morphine will be constant now to ease his pain. We will have to try and
say goodbye now before they start that process.'

Lisa's lips trembled as she eased herself into a chair next to Des's bed. She pulled out the letters from the twins and placed them on the bedside table. Zena pulled another chair from across the room and sat down next to Lisa.

'Dad, can you hear me, it's Lisa. We're all here.' She took his frail hand. His skin was almost pearl-like, translucent, and the veins could be seen so clearly. She remembered the vision of him when she was a young girl. Jet black hair, tall, strong and a real force. Who was this person lying here?

Des's eyes fluttered. 'Dad, it's Mark. Zena and Lisa are here as well.' There was a slight moan as he slowly opened his eyes.

'Lisa,' he croaked. 'My girl.' Lisa curled her fingers around her dying father's hand. 'Dad. I don't want you to go.' She buried her head on the bed. His weak hand stretched out and stroked her hair.

'It's alright, Lisa, it's my last journey. It will be a good death now you are all here.' Des looked at his sister, who was barely able to hold back the tears. 'You've done a great job, Zena. I owe you so much.'

'It's okay, Des,' Zena softly replied as the tears began welling in her eyes.

'And my son, you have achieved so much. Keep on achieving. I am so proud of you, of you both.'

Lisa pulled the letters off the bedside table. 'Dad, I asked Jedda and Jesse to write something for you as I told them you are going to the spirit world.'

Des managed a weak smile and murmured, 'Spirit world.' He closed his eyes and his head lolled to one side.

Lisa's face crumpled.

'It's alright, Lisa, he's still breathing. Why don't you start to read.' Zena took her hand.

'Dad, I'll read the letters to you, and you can hear their words as you sleep.' Lisa's eyes were now red and moist. Mark had to look away momentarily, trying to prevent the sobs from spilling out of his chest.

'This is from Jedda, and she says, 'Dearest Des, I hope you are not too sick and you feel better soon. I miss your stories. I am going to be famous one day and I love you.'

Lisa felt the hot tears spilling onto her hand, trails of tears running down her cheeks. Her vision blurred slightly, and she blinked them away, clearing her throat, her voice barely a whisper.

'This is from Jesse, and he says, 'Dear Des, you are a top person, proper true. Don't get sick any more but Mummy says you will go to the spirits, so I can talk to you there and you can see what I do. Will you be in the sky with Ume. I love you very much.'

Lisa folded both notes and placed them in his top pocket. Des did not move, and his breathing was peaceful as the morphine kicked in.

Mark quickly exited the room, barely holding it together. 'He'll be okay, Lisa. He just needs a bit of space and fresh air.' Zena tried to contain her own grief.

'I keep looking at his chest, willing it to keep rising,' Lisa said solemnly as she listened to the raggedness of his breathing. Her father lay so still, and she visualised the cracks and scars of his life that filled his soul.

Zena, her elegantly beautiful face now haggard, said gently, 'Let's find Mark, he may need a hug.' Zena took Lisa's hand. 'Come on, we won't be far away, and they have so many things attached to Des, so as soon as anything misses a beat, a buzzer will sound.'

As they came out into the corridor, Jenny the nurse pointed to the room they could see at the end of the corridor. 'Down there, it's a sitting room.'

Mark sat sipping tea in a room obviously used by visiting family, friends and relatives of those who were just about to pass. 'Hey,' said Lisa softly.

'Hey, yourself. Sorry, I just had to regain my composure, get a grip on things.'

'It's okay, Mark,' Zena murmured. 'We all have to prepare for Des's death. We can go back in when you're ready.'

'Luckily we got to have a quick chat. The morphine is so powerful.' Mark suddenly looked lost.

'Yes, it is, my dear,' said Zena sadly. 'But at least he's not in any pain now.'

'Right, I'm ready, let's go back in then.' Mark's tears threated to invade.

When they got back to the room, Jenny, the young nurse, was preparing the infusion.

Jenny advised, 'Dr Malvern said to start setting this up. This will make it easier for him now in terms of pain.'

When Jenny placed the cannula into Des's arm, he opened his eyes. 'I'm a lucky man,' he whispered as his eyes searched the three sad faces. 'I wish I'd have had the courage to be true to myself and live the life I wanted.'

He closed his eyes as Lisa took his hand and bent to kiss his forehead. 'It's okay, Dad. You did your best.'

'He'll rest now,' said Jenny.

'We'll stay here, thank you, Jenny,' added Zena. It was now early afternoon.

'His breathing seems to be getting more laboured,' observed Mark. 'It wasn't too bad this morning.'

'Yes, I've noticed that too, Mark,' agreed Zena. 'It's like deep, rapid inhalations that slowly decrease and then he doesn't appear to be breathing at all.'

'I'm going to call home and see how the children are. We may be here for a while. I hope Ningali picks up, but I know she doesn't like phones. Thinks they're strange things. Billy wouldn't be home yet but maybe Alan is there.' Lisa disappeared to find a pay phone and returned twenty minutes later.

'How did you go?' queried Zena.

'No answer.'

'We cannot do much here, and he looks to be comfortable apart from his breathing being a little laboured,' said Zena. 'It's been an exhausting day, let's go home and be back here early tomorrow.'

166

They nodded in agreement and Lisa kissed Des on the cheek. 'Be back soon, Dad.'

As they went past the nurse's station, a new nurse was behind the desk. 'Hi... err Susan,' said Zena looking at her name badge. 'We are just heading home. Should anything change with Des O'Connor, please call us.'

'Yes, of course. We always do,' Susan replied.

As they drove home, the same thought lingered in all their minds. *Will Des make it through the night?*

'What a very sad and draining day,' said Zena. 'A hot shower and dinner with an early night will make us all feel a lot better. What have you got in that fridge so that I can rustle up something for us.'

'There is some Bolognese sauce, so maybe a pasta,' said Mark.

'Super, I'll start and you guys hop into the shower,' said Zena taking control as they pulled into the driveway.

'I have to touch base with the children and Billy. He may be home now.' Lisa dialled the number to home once inside.

'Hi, Billy.' Lisa's face lit up. 'I'm glad you picked up. I called earlier but knowing Ningali, she probably avoided the phone. You know she has a phobia about technology.'

Billy laughed. 'Me too. Tell me da news, grasshopper.'

'Well, the news is not good. Des is perhaps meeting the spirits soon.'

Billy could hear the sadness in her voice. 'Des, he have da good death. He with his mob. Not in pain anymore, Lisa.'

'I guess so. There's not much we can do, Billy. Where are the twins?'

'Dey with Mum Shirl and Ningali down at the sheds. Dey like da glue. Mum Shirl telling 'em lotta stories. Dem twins dey not stop laughing. Wanna stay down with dat mob. Wanna sleep in Mum Shirl's tent.'

A smile spread across Lisa's face. She could see it so clearly. The children were obviously drawn to the women as she had been to Binna and Ningali.

'Love you, Billy. I'm very tired. Big kisses to you and the children.' Lisa took a deep breath.

'Be okay, Lisa. Da spirits dey always watch over. Des, he return to da earth. Sleep well.'

'And you too, my darling.' When Lisa hung up the phone, she doubted her grief would ever go.

As they drove to the hospital the following day, it was just after 8:00 a.m. No phone calls that night meant that Des was still with them.

'I hope he slept peacefully,' said Zena as she pulled into the car park.

'I'm sure he did. As Jenny said yesterday, Des is now on hourly doses of morphine,' said Mark sadly.

'I thought of him all night. It's funny how those we love most give us great joy but also cause the greatest pain. I feel guilty already in this world, this place, if my father is no more,' said Lisa.

When they got to the ward, it was Jenny who greeted them. A look of relief crossed Lisa's face. At least it was the same nurse that was caring for him.

'How is he?' Lisa asked hesitantly.

'He slept peacefully. Susan, the nurse who was on last night, has recorded there were no problems and the morphine has been monitored regularly. He has not been conscious though,' replied Jenny as she sponged his mouth and then left the room.

The three of them pulled chairs around the bed and sat down. His breathing was now a more rattled sound. Zena knew exactly what it was. She knew Des was in an extremely weakened state and now not physically strong enough to cough or swallow to clear the secretions from the back of his throat.

Lisa took her father's hand. 'Dad, we're here, and I'm not sure if you can hear me speak. I just wanted to tell you that I love you.' The tears fell harder with each word. 'I love you, Dad.' Lisa gulped as she held his hand in silence, letting her feelings for her father linger in the space of time that was now slipping away, deeper into an unknown mystery.

As Zena was about to speak, Des made a loud gurgling sound and his chest rose no more. Lisa squeezed her eyes shut and bowed her head to the sounds of the noises from the machines.

Minutes later, Jenny appeared. She looked at their grief-stricken faces. It was always a stressful experience and a sight she never got used to. 'I am sorry for your loss. Death and saying goodbye are very painful.'

No one could speak but sat almost transfixed at the events that followed. Jenny began removing the IV Cannula, as well as the indwelling catheter and feeding tubes.

'What happens now?' asked Lisa shakily, her luminous face now buried by sadness.

Jenny looked at the heartbroken woman clearly affected by her father's death. 'It may be best that you say your goodbyes now. Dr Malvern has been notified and he is on his way for the formal certification of death. I will have to wash your father's body and then he will be transported to the hospital mortuary where the funeral director will collect him. Have you spoken to anyone regarding this?' asked Jenny.

'Umm, yes, I have,' said Mark. 'I have made all the arrangements according to Dad's wishes.'

'Well, just let them know that your father has passed away and they will contact us about the collection of his body.'

There was an outburst of tears from Lisa as she cried into her hands. 'Please, there are two letters in his top pocket. They are from my children. They must stay with my father, please.'

'Yes, of course, Lisa. Now, I just need to help you fill out this final paperwork,' said Jenny softly. 'I will get a bag from reception that you can put all his belongings in.'

When Zena opened the top drawer, there were two old black and white photos. One was of her and Des riding when they were in their teens. She remembered the day so clearly. The other was Des holding Mark as a baby, with Lisa clinging to his thigh.

Through her grief-stricken face, she smiled. So sad, photos full of love and so full of what might have been. Now he was gone. It was then that she lost all control.

The funeral was simple and private. Des had requested to be cremated and his ashes scattered from The Jellore Lookout, Mount Gibraltar Reserve, in Mittagong. It was a collapsed volcanic core, and 150 million years ago it pushed through Hawkesbury sandstone to form the mountain. Billy said it was Gundungurra country that was bounded by the highest ridges of the Blue Mountains to the north and down to Goulburn in the south, Picton to the east and areas around Oberon and Bathurst. The Gundungurra people and their culture stretched back tens of thousands of years. Lisa hoped Des would find a spiritual connection to the land.

From a high, flat rock where Des and Zena had visited as children, his ashes were scattered to the wind. Lisa watched as her father's ashes blew high into the blue sky. 'I hope you are at peace now, Dad. Fly like the Spirit Bird.'

NINETEEN

TWO STRANGERS

It was very early when Zena dialled home, but she knew it was the only time she may catch Alan. 'Hi darling, it's me, I know it's very early, but it's the only time I could probably catch you with the day being so busy and the shearer's-do on tonight at Woodside.'

'It's all good, Zena. How's it going?' asked Alan, hearing the despondency in her voice.

'As can be expected. We scattered his ashes yesterday. It's all a process and the next task is just as bad. We'll go through his things tomorrow to help Mark and then I guess make our way home. How are things there? How is Kate managing? Please apologise for not being there to assist, Alan. I feel very guilty.'

'Don't be daft. No one can predict death. Kate will be fine. Dave and I will pitch in, and there's Tess, Polly and Olivia. Kate said things were good at the moment, fairly peaceful, and besides, it will give them something to do.'

'Do we have enough workers or are we borrowing?' asked Zena.

'Borrowing, my love, but I somehow knew that would happen. We'll finish here at Woori first and then see if Dave wants to keep some of our boys on and go from there. But he has a full crew, so not really sure if he needs any help from us. Anyway, Billy and Kev have it under control down there and the shearers have all settled in. He does have doubts about two new men though.'

'Oh, why is that?' Zena's curiosity was aroused.

'They are pretty hardened but a lot of shearers are like that, as you well know, and over the years we have seen them come and go. Tough nuts but they turn out to be good blokes. But these two, well, I just don't know. They brought their own working dogs, which we didn't expect, and Billy caught the dogs biting the sheep. Not nipping but really biting, causing them to bleed. He had words with them, which I understand caused a bit of a kerfuffle, but they have only been here a couple of days, so I'm hoping the dogs will settle, and the blokes.'

'How old are they, Alan? They don't sound too mature.'

'I'm guessing late thirties. James Griffin and Ernie Tubbs.' Alan hesitated. 'But I have to say these two blokes are odd, the bigger bloke especially. There's just something about him. I never trust a man who can't look you in the eye. Got a jagged scar running down his face. I might be guessing but it looks like a knife has been there.'

'Now you have me worried, Alan.'

'Don't be. Anyway, I'll leave it to Billy. He has a good handle on it,' said Alan.

'Alright, darling, we'll leave here in a few days. I'll miss being there tonight, so will Lisa. I always enjoy the start of the season shearer's-do so much. This will be the first one I'll miss in all these years,' said Zena wistfully. 'But I just want to make sure Mark is okay before we get on the road.'

'Stay as long as you like. We'll be fine. I'm heading up to see Kate and Dave this morning to see what I can do. But knowing Kate, she'll have it all under control. Love to Mark and Lisa. Oh, tell Lisa that she'll have a job dragging those kids away from Mum Shirl. They are like glue down there. Saw her piggy-backing Jedda around the sheds the other day!'

'Piggy-backing!' Zena laughed, grateful for some humour. 'She was not that mobile!'

'Yep, our Jedda was digging her heels in and telling the poor old girl to go faster. I thought she would have a heart attack or fall flat on her face! So, Mum Shirl is doing just fine. The kids are good for her,' said Alan. 'I don't know who is having more fun, the twins or her.'

'Thank you, my darling. I have that imagery now.' A smile swept across Zena's face. 'Be home soon.'

◊

When Alan headed down the long the driveway of Woodside, he had a tingle down his spine. These functions were always a lot of fun, and it brought back fond memories of Jack and the years they'd worked together. He could hear his words, 'Let 'em get shit-faced and then it's work.'

'Coooeee, anybody home.' Alan half-opened the back door. The smells of cooking wafted into the air.

'Coooeee back to you,' said Kate Walker, making an appearance. 'It's that time, Alan.' She gave him a peck on the cheek.

'Zena sends her love and apologies that she could not be here.'

'It's a sorry business death and funerals. Something we all must prepare for one day. Tough losing your dad or brother,' said Kate.

Alan nodded solemnly.

'Dave is up near the sheds, getting the spit ready. So, if you want, you can head there to see if they need a hand. I have things pretty much under control, and the girls are pitching in.'

'I heard that things were better,' said Alan.

'Yes, what a relief. We had a bit of a bump when Tess was in town not that long ago, but Mitch got Polly in quickly to see her psychiatrist and things were sorted. Fingers crossed it stays that way.'

'Right then, I'll be off to find your men. What time do you want us here and can we bring anything? asked Alan.

'About six, we'll start. Dave will have the lamb ready for the spit. We don't need anything really, Alan. You and Zena have organised so many things in the past, it's our turn,' smiled Kate.

'Okay.' Alan tipped his hat. 'Looking forward to it. 6 o'clock it is. I'll see you tonight with my crew but will head on up to catch Dave now.'

As Alan drove towards the shearing sheds, Dave came into view. He already had a beer. Under an old lean-to there was a sign that said, 'Grog Station' and a blow-up swimming pool was filled with beer and ice bags. A cold storage unit that contained ice had been hooked up to a long lead that ran to the power points into one of the sheds. Bales of hay were scattered, and the spit was set up ready for the roast. Just behind it were six long tables under another canopy that had roll-down fly screens. It was going to be a good night.

Dave looked up when he saw Alan's ute and waved.

'G'day mate, see you have things all sorted,' said Alan. 'Love the sign, "Grog Station",' he laughed.

'Yeah, it's a bewdy. Mitch's idea. But as if those blokes couldn't smell a beer from a mile away. Don't need a sign for that! Thirsty bloody shearers,' scoffed Dave as he passed Alan a beer. 'Been using the Quadrunner?'

'Yeah, a lot lately. Fantastic machines. Thanks for the tip.'

'Been up at the new dam today. It's a cracker,' added Dave. 'I know you said the sides were steep but we have evened them out slightly around the edges so it will catch every drop of rain. Always appreciate your opinion on things, Alan.'

A cloud of red dust billowed as Mitch zig-zagged across the pad-dock. 'What's he up to?' asked Alan.

'It's Olivia, she loves the quaddy. Hangs on for dear life but the faster he goes and the more he does stuff like that, the more she squeals. He took her up there for a swim. Trying to get her to like the water.'

As they pulled up, Dave shook his head and they all began to laugh. 'Mitch, you need to get some goggles. All I can see are the whites of your teeth. You're covered in red dust.'

Mitch guffawed loudly as his arm came around to help Olivia off.

'Hello, Mr Alan,' she said cheerfully, dusting her pants.

'Hello back, Miss Olivia. Having a good time with your father, I see.'

Olivia giggled. 'The best fun. Daddy makes me laugh, but one day, I'm going to drive the Quadrunner.'

'When you're older,' said Mitch, beaming.

'Have a swim?' asked Dave.

'Nope, this little cherub won't even stick her foot in the water, Dad. Says she hates the water.'

Dave scratched his chin. 'Well, Miss Livvy, how can we go for beach holidays if you can't swim?'

Olivia cringed. 'I don't like the water, Grandpa, please don't make me get in the water.'

Mitch laughed. 'Yep, she isn't a water baby at all. I don't know why she hates it so much. Just have to persevere. Anyway, all set for tonight, Alan?'

'Yes, mate, but I can see you, Dave and Kate have everything organised.'

'Don't I know that! I'm heading back to the house. See you a bit later then, Alan,' said Mitch as Olivia clambered back on the bike and they took off.

When Alan drove back to Woori, he headed for the shearing sheds. A small group had gathered, and Kev was talking to them about the do that night. In the distance, they could see Billy riding Jed, heading their way.

Alan noticed the two new recruits sitting together, obviously preferring not to mingle. They were a strange pair. James Griffin or 'Griffo' was hardened and mean-looking, and Alan wondered how he got that scar. Ernie, his mate, looked like he had a seat next to the fridge. His middle was like a wine barrel, the buttons on his shirt straining under his girth.

As the figure in the distance galloped towards them, Ernie nudged Griffo. 'That younger bloke, Billy, the boss, bloody good seat on that big black horse. Makes it turn on a five-cent coin.'

'A lot of them blackfellas do,' sneered Griffo. 'Trying to take over our jobs, those black bastards.' He lit up another cigarette, his eyes narrowing with the intensity of his gaze. 'Got a nice arse though.'

'You're bloody crazy, Griffo. Too many canaries flying around in your head,' said Ernie nervously. 'Mate, we don't want no trouble, not like that last place. We need the dosh, remember? As soon as we get paid, we can piss off to the Territory, like we planned. No one will find us out there. You always think with your dick, and it lands us in the shit every time!'

Griffo blew a casual ring of smoke, seemingly oblivious to Ernie's comments. 'How did he get this job, that Billy? Out here with his darkie mate Kev... choppers like a beaver. There's gotta be a story. We all have our secrets. Although I don't usually like them that old.' Griffo stared intently at Billy.

'Don't be talking your shit, Griffo. You're playing with fire. We need the job and we need the money. Like we said after the last place, keep our heads low, get some money and then clear out,' said Ernie. 'This is a nice set-up, ain't never seen shearer's quarters like this. And that Alan, he seems a decent bloke.'

'Yeah, yeah,' smirked Griffo. 'But I could give that darkie a run for his money. I was doing rodeo before shearing, mate. Nothing could buck me off. Like I had glue to me bum. That's a fact.'

Griffo watched Billy as he threw his legs off Jed and strode towards Alan.

'Not an ounce of fat on him, just like the last kid,' said Griffo, his voice dangerously low.

'Knock it off, Griffo. Now! Look at your bank account before you touch anything here.'

'Well, there's not much to touch here. A few fat old lubras, and nothing you wouldn't touch with a barge pole. Anyway, I don't need your bloody lectures,' muttered Griffo. 'Since when did you become a goody two-shoes? I told ya, that last kid wanted it. Just over jail-bait age anyway. His curiosity got the better of him, that's all.' He stomped out the burning cigarette butt.

'Shut up, here come Alan and Billy,' said Ernie.

'Gentlemen, good day,' said Alan. 'Everything alright, settled in?'

'Sure thing,' nodded Ernie. 'Being treated real nice here, you got a good set-up, Alan, and yeah, lookin' forward to tonight. Done a lot of shearing but we ain't seen nothing like this.'

'Yeah, people thought I was joking when I built these sheds. They all scoffed and said "You don't build stuff like that out here for shearers".' Alan laughed. 'But that's how I wanted them. Decent living, wages and treatment and you get decent people.'

'For sure, looking forward to working hard,' said Ernie.

'This was my father's property and from as far back as I can remember, we've always had a start of season get-together. It's a lot of fun, the first night, but after that, it's down to business. We've got a lot of sheep to shear,' added Alan. 'Got your dogs under control?'

Billy's gut instincts told him this pair were bad, especially the big bloke whose bloodshot eyes looked through him. Billy locked eyes with him. It was animal instinct. Animals do this in the wild when they're ready to fight.

'Yes, boss,' replied Ernie. 'Lookin' out for those dogs.'

'You men, you keep your dogs away from da sheep. Dey bite da sheep badly and bruise da skin. Don't want no bites or bruises. We lose money on dat stock,' said Billy calmly but firmly.

Griffo slowly got to his feet. He was taller than Billy and powerful-looking, built like a brick shithouse. His neck was thick like a bull's, and he stood in an intimidating manner.

Billy took a step back and clenched his fists. The two men seemed to be sizing each other up. Quickly Alan moved to stop the tension.

'Alright fellas, we'll see you tonight.' Alan nudged Billy to follow. He was slow to move and clearly there was no backing down from either of them.

When they got to the ute, Alan looked at Billy. 'What was that all about? Do you want to tell me, Billy? The air was crackling. I don't like those blokes much either, if that's what it's all about. But it's early days and you have to remember that they're here to get a job done and that's it.'

The storm in Billy's eyes quieted. 'Dem blokes, Alan, dey bad. Plenty trouble. Dat big one da most,' said Billy as he turned to watch them in the distance.

A cold shiver travelled down Alan's spine. Billy was usually right.

'What do you mean, Billy? Now you're making me nervous, son, real nervous. Don't go tangling with that bloke. Just give them direction, get the job done and they'll move on. And make sure Kev is with you whenever you do tell those blokes what to do,' said Alan.

As they drove towards Woori, anxiety crept through Alan's body. He knew Billy could sense and feel things long before others. He hoped they would get things done quickly. He hoped Billy was wrong.

TWENTY

OPENING NIGHT

It was just after six when Alan waited for Kev's car. He smiled as the red ute sped towards him. 'God, what a sight,' Alan said out loud. Ningali was sitting on Billy's lap as they pulled up. Mum Shirl and the twins were in the back of the tray, their giggles louder than the kookaburras.

'Dey all in da back,' giggled Ningali. 'With Mum Shirl, she musta cast a big spell. Dem kids, dey don't wanna leave. Like da little bugs, sticking to da old girl.'

Alan shook his head. 'Let's get going then, just follow me, Kev. Don't forget what I told you, Billy. I don't have any problems with our crew, apart from the two new blokes. Keep your eyes peeled. Grog, as you well know, can fire up a man. There is a slow fire burning in the gut of that big bloke Griffo. I can't put my finger on it. I just don't know why, and if Jack were here, he would quickly sort it out. But we are on our nelly, and I'm not saying you can't do the job. All I'm saying is I smell trouble.'

'Orright, boss,' replied Billy. 'Kev and me, we keep da good eye out.'

'I don't like dat rooster either,' said Ningali. 'He proper bad. He got da blackness in his eyes.'

'Have the crew all left for Woodside?' asked Alan.

'Yep, about fifteen minutes ago. Had to round up dem kids,' said Billy to the sounds of laughing in the back of the ute. 'Dey wouldn't get out Mum Shirl's tent.'

'Well, let's make our way up there.' Alan took the lead. 'Hop in, Billy. And Kev, you follow. Oh, and one last thing.' All eyes shot to Alan.

'What, boss?' Kev asked.

'Keep the kids with Mum Shirl and Ningali. Do not let them out of your sight. Did the other jackaroos take their lubras?'

'No, dem women, dey wanna stay here,' replied Kev.

'Probably a good idea. The blokes will probably want to get on the turps. Less hassle. Right then, let's go,' said Alan.

When they pulled into Woodside, Cookie was sitting with their crew and old Ned was playing his harmonica. The smell of the lamb on the spit wafted into the air, and he saw Kate under the lean-to tents organising bowls of food.

'Looking good,' Alan spoke aloud as Kev pulled up alongside him. Billy went around to help Mum Shirl and the kids from the back of the tray. Ningali stood still, taking in all the sights.

She clapped her hands like a child and twirled around. 'We gonna have da big fun.'

'Kev, control that woman of yours,' laughed Alan. 'Right, we're here, and we were all invited, so don't go and get spooked about eating with white people, Kev. And remember what I said, Ningali. Keep the kids close.'

Mum Shirl shot Alan a quizzical look. 'We got to keep da kids close? Mebbe dat rooster is about? Dat rooster he cause trouble tonight?

Ningali giggled. 'Sure, boss, me keep 'em here and teach 'em some dance moves. Mum Shirl and me, we gotta watch for da big roosters.' And she suddenly started strutting like a barn chook, clucking her arms. Everyone laughed.

'Come on, just this way then. Find a spot and get some of Kate's good tucker. I'll catch up with Dave and Kate first, so Billy, get this lot sorted.' Alan dusted himself off. As he strode on towards the tents, he saw Griffo and Ernie sitting alone and away from the crew. Alan waved to acknowledge them. *Bloody loners, bloody trouble.*

Dave handed the beer to Alan, and they looked at the crew who were now in full swing. 'That new bloke of yours is a giant of a man. Looks like an old wrestler, a mangled one at that. Doesn't look like a shearer,' said Dave.

'Yeah, I know, Dave. Bigger than Jack, but then I've seen men just as big, and then those who look like they couldn't lift a potato sack, all working well. Sometimes size doesn't matter. But I don't know. That one, the big bloke, he has trouble written across his forehead. Like he's ready to erupt.' Alan took a swig of his beer. 'But I don't care what they look like as long as they do the job.'

'Agree, mate. Nice to see old Cookie and Ned here again,' said Dave.

'Yeah, familiar faces. Just one missing though,' added Alan grimly.

'Who?' asked Dave.

'Jack. My good right-hand man. It all seems so different this season, but Billy has stepped up and is doing a great job. Everything changes, nothing, absolutely nothing stays the same. Zena always says that.'

'Yeah, she's right,' said Dave. 'If things didn't change, the boys here would be using old clippers to shear if it wasn't for that young Irishman from Dublin, Fred Wolseley. Came to Walgett in the late 1800s. Bloody ingenuity to invent mechanical clippers around that time. Mitch said he was smart for a potato-head!'

Alan laughed. 'Yep, it would be long, hot work using those old shears.'

'How are Zena and Lisa? Kate told me that Des had passed,' said Dave.

'Yeah, Zena has never missed an opening night with the shearers but is sorting things out down there. She'll be home shortly. Place is not the same without her. Pretty bloody quiet and it feels so odd without her here now.'

'Yeah, women. Lost without them, especially out here. Almost your right arm some days,' added Dave.

'Another beer?' asked Alan. 'That one hardly touched the sides.'

'Sure, mate,' said Dave. As Alan turned, he saw Tess, Polly and Olivia carrying food, heading towards Kate.

'Dave, I'll just quickly go over and say hello to Kate and the girls. I won't be a minute,' said Alan, walking briskly.

'Hello, you lot.' Alan took off his hat, smoothing his hair down.

'Oh, lovely to see you,' smiled Kate. 'Shame Zena and Lisa are not here.'

'Yes, sorry news about her dad, but none of us are here forever. They're home tomorrow. As I said to Dave, they're just getting things sorted down there.' Alan turned his attention to Tess and the two girls who were putting food into the big white bowls. 'Ladies. I must say you all look great and have done a pretty good job for the blokes tonight.'

It was hard to believe that Polly was only fourteen. She looked a lot older than her years. She was tall and lean with an athletic build and wearing lipstick. Instead of her hair being pulled back, it hung loosely around her shoulders, the same flaming red hair as Tess's.

Polly giggled. She did like the attention. 'Tess, you two are like peas in a pod,' said Alan.

'That's what everyone tells me. She even insisted on wearing my lipstick tonight. A little treat for her,' Tess smiled.

'So, I see,' said Alan. 'And Olivia, you're growing prettier by the day.' The young girl ducked her head and blushed.

Alan had to admit that Tess scrubbed up well, and it did not go unnoticed by all the blokes. Tess was enjoying the stares.

But it was Griffo who sat transfixed. Here was the mongrel bitch-whore from the pub. The prick-teaser. What the hell was she doing out here?

'Get a load of that redhead, Griffo,' nudged Ernie.

'Yeah,' he growled. 'I see.' He sucked on his beer. 'I see them both. Mother and daughter. This place just got a little bit more interesting.' His eyes never left Tess.

'Keep your dick in your pants, Griffo,' said Ernie anxiously.

'I was referring to the older one, she's a wild-looking bitch. Just what I need, a tall redhead.' Griffo growled.

'Remember what we said, Griffo. That's clearly the daughter, jailbait for sure.' Ernie jabbed a finger in Griffo's ribs.

Griffo smirked.

'That Billy is here with some of his mob,' said Ernie. 'Those little creamy kids are lookers. Where's the mother? Certainly not that fat old boong or the one with stick legs.'

Griffo snorted. 'Bloody boongs, should keep 'em all chained. I'm getting another beer.'

◊

Tess noticed the big man crossing in front of her to the inflatable pool filled with cans of beer. *My my, you're a big one.* Her eyes drank him in. *Might have a bit of fun with you tonight. That'll piss off Mitch.*

As Griffo ripped the top off the can and drank, he turned and locked eyes with Tess. He licked his lips deliberately, and Tess felt a shiver go up her spine, a mixture of fear and excitement igniting her body. The corners of her lips began to twitch. Griffo walked towards her, and it was Tess who spoke.

'Enjoying yourself?' she asked with a heavy dose of sarcasm.

Griffo's lips curled into a smile. Her jibe only intensified the urges he had to completely dominate her so she was powerless and naked under him.

Griffo's voice lowered, 'You have no idea.'

'No idea of what?' Tess mocked him.

'Of what I'd like to do to you. Lucky that table is between you and me.' He leaned against the pole of the lean-to, sipping his beer.

Tess stood motionless, nibbling her bottom lip, her heart pounding. She felt his raw sexual energy, a husky provocativeness that became entangled in her mind. She took a deep breath.

Suddenly, laughter and children's squeals filled the air as Jedda and Jesse raced towards the lean-to upon seeing Olivia.

'Livvy, Livvy,' squealed Jedda as Olivia came out from behind the table.

'Hi, I'm just helping Nanny, but I can come and play soon.' She smiled, happy to see her friends.

Jedda was so close to Griffo, oblivious to the big man who was staring down at her. She suddenly turned and looked up at him.

'You're big, like a mountain,' Jedda said cheerily. 'I'm Jedda and this is my best friend, Livvy. Who are you here with?'

Griffo half bent as his big hand reached for the little girl's long dark hair, curling it around his finger. 'Got a bit of the tar brush in you, kid,' said Griffo.

It was Mum Shirl who spotted them. Her head swivelled, looking for Ningali, but she was nowhere to be seen. Kev was a good distance away talking to the shearers. She started to move, hurtling towards Jedda as fast as her fat legs would carry her down the hill towards the lean-to.

She sang out loudly. 'Jedda, Jesse, you come dis way, come to Mum Shirl.' Heads turned at the commotion, and there was a roar of laughter at the sight of the large black woman bouncing towards the food tent. Everything was happening so quickly. Her weight and the slight downward slope of the hill increased her speed so much that she tripped and fell flat on her face just as she got to Jedda.

'Mum Shirl!' yelled Jedda as she squatted down to the old woman. Jesse came to her side and then Billy moved quickly to reach them.

Griffo's eyes narrowed. 'You didn't have to run that fast to get some grog, luv.' He threw his head back and laughed wildly.

Billy felt the anger run through his body but remembered Alan's words. He helped Mum Shirl up off the ground.

'You be right, Mum Shirl,' said Billy as the old girl dusted herself off. Jesse wrapped his arms around Mum Shirl's legs.

'Me okay, little one. Mum Shirl just get a lotta worry when you go missing like dat. Give me the heeby jeebies.' She tried to make light of it.

She looked at Griffo. 'I see you, Mister. I see bad. Badness all around you. Stay away from da picaninnies.' She pointed her finger at his chest.

'Touching,' the big man said in the shadows. His face hardened into a icy mask as he crushed the beer can and threw it on the ground. 'I could squash your fucken head like a watermelon, you black bitch.'

'You be careful. I call Kurdaitcha man. He finish you proper good.'

'What the fuck is Kurda... whatever? Ha! You don't scare me, old girl.' Griffo's lips turned into a snarl.

'Kurdaitcha punish you. When he come, you be very afraid. He point da bone. You be sorry.'

Griffo jammed his fists into the pockets of his well-worn jeans. He wanted Billy to make the first move. He would take great pleasure in splitting his black head open.

'Come, we go dis way, back up to Kev and Ningali, our spot,' said Billy tensing, his eyes now dark and fierce. He began to walk away with Mum Shirl.

'She's real cute,' said Griffo, knowing these words would be like a dagger to Billy's heart. Billy stopped. He was breathing hard, every part of him braced and ready to attack.

It was Mum Shirl who stepped in front of Billy, hands on her hips as she turned and spoke to the brute. All eyes watched it play out as she stood right before Griffo, who did not move. He looked down at her with disgust. Jedda and Jesse stayed behind Billy, the air crackling with danger.

'You da big white fella, you got da dark soul. I see you. See you proper good. Da spirits here. You on our land. Dey watch you. Da land swallow you up, take you back to da earth. You just dust then.'

'Fuck off, you mad black bitch,' said Griffo as he stomped back up to where Ernie stood watching him.

'I take da kids back up our spot. Gunna give dat Ningali da big boot in da bum. She not look lookin'. On da grog. Not do her job. Got no brain sometimes. Like a beetle.'

Billy took a deep breath and was about to follow when Tess called out to him. 'Billy, wait up.'

Her eyes were dancing as she turned her attention to him, remembering that day at the river.

'And how have you been, Billy? Nice little scene there?' Her voice was almost teasing him as she moved closer.

Billy stepped back away from the tent. 'Me good, Missus Tess,' he said hesitatingly.

'The missus not around tonight? What a shame. Hope you're not too lonesome,' said Tess, her voice dripping with charm.

Billy did not reply but quickly joined Alan.

'Well done, son. I think he was itching for some trouble. Good you kept your cool.'

'He make me so angry,' replied Billy.

Tess wandered over and joined them. 'Alan, who is that big bloke?'

'Name is James Griffin. He goes by Griffo. Him and his mate, Ernie, are two new recruits. Replied to the ad,' said Alan.

'He's huge. Bet he could shear a few sheep, very powerful,' Tess purred. 'Now Billy, you obviously have your hands full, but if you need some help down home.' She reached out to stroke his arm.

'Tess, that's enough!' snapped Alan. 'Get along and help Kate and the girls. She looks like she needs a hand dishing out all those meals.'

Tess pouted and then turned on her heels. 'Fucking men,' she said under her breath.

'That one is a handful,' added Alan quietly. 'Keep your distance, Billy, and I mean a lot of distance. Trouble oozes from her skin.'

'Sure, Alan. She likem trouble. I know from my feelings dat one not right. Keep my kids away from dat one too. Proper bad.'

Alan laughed. 'She likem da men too, Billy, that's her problem!'

As they joined Mum Shirl, they began to relax. 'Who dat red devil floozy?' asked Mum Shirl. 'She got da fire in her. Gotta big fire between da legs!' Alan, Billy and Kev all laughed. The old girl had a way with words.

The night wore on, and the men became louder, their bellies full of good tucker and beer. Tess had one too many as well and was desperate for a cigarette. She sat with Polly, Olivia and Kate, observing the men and the atmosphere, listening to Ned's harmonica. Why was it that men congregated with men, yapping about the same old bullshit? Mitch was up past the last food tent, and she could hear him guffawing madly with the shearers. Only two men didn't join the scattered groups. She smiled over at the big man who sat quietly drinking. He raised his beer at her.

'I won't be a minute, girls,' said Kate. 'I need to tell Dave that the beer pool is getting empty. Need to give it a quick top up or perhaps just let it empty and get the men on their way. Early start tomorrow.'

Olivia jumped to her feet and took Kate's hand as they walked towards Alan, who now stood with Dave and Billy.

Tess smiled. Finally, a chance to duck away. 'Polly, I'm dying for a smoke. Getting bloody boring now. You stay here, I'm heading behind that hay shed over there to light a ciggie. You know they make a bloody fuss when I light up. Make yourself busy and top up the food bowls or you can wander and have a chat,' said Tess, fumbling in her pocket for the packet of cigarettes.

Kate had reached her husband by then. 'Dave, darling, I'm sorry to interrupt, but the pool, I mean, the beer is low. Do you want to re-top it for the men or just let it run out, so they'll be on their way to their beds?'

'Still on the early side. Just a few more cartons, I think. They're not too pissed, so it should be fine.'

'Billy go. Happy to help, Missus Kate.' Billy tipped his hat and walked towards the shed. He smelled the smoke before he saw Tess. She sat on a few cartons, the cigarette embers glowing in the dark, the orange tip igniting as she dragged on it.

'Well, well, look who we have here. What a nice surprise,' Tess smirked. 'You're looking good, Billy. I'm sure you must be a bit lonely down there. I'd love to come and see you.' Tess tipped her head back and laughed. 'I have had some delicious thoughts about you after seeing you down at the river. My, my.' She dragged on her cigarette.

'You keep quiet, Missus Tess. Just here to get da beer for Dave,' said Billy.

'Well, don't let me stop you, gorgeous. Come closer. There's a carton of Tooheys right under my rump.'

Billy didn't move.

Tess suddenly pulled up her dress and opened her legs. She wore no underwear, exposing her nakedness.

Billy took a sharp intake of breath.

'Like what you see? Us redheads are a little different. Come on, don't be shy, baby.'

Billy turned his back and took off, searching for Alan and hearing the sounds of her mocking laughter echoing in the dark. Alan stared at the empty-handed man who looked like he'd seen a ghost.

'What the devil is wrong, Billy?' asked Alan as he pulled him aside.

'Boss, you have to believe me,' said Billy.

'Believe what? Billy, for once in your life, you're not making any sense.'

'It's Missus Tess. Tess over dere, near da shed, she smoking and den she pull da dress up. She got no knickers on. I got scared, boss. Take off.'

'What's going on?' asked Dave, immediately aware that something was not right. Anger took over Alan and he stomped towards the hay shed, followed by Billy and Dave.

Tess had not moved. 'Evening, gentleman, just having a quiet cigarette. Asked Billy if he'd like to join me.'

'Tess, don't try and get my boy into any trouble. You hear me?' warned Alan.

'What trouble, what are you talking about, Alan?' asked Dave.

'Billy came to get the cartons of beer and this... this little cow lifted up her skirts, didn't she?'

'Is that true, Tess?' thundered Dave, staring at her in disbelief.

Ned stopped playing his harmonica as the raised voices soon drew attention. People stood staring in the direction of the hay shed.

'No, it's not,' said Tess petulantly, getting off the cartons. 'That black, he had a go at me.' Tess stomped on the cigarette butt.

'You're lying. Get out, Tess, get back to the homestead and don't show your face anymore tonight!' warned Dave.

Mitch suddenly appeared, pushing past his father.

'What's going on?' said Mitch, slightly intoxicated. 'Him,' Tess said, pointing at Billy. 'Tried to have a go at me, didn't he?'

Mitch suddenly lunged at Billy. The two grappled each other and punches flew, Billy faster and ducking Mitch's fists. They fell to the ground, scrambling in the red dust.

Alan and Dave stepped in. 'Break it up, you two, for Christ's sake,' said Alan as Dave managed to grab Mitch by the shoulders and drag him away. Billy was first up on his feet.

'Billy don't touch. She lie.' He wiped the dust from his mouth.

Tess's smugness was irritating as she lit up another cigarette. Mitch came towards her, the smell of beer strongly on his breath. 'Is it true, Tess? Tell me!' Mitch demanded as he turned to look at Billy.

The men glared at each other.

'Well, Billy, what have you got to say?' asked Dave.

'She here when I come to get da cartons. Smokin' and dat. Den, she lift her dress up and I go away. Dat's it, boss.'

'I know which one I believe,' said Dave.

'You little bitch,' Mitch growled.

Tess ignored him, and he grabbed her by the arm.

'Let go, you stupid prick, you're hurting me.' Tess struggled to free herself. Mitch's grip was strong as he half-dragged her across the yards in the direction of the house.

'Now get the hell inside and don't show your face again.' He stomped away to get another beer.

Ningali stood next to Kev, and the children huddled up against Mum Shirl as they watched the scene unfurl.

'What are you lot looking at?' said Tess, glaring at Ningali.

'We come lookin' for Billy, hear da yelling. See dat big white rooster heading up here. Plenty trouble,' said Ningali.

'You da red devil, you bin bad,' said Mum Shirl. 'Put dat fire out between da legs!' She said, pointing her finger at her.

'Why don't you lot just piss off back with your mob.' Tess stomped past them, heading to the homestead.

'You da floozy... you cause da trouble, not Billy,' shouted Mum Shirl.

Griffo sat with Ernie and enjoyed the scuffle. They were the only two who didn't move. He stabbed out the cigarette under his boot. 'Something going on here, that's for sure. Like a bloody jigsaw puzzle. What piece slots in where? But one thing is for sure, the redhaired bitch wants it, wants it bad. Dirty little fuckbird.'

'Stay away, Griffo. That is trouble with a Capital T and a one-way ticket.'

Griffo's eyes narrowed. 'What do you mean a one-way ticket?'

'For shit's sake, Griffo, you stupid, dense prick. A one-way ticket out of here! So that means no work and no money.'

And that was the end of the evening.

TWENTY-ONE

THE AFTERMATH

It was just before sunrise when Lisa called. She hoped the night at Woodside had been a good one. She ached to be home and so missed the children and Billy.

'Hello, sleepy head,' she said as Billy's deep voice answered.

'Grasshopper, I miss you.' He rubbed the sleep from his eyes.

'Me too, my darling, but I'm packing now. Everything is done, and Mark is in a good space as is Zena. How was last night? I so wished I was there.'

Billy did not want to say anything on the phone about Tess. He would explain when Lisa arrived home. Alan said it could wait and they would tell the women together. Giving them that news after burying her father and then a long drive home was not a good idea.

'See you soon, my grasshopper,' he said as he hung up the phone.

Billy took a deep breath. There was work to be done. He strode out to the paddock basher and roared down to Woori, trying to erase the thoughts of the previous night. Tess was dangerous, especially for a black man.

As he pulled up, Kev was already discussing the day with Alan.

'Morning, Billy, how did you sleep?' Alan asked.

'Not good, boss. Me tossing.'

'Well, clear those thoughts. We know what happened, and I'm sure Mitch dealt with it when he got home or at least this morning. She's a bloody handful that Tess. A hurricane to put it bluntly. What a night with both Griffo and her. But let's get on with it. You both need to keep an eye on Griffo and his mate.'

Kev and Billy nodded in unison. 'Don't be alone with either of them. You always work together. I don't know what the problems are with the big fellow, but certainly, you, Billy, and Mum Shirl have a gut instinct for trouble. I would rather them both be gone, but they're here now and that's our lot.'

Billy's eyes were cast downward and occasionally flicked upwards. It did not go unnoticed by Alan. The man was clearly troubled by what happened last night.

'Work will be good for you, Billy, for that matter, everyone. Forget about last night and don't worry about Lisa and Zena. Tackle that one when we get to it.'

◊

Mum Shirl poked her head out of her tent when she heard the sound of the Quadrunner coming towards it. She looked at the sleeping children. 'Da boss man, Alan, he comin' here. You picaninnies better wake up. Mebbe he coming to get you. Mebbe Mum Shirl in da big trouble.'

She scrambled out of the tent and met Alan with a big toothless smile. 'Boss man, it da good day today?'

'Hope so, Mum Shirl.' Alan turned off the Quadrunner. 'That's better, much quieter. Where are the twins?'

'Da babies, dey sleep. Tired. Late night, too much excitement, but not da good way.'

'Yeah, Mum Shirl, that's why I thought I'd come and talk to you and Ningali. Where is she?' asked Alan.

'Ningali. She bin sleepin' too. Up all night with Kev. She got da smoochies. Dat poor Kev. He exhausted. Me go wake her.'

'That would be good, Mum Shirl.' He watched her waddle away towards a tent further down the bush track.

He lit up a cigarette and waited. By the time he finished his cigarette, Ningali was walking with Mum Shirl towards him. Alan smiled. Ningali clearly had not had much sleep. Her hair looked like a tangled broom.

'Morning, Ningali. Late night?'

'Yeah, boss, proper true.' She laughed girlishly. 'Kev, he get up or-right. I see him in da dark, he get his boots on ready for work.'

'No problem there, Ningali. Kev was on time for the job. Now tell me, ladies, what are your thoughts? You're like Billy. I know you see things, feel things.'

'Thoughts?' The women looked at each other and then back at Alan.

'Yes, your thoughts on last night,' Alan repeated.

'Dat Billy, he da true magic man. He see things like Burnu, his dad,' exclaimed Ningali, her eyes widening. 'He tell me da big man evil. Da red hair, she also evil.'

'Ha! We need da Kurdaitcha man,' shouted Mum Shirl. 'He take da evil away.'

Ningali gasped. 'Kurdaitcha?'

'I heard you say that last night. Who or what is that?' asked Alan.

'When you got da evil all around, things dey happen. Da Kurdaitcha man, he da type of shaman, he come and point da bone. He wear da special shoes, leave no footprints, da soles made of emu feathers and made woven with feathers and human hair, mix with da blood. He wear da kangaroo hair stuck to da body. He punish da guilty party by death.'

'Death! Whoa, wait on a minute, you two, just your thoughts. We are not killing anyone,' said Alan, taken aback.

'No, da evil big here. He point da bone, voodoo death. No trace,' added Mum Shirl.

'Okay, I get it. We have the big bloke Griffo and he may cause trouble, and we have Tess, who likes to cause trouble.'

'Yes, dat right,' said Ningali. Dem two, boss, get da bad feelin last night. I gunna dance my own corroboree to chase da evil spirits away.'

'Yeah, bad feelin',' added Mum Shirl. 'Dat Billy, he know too. He see more.'

'But do you really believe in this bone pointing? What type of bone?' Alan asked.

Mum Shirl spoke in a whisper. 'Da bone, made of human, mebbe kangaroo, emu. Look like a long needle.'

Alan shook his head. 'Well, not right now. We'll handle this our own way. But both of you, promise me one thing.'

The two women leaned closer, curious to Alan's asking of a promise.

'Never, ever, let those two children out of your sight. And if you have any premonitions or, or just anything, you let me know. Got it. You come to me first.'

They both nodded in unison. 'Yes, boss, we gunna tell ya, proper true,' said Ningali.

◊

Mitch and Dave were also up early at sunrise, directing the crew with what they needed to do.

'I'm starving, Dad, and geez my head hurts. I need food.'

'Too many beers and a shit of a night in terms of your wife. Just when things were going along not too badly.' They piled into their ute and headed towards Woodside.

'Is she up yet?' Mitch flung his hat onto the table when they arrived, sweat marks already appearing around the brim.

'No, she hasn't made an appearance,' said Kate. 'But I did hear water running, so there is some movement. I'm dreading this, and just when you think things are running smoothly. It's so disturbing. I don't think she understands or is incapable of seeing the consequences of her actions and how upsetting it is for everyone. I know

194

Tess is a handful, but Polly has been doing so much better lately. She is still your daughter and our granddaughter, so we just have to cope with Tess. '

'Mum, just because she has had children, my children, it doesn't necessarily equate to being a good and respectful mother or person. Tess is...Tess is on another level. There is a complete lack of parental fitness. I don't think I can stand it any longer. And as for lifting up her dress and exposing herself to Billy!'

They all looked up when the door from the hallway to the kitchen slowly opened. Kate inwardly groaned. She braced for the confrontation.

'Morning, everyone,' Tess said defiantly as if she had done nothing wrong.

'This is not a good morning, Tess, after the stunt you pulled last night,' said Mitch.

'Go to hell. I didn't pull anything. Like I told you, that black bastard made a pass.' She smirked.

'You embarrassed all of us, especially Mum. Why don't you think carefully about what you do, Tess? You're a grown woman with two daughters.'

The room fell heavily silent, and Tess's eyes sparked. She blinked at Mitch's words then hissed through gritted teeth. 'You've made me what I am, Mitch. I opened up my heart and you got inside and messed me up. It's ripped me apart. I've tried too, so hard. But you don't give me anything! No love, no affection and certainly nothing in the sack!'

'And you think flashing your beaver to someone is a good thing? Good behaviour from a mother? Tess, get out. Now! I don't want you around my kids if you keep behaving like you do,' Mitch said.

'Is that a threat? You Walkers think you can control everything with your money. Take my kids away? Don't worry, I'm going, and I will get advice from my own lawyer. Don't ever expect me to lie down quietly so you can take my girls. Expect to hear from my lawyer, you bastard! Just because you have money, you think you can treat people how you want.' Tess stomped her way to the door and down the back stairs. She looked up at the window. 'And by the way, Mitch, you're a dud in the sack, arsehole!' her voice thundered.

Kate's eyes were closed as she swallowed hard and clutched at her shirt, wanting the misery of the situation to dissipate. The only sound was the roar of Tess's car. Dave came to her side. 'It's okay, Kate, we'll go forward and handle things like we always do. Fair and proper.'

'Oh,' Kate cried. 'I just think terrible things lay ahead, the darkest of days. What do we tell Olivia and Polly? And when Tess goes, Polly always deteriorates. She has been so good of late, and I know the medication and the psychiatry visits all help. This is the final straw that will implode everything. I just have this feeling.'

Mitch looked ashamed at the pain he had caused his parents. He ran his hand through his dishevelled hair and cleared his throat. 'Sorry, Mum, Dad. Anger I can deal with, but I hate to be embarrassed and lose control of my emotions like I did last night. I have to apologise to Billy. I just lost control. I agree, Dad, we'll get through this. Who knows, we may just get some peace around here, and if Polly deteriorates, I will be the first on the phone to that Dr Adams. I really liked talking to her, and she was good with Pol.'

Kate dabbed her eyes. 'You two have your breakfast. I'll see if the girls are awake. They will have to be told.'

TWENTY-TWO

BAD FEELINGS

When Zena and Lisa arrived at Woori, it was just after five in the afternoon. They were both emotionally and physically exhausted. When they called, Alan had said to head to the big house where they had a BBQ waiting.

As Zena drove toward the homestead she smiled. 'That looks wonderful, doesn't it, Lisa?'

'Best sight in the world. No. Make that second best. Billy and my darlings are always first.'

At the sound of the car, Jesse and Jedda came running out of the compound with Billy and Alan just behind them. Mum Shirl, Ningali and Kev stood at the gates waving.

'What a welcome, a most heart-warming sight,' laughed Zena as she pulled up.

The children were at full throttle as their screams reached fever pitch. Lisa leaped out of the car and squatted down to hold them. Billy soon reached them, and Lisa stood as he swept her into his arms. He nuzzled into her hair and breathed in her smells. He didn't want to let her go.

As they all sat down, Alan knew the questions would begin. He was ready.

'So, how was the night over at Woodside?' asked Zena, sipping her beer.

Alan took a deep breath, and something told Zena all was not well. She put down her beer and looked across at Billy. 'Alright, you two, I can feel when something is not right, so best spill the beans.'

'Kate had everything all under control and was ably assisted by Tess and her girls. They were doing a fantastic job, really. No drama until Tess decided to, well, muck up.'

'What do you mean, muck up?' asked Lisa as she took Billy's hand across the table. Anything to do with Tess was always trouble.

There was momentary silence.

'Alan,' Zena spoke sharply. 'Do I need to tell the children to go?'

'Probably a good idea. Mum Shirl, can you just take a wander with them. Once around the house will suffice.'

'Yes, boss, no problem.' She got to her feet. 'You two picaninnies, come, come, you gunna take a little walk.' Jedda and Jesse jumped up and followed Mum Shirl out the back door.

'Get on with it, Alan, and like Queen Elizabeth tells her press secretary, don't sugar coat anything.'

Alan exhaled a long breath and tapped his fingers on the table. 'Billy went to get a few cartons of beer for Kate. They were stacked up past a hay shed, and Tess just happened to be there, smoking. Billy didn't know she was there. She came on to Billy and lifted up her skirt, and then Billy took off.'

Lisa stared gape-mouthed at Billy. She looked across to Alan. 'You'd better explain... more.' She was livid. 'I had a feeling something bad would happen.' She looked into Billy's eyes, whose clench around her hand grew tighter.

'For God's sake, what happened next?' asked Zena.

'Billy came to me and told me what happened and the next minute there was a bit of a crowd from the party and of course, Mitch came barrelling in, full of too many beers and had a go at Billy.

Lisa's hand flew to her mouth. 'What!'

'Dat Tess, she cause all da trouble,' said Ningali.

Billy saw the fire in Lisa's eyes. Then she suddenly took his face in her hands and kissed him softly. 'I'm alright, Billy. It was just a shock,' said Lisa.

'I sorry,' he whispered hoarsely.

Alan chimed in. 'She tried to tell us that Billy made a move on her, but everyone knew she was lying, and Mitch sent her packing back to the house. No doubt we will hear what transpired from Kate or Dave. Anyway, the food awaits, so let's get started. Let's put this behind us, now it's out in the open.'

Zena smiled. Alan had a way of making things sound simple but no doubt there would be repercussions, which, as he said, would eventually come out in the wash. She would call Kate tomorrow.

It was around noon the next day when Lisa called Zena. 'Have I got you at a good time?'

'Yes, my love. I was up early and got stuck into a few things. So good to be in my own bed. How about you?'

'Spoiled. I slept in and had the house to myself. The twins are with Mum Shirl. They left me a little note for when I woke up. I'm just calling after doing bits and pieces. Also, I'm curious to see if you had touched base with Kate.'

'You read my mind, Lisa. That I did. I wanted to know exactly what happened after the issue with Tess and Billy. Curious creature I am, but I thought you would want to know too.'

'Yes, you know me well,' she agreed.

'Well, as Alan said last night, Mitch told her to go home and they confronted her very early the following morning about her behaviour. Tess was apparently on her way out, probably to remove herself from the friction and arguments about the evening. Obviously off to Walgett, but Mitch told her not to come back. Kate said it was most unpleasant and that Tess would get a lawyer. So that's basically it.'

'A lawyer! How awful,' said Lisa. 'Very confronting for Kate, well, for everyone. But what will Tess do in Walgett?'

'She has a roof over her head, Lisa. We shall have to see what transpires. I'm sure Mitch will try to prove Tess is an unfit mother. Anyway, what are your plans for the day?'

'I was going to head down and see Cookie, he may need a hand, and of course find where my children are. Billy said they squat in Mum Shirl's tent listening to her stories. School work has flown out the door.'

Zena laughed. 'She is a bit of a character. I can see why the kids adore her. What say I head down about four? The men will be coming in by then.'

'Sounds good. I'll see you down there.'

When Lisa arrived, she sniffed the air. Cookie was underway. She looked out past the shearer's quarters and saw two largish tents down a bush track. So, one tent was for Mum Shirl and the other was Ningali and Kev. She could hear the sounds of giggling and smiled inwardly. Lisa headed to the shearer's kitchen.

She popped her head in the doorway. 'Hey, you,' she said when she saw Cookie, a grin lighting up her face.

'Hey, you back, Lisa!' Cookie launched himself at her, giving her a ferocious hug. 'How are you? Alan told me the sad news about your dad's passing. Sorry, luv.'

'Yes, he's on the other side of the stars now, Cookie,' Lisa said sadly.

'None of us are here forever, sweetheart, so make the most of every day. What have you got there?'

'I picked them up on the way home. Thought they would not go astray. There are cakes in boxes just on the log outside as well. Don't forget them or the ants will carry them away.'

'You get brownie points for that. It all helps,' said Cookie.

'Now I have to find my kids and from what everyone tells me, they have taken up residence in Mum Shirl's tent.'

'That they have. They are real crackers.'

'Thanks, Cookie. So lovely to see you here.'

'Likewise, Lisa, likewise.'

When Lisa opened the flap of the tent to step in, Mum Shirl sat with her legs extended in front of her and the children were cross-legged just at the end of her feet. She was showing them a seed of some sorts and they all looked up when she stepped in.

'Mummy,' yelled Jedda.

'What are you two doing? No schoolwork, huh?' asked Lisa.

'Dey do da school work with Mum Shirl.' Her toothless grin flashed.

'Alright, I'll sit and have a lesson with you.' Lisa lowered herself to the floor and sat between her children.

'Us peoples we know da seeds deposit here on da earth. Whatever we do, we leave something here, just as da plants and da bush do. Da land and da mountains and all da rivers. Da flowing waters are da women. All dem things on da earth, dey all make da earth. Everything all forming. Da seeds dey strong in da ground and our spirits, our ancestors, dey create dis world. Dis da Dreaming. Each tribe dey have own land and totems and da Dreamtime. Some believes da ancestors were animal spirits. Some believe da ancestors were huge snakes. And some believe da spirit who created da earth was da Wandjina.'

'What do you believe, Mum Shirl?' asked Jesse.

'I believe dat all we see, da mountains, hills, rivers, plants, animals, people and da big sky above was made by da great spirits. My peoples we bin on da earth for thousands of years, since da spirit people,' she said, her arms extending upwards. 'Long time ago, we walked with da Gods and da humans. Da Spirit people created da land, da sky and da seas and all da creatures dat live in them. In making da world, da spirit people became a part of it. Our mob, da Aborigines, dis land owns da people who live in it.'

Jesse puffed his chest out. 'I believe that too! You speak like my daddy.'

Mum Shirl started laughing. 'Can you tell us more?' pleaded Jedda.

'No more, you two. Mum Shirl needs a break. Come out now. Thank you, Mum Shirl, for looking after my picaninnies. They just adore you. Off you two go and say goodbye to Cookie.'

'Dey special. Make Mum Shirl laugh. Ningali, she teach dem to dance when she not out with Kev or down by da bore catching yabbies. She bin helping Cookie a lot too and da little one, she sing to me. Like da bird. Da little willy wagtail. He sing all day.'

Lisa laughed. 'Yes, she does love to sing. Zena has been giving her a few lessons. Next year she will have some professional assistance.'

'You go first out da tent and I follow. You don't wanna be behind me. I got da slow legs and da big bum,' giggled Mum Shirl.

As Lisa stepped out, the shearers were coming down from the sheds. Sheep, newly shorn, were being pushed down the exits and scattering. 'Must be just about the end of the day, Mum Shirl.'

Griffo was last out when he looked across at Lisa. 'Get a load of that, Ernie, look over there, mate.'

'Mate, I've got bloody eyes. Must belong to someone here,' said Ernie.

The penny suddenly dropped. Griffo scowled. 'That must be the black bastard's bitch, and they are her creamies. Fuck. That black bastard. He's got the lot, hasn't he!'

'Mate, touching that would be even worse than messing with that wild redhead. Come on, let's wash up and get any thought of that pussy out of your messed-up brain. We've got no money, remember, and we don't get paid until we finish the job. So don't fuck this one up.'

Lisa watched the men coming out as Mum Shirl came to her side. 'My goodness, what a giant of a man. Who is he? Obviously one of the new faces.'

'Lisa, he got da evil inside. Da bad spirit. You stay away. Kids stay away.'

'What are you talking about, Mum Shirl? Jesse, Jedda, where are you? Come here, please.'

Jedda poked her head out from Cookie's kitchen. 'Here, I am, eating cake. Jesse is too.'

Lisa brought her attention back to Mum Shirl. 'Tell me, Mum Shirl. What is it?'

'Ningali and me. We see da things. Feel da things. I go into da trance and I see da bogey man. He got da unclean spirit. He da bogey man. Bring da bad things.'

Lisa shivered. Griffo and Ernie walked past her and Mum Shirl. Griffo raised his hat and smiled. Mum Shirl glared back at them as they headed towards the wash-room. 'Kurdaitcha,' she hissed under her breath.

'God, I'd love to be grinding away at that,' Griffo smirked. 'Bloody meat-head boong surely can't give her what she wants.'

'Shut up, Griffo. Keep walking,' said Ernie.

Lisa watched the men walk away. 'You're right, Mum Shirl. I think my appearances down here will be infrequent. He just made my blood run cold. I'll get the kids and head home. Jesse, Jedda, come. We have to go, and Cookie has work to do.'

Lisa stopped when she saw Zena heading towards her. They both slowed down. 'Sorry I'm late. I had Kate on the phone. Tess called and gave Kate a serving and was threatening to come back and do damage to anyone and everything. Kate said she was drunk so had to hang up on her. And Polly is starting to act up. It never stops for her.'

'Poor Kate,' said Lisa. 'But I don't think Tess would be brave enough to do anything silly or even front up here.'

'No, but when people misuse alcohol, anything can happen. I'll go and see Kate tomorrow. Her nerves are a mess.'

'I had a funny feeling down there. You know, without Jack, and with the new faces. Mum Shirl definitely doesn't like the big guy. I had an uneasy feeling about him as well.'

'Was Alan there?' Zena queried.

'No. So he may still be out with Billy and Kev. Ningali goes along for the ride now in the old paddock basher, so she's out there too when she's not helping Cookie.'

'Well, he shouldn't be long. I'll head down just to say hello to the old faces, and of course, Cookie. I'll call you tomorrow.'

When Zena pulled up, a few of the men were already seated at the outside table under a large peppercorn tree, just opposite the kitchen.

Ernie and Griffo sat on a log outside Cookie's kitchen. 'Who's this then?' queried Ernie as Zena pulled up. 'Cripes, that's a bit of alright too. Shit, where are all these women suddenly coming from?'

Griffo dragged on his cigarette. 'I wouldn't mind tangling with that one either. Got a bit of age on her, but gravity hasn't got her tits or her arse yet. Give her a run for her money. I so need to fuck something,' said Griffo. His eyes flashed a dangerous glint.

'There's nothing here, mate, unless you want to try that old darkie who lives in the tent over there,' laughed Ernie. 'But it would be like wrestling with a black snake!'

Griffo grunted. His thoughts turned to the redhead. He knew where he could find her when he finished his work at Woori. He would wait in town until she showed.

'Hey, you two!' Cookie suddenly appeared at the entrance to his little kitchen. 'Heard every word you said. You blokes better watch your language and your manners,' he snapped. 'Don't want no trouble here. Always been a good camp. That fine lady is Alan's missus and if I hear any bad words, you'll be answering to me.'

Griffo grunted. 'Now what's a pint-size chef gonna do to me? Be like swatting a fly if you get in my way.'

'Yeah, bloody tough talk. Seen blokes like you many times. Bloody goat humpers. They never last long. But I don't need to do anything physical to you, mate, brawny piece of shit that you are. I just won't feed ya. See how long you'll last!'

'Fuck off and stop flapping your gums. You're starting to really give me the shits,' snarled Griffo. He stubbed out his cigarette and blew a ring of smoke. 'Could squash that little Cookie like a gnat.'

'Cool it, Griffo, she's heading towards us,' said Ernie.

'Gentlemen,' said Zena as she passed by them, carrying a few small boxes.

'Hello, Cookie.' Zena stepped into the shed. 'So lovely to see you here, and I'm so sad this is your last season with us. It won't be the same without you.' Zena leaned forward and kissed him on the cheek. 'If you need a hand with anything, Lisa and I are always here.'

Cookie took the boxes and placed them on the bench. 'Got it all under control, Zena. Ningali and Mum Shirl have been helping. Got no problems at all. Just trying to keep these boofheads in line.'

Zena laughed. 'I'm sure that's not a problem either, Cookie. Well, let Alan know I've been and gone. I won't wait as who knows how long he will be. I'll just duck over to see Mum Shirl and I'll be on my way.'

As she walked towards Mum Shirl's tent, she felt the piercing eyes of the big man, a vicious, predatory stare. She had a bad feeling about him too.

TWENTY-THREE

A KNIFE ATTACK

The heat hit the shearing sheds by mid-morning. The men were working hard, and Griffo was one of the fastest shearers Alan had seen. He moved quickly for a big man, and the sheep were coming down the chutes one after another. He had no time for small talk and stuck closely to Ernie.

'Bloody odd if you ask me, the odd couple,' laughed Cookie. 'A bloke that looks like a gorilla and a sidekick who would look good in a tutu. Bloody goat humpers if you ask me. Better not cause any trouble. The rest of the crew are fine, Alan. Billy's doing a great job. He has their respect and has stepped up into Jack's role. But those two blokes, they're a worry.'

'Yeah, I agree, Cookie. Every time Billy looks at him, they size each other up. Be glad when they have both gone. But for now, as I said, he's one of the fastest blokes I've seen for a long time. About ninety seconds per Merino.'

Alan looked at his watch. 'Must be time for morning tea. Hit that triangle of yours and put out a few of those delicious cakes my woman has made. I could eat a few. No breakfast this morning. Billy and I were up early with the jackaroos bringing that mob of sheep down. He's not far behind me with Kev and Ningali.'

Cookie rang the triangle as Alan pulled up a chair. Men in blue singlets began to appear as they headed towards the table.

'As usual, good tucker,' said old Ned as he swatted the flies away from the creamy sponge cake. 'Goes down a treat with a cup of Bushells.'

'Yeah, Ned, she's pretty good in the kitchen, my woman.' Alan helped himself to another piece of cake.

'Can hear the old paddock basher roaring in the distance now. Better be quick or they will miss out,' said Alan.

'Nah,' said Cookie. 'Plenty of sweet grub here, thanks to Lisa and your missus.'

They all looked up when the mob of sheep suddenly scattered in the yards to the sound of dogs howling and barking. There was a screech of tyres, and billows of red dust raged across the landscape.

'What the hell is going on?' said Alan as he scrambled to his feet, racing to the yards at the other side of the main shearing shed followed by the crew.

Billy and Kev had seen the sheep scattering from a distance and then saw the dogs. Kev drove hard at the yards and came to a screaming halt. Billy leaped out of the ute, yelling at the dogs attacking and biting the sheep, some of them rounded up in a corner. Ningali sensed danger as she exited, her eyes scanning for Mum Shirl as she watched Billy trying to take control.

'Get back, get away, back!' Billy roared at the dogs, cracking the stock whip, sheep scattering in all directions. The dogs leaped for the fences and took off into the scrub.

Billy was breathing hard as he stood in the paddock, his eyes searching for Griffo. They were his dogs.

'Where dat idiot Griffo? I tell him before to keep dogs away and he don't listen.' The anger in Billy's voice was rising. He hurdled over the fence and headed towards the remaining shearers in the shed.

'Slow down, Billy. I'm right beside you,' said Alan.

'Where dat Griffo?' shouted Billy.

Tom, one of the new shearers, called out, 'They headed outside just a few minutes ago.'

Billy stomped towards where he knew Griffo and Ernie would be sitting, Alan directly behind him.

'You, big fella. You got no brains,' Billy shouted, pointing the stock whip at Griffo. 'I tell you before about dem dogs,' he said as he confronted the pair.

The big man stood up and folded his arms across his chest, giving Billy a deathlike stare.

'Tell me what, you stupid black cunt?' sneered Griffo. He wanted to beat the shit out of Billy. He would enjoy it so much.

Billy stood his ground, raw and angry as the words fell from his mouth. 'I tell you before, dem dogs, keep dem away from da sheep! Dey bruise da sheep.' Alan grabbed Billy's arm to stop him from getting any closer.

'Come on, you black bastard, wanna have a go?' sneered Griffo.

Billy dropped the whip and clenched his fists. There was an almost deathly hush.

'Alright, you two,' said Alan. 'Back off, both of you! We've told you before, Griffo. No dogs. So, keep them chained or pack your bags. Do you hear me?' said Alan.

Griffo's eyes slowly turned to Alan as his snarling mouth said, 'Yeah, I heard ya.'

'Right then, let's get back to work. No more of this bullshit and keep your damn dogs tied up.'

As Billy turned to walk away, Griffo suddenly lunged at him, knocking him to the ground. Billy fought for breath as he tried to shake the big man off and felt a painful blow to his skull. The sounds of men yelling filled the air as suddenly Griffo pulled a knife, the blade ready to strike, slashing in the air as it came slicing across Billy's face. He rolled, pushing Griffo's weight slightly and then brought his knee up between the big man's legs. Griffo roared in agony and brought his hands to his testicles as Alan kicked the knife out of his hand to one side.

Billy scrambled to his feet, enraged. He shook his head to clear it as the blood seeped from a cut under his left eye. The big man had tried to kill him.

'Get out,' Alan bellowed, his eyes bulging. 'Pack your things and get out! Both of you.'

Griffo still lay on the ground, his hands clutching his crotch, barely suppressing a groan as a spike of pain ripped through his balls. His voice was ragged as he half sat up. 'You better make sure our paths never cross again. I'll strangle you with my bare hands and watch the life go from your fucking dead black eyes.'

'Knock it off, Griffo. It's over. Now get out! Get your dogs and get out of my sight. Ernie, stop by the main house on your way out.' Alan looked at his watch. 'If you are not gone within thirty minutes, I'll make that call to the coppers. I'll give you a cheque you can cash at the pub or the post office. It will be in an envelope I'll pin to the gate,' said Alan, clearly rattled. 'Kev, take over. Billy, you come with me. I need Zena to look at that cut.' He wanted the men separated until Griffo had well and truly gone.

Every muscle in Zena's body stiffened as she saw the blood trickling down Billy's face. 'My God, what's happened?'

'I'll explain as we go but for now, just have a look at the cut below his eye. Does it need stitches?'

'Billy, sit down, please. I'll just go and get the medicine kit.' Zena dashed away.

'You okay, son?' asked Alan.

'Yeah, sorry, boss. I just got real angry,' apologised Billy.

'So, I noticed. Anyway, don't be sorry. You did us all a favour. Seems everyone was of the same opinion. No one liked the big bloke. But you're lucky. He would not have hesitated plunging in that knife, regardless of the consequences to himself. That's madness. And we don't need madness here.'

Zena reappeared and began unpacking cotton balls, Dettol and anything else she could find. 'Now, can someone please provide me with an answer? What on earth has happened?'

'The big guy,' said Alan as Zena took a sharp intake of breath.

Billy winced as she applied the Dettol to his wound. 'A bit of bark lost but nothing that needs sewing. Superficial cut under his right eye. So very lucky. I can use butterfly tapes to close the wound. Where is Griffo now?' asked Zena.

'They're packing, him and his mate. Just excuse me, I need to put a cheque in an envelope.'

Alan headed out the door and as he got to the entrance gate to the compound, he saw their car coming in the distance. He rolled the envelope up like a bon-bon and stuck it through the cyclone wire. 'Good riddance,' he said as he walked back inside.

'Does Lisa know?' asked Zena as Alan sat back down.

'Nope. I'll leave that to Billy to explain. For now, Billy, I think you better head home and take the day off. Sometimes a knock to the head will have a few side effects. So, to be on the safe side, I will drive you home and you can rest.'

'Thank you, Zena,' Billy said sheepishly. He drew a shuddering breath. 'Lisa be angry with Billy.'

'It will be fine. She only commented today that there was something about Griffo. I agree. He frightened me. Go to her. The painkillers may make you drowsy. Sleep will do you no harm.'

◊

When routines change in the bush, there is always a reason. Lisa had just stopped for a break after School of the Air with the twins. She saw the paddock basher heading towards home and knew it was not the norm. Billy went from sun up to sun down. He never stopped. Neither did Alan.

The back door opened, and Lisa gasped. 'Billy, your face! My darling, what happened?'

He didn't answer right away, and Lisa could feel him struggling. Finally, he spoke, 'We fight, and da big guy, he pull da knife.'

'I know you are not telling me everything, and I just know this could have easily been a much worse outcome.' She shuddered.

Lisa took his hand, and they walked to their bedroom. She needed some space and quiet time with him. She lay next to him as her fingers gently traced his face. His lips suddenly parted and his mouth, soft as velvet, kissed Lisa tenderly. After a while, his breathing slowed, and his hold relaxed. Sleep came for Billy.

TWENTY-FOUR

MURDEROUS INTENT

As Griffo drove, his expression contorted into sheer venomous anger. His face was one of white rage. He knew he was entering a dangerous and murderous wave that would soon be out of control. The monster inside him was awake, and he was fighting back a powerful urge to maim or kill.

'How much did the bastard pay us? Bastard king dude he thinks he is. Big land, big dollars and soft in the head for those black dickheads. How much! Open that fucking envelope. Open it!' shouted Griffo as the veins in his neck bulged.

Ernie opened the envelope. 'Four hundred bucks, so that's two hundred each. And that's it.'

'What do you mean that's it?' spat Griffo.

'I've had enough. That's the last time you fuck something up for me, Griffo. We go our separate ways. You didn't have to get into a fight. You should have kept the dogs tied. You did it deliberately, didn't you? Just to get under that black bloke's skin. Well, you achieved that and more, you stupid prick. Now we're out of a job again, and two hundred bucks won't last long. I always like to send money home to my mother. She's getting on now. How am I supposed to do that with this shit lot of money?'

Griffo stared at the road straight ahead and grunted.

'You were going to kill him, weren't you? Answer me!'

'Yeah, I was, but the black fucker was too strong,' replied Griffo, his voice stony. 'I'd love to get another crack. Not hard to track him down. Bastard Alan needs to have his skull cracked too. Mr Big Shot!'

Ernie met his glare. 'You're not right in the head, mate. You can't go back there. Havoc and destruction follow us, and it's all because of you. I've been your bloody sidekick for what, ten years now? And it's not better, it's getting worse. I thought you were odd, Griffo, when I first met you. I put it down to all those stories you told me about your shit, abusive childhood and ending up in Homes. But mate, now I know for sure. You're bloody crazy. You need help. You nearly killed that kid the last joint we were at and now we're ducking and hiding again, and fuck, with no money left! This old ute is on its last legs and $400 won't get us far. We are never gonna get any work after the shit you just pulled. Never get a reference.'

'I told ya, that kid at the last place, he wanted it, so I gave it to him.'

'Griffo, he was just a kid, and you didn't have to rough him up like that. It's a wonder the cops weren't involved!' yelled Ernie.

'Parents wouldn't want the cops, too embarrassed. The privately educated little bastard was not Mr Perfect.' Griffo burst into laughter.

'As I said, I'm out. When we cash this cheque in Walgett, I'm dumping you. Want nothin' to do with you anymore,' said Ernie. 'You're a bad egg, mate, and I don't wanna be involved. Bloody accomplice or something like that is what the cops would charge me with, getting roped into your stupid shit.'

A black fury began building. Griffo knew he was bordering on the edge of losing control. He suddenly slammed his fists on the steering wheel of the old Holden, anger spiralling from the pit of his guts.

'You're not so fucken great either, you know!' he exploded. 'I've had a gutful of your whingeing and whining. It's me that finds all the work. Me that everyone thinks is the best worker, not you, you bloody stupid, fat sloth.'

'That's what you think. Stick it up your arse, Griffo,' yelled Ernie. 'Drop me off at Walgett. You can get on your way.'

Griffo seethed and remained silent until the last gate came into view. 'Last gate out of Woori,' he sneered as he slowed the car to a halt. As Ernie went to open the car door, he felt the blade of the knife plunge deeply into his back. He exhaled in a gasp and his piercing howl tore from deep within, falling on the deaf ears of the bush as his bleeding body fell out of the car and sprawled into the red dirt.

Griffo came around to where the bleeding man was trying to crawl away. The dogs in the back of the ute were barking incessantly. 'Sit down, ya mongrel dogs!' Griffo roared.

'Not so mouthy now, are we, Mr Ernest Tubbs. You fat fuck. It takes courage to kill, Ernie. Real fucken courage,' he bellowed. Ernie tried to drag his body along the dirt, but Griffo plunged the knife repeatedly into his back until there was no movement. He looked down at Ernie's lifeless body. 'Pigs will get a good feed, mate, and those fat sows will happily eat your face off. You'll be unrecognisable.' Griffo dragged him by the ankles deep into the scrub and returned to his ute.

He rummaged in his duffle bag and pulled out a clean shirt, stuffing the blood-splattered one into a plastic bag. He looked at the dogs in the back of the ute. 'Have to shoot you, mongrel dogs, can't take you with me.' Griffo looked into the bush and then back to the dogs. 'On second thought, fuck off the lot of ya.' He let the dogs off their leashes and watched them take off into the bush. 'You'll get a feed as well. Chomp chomp.' A beastly smile crossed his face.

When Griffo got into the ute, he grabbed the cheque. 'I just made myself another two hundred bucks. Thanks, Ernie.' But he knew he did not have enough money to go far and he would have to stay in the area getting odd jobs. Revenge was also on his mind.

As he hit Walgett, he pulled over to a council rubbish bin and threw the tied plastic bag into it. 'Goodbye, Mr Tubbs.' He mockingly looked up to the skies and made a sign of the cross. He looked for a clothing bin and found one at a local church, throwing Ernie's clothing into it. 'Thank you for the clothing donation, Mr Tubbs. The minister and his congregation thank you.'

Griffo began to laugh as his thoughts quickly turned to the red-head. 'Let's take a drive into suburbia and see if anyone's home. He drove down the street where Tess lived. The front door was open. Lust gnawed at him like vicious little teeth. 'I'm in luck,' he said as he rubbed his crotch. Griffo drove off slowly and knew he would have his opportunity. It was just a waiting game.

◇

Tess dressed slipped into a black dress that showed her cleavage. When she looked in the mirror, she smiled. *Not bad.* She finished her drink and headed to the pub.

Griffo sat waiting patiently in a far corner of The Thirsty Dog. She hadn't shown last night. He had heard the lads talking about her. A man by the name of Johnny was the most verbal, giving a graphic description of his sexual encounters with Tess. He smiled. She would be enjoyable.

When she came into the pub it was just after 7 p.m. Like bees to honey, the men they swarmed around her. *Pick me, pick me.* The woman was clearly enjoying her power and dominance over these drooling fools.

Griffo enjoyed the game, and he watched quietly in the back-ground. The young man chatting to her looked about nineteen, and she no doubt would teach him a thing or two. After they left togeth-er, he followed them to her house. He stopped and crossed the road, waiting for an hour, then headed in the opposite direction as he saw the front door open and the young man step out. When he disap-peared around the corner, Griffo made his move.

He went up the stairs to the front porch. Music was playing, and he peered through the tattered fly screen. She wore a floral dressing gown and was swaying to the music. He knocked roughly. She spun around and stared at the masculine form standing at the door. The light on the front porch was not working, so all she could see was the silhouette of a large male.

'Are you making a house call? Looking for something in particular?' Tess sauntered to the front door. 'Hey, it's you. What are you doing here? How do you know where I live?' Her dressing gown was loosely tied, barely covering her.

Griffo just stared at her, lust written all over his face.

'Oh, never mind that. What can I do for you?' She took a swig from her glass. Tess ogled him through the screen door. 'Big dude, why aren't you working?'

'Finished up,' he growled as he made his move and pushed the fly screen door open.

'Never got your name at the shearer's do,' said Tess teasingly.

'Don't need a name.' He slipped his fingers around the belt of her robe and pulled her towards him.

Tess felt a rush of excitement. He was hungry.

'Had enough for tonight, playing with little boys?' guffawed Griffo as his big hands held her tightly.

Tess threw her head back and laughed. 'He was a baby, couldn't get it up. Sent him home. Told him to come back when he's all grown up.'

Her eyes gazed over Griffo's strong body. 'I don't think you would have that problem. Would you like a drink? Let me get you a beer.' She walked to the kitchen.

Griffo followed and came up behind her. 'You need a real man. Ever since I saw you at that party, I thought of all the things I'd like to do to you.'

Tess leaned her back into his chest as his fingers roamed her body.

'Like it rough? Yeah, I bet you do.'

'Yes,' she purred, a soft moan escaping from her lips. She so needed sex.

'How rough, baby?' He bit hard into her neck.

'Not that hard. Easy, we've got all night,' Tess whispered. She turned to face him, well aware of his erection.

'I'm gonna enjoy hearing you scream with pleasure.'

Tess felt her heart racing with sexual excitement.

He was dominating her, pulling her in. She was highly aroused and wanted more. He ripped her gown open and hungrily kissed her breasts.

Griffo displayed a ravenous urgency. His fingers curled around her hair, holding her to him. 'Want more?'

'Oh, yeah,' replied Tess huskily. 'I want dick and lots of it.'

'Undress me then,' he commanded.

Tess pulled the T-Shirt over his head and undid his jeans, his erection springing out. 'I want that so bad.'

He ripped the gown from her and made Tess stand with her hands on the sink, her back facing towards him. He bent down and pulled out the gag and pantyhose from the pocket of his jeans.

'Hey, what are you doing?' Tess asked a bit nervously.

'We're going to play a game, you and me. Do you like games?'

Sexual tension filled the air. 'I don't know any games. What do you mean?'

'I'm going to gag your mouth, baby, so you can watch but you can't speak. I want to completely dominate you and do what I want with you.'

Griffo pulled the white cloth around her mouth and fastened it tightly. He was exciting and no one had ever aroused her or done what he was doing to her. His mouth roamed all over her body making low growling noises in his throat.

'Spread your legs.' He started to repeatedly spank her buttocks. Tess moaned, her body greedily taking pleasure. He spun her around and kneeled between her legs. His tongue was like an electric shock and she came to a shuddering orgasm.

'Yeah, you like it. They all do.' He grabbed her roughly by her hair and dragged her to the bedroom, throwing her on the bed.

He felt her stiffen. 'Relax, baby, just a little bit of bondage.'

Tess tried to speak but it was just a muffled sound under the gag. Being powerless turned her on. He was right.

'You'll love this, so relax. I get real hard and I go all night. You want that, don't you?'

Tess nodded, her heart beating rapidly. He tied her hands with the pantyhose to ends of the old brass bedhead.

He stood up and looked at her spreadeagled on the bed. The marks on her neck were turning red and blue from bruising.

'Now I'm going to fuck you and fuck you hard.' Suddenly his hand come down hard and slapped the side of her head. 'Rough, yeah? I'll give you more, you dirty little fuckbird.'

Tess gasped when he penetrated her. He felt huge, and she rocked her body with him, her legs entwined around his waist. He didn't stop and thrust violently again and again into her until he ejaculated wildly.

'Ready for more?' his gravelly voice asked. 'This is your last ride, baby.' He suddenly reached up and began to undo the panty hose and then removed her gag. His mouth crushed hers violently, smearing what was left of her red lipstick across her face. Tess's back arched, her hips undulating and demanding more. She breathed heavily as she met his lips hungrily, his tongue scraping the roof of her mouth.

'Turn over. Get on your knees.'

'Doggy style, hey,' panted Tess.

This was his favourite part. The stalking of the prey, the excitement and then the kill. He slapped her arse and wound his big hands through her hair, pulling her head back until she rocked with him again.

He ground himself into her and then reached for the panty hose on the bed.

'Do you like this, Tess? No more playing games with us men. Teasing us. You fucking bitches, prick-teasers. All the same.'

'What... what are you talking about?' As she tried to get up, he held her tightly. With one hand bracing her against his body, he wrapped the panty hose around her neck, quickly pulling it tighter so she could not speak or yell. She raised up on her knees, her hands desperately trying to pull the panty hose away, struggling furiously, her choking breath gasping for air. He could feel her getting limp.

'It doesn't take long, fuckbird, and in six minutes you'll be dead.' It excited him more as he watched her life ebb away. It was such a strong physical release, the power to end someone's life.

PART THREE

FRACTURED SPIRIT

TWENTY-FIVE

CHAOS REIGNS

Mitch sat stony-faced by the grave site as they waited for the minister to deliver the service. He refused to have it in a church, and Kate was aghast at his decision.

'She didn't believe in church or religion, Mum, so she's getting the service she wants.' He could finally get on with his life now Tess was out of the way, yet not even he had wished murder upon her.

Zena sat with Alan, and all she felt was great sorrow for the young girls at losing their mother in such an horrific way. They had made the decision not to tell the girls the exact cause of death. Kate felt it would have been too traumatic. Polly never said a word at the service and greeted no one. Waves of suppressed energy surrounded her. She moved like she was in a trance, the dark circles under her vacant eyes clearly visible. Olivia sat huddled against Kate, whose face was gaunt. Dave looked exhausted.

'Murder is an act of evil,' Zena said softly. 'No one deserves such a death. Tess was a handful, no dispute there, but to think someone is walking amongst us that could do such a thing. Kate told me she knew something was terribly wrong. She called for nearly a week, day and night, with no answer.'

'Would have been a gruesome sight for the coppers,' replied Alan. He shuddered. Maggots would have covered her rotting, swollen green-tinged body. The fluids from gas would have built up to give off an unbearable stench that permeated the room. Animals were bad enough, but the coppers said humans were worse. 'They said her body had been subjected to extreme violence and violation.'

Tess's casket lay next to the open hole in Walgett Cemetery. The minister stood next to it and opened his bible. It was just after noon. *'Ladies and gentleman, let us begin. We bring Tess's body to this place, which has been prepared for her rest. Ashes to ashes, dust to dust. God, you are a refuge for us. You rescue us when we are in distress, and we take relief in knowing Tess's suffering has ended. We release you now into the Everlasting and Loving Arms of our Lord. May you know wholeness and peace now and throughout all eternity. This concludes our service for Tess Walker.'*

Polly and Olivia walked slowly over to the casket with Mitch and each placed a small yellow rose on top. 'Come on, let's go,' he said, ushering them away from the coffin. Olivia reached for his hand, but Polly suddenly turned and spat at him, her fists clenched and eyes blazing.

The minister's mouth flew open. Zena and Alan got to their feet. 'What on earth is happening now?' said Zena, concerned for the young adolescent who was now hysterical.

'You did this!' Polly wailed. 'You did this, it's all your fault. You killed my mother. She'd still be here if you hadn't sent her away.' Polly threw herself at Mitch, knocking the minister to the side, her fists flailing at Mitch's abdomen.

Kate summoned what strength she had and went to Polly, trying to soothe the girl. 'And you stay away from me too, all of you. I hate you. The voices say you are all evil.' She screamed into to the sky, tears streaming down her face.

'Dave, give me a hand here,' said Kate as she tried to put her arms around Polly. The girl's mind was again clearly in a state of crisis and chaos.

'Leave me alone, *grandmother*. You hated my mum.' Her hand lashed out across Kate's face, her fingernails drawing blood.

Mitch suddenly scooped Polly up, and she began screaming and kicking. 'Dad, will you drive straight to Walgett Hospital while I restrain Polly in the back seat.'

Zena tried to console Olivia and Kate.

Mitch looked out the car window at Zena as he tried to contain the struggling Polly. Zena waved them on. 'Go, just go. Alan and I will get Kate and Olivia home.'

Silence filled the car on the journey back to Woori, and Zena was adamant Kate and Olivia stay with them until they heard some news from Mitch.

The phone rang just after 4:00 p.m. 'Mitch, what's happening?' Alan braced himself.

'They put Polly under sedation. The psychiatrist, Dr Adams, who has been treating Polly, is coming tomorrow. Dad and I will stay in town until things are sorted. Can you please let Gus, my head guy, know? He and the farm crew will just get on with it. Gus knows what to do.'

'Sure, Mitch. I'll head over after I get off the phone.'

'How are Mum and Livvy?'

'Zena is with them. She wanted them to stay at Woori until we heard from you.'

'Good idea. I can't thank you enough. You... you've always been there for us, Alan.'

'That's what friends are for. Now try and rest yourself, you and Dave. All under control here.'

Alan walked to the living room where Zena sat with Kate and Olivia.

'Well?' asked Zena as he stood at the entrance door.

'They've sedated Polly and the psych she was seeing is heading over to the hospital tomorrow. They're staying in town so I'll duck over and let the boys at Woodside know.'

'Okay,' Zena nodded. 'I'll sort things here.'

Zena took Kate's hand. 'The worst is over, Kate. Polly will get good care, and her grief will pass. For now, I think a warm shower for both of you and a good cup of tea is what's needed. You can slip on one of my spare robes and I know I have some of Jedda's gear here for Livvy.'

Kate rose to her feet. 'I don't know how we will ever get through this, Zena. Polly had been doing so much better, but now?' She took Livvy's hand.

'You will. Polly is getting the help she needs right now. Perhaps her meds had stopped being as effective, or it was just the stress of her mother's death making her lash out?'

The women stood and faced each other. 'It will get better, Kate.'

◊

Polly came home to Woodside after a month of intensive psycho-therapy, change of medication and some electroconvulsive therapy at Walgett Hospital. Kate had travelled in every second day, either with Mitch or Dave, for the counselling sessions with Dr Rebekah Adams, the psychiatrist. Kate found the peer-group sessions with other young girls the most helpful for Polly, and Polly seemed to be emotionally lifted by the fact that there were other girls, like her, who suffered with mental illness.

It was during one of the group sessions that Dr Adams asked the girls, one by one, how they felt about going home.

Polly looked at Mitch. 'Yes, I think I'm ready. I want to go home,'

'That is wonderful, Polly. I believe you are ready. You have re-sponded well to the intensive treatment regime. I'll let the staff know and will arrange for your discharge papers to be signed. I'll see you and your family in my office before you go. I just want to run over your medications with everyone on board.'

Mitch felt his stomach churn. It has been so peaceful without Tess and Polly. The meds masked a lot of things, but deep in his heart, he was guarded. He knew how quickly things could change. Schizophrenia. They hadn't been expecting that. He was glad he had touched base with Dr Adams when Polly had had a short relapse. He felt comfortable talking to her and would involve himself more with Polly and make sure she continued to take her meds.

Dr Adams looked at Mitch. 'Polly has responded well, Mitch, but you will all play a role in her healing. As always, please feel free to contact me of you have any concerns. Kate, I'll leave you to pack what she has here, and I'll then see you in my office. Don't head to my private practice, just the rooms I use here in the hospital are fine.'

'Thank you, Dr Adams,' said Kate, grateful for the fine doctor who had assisted her to also come to terms with everything that had happened.

When they pulled into Woodside, Dave stood chatting to Alan, who had been there to help out with the end of the season.

'We're home now, Polly. Let's say hello to Alan,' said Kate.

'G'day Pol, nice to see you back home,' said Alan. 'We were just chatting about the end of the season. All the shearers have packed up. Didn't even have a farewell either, so it's pretty quiet now.'

'Thank you, umm, yes, quiet, but I'm looking forward to being home and riding again,' Polly replied. 'Hello, Grandpa.' She turned her gaze to Dave. It was unnerving, her eyes were alive but somehow at odds with the rest of her face. It must have been the effect of the meds.

'Good to have you home, Polly,' Dave said.

Mitch could sense his father's apprehension. Everyone was making an effort but the atmosphere felt somewhat strained.

'Alright, I best be on my way. Good luck with everything,' Alan said before he headed home. The only word that sprang to mind was 'awkward'.

'Cooeee,' Alan yelled out as he flung his hat on the table.

'Cooeee, my love,' Zena sang out as she appeared. 'How was Dave?'

'Looking good, and we had a long chat about expanding and diversifying. Took a run out to that dam. More like a deep, small lake.

Had the water tankers there a couple of weeks ago, filling it to the top. Great swimming hole. The kids will love it.'

'How did Kate look?' queried Zena. 'I'll give them some space before I head over there.'

'Kate looked on edge, and as I drove home, my gut feeling was it felt awkward. Like everyone was on their guard or something. I was glad to be out of there.'

'Of course it would be awkward. Their mother murdered. Coming back to family life and trying to be normal. It would be difficult, and it will be difficult. The road ahead will not be easy, especially as Polly does have a diagnosed mental disorder and needs medication permanently. Kate told me about her having schizophrenia. That's a challenge and a half to treat. How they will make sure she is taking the medication will also be hard. I always try to be positive, but somehow, I feel the road ahead will be tough, very tough, for them.

TWENTY-SIX

WALKING ON EGGSHELLS

It was coming to the end of November 1985, and over the ensuing months things were somewhat quieter. Yet although Polly was co-operating, there was still an edge about her. Olivia enjoyed riding with Polly, and it was always a race to see who was first home. Mitch now included Polly in some of the chores but it was his gut feeling that she could turn at the slightest provocation.

The days were getting hotter. 'Let's ride to the new dam, Livvy,' said Polly one day. 'I feel like a swim.'

'I'd like to ride but I don't like the water. I thought you didn't like the water either? I can watch you,' replied Olivia.

'I've been dog paddling and trying to teach myself. Come on, sis, don't be a baby,' Polly chided.

'No! I don't like the water. Not even Jesse can get me to swim. I can't swim,' said Olivia, exasperation creeping into her voice.

'Jesse? Creamies are not good swimmers!' teased Polly.

'Yes, he is, he's great at swimming, and why are you being so horrible? Stop calling them creamies!'

Polly laughed. She enjoyed teasing Olivia. 'Someone's got a crush, someone's got a crush.'

'He's my friend, Polly, so is Jedda, that's all. And you used to play with them too, you know. They were your friends as well. Nanny said it's good to have friends.'

'Yeah, sure Livvy,' Polly drawled. 'I'm hungry. Let's get some lunch and we can ride this afternoon.'

'Hello, you two. I was wondering when you would come in,' said Kate as they appeared. 'Did you see any holes in the fences?'

'Just a few.' Polly pulled out a crumpled note from her top pocket. 'I've written down where they are by my compass.'

'Clever girl. Your dad will be grateful. I was thinking, Polly. If you wanted to, when we go into town next, we can perhaps visit your mother's graveside. Would you like that?'

Something clicked in Polly's head. Her eyes widened and then narrowed. 'My mother's death was like a thousand cuts,' Polly scowled. 'I know where she's buried, but I have no desire to visit her grave. All I can say is I hope she rests in peace. My mother only had need for herself.'

Kate made a mental note to let Mitch know her reaction to this suggestion. He had been taking Polly monthly to see Dr Adams, whom he now fondly referred to as Rebekah. He seemed to enjoy the visits more than Polly.

'I'm sorry, Polly. I didn't mean to offend you. It was just a thought.'

Kate had an uneasy feeling and had been waiting for this reaction with every passing day. The minute Polly disagreed with something, or something was wrong, it was like a snake uncoiling. She wondered when the girl would strike. Since her release from hospital, and the sessions with Rebekah, things had been good, almost perfectly pleasant, but there was always an undercurrent of danger lurking beneath the surface.

Polly, I was only... I just thought it might be something you might like to do,' apologised Kate.

'No! I never want to go there,' Polly snapped, adamant.

'Polly, Nanny was only trying to do something for you,' said Olivia.

Kate knew then that she would have to be always be wary in Polly's company. She trusted Dr Adams and her treatment protocol, but she just could never let her guard down around her granddaughter. There was a sense of pervading threat, and her mood could change so dramatically.

'Anyway, we're going for a ride out to the new dam after lunch, aren't we, Livvy? Going to have ourselves a little swim,' Polly said smugly.

'I said I didn't want to go, Polly. I told you I hate the water!'

'Yes, I don't think that's a good idea, Polly. You know Olivia cannot swim. And besides, Olivia is staying with Jedda and Jesse tonight. So, I think she best stay put.' Kate's voice was firm but laced with nervousness.

Polly watched Kate closely, observing the effect on her nerves with each word she uttered. She inwardly smiled.

'Nothing changes, it's always Olivia, Olivia, Olivia!'

Kate grimaced. Polly's anger was swift. 'What's brought all this on? I'm just telling you that Olivia has plans for tonight. And it's not safe for you to go swimming when Olivia cannot swim.'

Polly's lips curled as she shot Kate a warning glare. 'I'm riding on my own then!' She stomped off.

Kate shifted anxiously as she watched the back door slam. She sat down with Olivia. 'She's just having a moment, Livvy. She's well and truly a teenager now and sometimes teens get a little moody. Their bodies are changing. You might go through that stage too.'

'She frightens me sometimes, especially when she can't get what she wants!'

'Well, let's concentrate on the weekend. Lisa said the twins are so thrilled to have you over and that they have lots of plans.'

'Oh, I'm so excited,' Olivia's heart hummed. 'I really didn't want to go swimming. I hate the water. I wish I didn't, but I do.'

'It's all good, Livvy. We all have something we dislike. Finish your lunch and I'll drop you off. A little early, but that will be fine.' Kate felt her heart racing. *Please don't let things spiral out of control.*

Was it just petulance and puberty or were these signs Polly was on a backslide? Soaring one minute and then spiralling straight down. Kate hoped she was wrong, and it was just a tantrum. She feared there would be more of these outbursts.

As Olivia got ready, Kate checked Polly's room for any signs of something not being right. She knew the girl had been taking the medication as she herself administered it every night with a glass of water at the dinner table. She searched high and low in Polly's room for anything remotely wrong. Nothing. She took a deep breath and closed her eyes. *Don't panic, Kate. Breathe.*

TWENTY-SEVEN

DOWN BY THE RIVER

The Garretts, plus Olivia, set out early before the flies and the heat arrived. Laughter followed them all the way to the river. Lisa still felt a strike to her heart when she passed by the big old tree where she had often sat with Binna and Ningali. It seemed like years ago now.

As they came around the last bend, it was Jedda who squealed, 'Look, look, there's the river,' She pointed her finger.

'No galloping, a light canter please,' yelled Lisa as all three children took off after Billy. She watched them as they disappeared into the distance. They had perfect control of their seats in a saddle. Perhaps on the way home, she would let them really stretch out. Always in the back of her mind was the inherent danger of falling off in a gallop and breaking bones. Medical help was so very far away. Her thoughts turned to Burnu all those years ago when he was bitten by a brown snake. Death came quickly, and he knew as he lay against a tree that there was no hope of getting to a hospital.

By the time Lisa caught up, Billy was in the water with Jedda and Jesse. He was throwing them into the air, and they laughed dizzily when landing back into the water. Olivia sat and watched. She looked up as Lisa approached.

'Still shy of the water, Livvy?' said Lisa, dismounting. Olivia nodded.

'I'll just tether Topi and come and join you. Some days I just like to watch as well.'

When Lisa sat beside Olivia, Jesse was pleading for her to get in the water. 'Come on, Livvy, it's nice and cold and sometimes you feel the fish.'

Lisa started laughing. 'Go on with you, Jesse. What a big story.'

'It's true. I feel the things touching my legs.'

'Oh, silly boy, it's probably just reeds,' said Lisa.

'Olivia,' called Billy. 'I keep you here with me, all da time. Safe with Billy.'

'That's my darling husband,' said Lisa. 'Who could resist that offer, Livvy? You know Billy would always protect you.' She drew her arm around the timid little girl.

'I think that... I think that might be alright. I love Billy, almost as much as I love Daddy and Nanny and Pop.'

Lisa looked bemused. 'It's your decision, Olivia.'

Billy swam and then half-crawled to the water's edge, his body still submerged in the lapping waters. He beckoned Olivia with his hand. 'Come, Livvy. You put your hands around Billy's neck. You swim on my back. Keep you safe there. I be like da turtle.'

Olivia started to giggle and then slowly stood up. She walked haltingly to the water's edge and looked down at Billy. 'You da brave one, Livvy. I turn around and you hop on.'

Lisa was sure Olivia would not proceed but to her surprise, she squatted down, strode over Billy and then gently lowered herself into the water, wrapping her hands around his neck. Billy glided out further as she hung on tightly. She shrieked as he went further out.

'Be orright, Livvy, no harm. Gotta be strong in da water, like da fish. We go swimming in da billabong, sometimes leave you. So you gotta swim.' Billy felt her grip loosen, and she began to relax as he moved from breaststroke to freestyle. Slowly, Jedda and Jesse joined in.

It was such a beautiful sight watching Billy with the children. Lisa touched her belly and remembered last night. *Why does nothing happen? If you can hear me, Binna, please bring me another gift.*

'Livvy, I put you on your tummy. You try to kick your legs,' said Billy as he stood in waist-deep water.

'No, I'm afraid.' She suddenly tightened her grip.

'Billy not let you go. I show you.' His voice was gentle encouragement.

As Billy began the process, Lisa suddenly sat bolt upright, turning to the direction of the road. 'Billy, a horse or horses!'

Billy swung his head around momentarily to see where Jesse and Jedda were and then Olivia panicked, her head going under the water. She tried to squeal but took in water. It all happened in seconds. Billy lifted her out of the water coughing and spluttering. She began to cry from fright and Billy cradled her to his chest as he waded to shore. Jesse and Jedda followed.

'There, there, Livvy, it's alright. Let me wrap you in this towel.' Lisa came towards them.

'I hear the horse. Just one rider, Lisa,' said Billy. No sooner had the words been said when the flame-haired rider came into sight.

'It's Polly,' whispered Olivia.

'Yes, Polly,' said Lisa. 'I wonder how she knew we would be here today.'

'Hello, everyone.' She lifted her brown Akubra hat. 'Oh dear, did I interrupt you, here?' she asked smugly as her horse stomped up and down in the river sand.

Lisa was thrown off by her directness. 'No, not at all Polly. We're just having some time out. Did you know we were here today?'

'Nope. I just felt like a swim. I see you got my sister in the water. Well done,' said Polly, her lips twitching uncontrollably. 'She's always so scared of it. Terrified of drowning, aren't you, Livvy?' Her tone of voice was almost mocking.

Polly turned her eyes to Billy. 'And you, Billy, well everyone knows you're just amazing. No wonder my mother liked you so much. Do you remember the day we came down and you were here swimming. Not a stitch on. Mum never stopped talking about you!'

There was a sudden lull, a silence that crept over all of them, as Polly's defiant stare cast about them, her actions screaming for attention.

'One big happy family down by the river. Oh, wait a minute, Livvy is part of my family. Isn't that right, Livvy!'

'Yes,' Olivia replied. 'Polly, we are just having some fun.'

'Why don't you go away,' yelled Jedda. 'We don't like you when you are like this.'

Polly's body shook with laughter. 'Guess what, creamy? I don't like you sometimes! I prefer your cutesy brother.'

Jedda started to run towards Polly, but Billy was too quick and grabbed her by the arm.

'Be still, Jedda,' said Billy as she struggled to pull away. Jesse suddenly threw a stick towards Polly and her horse half-reared into the air.

'You little brat,' Polly yelled as something dark inside her uncoiled. She spurred her horse on towards Jesse. As she raced past Billy, Jesse dived into the water and began to swim towards the middle of the river. He could hear the yells of his parents and turned when he felt safe in the middle.

Billy was fuming as Polly's horse danced back and forwards along the riverbank. He was powerless. He could not lay hands on another person's child, and if he did try to apprehend her, it would be difficult halting her and the horse without causing her harm.

'Polly,' commanded Lisa. 'Get out of here! Go! Before I get you off that horse.' Lisa advanced towards the prancing horse, lunging at the reins.

'Stay back, Billy.' Lisa grappled with the reins of Polly's horse. But Polly dug her heels in and swung the horse's head back towards the roadway, knocking Lisa to the ground.

'I hate you all!' Polly roared. 'You should be dead, rotting in a grave like my mother.' Then she galloped up onto the road and disappeared.

Billy came to Lisa. 'You okay, Lisa?' he said as Lisa got to her feet.

'I'm fine, Billy, just a little shaken, like everybody else. Kate really has her hands full with that one.'

'She da bad one.' Billy sniffed the air. 'Smell bad.' The anger rose in his voice.

Lisa looked bewildered at what had just occurred. 'I just can't believe it. She's still so young but the voice, her voice, it's just so old. It sounded just like Tess spewing out that rage.'

'She have da big anger. Not good with dat devil inside.'

'Distraction needed, Billy.' Lisa looked at the three children squatting in the sand after Jesse had swum back from the middle of the river. 'Let's sit and have a bite to eat. Perhaps a story?'

'A story,' he smiled. 'But first we walk.'

'Come,' he called 'You too, Lisa, come. Polly not come back.'

'We go further into da bush, I show da insects and da fruits and seeds. Da bush tucker. Good tucker.'

The children followed Billy, and the quietness of the bush finally settled the rattled nerves, along with his soothing voice. The girls pulled faces when Billy mentioned eating witchety grubs, cicadas and caterpillars, and they marvelled when he showed them the bush tomatoes and plums, the mulga seeds and wattle seeds, snapping them off for them to try.

'I already know this stuff,' said Jesse. 'With my dad, we go to the bush alone and he teaches me.'

As they sat ready for the evening, the fire was well alight, the burning wood filling the air with a musky fragrance. The only sound was the crackling fire and the bird sounds.

'I love the willy wagtails,' said Olivia. 'I see them hopping around the bushes in our garden. They wiggle their tails so quickly and are always chattering.'

'I love them too,' said Jedda. 'My favourite.'

When you see the willy wagtails, it means a message of some sort,' said Jesse.

'He da cheeky bird, always busy and cheerful. He called Jitta Jitta and he listen to your secrets,' said Billy. 'He tell your secrets.'

The children sat in awe. 'Shoo willy away when you talking so he not hear. He a gossiper and tell all da secrets and tales. When he make da clicking sound, important news come. He da messenger from da Great Spirit. If you kill da willy, big storms come. He like you, Jedda. Woodland songbird. He sing through da night, especially on da full moon.'

Their eyes widened as the sound of a car came close. Billy smiled. 'Surprise.'

A red ute pulled up at the top of the riverbank. The children were on their feet, running and squealing, their faces flushed with pleasure. Ningali's long legs hit the ground, and they ran into her outstretched arms.

'Ah, da picaninnies. We bring da swags too. We gunna have da big campout tonight. We gotta lotta stories. Bring da clapsticks, we gunna make da music. Dem spirits, dey join us,' said Ningali excitedly.

Kev had already gone to the rear of the ute to help Mum Shirl out. Excitement was at fever pitch as the children almost dragged Mum Shirl down the embankment.

'Whoa, you picaninnies. Mum Shirl, she going as fast as da legs can carry her. Slow down or Mum Shirl, she gunna be da big ball and roll over!'

Kev carried the swags and Ningali followed, finding their place by the fire, which burned loudly and fiercely, the embers dancing high up into the night sky. The night air spoke to Billy, whispering secrets as it carried the scent of trouble. As they all sat down, Billy spoke.

He pointed to the sky, the stars twinkling. 'We all come from da stars and to da stars, we all return.'

'Are you going to tell a story now?' asked Jedda.

Billy smiled. 'I tell you about da moon. How da moon was made. Da girl, Bindi, she love to dance, like Ningali, and she dance all night long into da night but den, she lose her favourite necklace. She love dat necklace. It special. She ask her friend Cloudskipper and da other clouds to help her. Da big wise cloud, he very old, gave her some cloud and shaped it. Da cloud was soft and fluffy and it drift up to da sky where it became da moon and da moon lit da world. Bindi find her necklace and she so happy, she danced under the moon.'

'Oh, I so loved that. Find me a cloud, please Jesse,' said Livvy.

Jesse looked shyly at the exuberant girl. 'Jesse give you everything.' His smitten openness was obvious as his eyes gleamed.

'Lovebirds,' giggled Jedda.

'Jedda, silly wild goose, being good friends is a gift in life. We all need good friends. Always,' said Lisa, although Lisa and Billy knew Jesse was so very attached to the little blonde girl.

The night wore on, their laughter filling the evening. The children used the clapsticks and were dazzled by Ningali dancing around their campfire, but tiredness soon came upon them.

Billy opened their swags, one by one, and then helped Mum Shirl up into Kev's ute.

As the cicadas grated their song into the evening, and the stars fell deeper into darkness, a lone soft voice whispered into the earth, 'Sleep well, my darlings. Have beautiful dreams.' Then Lisa gently rolled over into Billy's arms.

TWENTY-EIGHT

DESTRUCTION

When Polly returned from her ride, she was clearly agitated, but dinner, although having an air of tension, was completed without any arguments. She then retired to her room, and Kate breathed a sigh of relief as she disappeared down the hallway. Her wearied patience was being tested lately.

'What's up with her?' asked Mitch.

'I really don't know but I wish I could answer that,' replied Kate. 'All I know is that something is not right. I can find no evidence to the contrary, but it's just my gut feeling. Like she's about to destroy something. I simply asked her if she wanted to visit Tess's grave, and she had this huge outburst of anger. It just triggered her off.'

'I'll call Rebekah tomorrow. Maybe it's puberty, and Tess's death would still be very raw for her. I know it is for me. I do think about Tess and what happened. Did you get Livvy off to see her mates?'

'Yes, she was so eager to go. Apparently, they were camping out down by the river. She'll come back with many stories. Always does,' said Kate.

'Let's go sit in the family room. I'll pour a few drinks,' said Dave.

As they sat in the big room, Kate switched on the record player and played some classical music. Dave poured three cognacs. The music drifted throughout the house and Polly came out of her room to listen. The voices in her head were getting louder and stronger, so she slapped her hands over her ears, shaking her head from side to side. She could hear Rebekah's words: Just sing or hum your special song, Polly. *Happy Birthday to me, Happy Birthday to me.* She stopped momentarily but then moved closer. The voices told her to listen and see what they were talking about. She moved down the hallway in the direction of the sitting room, stopping as she heard the voice of her grandfather.

'Do you think Polly found out her mother's exact cause of death? I know we sort of smoothed it over, saying Tess had passed away of natural causes. But she doesn't know it was a matter for the NSW Coroner and the police.'

'No, when she asked me I said it was perhaps her mother's heart. We were not sure, and I left it at that,' replied Kate. 'It's too traumatic for such young girls to be told the manner in which she died. Really, Dave. Mitch.' Kate's tired eyes looked across at them. 'How could I possibly tell a young teenage girl that her mother had been found naked and strangled to death.'

Polly's face contorted in shock. She covered her mouth with her hand as she made her way back to her room. Then she rocked herself to sleep, the image of her mother brutally murdered dancing horribly across her mind.

◊

The house was unusually quiet the following morning. Dave and Mitch had left early. Kate decided to rouse Polly from sleep at about nine. She sipped her cup of tea and looked at the chair Polly always insisted sitting on at the dining table. It was fraying, with the fabric open and slightly raised in one corner. She'd have to get that fixed. On closer inspection, the fabric had been deliberately cut. Kate's hand went to her throat.

She ran her hand over the chair and down the sides, finding little lumps. As Kate pushed her fingers into the stuffing of the chair, she pulled out the pills. 'No, no, no!' Kate cried in her mind, wringing her hands in anguish. 'Polly, you've been stuffing your pills into this chair instead of swallowing them!' She shook her head and felt the anguish in her heart, gathering herself to confront the girl.

As she headed towards Polly's room, she heard her granddaughter muttering to herself. But nothing could prepare Kate for the scene that unfolded when she opened the door. Her eyes were immediately drawn to the words FUCK and WHORE written in what appeared to be red lipstick on her bedroom wall.

Polly swivelled her head around as she turned to face Kate. Her face was flushed, and her eyes narrowed, with the red lipstick grotesquely smeared across her lips. Her voice was gravelly but filled with pain and despair. 'Get out! Get out of my room! I hate you all. I hate everybody. The voices tell me what you are all really up to. My mother was murdered. Who murdered her! Why didn't you tell me?'

'Polly, my God, what have you done. Let me help you,' Kate pleaded. Her heart began to beat faster as she bent to console the young girl. 'Polly, darling.' But she pulled back swiftly when she saw the amount of blood oozing from Polly's wrists.

'What have you done to yourself! Dear Lord, I have to stop the bleeding. Polly, come with me!'

But Polly's red-hot anger was so fierce that she lunged at Kate, striking her face. Kate fell backwards in surprise, striking her head against the door. She lay on the floor momentarily, trying to gather herself as Polly hurled abuse at her. She managed to get to her feet and ran to the laundry where they kept bandages and the First Aid box.

Polly laughed hysterically, again slashing up her arm with a razor blade, the cuts leaking blood all over her.

When Kate returned to Polly's room, her granddaughter stood banging her head against the wall and screaming, 'You killed my mother!'

'Polly, please, I have to put these bandages on your wrists.' Kate began to grapple with the agitated girl.

Polly grabbed the bandages and threw them across the room. 'I don't want any damn bandages. I hate you all. You killed my mother. You and this whole shitty family.' Her eyes blazed. Polly began to hurl objects and books and anything she could find around the room and at Kate.

When a small glass vase struck Kate's head, she staggered back, clutching her chest, gasping for breath, the searing pain ripping through her heart as her knees gave out. She gasped for breath as the room began to spin and then she fell to the floor.

Polly wailed and then continued beating her head again against the wall until she passed out, Kate's lifeless body, still and cold, lying next to her.

◊

'It's bloody quiet in here this morning.' Dave threw his hat on the kitchen table. 'Kate,' he called out, 'We're home for morning tea.'

'I'll go wash up and start morning tea,' said Mitch.

'And I'll just see if Kate is in her room,' Dave suggested.

After walking up the hallway, Dave suddenly reappeared, staggering, his face ashen. 'Mitch! Oh God, call the Flying Doctor!'

'Dad, what is it?' Mitch's heart was hammering at the deathly signs his father was giving.

'Just call, Mitch, for God's sake! Your mother is lying dead and Polly is unconscious and bleeding.'

Mitch's face went white. He raced up to the office and switched on the radio to contact the Royal Flying Doctor.

'This is Mitchell Walker from Woodside, Carinda. Do you copy?' The line crackled and the voice responded.

'Mitch, yes, we copy. It's Derek. What's the issue?'

'Thank God it's you, Derek. It's... I don't know. Dad said one dead and another unconscious and bleeding. Please hurry.'

'On my way. Until I get there, apply bandages and tourniquets, direct pressure, and elevate above the heart. I'll be there shortly.'

Tears sprang to Mitch's eyes. His whole world was spinning. Since he had met Tess, his world had been a storm, and that storm had never ended. His mother dead? It wasn't possible! He rushed towards the room he knew his father would be in and pulled up in shock when he saw the scene that opened up before him.

The door was ajar and the smell of blood permeated the air. He cringed, dying a thousand deaths, when he saw the walls scribbled with obscenities. Dave cradled his mother's limp body in his arms. Her skin was cold to the touch and her lips were blue. His father wept bitterly as the only woman he had ever loved now ceased to exist. He looked up at Mitch standing in the doorway, his face flooded with misery.

'Dad, I've called the Flying Doctor, and we have to apply pressure and tourniquets to Polly.' He frantically gathered up the bandages on the floor.

Dave was oblivious to the sound of Mitch's voice, his sobs filling the room. 'This is all your doing,' he lashed out. 'Bringing that trash into our home so many years ago. This is the price. Nothing can bring Kate back. My Kate.'

Mitch wanted to howl with grief at his father's words. His heart filled with pain, even though he knew his father was just lashing out in his grief. He dutifully applied the bandages to Polly's arms and kept the pressure. Polly had lost a lot of blood and was pale and unconscious. Did he let her die? His daughter was so like her mother, but worse. It would be so easy to let her drift off. With every roll of the bandage, his despair deepened, but then something clicked. He could hear his mother speaking, 'Do the right thing, son.'

The Flying Doctor landed about one hour after Mitch made the call. 'Dad, that will be Derek. I have to leave you and go get him.'

Dave made no response as Mitch scrambled out to go and pick up Derek from the open paddock they used as an airway. He was coming down the stairs of the plane as Mitch pulled up in the Land Rover.

'Derek, come with me.' His voice broke off as his sobs took his breath away.

'Take it easy, Mitch. Try and let me know what's happened on the way to the farm. The nurses will stay behind in the plane and will get everything hooked up once we have the patient in. Let's just get to the house.'

By the time they arrived, Derek knew what lay ahead. One attempted suicide by Mitch's daughter Polly and sadly, his mother, Kate, deceased.

It was a tragic scene, and Derek knew that these were deep cuts. But with no arterial spurts, Polly would no doubt survive.

'You did good, Mitch. Tourniquets are applied well. Are you able to help me lift and carry her?'

'Yeah, Derek.' He gently lifted Polly into his arms.

'I'll administer IV fluids when we get into the plane and from there, we'll head to the Emergency Department. Some of the wounds may need stitching.'

'And after that?' queried Mitch.

'I'm afraid it will be involuntary admission to a psychiatric unit. She is clearly a danger to herself and to others.'

Mitch nodded. 'She's been seeing a psych in Walgett, Rebekah Adams. We thought things were going reasonably well. Or they were, but now this.'

'Always when you least expect it,' said Derek. 'From my experience, they can have relapses, despite being on medication.'

'Can you take her out to the plane as the nurses are waiting. I have to talk to Dave,' said Derek solemnly. 'Just head back here when you can. I may need a hand.'

Mitch carried Polly out to the Land Rover and drove towards the plane.

Derek grabbed the large black body bag that he had rolled up and carried under his arm. Initial sighting of the bag was often too traumatic for relatives to deal with.

Derek turned his attention to Dave, who had not uttered one word. He sat stroking Kate's face as rigor mortis set in.

'Dave, I know you can hear me. It's Derek from the Royal Flying Doctor Service. I have to take Kate with me now. You know that. She's gone, and her body will have to be delivered to the coroner. I suspect she has had a massive heart attack.'

Dave turned to Derek, his eyes red and swollen. 'I know all that, Derek. I just knew one day her heart would give out with all the stress she's been under.'

'Come on, mate. Why don't you wait outside in the kitchen and let me do what I need to do,' Derek said softly.

Dave let Kate gently down and got to his feet. 'My beautiful woman is gone. I don't know how I can live without her. She was my rock. I want to hit something.' His voice quavered.

'You have your family here, Dave. And close friends. You'll get through this.' Derek put a comforting arm around the grief-stricken man. He shuffled him out of the room and sat him down in the kitchen, then headed back into the bedroom as Mitch came back up the stairs.

'Dad... I.' But Dave waved his hand in the air as if to cut Mitch off. Mitch headed to the bedroom just as Derek was zipping up the body bag.

'You'll need to give me a hand, Mitch. I know Kate is your mother, but this will be very distressing for your father. I need to get her to the Land Rover and onto the plane. As I said to your dad, the coroner will need to look into her death.'

Mitch fought back the tears as they carried his mother's body out to the kitchen. Dave suddenly leaped to his feet, taking the load of Kate's feet.

'I can do this,' said Dave, his voice filled with despair.

Mitch stood dumbfounded, a wrenching hollow ache in his chest as he watched his father and Derek carry his mother's body away.

He dropped to the floor and let the wracking sobs rip from his heart.

TWENTY-NINE

LOVE AND GRIEF

The coroner's report was conclusive: The cause of Kate's death was a massive heart attack. Kate would have been dead by the time she hit the floor.

Zena helped Mitch to organise the funeral, and it was standing room only in the Walgett Church, with speakers being set up outside as well as chairs.

Dave looked at his wife's body in the casket. She looked so peaceful, and he pondered the thought that death was really the tragedy for those left behind. For Kate, she had no problems now.

'Dad, it's time to sit for the service,' said Mitch gently. His father had aged considerably with the loss of his wife, and his spark and energy had gone. Mitch hoped it would come back with time, but he knew he could never forgive himself. His father was right. It was all his fault. Little Olivia was also devastated by the loss of her beloved grandmother.

Mitch allowed her to stay with Jesse and Jedda as he thought the funeral would be too traumatic. Polly had been flown to Dubbo Hospital where she was still an inpatient. It was the only bed available, and she was being transferred back to Walgett Hospital to be under the care of Dr Adams.

'Grief is forever, Mitch,' Dave had said sadly. 'It becomes a part of you. Grief and love are conjoined. You don't get one without the other.'

Dave followed Mitch to their seats as the minister began his service. *'Thank you, everyone, for joining us here today to remember a wonderful lady, Kate Walker, who did so much for our community. I read this poem now, a selection from Dave, her husband, as we begin our service:*

'Though your smile is gone forever and your hand we cannot touch, still we have so many memories of the one we loved so much. Your memory is our keepsake with which we will never part; God has you in his keeping, and we have you in our hearts. It is sad to walk the road alone, instead of side by side, but to all, there comes a moment when the ways of life divide. You gave us years of happiness, then came sorrow and tears, but you left us behind beautiful memories we will treasure through the years.'

The readings and eulogies from various friends and relatives were also read out. Although Zena wanted to speak at the service, she knew in her heart that she would break down. Alan held her hand tightly as the grief and loss clearly took its toll on his wife. They sat with Lisa and Billy, and it was apparent that Kate's death had shaken Lisa. As Zena had said on the way to the church, it was like a bad dream, your worst nightmare.

The service lasted well over an hour, and then the minister announced the burial. 'We would all ask you to respectfully proceed to the Walgett Cemetery for the final resting place of Kate Walker, and as I understand it, this will be followed by a wake at the RSL. Everyone is welcome.'

'This will be both a happy and sad time, Aunty,' said Lisa as she wiped the tears from her eyes.

'Why do you say that, Lisa?' asked Zena, dabbing her eyes.

'It's where I first met Billy,' Lisa said softly.

'Goodness, that seems like so many moons ago now, doesn't it. Where does the time go?'

'That's the ironic thing about funerals,' added Alan. 'You general-ly catch up with people you haven't seen for years, for all the wrong reasons: someone's death.'

As they came out of the church, Mitch and Dave stood side by side as people offered their condolences. Lisa hugged Dave first and then came to Mitch. Her heart went out to him. She had never seen him in such pain; his eyes said it all. She leaned into him and held his hands, trying to find words of comfort, when he suddenly put his arms around her and cried softly into her hair. Lisa didn't pull away. She felt so much compassion for him. His life was a mess.

'It's going to be okay, Mitch.' She stroked the back of his head. 'We are all here for you, Livvy and Dave,' said Lisa as she slowly pulled away.

Mitch wiped his tears and gained some composure. 'Thanks, Lisa, that means a lot to me and Dad.'

◊

When they finally reached Woori, it was just after 5 p.m. 'Do you want to come in for a drink?' asked Alan.

'No, but thanks for the offer,' said Lisa. 'I think we just want to get back to the children. I'm sure Mum Shirl and Ningali will be ex-hausted.'

'Okay, another time, you two,' said Zena as Lisa and Billy hopped into their car and headed home.

As the Wooribilly cottage came into view, the children were al-ready running towards the entrance gate at the sound of the car. They were filthy, covered in dirt, and had their faces painted with Aboriginal patterns.

Lisa burst out laughing, despite her sombre mood. 'And to think, Billy, I was so worried. Just look at these children!'

Billy hopped out and came through the gate, swooping Jedda up in his arms. Jesse clung to Billy's legs, which made it difficult to walk.

Mum Shirl held Olivia's hand and waved as she waddled towards them with Ningali and Kev.

'I see you have kept them amused,' Lisa smiled.

'Ningali and me, we do da painting on da faces. Da picaninnies, dey love it and den dey want to learn da dance, like Ningali. She have legs like a bird, long and skinny. Dey sit looking at her all day. Jesse call her bird legs and we all do da dance like Ningali.'

Ningali stood with Kev, her hands on her hips, and then wiggled her bum like she was dancing. 'Hey dat Ningali, she gunna make me laugh,' said Mum Shirl as she imitated her friend. 'Sometimes think something bit her. Anyway, much fun, Lisa. Dey special dem kids. Jedda, she sing sing and I do da dance. She got da gift.'

Lisa smiled. 'Yes, that she does Ningali. And how are you, Livvy? Have you had a good day?

'Yes, I have,' she replied in a small voice, 'and I want to stay here.'

Billy kneeled down to her, and Olivia wrapped her arms around his neck. 'I don't want to go home with my nanna no longer there. I miss her already,' her little voice pleaded.

'Be okay, little one, little lady beetle,' Billy whispered.

Jedda and Jesse smiled. 'Lady beetle!' they said in unison.

'Yes, Livvy is da pretty lady beetle who can come and go. She love da waratah flower. Waratah is magic for my people. She fly here, and she fly there. She magical. She always ready to spread her little wings. Our home always open, but da lady beetle knows where she belong is with her family.'

Mum Shirl stood transfixed with Ningali. 'Dat Billy, he truly a messenger of da Great Spirit. He guide da people to da right things,' said Ningali.

Billy stood and carried Olivia towards the house, Lisa by his side with Jesse and Jedda. 'We rest inside now. Lisa and me have da big day but we happy to be home.'

'Alright, lady beetle and crew, time for a wash. War paint off,' said Lisa. 'I'll just make a quick call to Mitch and see if Livvy can stay one more night.'

When she made the call, Mitch's voice was very solemn and tinged with sadness. 'Hi Mitch,' said Lisa. 'It was a lovely service to-day.'

There was an awkward silence. 'Yes, it was, but the house seems really quiet now. How is Livvy?'

'That's why I'm calling. She asked if she could stay an extra night, but if you're not happy with that, I can bring her down after she's cleaned up a bit. They had some fun today with face painting.'

'That's fine, Lisa. I really appreciate you looking after her. I'd like to sit with Dad, and maybe have a few quiet beers and discuss the arrangements for Polly. So it's good that Livvy is not here.'

'Okay then. Let me know if you need anything. I'll bring her down tomorrow.'

'Lisa, thank you for being there today. It's been an awful time, and Dad's heart is just broken. And it's all my fault.'

'Mitch! Please don't say that. Kate's heart has been a worry for some time. You know that. Who knows if Polly was the catalyst or if it would have happened anyway,' said Lisa, her voice softening.

'Yeah, Lisa, who knows, but thank you. I'll see you tomorrow.'

THIRTY

A NEW INVESTIGATION

Olivia was very quiet as they headed to Woodside. Jesse didn't want to let his lady beetle go, which made the little girl cry. 'Livvy,' said Lisa softly, 'please remember that Daddy and Poppy have also been through a lot, and right now they need lots of kisses and cuddles.'

She nodded as they turned into the driveway and headed towards the big house. Mitch came out to greet them, and he looked tired. His boyish good looks were diminishing with the passage of time, but the grief and stress were also taking their toll. Kate had told Zena that he had been drinking heavily for a while, and no doubt this was playing a part in his appearance.

'Here we are, as promised,' smiled Lisa. Olivia stayed in the front seat.

'Hey, my lovely girl, where's my hug?' asked Mitch. He opened the car door and reached for her hand.

'I'm a lady beetle,' she giggled, taking Mitch's hand.

'Why a lady beetle?' asked Mitch.

'Billy gave her the name, Mitch. I think he was trying to cheer her up at the time. It worked as the children all started laughing,' explained Lisa. 'Right then, I had best be on my way. Bye, Livvy.

Thanks, Mitch, for letting her stay. She loves the twins, and they all get on so well.'

'Sorry, Lisa, manners. Forgot my manners there. Would you like to come inside for a cup of tea?'

'Mitch, another time. I have a few things to do this morning but thank you.'

Mitch stood with Livvy as they watched Lisa drive away. 'I love Lisa, she's so nice,' said Livvy.

'Yeah, I do too, Livvy. She's special. Come on, Poppy needs a hug.'

When they came inside, Dave stood talking on the phone. It was clear that he was discussing Polly and the transfer to the hospital in Walgett. Dave held up his left hand and indicated five or ten minutes. Mitch nodded.

'Let's make ourselves busy, Livvy. You grab some cookies and plates, and just for a change, let's sit out on the big veranda.' Mitch wanted Livvy out of earshot of the conversation Dave was having. He followed her out to the veranda, and they both flopped into the big, soft chairs.

Dave appeared about five minutes later. 'How's my granddaughter?' His tired face lit up as Livvy came over to him.

'I'll sit on your lap, Poppy, as you need a hug,' said Livvy, snuggling in.

Mitch saw his father take a deep breath inwards and his eyes became watery. 'She's a little gem, this one.'

'Don't I know that, Dad,' smiled Mitch.

'At least you got one right,' Dave said. 'Why don't you go wash up, Livvy, while I discuss something with your dad.' They both watched as Livvy disappeared from view.

'Polly just needs help, Dad. Lots. So, are they on their way to the hospital?' queried Mitch.

'Yes. Rebekah seems to think the whole treatment process will be lengthy due to Polly's mental state. She is talking years. Said she may be wrong, and she hopes that she is. I do too, Mitch, for the sake of her own health.'

'Years! God, Dad. Why?' Mitch threw his head back into the big lounge chairs, looking to the ceiling, exasperated.

'Rebekah said she is almost catatonic with severe auditory hallucinations. So, the whole process will be anti-psychotic medication, some sort of therapy to reduce the distress of hearing the voices and then she mentioned ECT.'

'Honestly Dad, I hate the sound of that ECT. I know it has something to do with an electrical pulse to the scalp in order to produce a seizure. Rebekah did explain. I just wish this would all go away.' Mitch buried his face in his hands.

'Have to see it out now, son. She's your daughter, my granddaughter, and Kate would have wanted it. Rebekah will get it all under control.'

'She's fifteen soon, Dad. Mum and I discussed her going to Koombala when she turned sixteen. Kate had her booked in as a boarder even though Polly was refusing to go.'

Dave took a sip from his mug of tea. 'One foot in front of the other, son. By the way, Detective Jon Lynch called here asking if I had seen, hired or had anything to do with a big bloke, or seen a stranger in the area. Detective Lynch is running an investigation, trying to link someone to murders similar to Tess's. There have been two other women also murdered by strangulation with panty hose. All the victims had been seen in the Walgett pub before the night of their murders, and witnesses also report a stranger at their local. A big man who drank alone. So, he obviously prowls the bars to find his victims. Apparently, Owen, the publican, said he saw a bloke of that appearance in his pub a couple of times. Had never seen him before. It's his sheer size that jolts people's memories.

'Yeah, there was that big bloke who turned up at Woori, mean-looking dude. Scar down his face. Alan was right. He was trouble. No wonder he told him to pack his bags. Do you think there is any link between him and what the coppers were asking?

257

'Don't know, Mitch. Maybe, maybe not. Most of the truckies are usually on the beefier side. Anyway, I told them to call Alan. A lot of big fellas out and about these ways.'

'Yeah, Dad, that bloke was huge. But you know, when I was in town not so long ago, I thought I saw him standing next to a big rig. You know, those road trains.'

'If he wants to stay in town, that's his business,' added Dave. 'Maybe he likes Walgett. Plenty of work. Road trains, big stock trucks and the fuel tankers. He shouldn't have had those stupid dogs. They were the problem, attacking Alan's sheep. Anyway, I said Alan had trouble over there with a big guy, so the detective was going to call him and see if he had any information. And we really don't know if that bloke had anything to do with Tess's demise. Innocent until proven guilty, but I don't know how anyone can strangle another person and watch their life slip away,' shuddered Dave.

THIRTY-ONE

MAKING PROGRESS

Rebekah Adams had spoken at length with Mitch about Polly's psychiatric disorder. The reports from the doctor all indicated that Polly had responded well to the ECT treatments. They had also tried mood stabilisers and anti-depressant medication as well as cognitive behavioural therapy, focusing on loss and anger management. Polly just could not handle any confrontation with anyone, and the death of her mother and how she was murdered were catastrophic for Polly.

'I realise it is difficult for you to understand, Mitch. It can be a long process, but it's a path towards recovery and coming together again as a family.'

'So, Rebekah, you mentioned it could be years but roughly how long will this all take?' queried Mitch.

'I wish I could tell you that, but some people recover and respond well to treatment, while some people do not, and others, well, it just takes time. I do feel it will be a long, slow road, but I will always keep you informed with updates, Mitch.'

'I can't have Polly back until everything is sorted in her head. Dad is not well. He has high blood pressure, and I have a younger daughter, Olivia, who is progressing well. Not to sound uncaring, but we live remotely, and I think you get the picture.'

'Yes, I do.' Rebekah continued, 'Mental health is very difficult as opposed to an open wound. Fleshy wounds you can see and treat, but wounds of the heart and mind are a much different thing.'

When Mitch got home, he tried to explain to his father what he had discussed with Rebekah.

'I said to give Polly time and allow for her confidence to return with support from the therapists at the hospital. Confronting her right now is not appropriate. All in good time, it seems, but I'm sceptical, Dad, really sceptical.'

'Polly is still your blood, Mitch, and you know Kate would say to do the right thing. Maybe therapy and treatment will allow her to see just how much trouble all this emotional stuff caused. To me, Polly was always striving for attention or something, but obviously it was much worse than that. Finding out the way Tess died was also the catalyst for her recent episode.'

'I know, Dad, I hear Mum's words constantly about doing the right thing.' Mitch's voice was tinged with sorrow. 'Everything is going so well now: the crops, the stock, Livvy. I just don't want anything to change. It was so bloody horrible there for such a long time.'

Dave paused. 'I need to know that you have the place under control if anything happens to me. When I go to my grave, I want to know that I have done everything humanly possible to help my eldest granddaughter.'

'What are you saying? Going to your grave? What's that rubbish?' said Mitch, recovering from his father's statement.

'I'm not here forever, son. You know I've been struggling with my blood pressure. I hate taking all those pills. The doctor said to lose weight and cut down on drinking. Well, I enjoy my tucker and I like a drink. Take away all of that and there's not much enjoyment.'

Mitch took a deep breath. Kate had always monitored Dave in that regard and was always at him about blood pressure and taking care of himself.

'Maybe cut down just a little then, Dad.'

'You oughta talk! The Chinese always say you are born with so many breaths. I'll go when my time is up. Join Kate,' he said solemnly.

'But you have to stick around, old buddy. What am I going to do with two women in the house if you aren't here! Like, if Polly comes back and it's just the three of us?'

Dave laughed. 'Livvy wants to work the land, and she will be good at it, a natural. She's great now, and boarding school awaits. They will finish her off in terms of education. Like a good polish.'

Mitch nodded. 'It will be hard letting her go, and the only time we'll see her will be school holidays, but her heart is set here. She loves the land. I know that.'

'Women are just as good as men on the land; in fact, women are good at everything, if us blokes just give them a chance,' added Dave. 'Who knows, Polly may find something that interests her here too. She was good riding the fences and has one of the best seats I've seen on a horse. But let's not jump to conclusions just yet. We'll be guided by the advice from Rebekah and go from there. Polly has a lot in front of her. All the trauma, her mother's behaviour and her death, finding out about her mother's death, and of course, Kate's death. No hurry. Leave it to the experts.'

They were interrupted by Olivia who came and sat down.

'What are you up to, Princess?' asked Dave.

'It's a lovely day and I've finished School of the Air, so I'm riding over to see Jesse and Jedda. Is that okay?'

'Sure,' said Mitch. 'Dinner is about six and watch for the Joe Blakes on the road.'

'They always get out of the way when they hear the horses, Dad. I give them a wide berth too, you know. Snakes give me the willies, and those horrible goannas.'

Olivia stood and kissed Mitch and then her grandfather. 'Won't be long,' she said as she headed out.

'Gorgeous child,' said Dave.

'Yeah, she is. I'm so proud of her. Perfect grades. Everything she does is good.'

'Reminds me of Kate,' Dave said softly.

'Yeah, that she does. But I worry about the lack of friends that she has, and her association with Jesse and Jedda. She talks non-stop about that boy.'

'Just young, Mitch. We all have crushes, and secondary education is not that far away. She'll be eleven next year, and when she hits boarding school, she'll make loads of new friends. Let them just enjoy each other's company. She always comes back so happy after spending time with the twins.'

Mitch made a sound like a choked laugh.

'It'll be fine, son. Time flies. Don't let bitterness or jealousy take over. Bitterness is like a cancer. It eats upon the host. Keep the bitterness out. Let's enjoy the peace and let them have fun.'

◊

It was late afternoon and Alan was doing some bookwork when the phone rang. 'Hello, Alan Smith speaking.'

'Mr Smith, it's Detective Jon Lynch from Walgett Police station.'

'G'day, Jon. What can I do for you?'

'We're following up on the Tess Walker murder. We called Dave Walker and spoke to him about any information or anything he can possibly remember that may give us a lead. Our unit fingerprinted the old house in Walgett but there's nothing on the databases. Cause of death was strangulation. No one saw a thing. No one heard a thing.'

'Understandable,' said Alan. 'That old Dunphy house, I know she got it at a bargain. When it was built, it was supposed to have more houses around it but that never eventuated. Not enough demand. Dead-end street. Mitch Walker, her husband, has been out there a few times and said it was pretty deserted. Even the house next door had been vandalised. Windows smashed, and no other houses around, just all land. So how could anyone hear anything?'

'Yeah,' said Detective Lynch. 'It's pretty deserted. We asked the publican, Owen of The Thirsty Dog, if he had seen anything suspicious. That was the last place Tess was seen alive, so we put up a sign in the pub to contact us with any information. Usually truckies will head to the pub rather than the RSL, and that pub is also well known for cheap and cheerful pub grub. There have been two other women strangled, in very similar circumstances.'

'Was Owen any help?' queried Alan.

'Unfortunately, no, but sometimes something will jig with someone and then a lead suddenly develops. Right now, we don't have a lot of information apart from one thing, and a few different people have more or less said the same thing.'

'Which is?'

'It's very loose but a few of the locals from the pub seem to recollect a stranger. And this is a long shot as we both know outback pubs have people coming and going all the time. Truckies, itinerant workers. See them once and you never see them again, just passing through. But it was the size of the bloke that made him stand out.'

Alan took a deep breath. His gut feeling told him he knew where this was leading.

'The way Tess was murdered, strangulation with panty hose, as I said, there have been a couple of murders now like that, very similar over the past three years. No forced entry, single lady living on her own.' said Detective Lynch. "The decomposition of the other two victims was not as bad either as they were found sooner.'

Alan pondered. 'What a grim job you blokes have. I did have a guy here working for me. He answered an ad in the paper for shearers. He was as you said, big dude, and he had a sidekick with him. Name was James Griffin and the other bloke was Ernest Tubbs.

'Do you know where they were headed?'

'I actually asked them to go. They caused trouble with their dogs, biting stock. Paid them out and then basically booted them off the property. But the big guy is mean. Had a fight with my son-in-law and drew a knife. Should have called you blokes then, but I was just glad to see them go. A couple of the lads said they wanted to head to the Territory.'

'Yeah, those in trouble tend to head there. You can basically hide.'

'Never a truer word. How do you know that Tess was strangled if her body was so decomposed?' asked Alan.

'Haemorrhages from the eyes, mouth and something about the ligature marks on her neck. There's a crossing of the ligature marks. Makes sense if you envision someone standing behind you holding the panty hose at both ends and trying to pull it tight around the neck. Would you mind if we came out and took a look around? Maybe show us where his quarters were?'

'No, not at all, come when you like. I'll let Billy and Kev, my managers, know.'

'Well, if you can think of anything that may spring to mind Mr Smith, please call me at the station. Thanks for your time, and we will be out there maybe tomorrow or the day after.'

◊

Jon Lynch made plans for the following day. As he drove to the last gates of Woori, there was an object in the middle of the road. From a distance he thought it was a rock but he slammed the brakes on when he realised it was a human skull.

He got out of the car and looked down at the skull. It was large, so definitely not female. His head swivelled around the lonely landscape then he returned to his car and pulled out a plastic bag and some gloves, putting them on. As he examined the skull, he observed there were no fractures, no gunshot wounds. He placed the skull in the bag and opened the gates to Woori.

Alan saw the approaching car heading towards the house. Jon had called that morning and said he was on his way. He quickly went down the back stairs and across to the compound gate to greet him.

'Morning, Jon. I'm Alan.' They shook hands.

'Nice to meet you, Alan, and thanks for being so accommodating. As I said, I spoke to your neighbour Dave Walker and he pointed me in your direction.'

'No problem. Do you want to come inside or just get going?'

'Alan, thanks for the offer, but I would really like to just have a look around. I did find something rather grim at the entrance to your gate.'

'Oh? Grim? What could that be? You look a bit unsettled, mate.'

'Nothing I haven't seen before, that's for sure, and I've seen worse, but it's not often you see a human skull in the middle of the road out here.'

'A skull. My God!' Alan was trying to take it all in.

'I've got the skull in the car. I'll take it back for forensics. Definitely male, too big for a female. Generally speaking, male skulls are heavier, the bone is thicker and the areas of muscle attachment are more defined than in females. There are also key differences in the appearance of the forehead, eyes and jaw between men and women that are used to determine the sex of a skull. Sorry, been to a fair few autopsies over the years.'

Alan scratched his chin. 'I don't know how you do that as part of your job. Anyway, there are a lot of feral pigs out here, Jon. Big buggers. I've shot and killed 90-kilogram boars, and the sows are right bitches, especially with babies. We've also seen an increase in wild dogs. If you did get attacked out here or you died in the bush, there would not be much left of you. Everything out there wants a feed. Look, I'll take you down to the sheds, but there's not a lot to see. When I told them to clear off, they took all their gear.'

'Okay, just for certainty I'll look around but I'll be back tomorrow with a few more from the Force. We'll need to do a search of the area near your front gate.'

'No problem. Let's head out down there now. You can leave your car. We'll go in the Land Rover,' said Alan. 'Hop in.'

After a thorough search, Jon drew no clues. 'Nothing,' he said as he walked towards Alan, who stood chatting with Billy.

'This is my son-in-law, Billy,' said Alan, introducing him. 'The big bloke, James Griffin, he had a go at Billy with a knife.'

'Lucky you're still here, Billy. Knives are dangerous things,' said Jon.

'He was trouble from da beginning. Glad he gone.'

'Yeah, they weren't here for long before I told them both to go,' said Alan. 'You think he has something to do with the murder of Tess?'

'Look we're just investigating at this stage, Alan. There are similarities with two other women, both strangled by pantyhose and both last seen in pubs. The witnesses who have come forward all describe a stranger in the pub. A big man. When I spoke to Owen, the owner of The Thirsty Dog, he basically said the same thing. A stranger appeared. Very non-talkative, sat alone drinking his beer and the bloke had a long scar on his face.

'That would be Griffo, James Griffin,' Alan replied. 'Description fits perfectly.'

'Okay. I'll see you tomorrow then. I won't come down to the house as it'll just be a line of men going through the bush and searching for anything we can find.'

Billy glanced at Alan, surprised as his eyebrows furrowed.

'Right then, Jon. Do what you need to do and just call me if you need anything. The only info I can give you is what you already know. He is a big bloke, name is James Griffin, and he had a long, fine scar down the left side of his face. Like someone had opened him up. The other bloke was half-decent really. Ernest Tubbs. He was funny as he didn't like to wear the dark blue singlets all the shearers wore. He always wore these short-sleeve country-type shirts that were oversized. He told Cookie, our chef in the shearing season, that he loved his food but hated his belly. Singlets hide nothing, so maybe that was the reason. Strange pair. Kept to themselves. Ernie was certainly led by the other chap. I often wondered if they were a couple. Nothing surprises me.'

'Thanks, Alan. Any bit of information helps,' said Jon. 'Interestingly, we took a call from Mrs Tubbs, Ernie's mother, a while back. She said her son Ernie was travelling with this guy James Griffin. Seemed they had worked together for a long time, and Ernie said they had picked up work in outback New South Wales. But you're right, he was half-decent. Used to send money home to her, but she has heard nothing from him for months.'

'Shame. I didn't mind Ernie. I wonder what's happened him, to both of them?'

'Anyway, Alan, I best get going. But thank you, you have been most helpful.' Jon shook his hand and then handed him his card. 'Call me any time if you think of anything else.'

◊

The following morning, a dozen police officers arrived at the gates to Woori with Detective Lynch. 'Okay, officers, this is where I found the skull. Obviously, an animal has dropped it here on the road. So let's form a line and head across the paddock to do a full 360. Alan, the owner of this property, said to be mindful of snakes, so use those walking sticks in your hand and thump the ground to make some noise. If there are any near, they'll scatter. Snakes don't like us and we don't like them, and you don't want to step on a brown snake out here. Also, he said there are the big boars and sows to watch out for. Guns ready as the boars charge and can rip you open very easily.'

They proceeded in a long line, stretching out about two feet apart. As they headed further into the bush, about a mile in, one of the officers yelled, 'Over here!'

Jon started running in the officer's direction. 'Here, Jon,' said Martin, a probationary constable, waving frantically.

'Good spotting, constable.' Jon squatted down to the shirt and picked it up with his pen. There were old blood stains and holes in the back. He winced when he remembered Alan's words. It was a short-sleeve country-type shirt. Checked pattern, the sort you see on the country singers.

'If I'm not wrong, by the jaggedness of the holes, these are multiple knife wounds. Mission accomplished. We'll keep looking and see what else we can find.'

As the police officers circled the area, they found more human skeletal remains. The bones were carefully placed into bags. 'It's not a complete skeleton,' said Jon to the officers, 'but you would expect that out here. He would have been gone in a few days. Poor bugger. I hope he was dead by the time anything got to him, but I suspect from the multiple holes in that shirt that he would have been. Let's head back to the station.'

As Detective Lynch drove, he knew James Griffin was a person of suspicion in the missing persons case of Ernie Tubbs. Certainly, after talking to Owen the publican at The Thirsty Dog, a man fitting his description had been there a few times. A large man with a scar down his face. Was he linked to the death of Tess Walker? His gut instincts told him yes. An APB for him was issued that evening. He knew Griffin was definitely a person of interest and he would do everything he could do to bring him in and question him. It was always a long process following leads, but he knew he was onto something.

Jon Lynch called Alan first to give him the grim news that further skeletal remains were found in the bush. He then called Mitch and Dave. The NSW Police Force and the powers that be in government believed they had a serial killer with the three womens' murders being so very similar. A reward of $500,000 was offered and posters were placed in all of the pubs in the Central West Regions.

THIRTY-TWO

LAYING LOW

Miss Upjohn, the music teacher in Walgett, called Wooribilly early one morning. Jedda was so looking forward to the music lessons next year that she could barely contain herself. Her musical voice was lovely to listen to, and she almost sang her words, even when she was talking.

Miss Upjohn said, 'I've just had one of my pupils drop out, so I now have a vacancy for your little nightingale on a Friday for a couple of hours if you like? No need to wait for next year.'

'Marvellous, we'll take it,' Lisa said happily. 'Jedda continues to have singing lessons with my aunt and if her musical instincts are right, our girl is a natural soprano.'

'Oh, splendid, my dear. I look forward to seeing you this Friday then. Is that too early or shall we start the following week?'

'No, not at all, this week is fine, Miss Upjohn. Thank you. Jedda will be delighted.'

'Oh, just one more thing, please call me Lydia. Apart from being so formal, Upjohn is such a mouthful.'

Lisa laughed. 'Yes, of course, Lydia. We shall see you this week.'

The smile never left Lisa's face all day. She would wait for dinner to give the good news. There would be squeals, no doubt. Everything was going to plan for Jedda. She was enrolled for Fernhope in the Southern Highlands, and their music department, according to Mark, was superb and had a rich culture of musical excellence. Jedda could not wait. Whenever Mark called, she would incessantly ask the same questions about their music teachers. But it was Jesse who concerned her. He refused to go anywhere but Woori. He wanted to stay on the land and be like Alan and Billy. When Orange Ag School was mentioned, he pulled a face and simply said no more classrooms, just bush and land.

Zena and Alan joined them for dinner that evening as well as Ningali, Kev and Mum Shirl. They had planned on an outdoor BBQ but the flies were now building up for the summer heat and threatened to carry the food away.

'Better idea to stay inside, what do you think?' said Zena.

'I agree! I've eaten too many flies myself so far this season. As soon as you open your mouth, bingo!' Lisa admitted.

As they sat down, Lisa clanged a glass with a spoon. 'Just a little announcement. I am so thrilled as I know you will all be. Our Jedda, our little wild goose, will start her official music lessons with opera teacher, Miss Lydia Upjohn, this Friday.'

There was momentary silence and then an ear-piercing scream from Jedda, who jumped up, knocking her water over. She stood clapping her hands then raced around to Billy, clambering onto his lap.

'You too heavy now, little goose. You da big girl, nearly,' smiled Billy, his heart bursting with pride.

'Ha! Jedda a big girl but not like me,' giggled Mum Shirl. 'Da nightingale, she go to da big school now?'

'No, not really. But this lady who teaches in Walgett lived in Sydney and trained at the Conservatorium of Music and then went on to appear in musicals and operas all over the world. She has a beautiful soprano voice. But she is also such a warm, lovely lady, so I'm sure she will bring out the best in Jedda.'

'That's wonderful news, Lisa,' said Zena. 'I can't go any further with her and if she has a chance to really exceed in something she loves, then we have to give her the best shot. We're so lucky to have Lydia way out here. I was intrigued as to how she got here when I first spoke to her on the phone. She said she came to fill in one summer for a music teacher and loved it. When she went home, she could not stand the feeling of being so crowded in suburbia. She now has a lovely little white cottage at the end of town.'

'That I understand,' said Alan. 'A toast.'

Glasses and beers were raised, and it was Ningali who spoke. 'Dis little one, me and Mum Shirl, we see in da stars. She gunna fly like da spirit bird, high and high into da skies. Everybody see and hear da little wild goose.'

Billy took Lisa's hand. 'Grasshopper, we raise da beautiful pica-ninnies.'

'That we did, Billy. I so wish for more babies, as these ones have grown so quickly,' she whispered.

'I hear dat... what you say... more babies, eh?' queried Mum Shirl.

Lisa looked embarrassed, and Zena quickly stepped in. 'Probably not the time to discuss more babies. Let's just enjoy our meal and celebrate the new adventure that awaits our young Jedda.'

'Proper true,' said Ningali. 'And you, Jesse, bush baby... what you gunna do with yourself? Be like my Kev? He da crack shot, teach you good. He say your aim deadly.'

Jesse paused for a moment. 'I'm going to be like Daddy. I'll stay here and I'm going to marry Livvy and we can make babies like Mummy and Daddy.'

It was weirdly quiet for a few seconds until finally Alan started laughing and then the whole room broke out with peels of laughter.

'You love da Livvy? asked Mum Shirl. 'But you just da babies.'

Billy looked across at his son. 'She da little lady beetle and she find a way into hearts. Good to feel love. Always come unexpected. Sometimes too young, sometimes not right timing, but love in da heart better dan hate in da heart.'

As Lisa began to clear, Mum Shirl followed Lisa into the kitchen. 'My Lisa, you come see me. I feel da womb is empty. I gunna talk to da spirits. You come come when you ready.'

Lisa was momentarily taken aback. 'I will, thank you, Mum Shirl. You always see everything so clearly.'

◊

As they lay in bed that night, Lisa came into Billy's arms, their bodies wrapping together. 'Nice words you said tonight, darling, about love in the heart.'

'Just speak da truth, my grasshopper. Love better dan hate.'

'Yes, I know that. But what did you really think about what Jesse said.'

'Just young, da babies, always like each other too much and den as dey grow, it find another direction, like da river.'

'We call it puppy love,' said Lisa.

Billy laughed. 'Yes, dey da pups. True talk. Just let da picaninnies enjoy da laughter and da gift of friendship. Burnu always tell me, life a hard road. Always important to have da mates, dey always there for you. No matter where we travel, he always have dat. All da mobs, dey always welcome my Burnu and me.'

'You're right. I'll try not to read too much into it. Kids being kids and friends, I guess. Jesse just seems so besotted,' said Lisa. 'But everything sorts itself.'

Billy brought his finger to her lips. 'Shhhh, talk too much.' He softly ran his lips over her forehead and placed a gentle kiss on her lips. He sighed with pleasure and deepened the kiss.

A whimper escaped Lisa's mouth as her hand traced the length of his back. 'I love you, Billy.' She closed her eyes, lost in the feeling of the tenderness of his lovemaking.

◊

After an eventful morning in Walgett at the General Store while Jedda was at Miss Upjohn's for her first lesson with the vocal coach, the Garretts and Smiths stopped in at the pub for lunch. As they left the pub, a big fuel tanker pulled up and parked on the other side of the road. As he went to switch the radio off, the news was broadcasting missing persons from the Central West.

Shit, Fuck! Shit! Ernest Tubbs was on that list. Griffo knew then he had to lay low. They weren't ever going to find him. Dumb coppers. He ran through his head the evidence that he knew he had destroyed. The pigs would have got Tubbs as well as the other feral animals out there. He'd ditched his blood-splattered clothes and burned the ute once he got work with the haulage company. The coppers had nothing. He decided to work mainly up through Darwin and Broome until the heat settled.

As Griffo grabbed his sunglasses, ready to get out, he momentarily froze. *Well, well, looky at what we got here. It's those rich fuckers from Woori.* He sat and watched them. *Rich bastards who had not a worry in the world. Flick people off whenever you want. I'll give you all the worry you can handle.* His eyes narrowed as he felt the urge to squeeze the life out of all of them. He knew the most pain and suffering was through a child. He looked at the little girl, recalling her at the party. That black bastard would die a thousand deaths if he took the girl. He sat high in the cabin of his truck as he watched them. His body tensing, the hate spilling from his body. *Little creamy. Cute little creamy. You'll all keep. I know where you are.*

PART FOUR

FATAL ENVY

THIRTY-THREE

GRIFFO RETURNS

Two years later

Towards the end of 1987 everyone was preparing for Christmas, the most hectic time of the year. After hearing Ernie Tubbs on the Missing Persons bulletin two years ago, Griffo had grown a full black beard, which was thick and covered most of his face. He had shaved his head and travelled under a different name on his licence, forged when he was up in the Territory. He was now Gregory Cooley. He mainly worked in Perth, Broome and then Darwin.

Griffo had laid low for two years, hoping the heat from the coppers passed, and then he took up the route across the New South Wales outback again. He had unfinished business. But he never went back to The Thirsty Dog when he travelled through Walgett with the road trains. He went to the other pub, The Royal, where the blacks drank frequently. But always in the back of his mind was revenge. He should have run over those rich fuckers and their creamies when he saw them on the streets in Walgett two years ago. Sometimes he could see himself cracking Billy's skull open. That black bastard Billy. Maybe make his white bitch wife watch. Then rape her. Or maybe the other way around. Do her first and let him watch. He could feel an erection every time that thought crossed his mind.

He drove on, the big wheels of his rig churning along the highway as he headed to Walgett. He was glad to be out of Alice Springs. He felt the scratch marks on his face. That last bitch had put up a good fight. Toe-rag hooker. He'd picked her up on the outskirts of town and fucked her hard behind his rig. When she'd demanded money, he beat her so severely that he'd heard on the radio she was close to death. As if he was going to pay her for sex. Griffo laughed as his cavernous eyes fixed on the road ahead. He was wired for destruction.

When Griffo pulled into Walgett, he was hot and thirsty. The beard made him itch as he headed to The Royal. He kept his hat and sunglasses on and parked the big rig just up the road. As he entered the pub, he kept his hat on. There was a loose rule that you removed your hat, but no one had dared ask him to remove it.

'What it will be, mate?' asked the barman as he eyed Griffo's hat.

'Bloody hot out there. Give me a schooner of Reschs. Make that two. The first one will hardly touch the sides.' Griffos eyes darted around the pub. Pretty empty for a Tuesday. A few locals and a few blacks getting pissed. He took a chair in the corner and gulped the first beer down.

Picking up *The Walgett Weekly*, his eyes were drawn to the article on the second page. It was the little creamy, Jedda. *Local 12-year-old girl sings up a storm. Local music teacher Miss Lydia Upjohn calls her student Girl Friday as she has provided her with singing lessons at her home every Friday*. Griffo grunted as he grabbed the next schooner, wiping the froth from his beard. He went to the phone box and pulled out the yellow pages, flipping through music teachers. He smiled when he saw the advertisement for Miss Upjohn, ripping out the page and stuffing it into his pocket.

As he drove down the road, he saw the white house with a sign outside advertising Miss Upjohn's musical services. A menacing smile crossed his lips. It was on an isolated road that seemed to stretch forever. There was a home further in the distance on the opposite side.

He had picked up the livestock from Carcoar at the Regional Livestock Exchange and was travelling to a property near Grafton, some
eight hours away to offload them for the new owners. He'd had
enough of carting beasts. It was always a slow trip stopping for feed
and water, and he was sick of the smell that emanated from the truck
when sleeping in his cabin. He would commence working next week
as a fuel tanker driver for Monaro Fuel Haulage. Better pay, and he
was driving the big Kenworth trucks up to central Queensland and
regional areas of New South Wales. He would head back to Walgett
and wait after getting back late Thursday afternoon. No one would
question a big rig by the side of the road. Friday could not come soon
enough.

It was just after 1:00 p.m. when Lisa pulled up at the little white cottage. Griffo's eyes narrowed as he watched Jedda saunter up to the
gates of the cottage. He smiled when no one else got out of the car
and slid further into his seat, pulling his hat down as the Land Rover
did a U-turn and headed towards the rig. He tilted his hat slightly
and peered out under it so he could see the occupant. An inward
growl rippled up through his chest. Lisa. He mouthed her name. He
could almost taste her. But for now, he wanted the creamy. It would
inflict the most pain.

He started his rig and followed the road slowly towards the cottage, parking further down amongst some large gum trees. As he
passed by the cottage, he could hear the banging of piano keys and
voices. Griffo looked left then right. Not a soul. He opened the truck
door and stepped down, moving briskly. His heart was thumping at
the excitement of taking the girl. The black bastard would howl all
night like the lubras when someone was dead. A malicious smile
crossed his face as the monster within begged to get out.

The floorboards creaked as the old wooden porch protested under
his weight. He peered through the fly screen to make sure it was only
the two of them inside. His big hand moved slowly to the screen door

as his breath came in rasps. Excitement ripped through his body at the delight of causing pain.

The music suddenly stopped as Miss Upjohn flicked the music sheets. She cocked her ear as she brought her finger to her lips. 'Shhh for a moment.' There was something out there on her porch. She got out of her seat and looked up the long hallway, freezing where she stood. A hulk of a man stood at her doorway rattling the handle.

She whispered to Jedda, 'Go into that room and lock the door. Quickly go now, do as I say.' Jedda slinked off as Lydia walked hesitantly towards the door.

She stopped halfway down the hallway as her eyes fixated on the huge stranger. 'What do you think you are doing on my doorstep?' she demanded. 'You are not expected here. Get away from the door and my house or I'll call the police. They will be here very quickly once I make that call. Now get away with you!'

Griffo laughed and then gave her a hideous snarl. 'You fucken old boiler. You don't frighten me. I want something inside and if you don't fuck off, I'm gonna break the door down.' Griffo felt the anger rising in him. He didn't expect the door to be locked, nor did he expect it to be better quality than the flimsy screen door that had led to Tess. He began banging on the door and trying to force the lock, shaking it violently.

He gritted his teeth. 'Open the fucking door!' his gravelly voice roared. Lydia took a deep breath, her face white with fear as she mustered all her courage, trembling as she ran for the door. 'Get back, you, you deranged moron! You have no business here.' She slammed the thick wooden door shut and raced back down to the phone and dialled 000.

Griffo went around to the side of the house, looking for a way in as he heard Lydia on the phone shouting the details of her location.

'Yes, please, please hurry!' She slammed the phone down. Her eyes frantically scanned the windows for any movement outside. She froze when she turned and saw him at the back door. Thank God that screen door was locked. Her heart was pounding as her hand went to her throat in fright. He was taking pleasure in her fear as the dark forces within him rose up to strike.

'Get lost! I've no money here if that's what you want. I've called the police and they will be here any minute!' Her voice was now shrill.

'Fucking old bitch,' Griffo bellowed as he made his way over the fence and ran for his rig. There would be another time, but for now he knew the cops would put out an APB on him and have a description. His heart was pumping as he reached his rig. He jammed his foot on the accelerator, the dust flying behind him. He had to change his appearance again. The beard had to go.

Lydia ran across to the room where she had sent Jedda. 'Open up, Jedda, it's me. Unlock the door. Hurry!'

The soon-to-be teenager looked bewildered when Lydia came into the room and locked it behind her. All colour had drained from Lydia's face.

'I think he's gone.' She shuddered, trying to catch her breath. 'The police, they should he here any minute now.'

'Who on earth was it?' asked Jedda, confusion in her eyes.

'I don't know but, oh, it was most frightening.' No sooner had Lydia said that when they heard the police siren.

◊

When Lisa arrived, she gasped when she saw the police cars. *My God, what's happened,* she thought as she sped towards the home and leaped out of the car, racing up the front steps.

'Jedda! Lydia!' She bounded up the front steps yelling their names as she flung the screen door open. She took a deep breath and exhaled when she saw them both sitting with the police.

'What's happened?' She looked back and forth between the two constables.

'It's alright, Lisa,' said Lydia, her voice still shaky. 'The police have been most helpful. I'm just trying to stop my nerves from fraying. Please sit.'

'Lisa, I'm Sargent Tony Roycroft and this is Constable Troy Seaton. Triple zero directed us here from the station.'

'Okay, so no one has been hurt?' Lisa sat next to Jedda and put her arm around her. Jedda was thirteen in six months, but she was already nearly as tall as her mother. Long-limbed and slender, with long black hair, she was a lot like Lisa in appearance, but with slightly darker skin and eyes like Billy's. There was no doubting that physical beauty would be gifted to her, but her real beauty was her ability to make other people smile and the wild sparkle in her eyes when she talked about the things she loved.

'Fortunately, no,' replied Tony. 'We have taken all the details and will head back to the station. But we'll be in touch. Thank you, ladies. Just always keep your doors locked, Miss Upjohn, and if you have any concerns, please call the station.'

'Oh, thank you so much, and for coming so very quickly,' replied Lydia.

'We will let ourselves out. If we need any more info, we'll be in touch,' said Tony.

Lisa looked confused. 'So, what happened here?'

'We were rehearsing and then stopped momentarily. I heard something at the door so quickly jumped up and looked down the hallway. What a frightful sight to see this hulk of a man at my door. I told Jedda to go to that room next to the laundry and lock the door. I had on one occasion a scare when I first moved in, so my bedroom up the hallway and that room Jedda was in both have solid locks. The screen doors as well.'

Lisa was aghast. 'But... what did he want?'

'Something inside, his exact words,' said Lydia. 'I don't know what he meant by that. I'm still puzzled. But he was a ghastly looking brute of a man. Terrible stench about him, a really foul smell like he had never washed.'

Jedda remained quiet, chewing her lip.

'What did he look like, Jedda?' Lisa asked.

'I didn't see him, Mum. Lydia sent me to that room.'

Lisa turned her attention to Lydia again. She said, 'He wore a bushman's hat, you know the type you see all the jackaroos and bushies wearing. Tan colour. Dark sunglasses. Jeans, black T-shirt. He had a very full black beard and moustache that almost covered his entire face. Hairy.' Lydia shuddered. 'But he was huge, I mean his frame filled the door. I was so terrified when he started violently shaking the screen door handle. I really thought for one moment the door would go flying off. I just charged down the hallway and slammed the wooden door.'

'You were so brave, Lydia. Thank you.' Lisa thought about the consequences if Lydia had not acted so fast. The description of the man suddenly clicked in her head. Huge and wanting something inside. She blurted out the name as she clenched her teeth, 'Griffo.'

Lisa and Billy curtailed the singing lessons much to Jedda's disappointment, but she understood their reasoning. Despite the APB and the police searching all the roads, no one of that description was located, and there were no sightings of anything that fitted James Griffin.

Jon Lynch kept in touch with Mitch, Dave and Alan when anyone remotely resembling James Griffin appeared. But seemingly, his trail had gone cold.

THIRTY-FOUR

INVOLUNTARY PATIENT

Polly Walker was now sixteen and had remained in hospital due to relapses and continuing auditory hallucinations. She had received two years of intensive treatment as she was considered dangerous to herself and others and seriously unwell. She was detained as an involuntary patient for treatment.

Dave Walker had hired private tutors so her education could continue, and Rebekah Adams would advise accordingly when she felt Polly was okay to proceed, but when she relapsed, the lessons would stop. It was an on-and-off-again process.

Her grandfather was trying to get Polly to finish the last two years of her education at boarding school. Both he and Mitch had tried to see Polly on numerous occasions but she had refused, until finally after twelve months of being hospitalised, she'd agreed. It had been a slow and awkward meeting, but Rebekah had assisted on re-establishing their relationship.

The twins were now going on thirteen and Olivia was only a few months behind them. Her bond with Jesse had become stronger, and she never missed an opportunity to be with him.

Jedda continued to excel in music, even without her lessons with Lydia, and looked forward to boarding school. She was also passionate about Aboriginal culture and spoke one evening in a broadcast on the ABC about inter-racial relationships. Of her own volition, Jedda had written a letter to the ABC to discuss the problems of integration, and they had contacted her on the telephone number provided.

The interview, by phone, was later aired on national radio and at the end, Jedda burst into traditional Aboriginal song using the clapping sticks, a gift from Ningali. She wanted to show and give people an insight into a culture that the majority of the audience would be largely ignorant of. As Zena and Alan sat with Billy and Lisa, listening to her being interviewed, they were enthralled.

Her upbringing on the farm had strongly affected Jedda. She had fallen deeply in love with the bush and was so proud of her Aboriginal heritage. She loved the stories about the Dreamtime and would sing late into the night with Ningali and Mum Shirl in the warming company of the flickering flames. Her father, Billy, was almost legendary in her eyes, and Jedda had the same love for horses as her father and mother. Every skill Billy taught her, riding, finding bush tucker as well as tracking birds and animals would always make her feel one with the outback.

Jesse would be going to Orange Ag next year as a boarder. He wasn't happy with that decision, but Billy explained he needed to finish proper schooling. Jesse could not understand their reasoning some days as he worked with Alan and Billy, absorbing all the knowledge that they imparted. He drew on his father's experience and teachings every day. Olivia had laughed and said her father had enrolled her at Central West Girls School in Armidale as they had a wonderful Equestrian Centre, so Jesse resigned himself to the fact that everyone, once the new year came around in 1988, would be packed off to complete their education.

Mum Shirl persevered with Lisa. There was no physical reason she could not fall pregnant, but Mum Shirl told Ningali there was a presence of darkness that was surrounding her. The darkness would strike at the very things she loved. She did not say who or where it was, but when she did the cleansing ceremonies with Ningali, she felt a presence. Something, someone here, she would say.

◊

It was mid-December 1987 when Polly said she wanted to go home. She had been in hospital for just over two years and for the last three months there had been no hallucinations or hearing voices. The potential for violence, self-harm or suicide was not evident, and the medications now controlled her symptoms by affecting the brain transmitter dopamine. Her schizophrenia was now effectively controlled at the lowest possible dose, and she understood the implications of not taking her medications. She had told Rebekah Adams that she hadn't wanted to take them previously due to their side effects, which of course led to the disastrous sequence of events. Her conversations with Mitch and Dave had been engaging and although she was slow in some responses and there were periods of awkwardness, she told Mitch that she missed Woodside.

'Good morning, Polly,' Rebekah said as she came into her room.

'Morning, Rebekah,' Polly replied softly.

'I called your father and spoke to him about your wishes. He is happy to have you come home, as is your grandfather and Olivia. I will make the arrangements for your discharge. Along with me, there will also be a social worker and a psychiatric nurse, Jill, who will make regular contact with you, and of course, I am always available. You have my card and contact numbers. Your father has also invited me out to Woodside, which I am very much looking forward to.'

Polly's face brightened. 'Oh, that would be great to have you out there, Rebekah. I feel less nervous now.'

'Okay then, I'll let them know that you can be picked up later today, anytime is fine. There's just some paperwork to fill out. So, if you have any concerns between now and then, please let the staff know, and I'll come down and have a chat.'

When Rebekah left the room, Polly breathed a sigh of relief. She wanted to go home. She'd had enough of hospitals. Looking across at the medication that sat on the bedside table, she grimaced. But at least the meds were better than the ECT she'd received. That knocked her around for ages afterwards, and the side effects were worse. The migraine headaches caused her to be violently ill, and she felt like such a zombie when she woke after the general anaesthetic.

THIRTY-FIVE

HOMEWARD BOUND

It felt strange to be home at Woodside, and Polly was grateful Mitch had invited her psychiatrist, Rebekah Adams, to stay. Mitch had gutted the old bedrooms that Tess and Polly had used, and Dave now slept in one of the rooms. His old bedroom was now for Polly, and Mitch had turned the family room into another bedroom for Olivia. As they sat down for dinner, Polly felt relaxed.

'It's so nice to have you home, Polly. I would love to go riding with you when you feel like it,' said Olivia.

'That would be lovely, Livvy. I look forward to that. It's been such a long time since I was in a saddle.'

'I'm riding out tomorrow morning to the river with Jesse and Jedda. Is that too soon? They're meeting me at the front gates at eight, so if you want to come along, we need to be up early.'

'Sounds good. I always loved the river.'

Mitch looked at Rebekah, who was enjoying the banter. She was the first woman in a long while who had gained some attention from him. She wasn't beautiful like Lisa or the other girls he was usually attracted to, but there was something about her. 'We thought we might drive around tomorrow, Rebekah, and just show you a bit of the property.'

'That would be lovely, I'd like that,' she replied.

Polly yawned. 'I'm a little tired now and if we're to be up early, do you mind if I go to my room?'

Sure, Pol,' replied Mitch as he stood up. 'Do you want me to come down to make sure everything is okay?'

'No, I'm fine. I've settled in already. It's a great room, and I appreciate you giving me my own ensuite. Thanks, Dad.'

'Getting older now, Pol, and you ladies need your privacy. I thought you'd like it.'

Rebekah watched Polly leave the room. 'I think I'll just pop down there to see that she's alright. The first night home is always the hardest. If you'll excuse me.'

Rebekah knocked softly on the door and opened it slightly. Polly was sitting on the bed.

'How are you feeling, Polly?' asked Rebekah, closing the door softly.

'There are lots of memories, not all good. Just thinking of Mum, I guess, and Grandma. There weren't many good times, so I can barely recall them. Maybe it was a mistake to come back here,' sighed Polly.

Rebekah sat down beside her. 'Of course it's hard to come home, Polly. Try and think of all the good memories. We all have to deal with things that have been unpleasant and difficult to come to terms with. Life can throw some wretched things in our direction.'

Polly sighed again, but nodded.

'Well, you are here now and from what I can see, you have a family who are eager to welcome you home and who love you. Let's go with that. And you also have my support.'

Polly nodded. 'Thank you, Rebekah.'

Later that night, after everyone else had retired, Mitch and Dave sat on the veranda enjoying a cold beer. 'What do you think, Dad?' asked Mitch. 'Did you get a feeling there is something still not quite right with Polly?'

Dave pondered. 'It's an adjustment, a big adjustment, coming back here to her old home. I'd be nervous too seeing all of us. But we can only rely on Rebekah's advice. Polly has everything ahead of her. It's been a long hard road of mental illness but she's lucky to have Dr Adams and the range of treatments that are available now.'

'True, Dad. I would hate that for a job. But boy, I would love to be just starting out again, the world at my feet. Hit the re-set button. I would do everything so differently in hindsight.'

'In what way?' asked Dave looking puzzled.

'I'd think more with my big head,' said Mitch, guffawing loudly.

'Bloody oath, son. But everything is good in hindsight. Come on, we'll drink to that one!'

Jesse and Jedda's horses fidgeted at the gate. They were keen for a run. When Polly and Olivia cantered around from the back barn gate, Polly could not help but stare. Although Jesse was younger than her, she marvelled at the way he'd changed. He was bordering on his teen years but there was something very masculine about him. He was so lithe and had a presence about him as he sat tall in the saddle. He looked like Billy with his beautiful brown eyes with lush, thick lashes. Her heart warmed at the very sight of him.

'Hi Polly,' greeted Jedda.

Jesse merely raised his black hat in acknowledgement.

'Thank you. Both of you. It feels good to be in the saddle again, and I'm ready to ride. It's been so long.'

They all took off and when they reached the river, Olivia pulled out some water and sat next to Jedda and Jesse after he tethered the horses. Polly sat next to Olivia.

'Good ride,' smiled Jesse as he nudged Olivia's ribs.

It did not go unnoticed by Polly. They had always been close but now there was something different about them.

'Polly, you still ride so well for not being on a horse for some time,' said Jedda.

Polly blushed. 'I think there are some things you don't forget.'

'We're all off to boarding school soon. Are you looking forward to it?' queried Jedda.

'Mmm, maybe. Dad said I have to go and finish off school at Koombala.'

'I'm so excited to go to boarding school, although I'll miss here terribly,' said Olivia as she yanked Jesse's hat.

Polly rolled her eyes.

'They do this all the time when they're together, Polly. You have to get used to it. Lovey-dovey stuff, I call it,' scoffed Jedda.

Polly wished she had Jesse's attention. She wanted him to tease her in that manner.

'Why are we going to different schools, Livvy?' queried Polly. 'Is yours better?'

Olivia was taken aback. 'No, I don't think so, Pol. It's just that Central West Girls School has great equestrian facilities that I'm really keen to pursue. I don't know why Kate selected Koombala for you, but Dad said it was excellent. You may have to ask him.'

Polly peered curiously at Olivia. 'The river looks inviting. Do you swim now, Livvy?'

'Umm no. Jesse is the best swimmer, and he's tried so many times to get me in the water but even he has just given up.' Jesse suddenly pushed Olivia backwards and straddled her body. Olivia could not stop laughing.

'Because she's a big scaredy cat, aren't you, lady beetle,' said Jesse as he began to tickle her.

'Come on, you two,' said Jedda. 'We have to get back. Mum said we had to be home by 11 or 12. So we need to leave now.'

'You could give me some lessons, Jesse?' said Polly. 'I'm okay at swimming, but I'd love some more instruction. I've never been able to master freestyle.'

Jesse looked embarrassed and not sure where to look. 'Sure, Polly, happy to help.' But as he met her eyes, a shiver ran down his spine.

◊

Mitch had asked Rebekah to stay for a few days, which she happily agreed to. It was early the next morning when the enticing smells wafted from the kitchen. Rebekah and Polly had made a pact to get up early and cook breakfast for everyone. It was also Rebekah's way of getting Polly to engage in some activity that involved everyone.

'Good morning,' said Dave as he shuffled in. 'Boy, that smells good. Why is it when someone else cooks it tastes better.' He pulled out a chair.

Mitch followed shortly after him. 'Morning all. The wonderful smells coming from here have driven me out of my bed.'

Rebekah laughed. 'Good to hear, Mitch.'

'I look forward to some more of your cooking then, Polly,' added Dave.

'Yeah, me too, Pol,' chimed in Mitch.

Olivia walked in, rushing like a zephyr breeze as she wrapped her arms around Mitch's neck, planting a kiss on his cheek.

'Liv, look what Polly and Rebekah have for us this morning.'

'Morning, Pol. Morning, Rebekah. Something smells amazing.'

'Yes, that seems to be the word of choice, Olivia,' said Rebekah. 'Okay, are we done now, Polly?'

'Yes, it's all cooked. I'll just put everything on these big platters, and everyone can help themselves.'

'It's a good day to be out today. Sorry I didn't get you out and about as planned yesterday, Rebekah. A few things got in the way, but today I'm all yours,' smiled Mitch. 'Brilliant sunshine, and it's getting hot, so we'll eat and clear and then head out. What do you all think?'

'You're on!' exclaimed Olivia.

'How about you, Polly?' queried Mitch.

'That sounds good. I'd like to see how things have changed.'

'Okay, we can take the Land Rover. Dad, you can drive that and I'll take the Quadrunner,' said Mitch.

'Oh, super fun. I love that quaddy. It's the best, Polly. You must learn to ride it.'

'Sure, okay. Is it difficult?'

'No, it's just fun,' replied Olivia.

'You just have to be a bit careful on the turns though, as sometimes they can roll. I've heard they're designing the next lot with a roll bar, which will be a good thing. Safer,' said Mitch.

As they headed out, Dave drove the Land Rover with Rebekah and Polly, and Mitch had Livvy on the back of the Quadrunner.

'Let's head out and take a look at the crops and stock, Dad, and head to the dam after that. The new swimming hole,' beamed Mitch.

'It's fascinating being out here with all the miles and miles of land. I think that's when you realise how big Australia is. What about you, Polly, what did you like to do out here? What was your favourite thing?' Rebekah asked.

'I love riding, Rebekah. I was good when I rode here and I love the open spaces too. I do like the look of that Quadrunner though. It seems like a lot of fun.'

'Yeah, Livvy just about breaks her neck to ride it or just gets on the back with Mitch. When we get to the new water hole, you can sit on the back with Mitch and see how you go.'

'Okay, I'll do that,' replied Polly with a grin.

When they pulled up, Mitch was already there with Olivia.

'My goodness, the dam is huge,' said Rebekah as they got out of the Land Rover. Mitch walked towards them.

'Impressive, hey,' said Mitch.

'Why, it looks like a small lake. Why so big?'

'We built it big before the bureaucrats got in and changed the rules about how big you can build dams. We've got a lot of stock now, and if we get another drought, we're better covered. We used to just have sheep, but Dad said to diversify, and it's been good in terms of profit. So, more water is needed. The sides are steeper, so we catch more water should it rain. But as you can see, it's a great spot to swim too if the water fleas don't get down your knickers,' laughed Mitch.

'Oh dear,' said Rebekah, looking somewhat perturbed. 'I seriously don't want fleas in my knickers. Do you swim here, Olivia?'

'No, I don't like the water at all. I like to feel the earth under my feet. Water just spooks me out. Billy, next door, and his son, Jesse, have tried to teach me, but I just panic. I think they've given up. Dad, can you take Polly for a spin on the quaddy. I'm sure she'd love it.'

'Want to go for a spin, Pol? You have to hang on tight,' said Mitch.

'I think I can manage that, no problem,' smiled Polly. 'Can you show me how to work the controls so I can manage it by myself.'

'Okay, I'll start her up and then hop on behind me. I'll go slow initially, and when you think you want to go a little faster, give my ribs a squeeze. Just keep in mind, the dust and bugs fly into your face and the faster you go, so it feels like a house-brick hitting your noggin.'

They all watched as Polly threw her long legs over the bike behind Mitch.

'All set?' His hand patted her thigh, reassuring her.

'All good,' said Polly.

'See you back home, then.' Mitch headed the bike towards the red dust road, the grin never leaving Polly's face.

'I'm pleased Mitch did that,' said Rebekah.

When they reached Woodside, Polly and Mitch were covered in red dust.

'So, young lady, you like a bit of speed,' said Mitch as they dusted themselves off. 'Your hair is the same colour as the dirt on your clothes, Pol.'

She grinned. 'That I do. Speed feels, sort of powerful, free. Thank you, Dad. I did enjoy it and thank you for showing me how it all works.'

'Here, get on it on your own and just do a few loops here while we wait for the others to show.'

Polly hopped back on and started to drive around. 'It is fun, maybe just slightly better than a horse.'

'Here they come now, Polly, why don't you crank it out a bit,' said Mitch as he watched her speed off towards the Land Rover.

'Look!' said Olivia pointing. 'There's Polly, look how fast she's going.'

'That's a worry,' said Dave. 'Gotta remind her about that rolling. It's so easy to do.'

Dave slowed as Polly came closer. Olivia was leaning out the window clapping. 'Well done, Pol, you're a natural.'

'Just take it down a couple of notches though, Polly. These things roll and there have been a few incidents where people have been killed. So just a touch slower as we head home,' said Dave.

Polly nodded and spun the Quadrunner back towards Mitch but did not heed the advice. She loved the speed. It was exhilarating.

◊

Mitch had warmed more to Rebekah, and she stayed the whole week. Her secretary Gail rearranged appointments but her schedule was almost entirely free as she knew Polly would need help settling in.

Olivia bounced in after washing up and joined them on the veranda.

'What are you up today, young lady?'

'I'm going for a ride with Jesse this afternoon, so I'll just do a few things before I go,' said Olivia.

'Where are you riding to?' asked Mitch.

'Nowhere in particular. Just riding with Jesse is the good part.'

Rebekah nodded knowingly. Olivia wore her heart on her sleeve. Jesse, her friend, was more than a friend, even at their tender age.

'I look forward to hopefully meeting him and his family at some stage,' said Rebekah. 'But for now, I may go and read some more of a great book I've found on the interpretation of dreams. Sigmund Freud called dreams the royal road to the unconscious, but some of my colleagues say dreams are a blind alley filled with the randomly discarded trash of a day's experience.'

'Interesting, Rebekah. I always have very vivid dreams,' smiled Mitch.

'Some psychotherapists believe dreams are a key to unlocking and liberating repressed memories of past traumatic experiences. So, gentlemen, if you will excuse me. Thank you for a lovely morning.'

THIRTY-SIX

OLIVIA AND JESSE

Olivia saddled up Tilly, a beautiful bay mare, and as she rode, she thought about Polly. She was not overly warm or friendly, but she was definitely friendlier than Olivia remembered her. However, she was still a little wary of her sister after everything they'd been through with her. She soon forgot about it when she saw Jesse coming towards the gate. It was just him and her today. Her heart began to flutter instantly as his beautiful smile welcomed her.

'You're early, lady beetle.'

Olivia laughed. 'I know. Do you want to get going? I really feel the need to ride!'

'Sure, got my beautiful horse Jacko ready to go. Wait here and I'll ride him around,' said Jesse.

As Jesse pulled up Jacko beside her, Livvy noticed a small sack. 'What's that you've got?'

'Mum says this belongs to her. She always carried it to the river with food for some ladies who used to live that way. It's special.'

'Is that where we're going, Mr Brown Eyes?'

'Yeah, it's a good ride. My favourite.'

'You're not going to try to get me in the water again are you, Jesse?'

'Nope, lady beetle, you'll fly away if I do that.'

Olivia laughed. 'Okay then, let's be on our way.'

Jesse treasured these moments when they were together on their own. He hung on every word, and Olivia chattered like a magpie.

When they reached the river, Jesse pulled off a rug and the sack and lay them down on the long grass under the shade of the eucalyptus trees. He tethered the horses and joined Olivia. 'So, how've you been going with Polly?'

'Funny you should ask that. Everything seems okay, but I still feel like I can't trust her completely. I don't really understand her condition fully, and am waiting for the other shoe to drop, just like it always would. But for now, she seems okay. Not overly friendly with me, and she did mention something odd about which boarding school we were going to. I think she feels I'm going to a better school. I don't know. That was my impression. But Dad says just be patient. What's in the bag?'

Jesse pulled the bag towards them. 'Water.' He pulled two bottles out. 'And some fruit. Mum said to take it. And... something for you.'

'Me?' Olivia exclaimed. 'What, show me!'

Jesse dug his hand into the bag and pulled out what appeared to be a circle of chocolate-brown dried reeds, all intricately woven like a plait.

'Oh, what is it?' said Olivia, looking puzzled.

'From the marshes at Carinda. Dad and I drove out there and I picked the blue flag iris and the cattails. Let them dry out. You see, this flower, it's wilted now, but you can see the colour of the iris. This is a crown.' Jesse smiled as he gently placed it on Olivia's head. 'Princess Livvy.'

They both laughed. Olivia jiggled her head from side to side as she brought both hands up to touch it.

'Do I look like a princess?' she jested.

Jesse nodded, the smile never leaving his face.

'It's beautiful.' She took it from her head and then ran her fingers over it. 'One of my treasures to keep forever. I shall hang it on my bed post so I can look at it every night.' She hugged the crown to her heart. 'You always make me feel special, Jesse. Come on, let's just lie here and look at this big, beautiful blue sky and those puffy white clouds. I feel like a princess,' smiled Olivia. She turned on her side and lay against Jesse, closing her eyes. Next thing, she woke to the feeling of someone tugging at her hair.

'Princess Olivia, we have to go now. You've been sleeping. The sun, she'll be making way for the moon now.'

'Oh dear, we better get moving. I'll be in trouble! Can you put my crown in your little bag? I don't want to lose it on the ride home.' Olivia threw her hat on.

From that day on, their worlds changed. They were young, but anything was possible when they were together.

◊

Although they rode swiftly, it was just on dusk when Olivia returned to Woodside. She watched Jesse ride away from her and all she wanted to do was follow. Taking a deep breath, she came into the house.

Mitch sat reading his usual newspaper, *The Land*, and looked up as she came into the kitchen. 'Where have you been all this time, young lady?'

'Riding,' said Olivia meekly.

'I know that, but it's just on dusk. You know the rules. Boars come out at night hunting. It's not safe. I've told you so many times, Livvy. They can charge at your horse and their tusks can do real damage. You would be on the ground flat on your back!'

Olivia shrugged her shoulders. 'Yes, I know, Dad. I'm sorry. I just fell asleep.'

'Fell asleep? With Jesse, I presume?' He took a deep breath and exhaled as he ran his fingers through his hair. 'No falling asleep, no dusk returns. Do I make myself clear? And if you keep shrugging your shoulders to every question I ask, you are going to dislocate one of them.'

Olivia relaxed. She knew he was angry, but only because he was worried. 'Yes, I understand. I'm sorry. Time just got away from us.'

'Alright then. Hop to it. I'm on BBQ duty tonight, so go clean up.'

He stared out the window, his fingers strumming the kitchen table, mildly irritated. Her attachment to the boy next door was growing. As he folded his newspaper, Rebekah appeared.

'Can I help with anything, Mitch?' she asked.

'All under control, Rebekah, nothing fancy,' Mitch replied, his annoyance still lingering.

'Did I come in at a bad time? Something seems to be bothering you. I heard you with Olivia. I can give you some space.'

'No, not at all. I was just worried about Olivia. She's still young and is getting quite attached to the boy next door.'

Rebekah laughed. 'It's usually the girl next door. Well, it is and it isn't. He is next door, and she is next door. Do you want to run it by me?'

'We used to call it puppy love,' he replied.

'It still is, Mitch. Young love. Do you think it is love? Is that what you're worried about? First crush or just good mates?'

'I think it's more than just mates. It's been growing steadily over the years. Plain to see,' said Mitch. 'But they are so very young, just bordering on puberty.'

'We can all recall a first love from way back. I know I can,' added Rebekah.

'Me too,' said Mitch, his mouth twitching.

'Young love carries a lot of emotion with it. It can be an incredibly wonderful and intense emotion. It can also be extremely confusing. Love is difficult for many mature adults to manage, let alone teenagers,' explained Rebekah.

'God, don't I know that!' said Mitch, rolling his eyes. It was the way he said it that made Rebekah think he had been hurt or had lost in love.

'The way you said that, were you in love, puppy love as they say, when you were young?'

Mitch paused as his eyes scanned the paddocks through the big windows. 'Yeah, I guess I was. It did hurt. But I messed it up.'

'That's okay, Mitch. What happened, or am I being too nosey?'

'Nothing happened, really. I wanted her, then did some really stupid things, and she chose someone else over me.'

'Love is a difficult thing, Mitch. It can cause heartache and so many problems.'

'Boy, do I know that.'

Rebekah sighed. 'Grown-up love is confusing, and young love is hard for teenagers. However, for teenagers, just because it's confusing doesn't mean that young love isn't real. Sometimes it is, and sometimes it's not. This may all dissipate when they go to boarding school.

'The first feelings that preteens and teens usually experience are feelings of infatuation, or a crush. These feelings are more intense than the young person is used to and are easily mistaken for love. Maybe that's what Olivia is feeling. Is he a nice boy?'

Mitch nodded. 'I have to say yes. The boy, Jesse, he has good people surrounding him.'

'Well, that is positive news. Why are you worried, apart from their ages? Is there something you don't want should they form a relationship?'

Mitch didn't want to speak the words. He knew Rebekah would be horrified. *Because he has a bit of the tar brush in him. And he's Billy's son. It's bad enough that I lost my first love to him, let alone losing my daughter to his son.*

'Relationships are confusing for young people because they are experiencing feelings of romantic love and attraction for the first time. They are just starting to figure it all out.'

'What do I do then? Just let her do what she wants, or rein her in? I don't know what to do. I feel helpless. If I tell Olivia not to see him, she'll turn away from me, perhaps. She would be really hurt. But the boy is slightly older, not by much, and I can remember my testosterone levels when I hit my teenage years. They went through the roof!'

'Sit down and talk with her, Mitch, when you get the opportunity. Ask her how she's feeling. Let her come to you. Be open. I know this is difficult when her mother is not there to guide her as well.'

Mitch faked a smile. 'Yeah, I guess you're right. I have tried before to explain the birds and the bees. She tells me they have sex education at school and that she knows all about it.'

Rebekah laughed. 'Just keep reinforcing, gently, that you are worried about her and not to take things too quickly, especially with boys. As I said, you may also find as she grows and develops her academic life, and while away at boarding school, she will grow out of this crush.'

As Mitch pondered what she said, Rebekah thought how vulnerable he looked.

'Good advice, Rebekah. You have my permission to stay. Permanently.' He laughed and so did she. 'Let me get you a drink. Wine, G and T?'

'A glass of white wine, that would be lovely.'

Mitch handed the glass of wine to Rebekah and then held up his beer to her. 'Cheers and thank you. Dad and I appreciate everything you have done over the years for us and Polly.' He took a swig of his beer. 'I did want to ask you something, Rebekah.'

'What's that, Mitch?'

'Is it possible Polly could revert back to how she was? You know, become quite crazed and violent, sorry, mentally ill. Chattering, self-harm, a danger to herself and maybe others?'

'Short answer: yes. There can be relapses even when a person is on medication. Sometimes they might need to change to a different one. Or people stop taking their medication and relapse. Unfortunately, if they relapse, they need hospitalisation and possibly scheduling if severe and they refuse treatment.'

'So is Polly a ticking bomb?' asked Mitch as he eyed Rebekah nervously.

'No. I have had patients who have remained steady throughout their lives. They have continual reviews with a medical professional, which Polly will need as her self-harming and mental state were profoundly severe. But who knows, Mitch? As long as she feels supported and loved, this goes a long way to creating mental stability.'

'So, this is a forever thing?'

'I'm afraid so, but medication and treatment continue to go leaps and bounds, and Polly has responded well. I will say this though: It is hard for Polly to adjust, especially after all the trauma, and I truly believe it will be a time thing. She had fun on the quadbike, she likes to ride horses and she is trying to prove to herself to you and her family that she is worthy. She spoke at length in group sessions, where I joined in. It took her a long time to make her mind up about coming back to Woodside.'

Mitch closed his eyes and exhaled loudly. Then held out his hand to Rebekah to help her up before they made their way outside for dinner. Rebekah smiled softly, looking into his blue eyes, and their gaze held. 'Thank you, Mitchell.'

THIRTY-SEVEN

JEALOUSY REARS ITS HEAD

Later that morning after the men had left for work, Lisa and Jedda saw the old blue Zephyr heading towards the house.

'Coooeee,' said Zena as Jedda greeted her at the front door. 'So, the men are not here?' she asked, sitting down.

'Long gone, so it's just the three of us.' Lisa poured their tea.

'I had a call from Dave,' said Zena.

'Oh, how are they doing over at Woodside? Jesse and Jedda rode to the river with Livvy and Polly and they said things were fine. That is, Polly was fine.' Lisa raised her eyebrows.

'Yes, Dave said she's doing very well, and Polly's psychiatrist has been a blessing. She's staying with them, Rebekah Adams, until the end of the week. He wanted to know if we, all of us, would like to go across to Woodside for lunch. Sort of an early Christmas get-together.'

'I think that will be fine,' said Lisa, 'but I'll check with Billy. It's good that things are settling over there. Dave even said Mitch seemed to be smitten with this Rebekah.'

'Good for Mitch.' Lisa laughed. 'He deserves some happiness.'

When Lisa broached the subject with Billy over dinner, he was not initially keen, even though he had long since buried the hatchet with Mitch, especially after everything Mitch had been through.

'I always worried about dat Polly. Mebbe something go wrong. Don't want no trouble.'

'It's just lunch, Billy, and as Zena said, it's all good over there.'

He finally agreed and Lisa called Zena the next morning. Lunch was arranged for Saturday.

◊

Rebekah had helped Dave set up the long table in a new outside area he had created. Under the big lemon eucalyptus wafted a beautiful aroma. Thick poles had been constructed to look like a long, large pergola but the pull-down fly screens were an amazing idea. They could sit outside and see the beautiful views across the plains and not get carried away by the flies.

'They're here,' said Mitch. 'Cars are coming up the driveway.'

Dave led the way for everyone to their new outdoor tent, as he called it.

'This is absolutely marvellous,' said Zena as she sat down. 'We must do the same. I love to sit outside in summer but the flies drive you mad and then at night the mosquitos feed on you!'

Polly made sure she sat opposite Jesse. She loved to peer into his eyes, picking out the flecks of gold, and her memory could vividly recall his father Billy naked at the river. She wondered if he looked the same. She had felt sexual urges, had tried masturbation and often fantasised about romance. Since she had started menstruation three years ago, her sexual urges had grown stronger. She enjoyed touching her genitals and experiencing the pleasure. She felt as if her emotions were on a roller coaster, the influx of hormones triggering so many things.

Polly desperately wanted Jesse to notice her. He was younger than her, but she had developed an infatuation for him. She admired him as he seemed so capable and confident for his age. *I want you to desire me, Jesse, not Olivia.*

Lisa sat next to Jesse and was slightly erred by Polly's intense stare at her son. It was almost an inappropriate interest, given their age difference.

'Jesse is going to teach me how to improve my swimming, aren't you, Jesse?' Polly smirked.

'No, I'm not,' he quickly replied.

'Yes, you are. You said down at the river that you'd help me.'

'I didn't, Polly. You know that.' Jesse shifted nervously in his seat.

Mitch quickly interjected. Polly's fixation on the boy had not gone unnoticed. 'So, next year, we'll have a few empty nests. You lot are all heading to boarding school,' he said.

'I don't want to go,' said Jesse. 'I want to stay here and work with Alan and Dad.'

Polly's eyes widened. 'I can stay here too, Dad, and help you. Jesse and I, here on the farms, helping out. If Jesse can stay, I can stay.'

'What?' Mitch was puzzled at her comment. 'Polly, what are you talking about? We've had this discussion before. You need to finish your education. It's important.'

There was silence across the table. 'Yes, Polly,' said Rebekah. 'I agree, and probably all of us here know the value of getting the best education for your children. All of the schools selected are fabulous, and you will meet and make good friends along the way. It will be exciting, Polly. Think of it as an adventure.'

'I can't wait,' said Olivia eagerly. 'I will miss here, and Jesse. My best friend. And Jedda too, of course.'

Jesse grinned at Olivia across the table when suddenly she yelled, 'Ouch!'

'Polly, did you just kick me?' Olivia bent down to rub her shin.

Mitch looked at Rebekah and she nodded. Polly's jealousy for Jesse's attention was developing.

'Polly! Did you really do that?' Mitch sounded exasperated.

'Yeah, I did. Sorry Livvy, it was an accident. I was just stretching my legs.'

Mitch and Rebekah glanced at each other, sensing there was more to the kick than that.

Apart from that incident, lunch was enjoyable, but there was no doubt the air crackled at times with the tension that emanated from Polly.

As Mitch sat with Rebekah later that evening, he wanted to know why the sudden outburst. Polly had been doing so well until then.

'I think Polly has developed her first infatuation. She seems smitten with Jesse. Remember I touched on this with you when you had concerns for Olivia and Jesse. But this is more to do with puberty. Polly's puberty and adolescence.'

Mitch groaned and rolled his eyes. 'Not both daughters, crushes on the same boy. Save me!'

'Romantic crushes are formed when finding someone attractive that they are then are excited to be around. In Polly's case, she seems to be seeking approval from Jesse and wanting to be liked. Girls usually experience crushes when they get to puberty. It's a journey all adolescents take, Mitch. It's more to do with fantasy rather than reality.'

'Will she grow out of it?'

'It's a potent mix of idealisation and infatuation, and it doesn't require knowing another person well at all. But in Polly's case, she has grown up with Jesse so it's probably a projection of valued attributes onto another person. There is a risky side though, given Polly's mental health.'

'What's that?'

'We just need to watch that this crush does not become a fixation as it can be self-endangering.'

'Oh great,' he moaned.

'Anyway, thank you for taking my advice about not making too much of it. Polly apologised to Olivia, and sometimes there is rivalry between sisters. Romantic crushes don't last very long once the magic of the person wears off. But it's crucial to discuss her feelings and what is appropriate behaviour. Rest assured, Mitch, I will be keeping an eye on Polly, not that I don't already, but due to her background. As an older adolescent going on seventeen, she's probably experiencing a flood of raging hormones, which just makes me, well, you too, more aware.'

'How do we know, Rebekah, what's what? A relapse or just being a teenager?'

'All teenagers have mood swings. One minute they are relaxed and reasonable and then they lose their temper in the next breath. Puberty makes them vulnerable. They get irritable, easily excitable and overly emotional, and anger is an emotion that teens feel strongly. We just need to navigate Polly through this tumultuous period as she progresses to young adulthood.

'I hope you're right, Rebekah,' Mitch said, groaning inwardly.

◊

It was January 1988 when Dave and Mitch travelled with Polly and Rebekah as they headed to Koombala to meet the boarding school principal, Dorothy Deerfield. She had emphasised that all the girls were important and were encouraged to participate and do their best. Rebekah had given her a history of Polly's condition and advised that a psychiatric nurse, Jill Fitzgerald, and herself would always be in touch during Polly's time at the school.

Surprisingly, Polly settled in to senior school and was paired with a buddy, Veronica, who helped her with the transition. The Year 12 prefects acted as mentors and would regularly discuss issues with the boarders. Polly suddenly found freedom, and the stimuli provided by the teachers opened her mind to explore more. There were nearly eighty other girls boarding, and the school overlooked the picturesque Sydney harbour. Mrs Deerfield described the school as old-world charm. No wonder her grandmother had selected the school. As she looked from her bedroom across to the harbour, Polly pondered how vastly different the view was compared to the dry red dusty plains of Woodside. Rebekah called her weekly, and she always looked forward to their chats. The only thing she did not like was not having her own bathroom. It was a common room with ten showers that all the girls used.

Polly made a few friends who were similar to her in that they were essentially loners, a bit different to the outgoing and bubbly nature of the other boarders. She called them all 'Olivias' as they reminded her of her sister, always bright and breezy. Polly particularly liked the extra-curricular activities and chose ceramics after an afternoon of working the pottery wheel. She loved the feeling of clay forming under her hands and her fingers working the designs.

When Mitch came to pick her up for the April school holidays, he could not help but comment how well she looked. He couldn't wait to let Rebekah know.

◊

Jesse went to Orange Ag College, and Jedda to Fernhope. Once Jesse got to the college, he was like a kid in a candy store. There was so much equipment and machinery, so many things to do and so many new friends he made as he immersed himself in the wonders of education.

Olivia was in overdrive as she made her way through the gates of Central West. Mitch knew it was the right choice once he saw the Equestrian Centre.

Jedda of course had been to Fernhope before, so it felt like she knew her way around. She could not wait to get started on the musical side of her education. Mark kept a watchful eye over Jedda and was with her at every opportunity. She gained many friends and would regale with her bush tales and yarns to all who would listen.

The principal of Fernhope School, Luisa Shaw, advised Lisa and Billy that there was now a busload of young girls ready to stampede to the bush to learn all these skills. Despite the joy of boarding, however, with every school holiday, Jedda could not wait to get home.

◊

It was now late November 1988 and the Christmas holidays loomed. Polly had noticed a young groundsman, Charlie, who maintained the lawns and gardens. The girls all liked him and openly discussed him. He was nineteen, tall with dark hair and olive skin, and had been at Koombala since leaving school at age sixteen. He'd been in Juvenile Detention for car theft and breaking and entering, and had had a fairly abusive and turbulent childhood. But when the case managers from DOCS approached Mrs Deerfield, she said she would give him a chance. He had been with the school for the past three years and was a good worker, but it did not go unnoticed that as he grew older, he was drawing attention from the female students.

Polly always knew his pool-cleaning days, which was when he stripped down to his swim trunks. She daydreamed about him as she watched his muscles glisten under the hot sun. She was becoming quite amorous, like her mother Tess, and she frequently fantasised about losing her virginity.

As she lay on her bed watching a romantic scene on TV she suddenly became aroused. She masturbated but wanted more, so thought taking a walk would take her mind off things. From a distance, she saw Charlie putting tools away in the large storage sheds. She wandered over and watched him load equipment off the back of the ute.

'Hi, Charlie. I've seen you around the grounds. I'm Polly. This is my first year here.'

'Nice to meet you, Polly. I have seen you too. You're not hard to miss with that hair.' He laughed.

'Yeah, it's kind of wild and red, isn't it?' Polly's hands stroked her hair in an almost erotic way. 'My mum had the same hair, so I guess that's where I get it from.'

Charlie just said, 'I have to keep moving and get these tools away.'

Polly looked around to see if any teachers were about, and then followed him into the storeroom.

'Hey, you probably shouldn't be in here,' said Charlie, sounding somewhat nervous.

'Why not?' Polly shrugged. 'I'm not doing anything wrong.'

As Charlie bent over to stack some equipment, Polly swiftly moved closer so that she could practically grind herself against him.

'Hey, stop that,' said Charlie as she suddenly lifted her thigh and hooked it around his waist.

'Come on, Charlie, I've been fantasising about you since the moment I saw you.' She pressed harder against him.

They were both breathing rapidly, pheromones and sexual desire filling the shed. Charlie suddenly pulled at her dress and lifted it up over her head. He gasped when he saw she wore no underwear. Polly pulled his head to her pale smooth breasts and let his tongue roam over her nipples. Her body felt on fire and she wanted more. 'Come on, Charlie, I want you to fuck me.' Polly's voice was low and she was breathing hard.

Charlie said nothing, but his breathing quickened as he stepped out of his jeans.

Polly looked at his erection. 'Yeah, that's what I want.'

As she lay in bed that night, the pleasure outweighed the slight pain at losing her virginity. It hurt at the start but it got more enjoyable. She wanted more, much more.

Just before Polly left for the Christmas holidays, she met with Charlie again. 'I'm going to get into serious trouble, Polly, if anyone finds out.'

'I won't tell anyone. I just want you and what you've got between your legs. It makes me feel so good, you sliding in and out of me. I've been fantasising about you for weeks since our last time.'

Charlie felt a flood of desire shivering across his body as he reached for her. Polly gasped as he entered her, trembling from exhilaration. 'You feel so good,' she murmured as his lips hungrily met hers.

Polly flew home to Woodside for the school holidays. She closed her eyes on the journey home and thought about Charlie. She wanted more from him and liked the sensation that sex brought to her body. Her thoughts turned to Jesse and she smiled. *When you're older, I could certainly show you what I've learned.*

◊

Mitch had been seeing Dr Rebekah Adams on a personal and intimate level. His relationship with her was entirely different than it had been with Tess. It was a real emotional connection, and not just sex. He was making love with this woman. Rebekah was a loving partner, and he trusted her without question. Each drew upon their own knowledge and experience to make their relationship work. For the first time in his life in a relationship, he felt nurtured and fulfilled.

They both waited at the airport and would tell Polly of their involvement in due course. As Polly walked cross the tarmac, there was an air of confidence about her. She walked tall as she made her way to the entrance door to the airport.

'Gosh, that's my girl. She looks great.'

'That she does, Mitch,' replied Rebekah. 'Koombala has been very good for her.'

On the drive home, Polly talked non-stop about the school. 'I'm happy there, Dad. It's been great for me. How's everything at home? Have you seen Jesse? How is Olivia?'

'That's a flurry of questions, Polly.' He smiled. 'Well, in that order, everything at home is good. Jesse rode over yesterday to see Olivia, and as always, Livvy is Livvy. A happy camper. They have both loved the schools they're attending.'

Polly rolled her eyes. 'And you, Dad? I can feel something happening here.'

Rebekah laughed. 'Very intuitive, Polly. Yes, your father and I have been seeing each other.'

'Not really intuitive,' replied Polly. 'I saw you holding hands as I came through the entrance doors.'

'Well then. The cat's out the bag. How do you feel about that, Polly?' Mitch watched her reaction.

'Mmm, I think it's great. You deserve to be happy, Dad.'

For the next four weeks, the house was noisy with both the girls and visitors from Woori. Lisa commented on how grown up Polly looked, and there was something different about her.

Polly was still very drawn to Jesse but all she could think of was Charlie and how he made her feel. She wanted to try different sexual things and was so preoccupied with her thoughts in this regard that she could not wait to return to Koombala. If she left now, she could have more holiday time at Koombala and more time with Charlie. The other boarders would not be there as they would all still be on holidays. Polly had been sexually awakened and she loved the feeling of power and control.

Rebekah spoke to Polly the night before she flew back to Sydney. 'Are you okay, Polly, with everything? School, here, your father and me? You know you can ask me or tell me anything.'

'No, I'm good. I like it there, Rebekah. I thank you for calling every week, and Jill the psychiatric nurse usually rings on a Wednesday. I am taking my meds, but I miss all the stuff at school. I don't have as much to do out here, and I have a little project I'm working on at school that I want to get back to.'

'I can understand that, Polly. There is not a lot to do unless you are inclined to do so from a rural perspective,' said Rebekah. 'But you know I'm here if you need me.'

THIRTY-EIGHT

AN UNSUCCESSFUL ATTEMPT

Polly was so excited when she finally returned to Koombala in the late afternoon. The school was almost deserted. There were no teachers and very few students. She could not wait to see Charlie.

She wandered around the ground after breakfast and finally found him at the pool complex. He smiled as he watched her approach. Polly was easy and up for anything, which he found sexually stimulating. He walked back towards the change rooms and waited for her, and the light that filtered through the windows gave a hazy appearance to the room. There was a lounge area that led out to the French doors, which he locked.

Polly slowly opened the door when he suddenly grabbed her and held her against him. He kissed her forcefully, and her body quickly responded to his urgency. 'I want to try everything that you know. Teach me. Teach me, Charlie.'

'Let's fuck then, my redhead tiger.'

Polly lay back on the lounge and let him roam her body.

The pool house became their regular meeting place, and Mitch queried why Polly didn't seem to want to come home for the April school holidays.

'I can do more here, Dad,' she pleaded. 'I get bored now when I come home.'

'Alright, have it your way. But the next break, you're coming home. No excuses. We all want to see you. If you won't come home, Rebekah and I will head down and take you out to dinner. Are you okay with that, Pol.'

'Yes, that's fine, Dad, and thank you for understanding.' When Polly put the phone down, she knew the next break was July, the winter holidays. *Nope, Dad, I'm not going back then either.*

Over the ensuing months, there was nothing Polly did not learn sexually. The more sex she had, the more she wanted. Even though she increased her sexual activity with Charlie, it was never enough. It was like an addiction. She remembered the times when her mother had taken men to bed, and the groans she'd heard coming from her room. Now she knew what that was all about.

When the next holidays came around, Polly again refused to come home. Mitch and Rebekah became quite concerned so drove down to Sydney and stayed for a few days.

There was nothing overt about her that caused alarm. 'I think she's just exercising her own rights somehow, Mitch. She seems perfectly normal to me, and your discussions with Mrs Deerfield only revealed that she was a studious and co-operative student. What more can we do or say? She's happy at Koombala. She uses the pool a great deal and mixes with the other boarders who also didn't want to go home. So it's nothing unusual, apart from expressing a desire to not come home.'

'But I want her home, so do Dad and Livvy.'

'All in good time, Mitch. She's seventeen now and clearly making her own decisions.'

◊

It was mid-spring, and the warmer days had arrived. The cool air in the morning was invigorating. Charlie had been missing for the entire month of August and two weeks into September. He had planned a surfing holiday to Bali with his mates. Polly became extremely anxious at his departure and was quite sulky and moody in his absence. She feigned sickness for some of her classes and preferred the solace of her room. She looked at the medication on her dresser and threw the bottle at the wall.

'I'm not taking this shit anymore!' she said, her agitation growing.

Mrs Deerfield called Mitch and advised him of her erratic behaviour, and Rebekah was in contact almost on a daily basis. Again, there was nothing to indicate anything that involved mental illness. Her conversations with Rebekah were steady and there was no formal thought disorder. She lied about her compliancy with medication.

'So why the change?' Mitch asked Rebekah, confused.

'I really don't know. Should this continue, I will go down there and see her, but I can only justify her behaviour as induced by hormones and going through different phases. Mrs Deerfield said that she has had the prescriptions filled for Polly that I've sent down. But Polly did say she was looking forward to coming home.'

◊

Polly struggled now to control her sexual fantasies, masturbated excessively and was continually restless and nervous if she did not engage in sexual behaviours. She paced her room such that the other students complained, and Belinda, the Year 12 prefect, was called in to chat to her about any issues. She had drawn a line through each day on her calendar until finally the last day was marked off. Charlie should be here tomorrow.

She skipped her lessons and wandered the grounds, desperately looking for him. Monday was always pool day yet he was nowhere to be seen. She returned later in the afternoon and was relieved to see him cleaning the pool. 'Charlie, I'm so glad you're back,' she said as she ran towards him.

From the window of her office, Mrs Deerfield saw Polly run across the grounds and then spotted Charlie. She watched their interaction and was astounded when Polly threw her arms around his neck. Her jaw dropped as she took his hand and seemingly dragged him towards the pool house.

'My goodness, this is not the right behaviour,' she said to herself as she hurriedly made her way to June Davey's office, the Assistant Principal, quickly explaining that she might need assistance. 'I'll tell you on the way, June,' she stated as they headed down the stairs to make their way across the grounds.

◊

'I've so missed you. I've missed you in me. I want you now. I just can't wait,' said Polly, wrapping her arms around him.

'Polly, maybe we should cool it,' said Charlie.

'Cool it! Are you for fucking real!' She was outraged.

'Polly, be quiet, someone will hear you,' Charlie said as he grabbed her arms, trying to steady her.

'Have you missed me?' she demanded.

'Yes Polly, I have... but.'

'No more talk. I want you to fuck me.' She pulled his swimmers down and then dropped to her knees, taking him into her mouth.

Charlie moaned with pleasure until he couldn't stand it anymore and pushed her back onto one of the lounges.

He was fucking her hard as the door slowly opened. The ladies gasped in shock when they saw the scene before them.

'What the devil is going on here!' Mrs Deerfield demanded.

'Get out, Charlie, and you, Polly Walker, will get yourself dressed and appear in my office. At once!'

By the time Polly cleaned up and got dressed, it was nearly 3: 30 p.m. She made her way to Mrs Deerfield's office and dreaded the confrontation.

Mrs Deerfield removed her glasses. 'Sit down, Polly. Suffice to say, what June and I saw just then is entirely inappropriate. This is not the behaviour we expect from students at Koombala. Needless to say, Charlie will no longer be working here, and as for you, young lady, I will call your father and advise him of the situation. I'll be recommending expulsion. As I said, this behaviour is not and will never be tolerated at my school! Go to your room and Belinda will look in on you later.'

Polly stood up. Her eyes were cold.

'Do you have any excuses for this behaviour?' the principal asked.

'No,' she smiled slyly. 'I simply enjoyed it. Lots.' The she turned on her heel and left the room.

It was just after 6 p.m. when Mrs Deerfield touched base with Mitch.

'I am flabbergasted, what can I say Mrs Deerfield? I'm so sorry she has humiliated herself and for any damage this may cause Koombala.'

'I have recommended expulsion, Mr Walker. I've sent Polly to her room, and you can collect her tomorrow.'

Mitch called Rebekah. 'Oh my God, it makes sense now. Polly has obviously developed some sort of relationship or an infatuation with someone who worked at the school, which is why she didn't want to come home. I will try and speak to her when I get off the phone with you.'

'That would be great, Rebekah.' His voice was tinged with sadness. 'I'm heading down there to pick her up tomorrow. Do you want to come?'

'Yes, of course, Mitch. Please swing by my home on the way through. I'll be ready.'

◊

Belinda knocked softly on Polly's door. There was no answer. When she opened the door, Polly lay on her bed with her back towards the door.

'Hey Polly, it's Belinda. Mrs Deerfield asked me to come and check on you. Are you okay?'

Polly's eyes were red from crying. 'I don't want to talk to anyone,' she said as she wiped her nose.

'Your father has apparently been calling you as well as a lady called Rebekah.'

'Yes, I know. I can see all the messages pushed under my door.'

'Why don't you have a shower and get out of your school uniform. Freshen up, Pol. I can get you some dinner and bring it up here to your room.'

Polly liked Belinda. She was always kind to the girls, and they all looked up to her. Dux of the school, tall and athletic, she never put a foot wrong.

'Sure,' Polly replied. 'The other girls are probably laughing at me.'

'No one is laughing, Polly, I can assure you. We all want to help. Come on.' Belinda helped her to her feet. 'Will you be okay if I duck across to the kitchen and find your dinner.'

Polly nodded as she collected her dressing gown and walked slowly to the shower block.

Polly stared at the floor and felt a great emptiness. She felt herself sliding down into the black hole of depression, and her old feelings of worthlessness and self-hate began to surface. *It's all my fault. What will Dad say? What will they all say?*

She dragged the stool across to the showers and stood on it, her head reaching the metal bar of the shower curtain. She pulled off her school tie and then tied it to the curtain rail, tying the other end tightly around her neck. She kicked the chair. Her legs flailed in the air, her toes not reaching the floor. As she did so, another boarder, Jenny, came into the shower block, and her loud, piercing scream filled the corridors of the dormitory. Belinda ran from the kitchen and down to the bathroom where Jenny stood pointing. Belinda grabbed the stool and stood on it, pushing Polly's body upwards to relieve the pressure. By the time she did this, the supervisor, Elaine, who lived on the same level as the girls, had entered the bathroom.

'Oh my God, Polly!' Elaine shouted.

'Help me, Elaine. Just grab her legs as I lower her down.' With Polly on the floor, Belinda ripped the tie from her neck and began vigorous and prompt resuscitation as Elaine sprinted off to call an ambulance.

Polly's eyes fluttered once, then closed.

'Come on, Polly, breathe.' Belinda kept on with the CPR.

◊

Mrs Deerfield dreaded making the call, and there was no easy way to say it.

Mitch was enjoying the solitude with an evening beer when he took the call. 'Hello, Mr Walker, it's Mrs Deerfield.'

Mitch took a deep breath. Why would the principal be calling at this hour? He knew somehow this was going to be bad news.

But he never expected the news that Mrs Deerfield delivered. When he put the phone down, his emotions were pushed to the point of agony. He slumped on a chair and cried for his daughter. Then he phoned Rebekah.

THIRTY-NINE

FORENSIC PSYCHIATRY UNIT

When Mitch arrived at Rebekah's home that same night, she was already waiting for him. They stood there momentarily holding on to each other. Then Mitch said, 'Come on, she's been taken to St Vincent's Hospital in Sydney for now, but later on we can transfer her back to Walgett.'

They were met at the hospital by the consultant psychiatrist, Professor Dianne Burnett.

'Please sit down. I'm sorry you're here under such sad circumstances, Dr Adams, Mr Walker. But it is a pleasure to meet you, Dr Adams.'

'Likewise, Professor Burnett. I have read a few of your papers over the years.'

'I'll get straight to the point. Polly is lucky she was found early. As you know, Dr Adams, consciousness is lost after about 13–14 seconds. Polly will probably have retrograde amnesia, which is no memory of the event. The amnesia occurs primarily on the basis of circulatory interruption. She had a weak pulse and shallow breathing when she arrived here, but her Glasgow Coma Scale was 4. I understand they acted swiftly at the school with resuscitation methods, so in terms of a neurological outcome, prognostically it may be good.'

Rebekah exhaled. 'Yes, it is fortunate she was found quickly. I have been treating Polly for some time and everything has been fine up until now. I kept in touch weekly, as well as a psychiatric nurse, and there was no indication whatsoever of any issues that were disturbing her. Apparently, she'd developed some sort of a relationship with a groundsman at the school, and they were caught in a fairly intimate moment. I will know more obviously when I talk to her. When can we transfer her to Walgett Hospital where I'm based?'

'I would give it a couple of days, Dr Adams. I gather you will be doing psychometric testing on her in six or seven weeks to check for any higher cortical dysfunction?'

'What does this all mean? You doctors have lost me,' interrupted Mitch.

'Sorry, Mitch, it's a test we do to check the higher deficits to see if there are any neurological sequalae. I'll explain a bit more in detail later,' Rebekah said.

'If she were my patient, I would cover any sexualised behaviour issues. For some teen girls, this behaviour can be a cry for help. Sometimes teen sexual behaviour involves self-esteem issues or can even be a sign of deep depression. It's also a way of getting noticed.

'Yes, I agree,' said Rebekah. 'She was developing a bit of a fixation for the adolescent boy who lives next door so I will cover all of those issues. I won't be afraid of asking any hard questions when I'm able to.'

'Is that why Polly came under your care, Rebekah? Because of depression?'

'Polly is schizophrenic, Dr Burnett, and has been depressed in the past with severe auditory hallucinations such that she was involuntarily hospitalised for just over two years. It was a long process but she responded eventually and was compliant with her medication. But really, we don't know the triggers for this suicide attempt. I will know more when we begin therapy.'

'Adolescence is a unique and formative time. So many physical and emotional changes, and of course, combined with a diagnosis of schizophrenia it becomes much more complicated. Good luck with it all.'

◇

Polly was transferred to Walgett Hospital three days later. She sat in the hospital bed with Rebekah in a chair next to her when finally arriving. 'I didn't really want to die, but I kind of wanted the pain to stop. The voices to stop. When Mrs Deerfield found me, I felt like everyone was laughing at me. I just wanted Charlie to like me.'

'Adolescence, Polly, is not an easy transition but any sexual activity should probably be given mindful thought rather than just driven by sexual thoughts and desires. We need to eventually discuss what is normal sexual behaviour.'

She stared blankly at Rebekah. 'I liked the feelings! I liked what he did to me. It made me feel good and I wanted more! I remember listening to my mother. The men groaned. So did Charlie. I have that same power.'

Rebekah was taken aback by her comment. 'You need to understand the relevancy and power of sexualisation, Polly, both from a mental, emotional and physical point of view.'

Polly ignored her and stared out the barred windows of the hospital.

Rebekah knew it would again be a difficult road. Most teenage girls believed that sex equalled love, but sexual preferences were learned behaviours, and the conversations she'd had with Mitch about Tess and her promiscuity came back into her mind.

For the next six months, Polly was up and down. She was frequently moody and aggressive with hospital staff, and when Mitch, Dave and Olivia visited, she would often refuse to see them.

She also refused her anti-psychotic medication, repeatedly expressing vehemently her desire to avoid all medication treatment. However, her schizophrenia symptoms worsened and she began having paranoid delusions. She yelled at the staff and refused to eat her meals, believing they were poisoned.

Rebekah persevered. She knew it would take patience and determination to try and persuade Polly to take the medication.

After joining in a group session, Polly suddenly became interested in an adolescent male patient. It did not go unnoticed by Rebekah, but no one expected to find them having sex in the facility storeroom.

'He's not the first!' Polly yelled.

It was heartbreaking to give this news to Mitch.

'What do we do now? For God's sake, what do we do!' said Mitch, intensely frustrated. 'This is her third admission and things seem to just get worse!'

'We persevere, Mitch.'

'Yes, but for how long? How long, Rebekah!'

'I cannot tell you that. For as long as it takes.'

They continued as they had done before with group and individual therapy, psychoeducation and rehabilitation. However, after Polly viciously attacked one of the young nurses and accused her of being an imposter, Rebekah advised that the current course of action was clinically and ethically inappropriate.

Polly was to remain an involuntary patient and was classified a danger to herself and others. She was transferred to a forensic psychiatry unit. As Rebekah explained, violent and dangerous persons who committed crimes but were found not guilty due to mental illness can be detained for as long as needed in a forensic psychiatric unit. Polly remained in hospital for nearly five years. She was psychotic and delusional and frequently attacked the nurses, often being sedated due to her actions.

Along with Rebekah, there was now a small team assigned to assist in her wellbeing, not only to help with Polly's rehabilitation but also for the safety of the public. The aim was not so much to predict violence but to prevent violence. Polly was assigned to hospital under the mental health legislation to detain people in hospital as opposed to getting a prison sentence. Charges were never laid by the people

Polly had assaulted, and the management of her now involved a team of professionals.

A specific legal order was made to allow Polly, who had ongoing mental illness, to be given medication by injection. Clearly, left to her own devices she would not take daily pills. Due to her behaviour and non-compliance, Rebekah had provided both injection and medication.

Dave and Mitch were beyond words. Their grief at the situation was profound. Polly has missed completing her education while the others around her flourished.

FORTY

FATAL ENVY

Five years later

Mitch Walker was quite nervous and full of apprehension when he arrived at Walgett Hospital with Rebekah. Polly was finally being discharged. It was 1993, and she was now twenty-two. It had been a roller coaster of relapses, and it had taken its toll on her. She had a lack of emotional expression with fewer facial expressions. As Mitch told Rebekah, she appeared almost 'wooden'. Polly would often wear the same clothes for days and showered less often. But the most significant thing was her the way she seemed to be in a dreamlike state, just not quite all there. This was a side effect of the new medication she was on to control her schizophrenia. She was also highly suspicious of everything. However, she had been deemed recovered enough to be discharged.

'I'll be with you all the way, Mitch. I have medications and injections, and I shall monitor her every day. I'm hoping she will settle at Woodside. If not, then I am afraid she may require further hospitalisation. But let's concentrate on giving Polly her best shot at life.'

'I am so tired of this, Rebekah. It's an exhausting process.'

'We have to continue supporting her, Mitch. Emotional support from a loving family will play a huge role in Polly's recovery. Studies have shown that patients are likely to recover sooner when a family provides support and care.'

'I'm not sure how that's going to work. Olivia, although a young woman herself, is frightened of her, and the time lapse has meant their closeness or what they had previously has gone. She's now always next door with Lisa and her family. I feel I have lost my baby girl because of all this shit. I hope things can get back on track. Dad is not well and cannot cope with any more upheavals.'

'I understand, Mitch, which is why I'm here. Why I closed my practice.'

◇

A few months passed, and the quietness and family support as well as Rebekah being with Polly finally saw results in her behaviour. She was now riding horses again and also enjoyed riding the fences on the quaddy. It was getting hotter in the day as the weather warmed up, so Polly was often up early. She had the place to herself as Olivia was sitting her Year 12 exams, even though she was almost six months younger than the twins.

When Olivia finished school and arrived home for the Christmas holidays, she was initially apprehensive to be with Polly. But with Rebekah's assistance and Livvy's good nature and empathy for people, she relaxed and made an attempt at rekindling the relationship with her sister.

'I'm pleased you're getting stronger every day, Polly. You've had a rough few years, and I'm so sorry this has all happened to you. It's nice to have you home.'

'It's good to be home, Olivia. You're all grown up now and look so different, so much like Dad. How are your friends next door?'

'Thank you. You're all grown up too. I guess we can't stay babies forever. I love my school and have learned so much.'

Polly stared blankly at Olivia, her voice almost a monotone, 'Yeah, I stuffed up there, didn't I? It's going to be a farm life for me. And Jesse, what does he look like now?'

Olivia was taken aback and did not know where to look or how to address Polly's question. She had asked so quickly.

She paused. 'Jesse is good. He went to Orange Ag and really excelled in everything. We should arrange a ride or something so we can all catch up.'

'I'd like that. Very much.'

Life settled over the ensuing weeks but there was un uneasiness that permeated Woodside. Mitch was grateful for his relationship with Rebekah and the fact that she had given up her practice to not only be with him but to monitor his daughter. He knew in his heart that Polly would never be the same, but for now, he was happy she was responding and both girls were home for Christmas.

◊

The Woori and Woodside crews, plus Lisa's brother Mark, had decided to all meet for a pre-Christmas lunch at the Walker's dam. When they arrived, it was just after three and some of the sting from the heat of the day was subsiding.

Zena threw some tablecloths on the benches, and they spread some food out, covering it with the fly veils.

Alan, Billy and the others wandered around the perimeter of the dam.

'It's so big,' said Jesse. 'How deep is it, Alan?'

'Maybe about twenty feet in the middle. It's the biggest I've seen but all for a good reason. A dam that is deeper and has steeper sides will retain water for longer, and the water is a lot cooler, so it reduces evaporation,' said Alan.

They all looked up at the approaching noise. 'Here they come now, let's head back to the shed,' said Alan.

Dave waved as they came towards them and slowly pulled up his Land Rover away from the sheds so he didn't get red dust over everything. Mitch and Olivia were following on the quadbike.

'This will do here,' said Dave. 'Don't want to get too close. Bloody dust gets on everything.'

Mitch roared towards them.

'He'd better not come too close, or the dust will get over the food,' said Zena. As she shooed the flies away, the Walkers and Rebekah made their way over to the table.

Jesse, now a strapping eighteen-year-old young man, stayed close to Billy and Lisa. He looked at Polly sitting next to Rebekah and still felt anger. Their eyes locked. Much time had passed, and she was now a woman, but he still felt the cruelty she had dealt to the little emu, Ume, all those years ago. And now she was back home after five years of institutionalisation. He could feel there was something very different about her.

Polly suddenly got up and came towards Jesse. She hadn't been able to take her eyes off him, even though he was still a few years younger than her. But he was beautiful, with something so earthy and masculine about him. His dark hair fell in waves to his broad shoulders. Her throat went dry as something stirred in her sexually. She could practically taste his lips on hers as she stared at him with an almost predatory intent. He was a sensual feast. Polly wanted him. Visions of Charlie flashed through her mind. She wanted to do those things with Jesse.

'Can I get you a beer, Jesse?' Polly asked.

His shoulders stiffened and there was no mistaking the tension in his frame. She just made him uneasy, even though he was physically so much bigger than her. She was tall, like her mother had been, but reed thin.

'That would be lovely, Polly,' said Lisa. 'How about it, Jesse?' She was doing her best to make the young woman feel welcome, even though even she couldn't help but notice the way Polly stared at her son.

'Water, just water is fine, thanks Polly.' Jesse's voice was abrupt. 'But I can get it myself,' he said, dismissing Polly as he strode past her. He wanted to move away from her.

'Oh, no problem.' Polly's eyes narrowed. She did not like being so easily dismissed. The young men she'd had sexual encounters with found her very alluring and attractive, and she had enjoyed her fair share of them. While in the hospital, there had been so many places she had fucked the cleaners and in-patients. A smirk crossed Polly's lips. *Shame I got caught.*

Mum Shirl nudged Ningali. 'Da devil here today.'

Olivia had quickly joined Jesse after he'd gone to get his drink. 'Hey, you,' she said.

He softened as they sat back down together. Then he started teasing her about throwing her in the dam. She laughed and bantered that he'd never get her anywhere near that dam.

Polly stared at them, her hunger intensifying for him. She wanted to feel his full mouth on hers. He looked like a man now, and he was so different to the men she had been with. *I want him. I want him to pay me some attention.* Polly got up and walked over to them. 'I'll swim with you, Jesse. I'm a good swimmer.'

Jesse stared at the young woman. He felt an energy coming from her that made him uncomfortable. He knew everyone had heard what Polly had said.

'Go on, Jesse, you can swim with Polly. I'm not getting in!' said Livvy.

Jedda laughed. 'Still hate the water, Livvy?'

But Billy's breath caught in his throat as he looked into Polly's stormy eyes. He felt danger. He knew that look. Polly was into Jesse.

'Maybe later. Not now,' said Jesse, with a tight smile.

Olivia quickly interjected. 'Let's ride on the quaddy, Jesse. How about we go for a spin around the dam instead?'

As Olivia took off, Jesse's long legs overtook her and then he swept her up off her feet.

'Those two are having fun,' said Rebekah.

'Yes, they have a special connection. Always have had. Olivia is a lovely young woman,' said Zena.

Polly watched them run off. A predatory calmness began seeping into her soul, the envy building. *Why does Olivia have all his attention? Why does Olivia have everything? No medication, no institutionalisation.* Despite her mental illness, she knew men found her attractive, and she knew she would be able to pleasure Jesse far more than her baby sister could. Olivia was probably still a virgin, after all. Polly had had much more experience with men. If only Jesse would give her a chance. She ached to feel him naked next to her, to touch his beautiful skin. *I could teach you some of the things I've learned, Jesse.*

Mitch stood up and yelled as Jesse roared around the top lip of the dam and off into the distance. 'You two, stay away from the edge. Those bloody things roll.'

'It's okay, Mitch,' said Alan. 'He wouldn't do anything that was dangerous. He's been driving every piece of equipment I've got for years. Sat his backside in the old paddock basher when he was about nine. Got his driver's licence a few weeks back.'

Rebekah looked at Polly as she sat motionless, watching the pair in the distance. Something told her there was a lot more background to this trio.

'Alright, Polly?' she asked as she got up and sat down next to the young woman.

'Fine, Rebekah. I just want someone to come swimming with me. It's so hot, so jumping in the dam to cool off would be fun.' Her voice trailed off as she watched her sister and Jesse in the distance, her fists clenching under the table.

Ningali nudged Mum Shirl. She sat quietly on the second table with Kev, Lisa and Billy. They both watched Polly, and they read each other's thoughts.

It was Mum Shirl who spoke, in their own language. 'Da darkness, she here. Got da black heart.'

Ningali nodded.

As Jesse and Livvy sat down after getting off the quad bike, the chatter began back and forth and for a while and it felt like old times to Dave. Lisa could see he was so happy and caught Zena's eye. She nodded with the sense of something achieved.

'Jesse, would you like to come for a ride with me on the quaddy? I love speeding around on that thing,' said Polly.

His eyes widened as a few seconds of embarrassment set in. Jedda looked at her brother and was about to say something when she felt Lisa grab her arm under the table.

'Maybe later? I just got back and want to get stuck in to this tucker.' He started to help himself to some food.

'If you can go with Olivia, why not me? I want to have some fun too.' Polly crossed her arms, fierce and serious. The table fell silent.

Olivia looked at her sister and felt sorry for her. 'It's okay, Polly, I can go with you if you like. I know it's always much more fun when you ride it with someone else.'

A million chattering voices were filling Polly's head, and she suddenly felt a cold calm settle over her mind. She stared across the table at Olivia. 'I'll drive,' she said as she rose from the table.

'Pol, just stay away from the dam and head out in the paddocks,' said Mitch.

Rebekah was nervous. 'Is it wise, Mitch? I mean to let them go out there? You said it was easy to tip.'

'They know how to ride it, so they'll be fine,' said Mitch.

The girls walked to the Quadrunner, and Jesse stood up. He didn't want Olivia on the back.

'Livvy, be careful,' warned Jesse.

'All good, Jesse, be back soon. We'll just have a bit of fun, won't we, Pol?'

As they took off, Jesse stared into the distance after them. He was clearly unsettled.

'Proper bad. I don't like dis. Something not good here,' said Mum Shirl.

Jesse walked over to Billy and Lisa. 'I don't like it,' he said.

'I feel da same, Jesse. Just watch. We make a move if any trouble,' said Billy.

'You men are frightening me,' Lisa whispered.

'Yes, you are,' said Jedda. They sat and watched the girls in the distance. Mitch opened a few more beers.

'Polly needs to slow down,' added Dave. 'She's going too fast now, way too fast.'

'I can see that, Dad. She can't hear me way out there but I swear I will kill Polly if anything happens to Olivia because of her stupidity. I don't know why she's doing those circles.'

'Showing off?' asked Dave, the fear lurking behind his words.

'I think we should start to pack up when they come back,' said Zena.

Jesse suddenly jumped up and started running in the direction of the two women. 'Livvy,' he yelled. Billy quickly followed.

Jedda jumped to her feet, scrambling for her shoes. 'You stay right here, Jedda,' said Lisa. 'I don't want you over there.'

Polly sped towards the group and then swung the quadbike to make a large circle halfway from where they were sitting. Faster and faster, she was trying to pick up more speed. Olivia's yells to slow down could be heard in the distance. It was plain to see that Polly was headed at breakneck speed towards the dam.

'What the hell she is doing! No, no Polly, stop!' Mitch roared as he began running after Jesse and Billy.

'My God, Alan, what is she doing?' Zena's throat constricted.

'No idea, but something is terribly wrong.' Alan threw down his beer and bolted in the direction of Jesse and Billy. Jesse was covering ground quickly, but he was a long way off.

Lisa shuddered as Rebekah came to her side. 'Dave, take the car and head that way,' said Lisa, the panic in her voice audible. Kev, please go with Dave. We best stay here, please hurry!' She willed herself to stay calm but she feared for the worst.

They all watched in horror as Polly was making no attempt to stop. She made one last large circle, almost toppling over with the rapid turn of the bike. Livvy was yelling as Polly had her shoulders hunched towards the bars of the bike.

'Stop, Polly!' Jesse bellowed, but as Polly reached the rim of the dam, the quadbike suddenly became airborne and flipped over. It was like a horrible nightmare, watching the machinery fly into the air and then disappear down into the murky depths of the dam.

Jesse dived in, with Billy and Mitch quickly following. Alan watched helplessly as they continued to dive and search, coming up for air. But he knew that the weight of the quadbike, some 400 kilograms, hitting the girls would have knocked them unconscious. He felt his heart was being ripped out. He knew the consequences. Visibility in any dam was virtually nil, and the water two metres under was very cold.

They dived for nearly twenty minutes, exhausted, until their lungs were screaming from pain. Jesse made one last dive until he felt something. Which girl was it? He pulled and began to struggle for the top, the blonde hair now visible as he reached the surface. He desperately swam to Alan who grabbed Olivia by both arms and pulled her to the rim of the dam, commencing CPR. Her lips were blue, but he kept pumping her chest while Jesse blew the air into her mouth.

'Wake up, wake up! Olivia! Keep going, Alan.' Jesse was wild with grief as his body shook from cold and shock. 'Please, my lady bird, come back to me.' The anguish in his voice was clear as the tears streamed down his face. 'Don't stop, Alan, press harder. Livvy!'

Their resuscitation attempts continued for what seemed like an eternity until Alan sadly looked across to a distraught Jesse. 'I'm so sorry, Jesse. She's gone.'

Jesse cradled her lifeless and broken body as he stroked her muddy hair, his breath coming in jagged gasps as sobs wracked his body. 'Livvy, my Livvy.' He kissed her face gently and rocked her slowly in his arms.

Mitch and Billy had dragged themselves from the water after not finding Polly. Mitch staggered across to Jesse as he saw him sobbing and clutching Olivia's lifeless body. His eyes were wild and reckless and he felt the pressure of grief would crush him to the ground. Billy stood dripping wet next to Dave, who had pulled up in the Land Rover with Mark and Kev. They looked at the young girl's lifeless body. She was dead.

'Olivia gone to da Dreamtime,' said Billy softly, tears forming in his eyes at the heartbreaking sound of his son's pain and the loss of this beautiful young woman that they had known since she was a young girl.

Mitch crumbled to his knees, frantically checking Olivia for a pulse as he cursed the air, the sky, the clouds, both hands brushing away the tears that fell from his eyes. His face twisted with grief as he looked across to his father, whose face had turned ashen, and he just shook his head. Kev caught Dave as he began to fall, his mouth open in a frozen scream as the exploding pain in his heart paralysed him.

Mitch's cries and gulping sobs carried across the plains. 'I should never have let her go, never let her go,' he sobbed into the earth, the grief nearly choking him. Sorrow and death filled the air.

FORTY-ONE

ANGELS SING THEE TO THY REST

Dave Walker had suffered a massive stroke, losing his speech and most of his sight. The whole right side of his body was paralysed. He had been transported to Walgett Hospital. There was not much they could do. It was a haemorrhagic stroke, where the artery had burst causing bleeding into the brain. Although surgery was performed and a drain inserted to remove the blood, there was catastrophic damage.

Rebekah tried to console Mitch as best as she could. Every day was filled with grief and agonising emotional pain for him.

Polly's body was recovered by the police the following day after it floated to the surface. She was buried next to her mother in Walgett Cemetery. Mitch sat solemnly by the graveside with Rebekah, Zena and Alan as the minister delivered the service. It was brief and swift. The distraught father of two, now none, stared into the distance as the minister spoke.

'Death reminds us that we live in a fallen and imperfect world. We are reminded of our failings, our flaws and our limitations. But always God has a solution, something greater than the painful re-minder.'

Mitch scoffed and suddenly stood up. 'What solution did he have for my daughters or my father? They're dead and he's a vegetable!' He strode off, Rebekah following him and trying to calm him down.

Two days later, the funeral for Olivia was held in Walgett with a memorial service to follow at the RSL.

Jesse refused to come. He did not want to see her body lying in a box. Lisa tried desperately to console him, but he had closed down, refusing to speak or eat. He was in a haze of shock. Since Olivia's death, they could hear Jesse walking the floors at night, pacing back and forth.

'My darling Jesse, I know you're hurting and the pain is unbearable, but Olivia would want you to be, well, she would not want you to be so sad. We are all hurting, Jesse, so much. I feel this horrible pain in my heart too, so does Billy, but sometimes it helps to say goodbye.'

'I don't want to say goodbye. I want her back. Why did this happen to her? Why, Mum? She was...' Jesse's voice broke into heaving sobs that wracked his body.

Lisa felt so powerless as she looked at her son. 'She will always be with you, Jesse. Olivia lives in your heart and soul. Emulate her by living with her spirit and joy for life. Please think about coming with us to say the final goodbye.' Lisa's tears spilled down her cheeks.

Billy pulled the Land Rover up at the main gates and came into the house where Lisa sat with Jesse.

'You come, Jesse?' he said, the sadness tearing at his own heart. Billy gently took his son's hands.

'After death, we believe da spirit returns to da Dreamtime. From da Dreamtime, it return through birth as da human, animal, plant or rock. Da shape not important, Jesse, because each form shares da same soul or spirit. Livvy always with us.'

'I will always love her. All my life,' said Jesse as his shoulders dropped in resignation. 'I don't want to come.'

'We best go now, Billy, or we'll be late.' As Lisa rose to her feet, she cupped her son's face in her hands and kissed his forehead.

'We will see you a bit later, my son.'

The white casket was carried into the church by Billy, Alan, Mitch and a few of the Woodside farm crew. Colourful flowers covered the top, and the church was filled with family, relatives and school friends who travelled from Olivia's school.

Jedda sat with Zena and her parents, the devastation showing on her face. She looked at her mother, the tears welling in her eyes. 'Livvy is with Ume in the sky.'

'Yes, I am sure of that Jedda,' said Lisa.

It was a gut-wrenching day. Mitch sat stony-faced, his eyes red and swollen as he listened to Alan delivering the eulogy and then the readings from her school friends. He became numb as the service went on, his shoulders hunched, a broken man. He stared blankly at his daughter's beautiful laughing face on the memorial pamphlet.

The last reading was done by Jedda. Lisa squeezed her hand as she made her way to the pulpit.

'Olivia was my best friend, and I loved her dearly. Jesse, my brother, did too. He asked me to say this for him as he could not be here: 'Fly on, my lady beetle, fly through the sky. I will be by your side again one day.'

Jedda wiped her tears and gulped. 'I have these thoughts that I will share with you. We shed tears because Livvy is gone, and our hearts are empty because we cannot see her, but she is with us. Livvy lives in our hearts, and we can all be full from the love and friendship that we shared with her. Goodbye, my friend, I will never forget you.'

The minister stood and moved to the casket. 'That concludes our service today for Olivia Walker. If anyone would like to pay their respects or come up and pray, please do so.'

Mitch stood up slowly, his face ashen as he walked to the casket, carrying a small round circle of woven sticks. He placed it on top of the casket.

'What is that, Billy?' croaked Lisa, her voice broken from sadness.

It was Jedda who spoke. 'Jesse.' She wiped her tears. 'Jesse made it for her a few years ago. It's a crown.'

343

Mitch wrapped his arm over the casket, his body wracked with wave upon wave of heavy sobs. 'Goodbye, my Olivia,' he whispered, 'May flights of angels sing thee to thy rest.'

Olivia was laid to rest next to Kate. Lisa waited until the majority of mourners had left and then walked over to Mitch, who sat with Rebekah. He stood up and tried to speak but the words would not come out. He merely put his arms around the girl he had once loved and held her tightly to him. Lisa closed her eyes and felt the wetness of his tears on her cheeks as he sobbed.

'It's okay, Mitch. Let it out, I'm here.' She sobbed as she listened to the rapid heartbeat in his chest.

◊

At that moment, Jesse walked outside of Wooribilly and stood staring at the sky. It was blue. Olivia's favourite colour. His eyes stung. He opened up his mouth, tipped his head back and roared at the top of his lungs.

When they all returned home, the house felt very quiet. 'Jesse,' Lisa called out. She went from room to room.

Billy and Jedda came inside. 'I can't find Jesse,' Lisa said.

'Jesse's ute gone,' replied Billy.

'Oh no, Billy. Where would he be, where is he?'

'Jesse need time. He mebbe go just short drive.'

'No, he is so distressed. I'm worried. Jedda, did he say something to you? Was he going somewhere?'

Jedda shook her head. 'No, Mum. He didn't. All I know is that he is heartbroken inside, like all of us, and so very sad.'

'I know, darling, we all are, but we have to go on.'

Billy came to Lisa's side, placing an arm around her. Her body trembled.

'Jesse strong boy. Just need time. I go see if I can find him.'

'Thank you, Billy. I just don't know where he can be or where he would go,' she said solemnly.

Billy traced the tracks of Jesse's car tyres, which led out of Woori. It would be devastating to Lisa if something happened to their son. He hoped Jesse was just heading out for a few hours, but his gut feeling told him something else. His son had gone walkabout.

Lisa paced the kitchen floor and stopped when she heard Billy heading home on the motorbike. It was nearly dark.

As soon as Billy came inside, Lisa knew things were not good. 'What did you find?' She was almost terrified to ask.

'Jesse, his car tyres lead out da gates.'

Lisa's tears fell as Billy pulled her to him. 'Billy, where would he go? We have to find him.' She sobbed into his arms.

FORTY-TWO

EVIL COMES KNOCKING

Two months went by and there was still no sign or word from Jesse. He had gone walkabout.

'Jesse will come back. Billy feel it. He just need to get away, my grasshopper.'

'But he's only young. Anything can happen to him,' said Lisa.

'He be fine. Jesse a survivor, learn good from me. He come home when he ready. Spirits look after our boy. I feel in my heart he be okay. Mum Shirl say da same.'

Jedda, having finished Year 12 at the end of 1993, would be studying at the Conservatorium of Music for vocal and opera studies. She was deeply affected by the loss of her friend Olivia and then Jesse's disappearance, but was looking forward to university. She was currently away for orientation in Sydney, and staying with her Uncle Mark.

Lisa and Billy counted down the days until Jedda returned. Billy drove out to the airport and waited patiently, watching the plane land. As Jedda ran towards him, he felt immense pride. 'I am so glad to see you, Dad,' she said as she let his strong arms hold her.

'You good, wild goose?' His brown eyes searched her face.

'Yes, I'm good. University orientation has been a saviour; everyone has been great. But every day I have thought of Olivia and that horrible day.'

'We do too, Jedda. But Livvy in da Dreamtime and always with us.'

Jedda sighed deeply. 'Any news of Jesse? And how is Mum?'

'No news of Jesse, and Mum, she wait for you.' Billy collected her bags. 'Come, we go. Jesse safe.'

'How do you know that for sure?' Jedda queried. Even though she also felt in her heart that her twin was safe.

'Because I do. Spirits tell me. He be safe. I would feel if something wrong, Jedda. You would too. You da twins. You connected.'

'I hope you're right. I miss him, and I miss home. Love you, Dad.'

As they turned into the last Woori gates and headed for home, Jedda saw the old familiar blue Zephyr.

'We have company tonight,' said Jedda. 'Gosh, Nan loves that old bomb. Pop always tries to get rid of it but Nan won't have a bar of it. It makes me laugh.'

'True talk. Zena, she love da car.'

'There's something sentimental about it, I guess. I must ask her one day.'

Lisa came running out when she saw them pull up. 'My darling girl.' She flung her arms around her daughter, the spitting image of her mother but for her darker skin and eyes. 'And you have grown even more. Come inside.'

It was a good night, full of stories, and it would have been almost normal if it were not for Jesse's absence.

'I asked Dad on the way home. Still no news,' Jedda said sadly.

'We hope to have him home soon. Billy said he's safe. Mum Shirl says he's safe. I wish I could feel it. But we all know that some can see and feel things that others cannot. So, I put my faith in this beautiful man sitting here.' Lisa reached over, taking Billy's hand, and he kissed it softly.

'Anyway, I think it's a great idea to catch up with your old music teacher, Lydia Upjohn, and then go on and have some lunch. Just us,' said Zena. 'Be lovely. So good to have you home, Jedda.'

When Friday came, Alan had a list of the things they needed.

'We can't fit what we want into the Land Rover and all of us, so we'll have to take separate cars,' said Alan.

'That's fine, my love. I'm taking the Zephyr as it needs a letter from the mechanic to pass inspection. Won't take long. She's in perfect running order. Old but perfect. Bit like me,' she laughed.

'Give Lisa a call then and let her know we're ready so we can get going,' said Alan.

Billy hopped into the Land Rover and waved as they took off. 'See you ladies in town at the pub,' Alan called out.

Lydia was thrilled to see Jedda and had allowed time to sit and chat with Zena and Lisa so they could all catch up. 'Such wonderful news that you have been accepted into the Conservatorium of Music. You will fly from there, Jedda. They are renowned for producing singers of exceptional quality for concert and opera stages worldwide. You'll learn so much, my dear.'

'I'm looking forward to it, Lydia. The forms that they sent to me were amazing. They cover everything from singing to languages, role-preparation acting, dance, everything. I'm very excited.'

'So you should be,' said Lydia. 'I'm sure we will see you on stage one day. All I ask is to be in the front row.' They all smiled at that.

'Right then. The usual place for lunch,' said Zena. 'Alan and Billy are probably waiting for us. It's been lovely to see you, Lydia.'

◊

As they entered the pub, the figure in the corner startled. He suddenly threw his hat on and drew the newspaper up to cover his face. Three little birdies.

Griffo had been ducking and weaving the police for nearly a decade, covering big Territory and keeping low. It was easy to avoid contact. Sleep in the cabin, pull into a pub for a feed and keep moving.

He was about to get up when he saw Alan and Billy on the street coming towards the pub. He sat down quickly and pulled the newspaper up again. But it was like an instant switch, the sensations of hate clicking on, the anger flowing into his head like a liquid nightmare, seeping. His eyes glazed as he felt his skin prickle, and the demons howled to get out. He knew he had to stay out of trouble but he felt his big hands shake as the fury began to build. *Mr Kingpin himself. Dickhead who sacked me and his black bastard.*

Griffo left the pub and walked to where he'd parked the big fuel tanker. Bastards. His pupils were dilated. Rich bastards who never have any fucking worries. Treat us like shit all the time. Getting kicked out from every fucking place.

A fierce, violent anger boiled inside. He cranked the engine of the big Kenworth tanker. He knew the way they would head home. The cars on that road were basically nil unless making deliveries to Woori or Woodside. He found the bend in the road where he sat, waiting. He looked at his watch. He wanted to hurt them. Badly.

Griffo's eyes narrowed and his heart beat rapidly as he saw the two cars approaching in the distance. The monster inside was ready to kill. He hit the ignition and revved the big Kenworth tanker, the roar from the engines howling a murderous, high-pitched noise.

When he saw the old blue Zephyr, his foot planted heavily down on the accelerator. 'Come on, baby, give me some guts,' he roared.

Zena saw the big fuel tanker heading towards them as they came around the bend. She looked into her rear vision mirror and could see Alan's Land Rover behind them, a little way back.

'Zena, what is that tanker doing?' asked Lisa nervously.

'That I cannot tell you. He's in a hurry, and that Kenworth is going too fast for these roads. The fool has taken the bend at breakneck speed.' Something turned over in Zena's stomach. 'Look at the way it's swivelling and swaying. Oh my God, Lisa!' Her eyes widened in fear. The driver of the big tanker suddenly crossed the lines and was heading directly in their path.

Griffo pressed hard on the accelerator. 'Fuckers,' he roared. 'Prepare to die. Squashed and mangled into a million fucken pieces.' His mouth was frothing as his big hands thumped the steering wheel.

'For God's sake,' bellowed Alan, watching the scene unfold up ahead. 'He's heading straight towards the women! What is he doing, that bloody reckless bastard!' He knew that any accident involving a fuel tanker would lead to catastrophic injury or death.

Alan stopped the Land Rover, and Billy yelled, 'What you doing! We need to help!'

Alan's knuckles gripped the steering wheel, feeling helpless as he restrained Billy from getting out.

'Billy, stay here, those big trucks have much longer stopping times, and we need to see what the hell he's doing. He'll collect us both if we keep going in his direction. Zena, for God's sake, swerve. That bloody old Zephyr cannot out run him!'

◇

Jedda screamed in the back as she saw the big truck bearing down on them.

'He's trying to kill us,' shouted Lisa.

Zena slammed her brakes and pulled to the left, just split seconds before she avoided the big tanker hitting them head on. It clipped the rear of her car as it fish-tailed, skewing the Zephyr sideways where it glanced off an old gum tree. The car rolled and rolled down the embankment, the windscreen shattering, the screams of Lisa and Jedda filling Zena's ears. It was the last thing she heard before everything went black.

Griffo roared and turned the steering wheel in a maddening rage. He accelerated harder, going up through the gears, his gaze settling on the Land Rover. Griffo laughed wildly as he shouted, 'Coming to get you, arsehole, and your black cunt!'

Billy wanted to get out but Alan restrained him. 'No, Billy, I said wait! Wait, he's not finished yet and they are the other side of him now. He knows what he's doing. He's blocked us.'

A yell escaped from Billy's clenched jaw. 'We go now!'

'No, I said no! For God's sake, listen to me,' Alan roared. 'We can't do anything for the women now. God, what is he doing?' The big rig hurtled towards them. Alan reversed, desperately thinking of the best way out to reach the girls. 'This is no accident. This bastard has an agenda.'

'Maniac, bloody maniac!' raged Billy as his fists banged the dashboard.

Alan's heart was pounding, and he felt a sweat breaking out. 'I'll head back across the paddocks and try and get past him that way. The mongrel can't turn as quickly as us and those rigs are not meant for paddocks.'

No sooner had Alan had done that when he heard the big engine roar louder as the unknown trucker went down through its fifteen gears, faster and faster as it charged at them, a wild beast intent on killing.

As the tanker picked up speed rapidly, attempting to cut Alan off, they saw the front tyre suddenly shred, the rubber flying into the air and blasting out, causing a loud explosion. The front wheel of the rig blew out, catapulting the tanker 100 metres and then landing on its side, skidding in a shower of sparks, the air filling with the smell of burning rubber along the hot tarred road, the 10,000 litres of fuel spilling out. The tanker came to a shuddering, screeching halt.

'Christ,' said Alan. 'Let's get to the women.' He veered around the truck racing towards the embankment where the Zephyr had rolled down.

When Alan and Billy reached them, the car was resting on its hood. Alan raced around to the driver's door and grimaced at the sight of blood dripping from Zena's mouth. There was no movement from Lisa or Jedda. They pulled at the doors, but the twisted metal was resisting their efforts. Billy roared their names, 'Lisa, Jedda,' as he yanked hard on the doors, but to no avail.

'I need a crowbar, Billy, to get these doors open. Keep trying, but I'll get the one in the Land Rover.' Alan sprinted back to his car.

When he returned, Billy shouted, 'Hurry, dey moving!' He bashed on the windows.

'Step back.' Alan jimmied the driver's door open and came to his wife's side. 'Zena, are you hurt, does anything feel broken?'

'No, I think I'm fine. I'm alright, just hit my head,' Zena groggily replied.

Billy ran around to the other side with the crowbar. 'Lisa, Lisa.' The tears spilled down his face as he prised the door open, falling to his knees, cradling her.

'My girl, Billy, my Jedda. How is she? Is she hurt?' Lisa fumbled with her seat belt, the pain dancing across her forehead.

'She unconscious,' replied Billy, his voice shaky and disbelieving.

Alan looked at Jedda. She was still alive but flopped like a rag doll as Billy began to slowly try and move her. Billy's heart was thumping so loud, he suddenly lost control, his eyes wet with tears.

'Keep it together, Billy, she may have internal injuries,' said Alan. 'We'll get them out one by one. Just support their heads as I undo the seat belts.'

After what seemed like an eternity, Alan and Billy managed to pull the three women from the wreckage. He found the travelling blanket from the Zephyr and covered Jedda, who was still unconscious. Lisa leaned against Billy's chest as she held Zena's hand. They sat on the embankment, badly shaken and shocked but no broken bones and no significant pain to reflect internal injury.

'Do we know who it was?' Zena asked.

'No, but the tanker is on its side. Blew a tyre. Someone's still inside,' replied Alan.

'Someone's inside? Oh, God no. And what is that smell?' asked Zena as she passed the water bottle to Lisa.

'Burning rubber, leaking fuel,' replied Alan.

'You should go and see who it is,' said Zena.

'I don't feel like doing that. The mongrel could have killed us. More important is what is here,' Alan said. 'I'll leave shortly and head back to Walgett for help. Billy can stay with you, but it's important you all just do as little movement as possible until medical help arrives.'

Lisa poured some water into her hands and dabbed Jedda's face. 'My darling little goose. We are all here for you.' Her body wracked with sobs, which made her head feel like it would split open. 'Oh Billy, why doesn't she wake up?'

Billy's chin trembled. 'She wake soon, Lisa.'

Jedda's eyes suddenly fluttered.

'Oh God, Jedda we're here, my darling.' Lisa held her hand and kissed her forehead.

A gut-wrenching sob escaped from Billy as he wiped his face with his shaking hands. He looked up to the sky, his eyes searching. Alan hadn't left yet and let out a huge breath of relief.

'Jedda okay?' Billy asked.

'Um, my head hurts, that's all,' Jedda whispered.

'Alan, we're fine. Shaken. If there were internal injuries, we certainly would be feeling pain, a lot of pain by now. Now please, just take Billy and see who the devil is in that cabin before you leave for Walgett.'

'Come on then, Billy,' Alan said as they headed up to the Land Rover. As they got closer to the fuel tanker, they could see movement in the cabin

'God, whoever he is, he's still alive. I'll park here, and we'll head over on foot. Don't want to leave the car too close,' said Alan. He opened his door and got out. 'Take your time, Billy. We don't know who's in that cabin. What I do know is that he wanted us all dead. Don't get too close. There is movement, but God knows what else we'll find. It could be a mess.'

As they got closer, the bloodied face of a large, bulky figure was pushed up against the shattered windscreen. The eyes glared at them as he continued to slowly move around the cabin.

'He's either trying to get out or—' Alan froze as he saw the fuel now running along the gravel road. He looked back at the shattered windscreen, and his eyes widened with fear. There was no mistaking the barrel of a gun now poking through the gaps of the broken glass.

'Get back, Billy. Run! For God's sake, run and don't stop!' Alan shouted. He grabbed Billy's arm as they turned and raced towards the Land Rover. A single gunshot rang out just before the tanker exploded. The loud wailing noise of the explosion sounded like the roar of an express train. Fiery pieces of debris flew everywhere, and there was the sickly smell of burning rubber as black smoke and orange flames swirled high into the air.

The explosion knocked them both to the ground and shattered the windows of the Land Rover. Billy lay motionless, face down in the red dirt.

Alan rolled over, his ears ringing loudly from the explosion. He shook his head and sat up to survey their surroundings, trying to make sense of the lightning-fast horror sequence of events that just befell them.

'Oh God, no!' Alan cried as he saw the blood seeping through Billy's tattered shirt. He crawled across to him and gently shook him. 'Billy, wake up!'

◊

The fireball was visible from the town as the billowing black smoke circled into the sky, and the scene was catastrophic. The tanker was reduced to a tangle of smoking, charred metal, a mangled wreck, the fire so intense that parts of the tanker melted into the bitumen. An ambulance, fire brigade and the police arrived shortly after.

After X-rays and overnight observations at Walgett Hospital, the women were discharged home. Billy only became conscious upon arrival to hospital. He was severely concussed, but the bullet had entered the rear of his left shoulder with a clean exit. The gunshot had missed any main arteries, and he had fortunately only suffered soft-tissue injury involving the muscles and ligaments. His wound was debrided to remove any remaining bullet fragments and to check for additional injuries.

Detective Lynch headed the investigation into the wreckage and confirmed the body was that of James Griffin by the dental records. His gut feeling told him that he was responsible for the death of Ernie Tubbs along with the women who had been so brutally murdered. He deeply regretted that he could not bring the man to trial to be punished to the full extent of the law and serve the rest of his days in a cell. Nevertheless, he was consoled by the fact that after all those years of evading law enforcement, the trails and leads continually going cold, justice had finally been served to the evil monster whose soul belonged to the devil.

FORTY-THREE

A YOUNG MAN RETURNS

During the year 1994, Jedda settled into the conservatorium, and it was a complete cultural immersion for her. She felt both musical and powerful, and the teachers quickly embraced her early genius for both melody and harmony, a voice combining agility, accurate intonation and a trill with a strong upper register. A natural soprano. All the early-life lessons with Zena and then Lydia had provided the source of her innate vocal prowess. Jedda could not wait to get on stage. During the first year of university, she was extraordinarily disciplined and quickly mastered the art of acting and stage presence. Her days were filled with voice lessons, acting, languages, dance classes and exercise.

Every week, Jedda would call her mother, father and Lydia to tell them of her news. She was grateful for Lydia's knowledge and assistance, being forewarned that the four years of study to obtain her degree would be intense.

After singing her first solo, her vocal teacher, Vivian Moore, knew she was ready.

'Jedda, I believe you should perform in an opera we are putting together. Do you feel you would like to do this?' asked Vivian.

'Oh, Vivian, yes. I so want to perform,' said Jedda.

We all see that, Jedda, very plainly. I have never heard such a big, wild voice, and you have seemingly endless cascades of full tone. Would you be nervous singing in front of people you don't know?'

'Not at all, Vivian. My Nan, well sort of Nan, Zena, always called me an entertaining gasbag.'

Vivian laughed. 'Okay, the role I have is Rosina from the Barber of Seville. A Rossini piece. It's a very popular opera that offers the audience a delightful romp of farcical frivolity. It's quite a madcap delight and always brings joy to the people who perform as well as the audience. The Count Almaviva is wealthy and hopelessly in love with Rosina. He wants her to fall in love with him and not for his money, so he disguises himself as Lindoro and begins to serenade her. He must prise her from the clutches of her guardian, the lecherous Bartolo. And of course, the barber Figaro has a few tricks up his sleeve.'

'It sounds wonderful,' said Jedda. 'Why did you mention wild when describing my voice?'

'Because it is this that I feel when I listen to you. Your voice is wild, raw and still developing, but so beautiful. I simply cannot wait as your singing voice matures.'

'My name in Aboriginal means little wild goose.'

'Well, there you have it, aptly named, a perfect description then. I'm delighted you said yes, Jedda. I could not imagine a more suitable role for you. We have about two months of rigorous rehearsals so eat well and exercise. I shall bring you the material but just head to the Opera Production room on Monday. You'll find that our productions have become a creative outlet for students to challenge themselves.'

Jedda gushed. 'Oh, thank you. I can't wait!'

'Don't forget to tell your parents well in advance for tickets. We'll advertise this production as it will be at the Sydney Opera House. I have an inkling they would want to be there.' Vivian smiled. 'See you Monday.'

Jedda danced around the room. 'The Sydney Opera House!' she yelled and went racing down the hallway to find a phone.

◊

Twelve months earlier, Jesse did not know where he was headed when he left Wooribilly. All he felt was desperation to get away from any reminder of Olivia and the horror of that day. He crossed the border into South Australia and kept going until he came to Coober Pedy. As he ordered a beer in the pub, the publican told him about Anna Creek Station and that they were looking for good jackaroos. 'Great place to work, and the Kidmans treat their employees well.'

When Jesse drove out to Anna Creek Station, he was met by Fred, a big, burly, ruddy-faced man who was one of the overseers. Fred laughed when Jesse first asked him how big the property was. 'Only about 24,000 square kilometres, mate. Bigger than Israel, which is only 21,000 square kilometres.'

'Who owns such a place?' asked Jesse.

'The Kidman family run it now. Good people. But Sidney Kidman started it all. They called him the Cattle King. He was a bit of a legend. He ran away from home at age thirteen with five shillings and a one-eyed horse. Sid then picked up itinerant work and earned enough to buy a bullock team, setting himself up as a carrier. Got on well with the Aboriginal people, earning their trust, working with them and learning much of their bushcraft. Worked as a drover, stockman and livestock trader and saved until he bought his own stations. Smart bloke, you should read up on him. Gave fighter planes to our armed forces during World War One, and even gave the Salvos a half share in one of his cattle stations. Wealthy but good-hearted. Lived a long, full life. You would have got on well with him, Jesse. But Sid fell off his perch long before you were born. Think it was around 1930, something like that, but he was knighted. All the family continue to run it now. You got a bit of the black stock in you?'

Jesse was taken aback. He had never heard that said before. 'Yes, Aboriginal, if that's what you mean.'

'Hey, kid, I didn't mean to offend you. Just the way I speak. When can you start?' asked Fred.

'Straight away.'

'One more thing, you're not running away from anything are you? Not in trouble with the law?'

'No. I just wanted to get away from home,' Jesse said softly.

That was twelve months ago, and Jesse proved to be one of Fred's best workers. He worked tirelessly, even on his days off, and he quickly earned the respect of his peers as well as Fred.

It was now early December 1994, and Jesse was beginning to miss home. He was now nineteen and had grown up even more working on the station. Jesse sat with the other jackaroos waiting for the cook to serve up dinner. They were a good crew, and he loved the fact that he could ride for days, see no one and still be on the same property.

'Hey, did you read this?' said Scotty, one of the crew. 'This article. Some Aboriginal girl from out west of New South Wales is causing a stir in the opera world. It shits me. Just because we live in the bush doesn't mean we don't have talent! I mean, look at me, I'm the most talented jackaroo here.'

The men started laughing as Jesse reached across for the newspaper. His eyes widened as he looked at the picture of his twin sister Jedda. He felt a deep swelling of pride. His amazing sister. She was studying at the Conservatorium of Music, and her first show was scheduled in December at the Sydney Opera House. He smiled. When he finished his dinner, he took the newspaper.

◇

The bright stage lighting made it difficult to see the audience filling the seats. Jedda knew Zena had organised a box just to the right of the stage so that they could all be together to watch the performance. She peeked from behind the curtains and saw her parents, Zena, Alan and Lydia up in the box. She was so excited and went backstage to do her vocal exercises. She took slow, deep breaths trying to ignore the quivers of nervousness, but inside she could not wait to make her debut appearance. The Concert Hall of the Opera House had 2600 seats. Vivian was backstage with all the singers, supporting and encouraging.

'How are you doing, Jedda?' she asked as she patted her gently on the back.

'I'm fine. A little nervous, but more excited.'

'That's perfectly natural. Opera can inspire so many emotions. Don't be surprised by people's reactions. Okay, everyone, we have about fifteen minutes before stage call, and people are coming to find their seats as I speak.'

◇

Zena sat reading the playbill and synopsis. 'It's going to be wonderful,' she enthused as she passed it to Lydia. 'It's been a long time since we were in black tie. Not quite sure if you like it, Billy?'

Lisa laughed as she hugged Billy. 'You look so handsome, my darling.'

Billy grunted. 'I look like da penguin.'

'Such a magnificent concert hall, isn't it, Alan?' Zena cast her eyes around the room. As she looked down into the stalls, a young man was making his way across to the middle of the row.

'My God, Alan, Lisa, everyone, look down in the stalls. There!' she said, pointing. 'The fourth row. Am I seeing things? Is that Jesse? Oh my God. It is Jesse!

Lisa stood up and watched the tall, striking figure take his seat. The tears began welling up as she tried to speak. 'Billy, it's our son. It's our Jesse.'

Billy's eyes widened. 'Jesse. I go to him.'

The lights started to dim as the chimes began. The conductor walked out to his stand and the applause of the audience resonated through the great hall.

'Lisa, sit down. We can't do anything now. We'll have to wait for intermission. He's not going anywhere, and we can see him from here,' said Alan. 'We'll catch him at intermission.'

For the next forty-five minutes, they were swept away by everything. They laughed, gasped, applauded and sat in awe of Jedda's beautiful voice, which soared out over the audience, holding them spellbound and enraptured.

As the curtains came down and the lights grew brighter, it was time to make a move. Lisa and Billy stood up quickly, as did Zena.

'Wait, can everyone just settle for a moment,' said Alan. 'Jesse has been gone for a long time after tragic circumstances. We don't know where he's been or what he's been up to, and he certainly didn't tell us he would be here. So, let's not charge at him all at once. Can I suggest that Billy head down there and speak to him alone?'

Lisa took a deep breath as she looked at Zena and Lydia. 'I just want to run down there and hold him. Hold my Jesse.'

'I know you do, but please, leave it to Billy,' said Alan.

'I think you're right again, my love. You best go down, Billy. We can see from here. Intermission is usually anything from fifteen minutes to half an hour,' said Zena.

Billy made his way down to the stalls, and the majority of the people in that row had fortunately gone down to the bar. Everyone watched from the box as Billy walked towards his son. Jesse sat reading the synopsis when he suddenly turned his gaze in the direction of his father.

Billy stood stock still as Jesse slowly rose to his feet. His boy was now a young man and he had never been prouder as a father as he was right now.

'Jesse.' Billy's voice was tight with emotion.

Jesse smiled and stepped forward, then Billy placed a hand on each shoulder. 'My son.' As they hugged, Lisa and Zena broke down when Billy extended his arm and pointed to the circle box just above them. Lisa stood up and waved to her son, the tears streaming down her face.

'Come, Jesse, we go,' said Billy, collecting his strength.

'I think we better make a move into the hallway, ladies. There's going to be tears. No room for group hugs in this box,' said Alan.

Lisa stood waiting, her heart thumping loudly. As Billy and Jesse came up the stairs and into the hallway, Lisa ran towards them.

'Jesse, I've missed you so. Where have you been?' Lisa threw her arms around him. She lifted a hand to his face, exploring every beautiful angle. Something was untangling inside him, the sadness he had carried for too long. Lisa clung tightly to him, sobbing quietly as she listened to the slow steady sound of his breath.

'We have all missed you,' said Alan.

The lights began to dim. 'Stay with us, Jesse. There are plenty of seats in this box,' said Zena. 'Jedda sings beautifully, doesn't she?'

Jesse nodded and his smile got wider.

'Jedda will be thrilled you're here, Jesse. We all are,' said Lisa.

Jesse sat next to Billy, who held Lisa's trembling hand. 'Grasshopper,' he whispered, 'Jesse home now.' He kissed her softly on her cheek.

Lisa's teary eyes looked at him. 'You were right,' she said her voice cracking. 'He's been safe.'

When the opera finished, a large bouquet was handed to Jedda, and she blew kisses to the standing audience. Their feet stomped and the applause grew louder. 'More, more.'

Jedda ran into the wings with the other performers, and Vivian stood watching. 'You were marvellous, Jedda, just marvellous. The audience obviously want more. Do you want to do one more song? Anything you like to sing. I can go down to the conductor and let him know.'

'Yes, Vivian, there is one song I would love to sing.'

'And what is it, my dear?'

'O mio babino caro. I would love to sing that to my father.'

Vivian nodded. 'It's a beautiful choice, Jedda. Will he know the meaning of those words?'

'No,' she laughed. 'I will sing it for him at home. He is my dear papa.'

'But you have the translation across in printed form with the program as well as the subtitles that are projected above the stage. He will quickly realise,' said Vivian. 'Just give me a moment. The curtain will go up and that is your cue to come out.' Vivian hurried away.

The lights went down, and the curtain was raised. Jedda stood alone centre stage, a sole light beaming down on her from above. It was almost spiritual, ethereal. As she sang, her eyes directed towards the box where her parents sat. It was a heart-wrenching and emotional experience as she sang to her father. The song was deeply moving and when Jedda finished, she blew a kiss to the direction of the box.

When the lights went up, Jedda saw her family standing and clapping. Her father blew a kiss back. It was seconds later, and with a feeling of disbelief, as she suddenly realised it was Jesse standing next to Billy.

Her hand flew to her mouth and then she rushed off stage.

'Vivian, my brother is here. It's my twin brother!'

Jedda changed quickly with the help of Vivian and wiped off her make-up as she rushed outside.

The group had made their way down into the stalls area and stood waiting opposite the orchestra pit. 'She will come bounding out of one of those doors any minute,' said Alan.

The door opened suddenly, and she yelled, 'Jesse, Jess!' as she flung herself at him, sobbing into his chest. 'I've missed you so much. We all have. I never stopped hoping you would come home.'

Jesse lifted her chin. He had not been so happy for months. He took a long breath. 'Little wild goose, I am home.'

When they all finally left the Sydney Opera House, they headed to the Hilton, where Alan arranged a room for Jesse. 'The Marble Bar will do,' said Alan. 'Champagne and a few beers before retiring.'

'Cheers to our songbird.' Alan lifted his glass. Jedda beamed. 'And most of all, cheers to having our Jesse back.'

'Yes, it is so wonderful,' said Lisa, wiping her eyes.

'I can say without doubt that Jedda is gifted and Covent Garden awaits. Well done, Jedda. It was superb to watch you,' said Lydia.

'I am just so happy,' said Jedda. 'The opera was, well, it was great, but what can I say – the most special thing is having Jesse here. My Jesse.' She hugged her brother. 'You have to tell us your stories. Where have you been!'

Lisa smiled warmly. 'It's so lovely to have you here with us, Jesse. We want to hear what you have done. I know you mentioned earlier that you were at Anna Creek Station, but we want to know all the details.'

'Happy to be coming home now,' replied Jesse.

They talked until they could talk no more. As Lisa and Billy reluctantly made their way to their room, it was like a valve had been released. So much tension and worry gone, and whether it was the exuberance of the opera or Jesse just being with them, they made passionate love. Billy was hungry for Lisa and their union was euphoric after months and months of worry.

EPILOGUE

During the year 1996, Jesse slotted back into life at Woori like he'd never left, and his experience on Anna Creek Station had only enhanced his skills.

Mitch had not recovered from the loss of his family. His laughter had died, and his body was weary. Some days he never got out of bed. Rebekah had stayed on and looked after him, but he remained morose and heartbroken. He told Gus and the workers to fill in the dam and rip down the sheds and tables. The quaddy had been sold and he never had another one on the property. He built two smaller dams in different paddocks for stock but no matter what he did, he remained haunted and grief-stricken.

Dave Walker died in hospital six months after Polly and Olivia, and he had told Mitch he never wanted a fuss. It had been a very sombre service as he was laid to rest next to Kate and Olivia.

While Rebekah sat with him one afternoon, she took his hand as he stared across the red dust plains. 'Mitch, I really think the best thing you can do is leave here. You know your heart is not in the place anymore. You can go anywhere you want, an entirely different location, any part of the world. But I think from a mental health point of view, this place is destroying you.'

He took a long time before he answered. 'Yeah, you're right, Rebekah. I'm no longer connected to this place or this world. I have lost all reason as to why I'm here. Some days I feel like loading a gun to my head. If you weren't here, I don't know what I would do.'

'You have a place on this earth, Mitch, like everyone. But as I said, I really feel you need to leave Woodside. If you don't, and it is entirely your decision, and if you want me to stay with you, that is fine. You know I care for you, deeply, but if you want to be on your own, then I completely understand.'

'No, I don't,' said Mitch shaking his head. 'I hear what you say, Rebekah. And no, I don't want you to go. You've been so good to me, were so good to all of us. I want you to be with me. Maybe we can move to Sydney and you can open up another practice? I really don't know what I would do in Sydney though. All my life, I have worked the land. But I know you're right. I'll call Alan tomorrow. He may know of someone who wants to buy the place.' A deep sadness resonated in Mitch's voice.

It came as no surprise to Mitch when Alan put up his hand to buy Woodside. He had wanted to increase his acreage for a long time. He bought the property two months after the finance was approved.

Mitch took no possessions. He wanted no memories, and the contents of the home were sold to Alan. He left with his clothes and Rebekah.

A few months after the sale, Mitch sent a brief letter of thanks to Alan and Zena and said he was travelling through Europe with Rebekah, whom he had married in Italy, and they were now expecting their first child.

Billy and Lisa moved across to Woodside, and Jesse remained at Wooribilly, staying in their home and taking up management of Woori with Alan.

Kev stayed on with Ningali, and Alan built them a small cottage so they did not have to use the shearer's quarters.

Mark, Lisa's brother, had moved to Paris to teach and had settled in well, fulfilling his dreams.

As a few of the old staff had left Woodside, Billy and Alan hired a few new crew members. One of the applicants for a jillaroo position was a young Irish woman. After reading her CV, Alan called the manager at Brunette Downs, who promptly advised that he had never seen better. Lily O'Shea, an exuberant 20-year-old, was at Woodside within four weeks.

'She'll be a little ripper, and it'll be nice to have a woman thrown in the mix, Billy. Brunette Downs is about 600 kilometres north west of Mount Isa in Queensland. It's huge,' said Alan.

Lily went above and beyond their expectations. Tall and slim, her long blonde plait trailed down her back. She was strong in character, full of life, patient and very kind. Like Lisa, she had a real affinity with animals, and she would quieten her mind to hear the horses. 'You have to hear what they are saying, Jesse, however quietly they are speaking,' she would say to him.

Lily made Jesse laugh, a laugh that roared from his belly once he got to know her. He adored her accent and, on her day off, Lily would either ride with Jesse or sit with Ningali and Mum Shirl, fascinated by their stories. Lily reciprocated by telling some Irish yarns. Sadly, Mum Shirl had a massive heart attack early in '96 and was buried where her little tent had stood for years.

As Lisa watched her son, it was clear that he was gently letting go of Olivia, the scars of his heart being replaced with wings. He was almost twenty-one, and over the next six months, since Lily's arrival, they were almost inseparable, with Jesse spending more and more time at Woodside.

Jedda had her first full-length dramatic performance at Covent Garden, and she was intent on completing her degree. Her desire was to commence philanthropic work after graduating and to help her Indigenous people, a cause so very close to her heart.

It was early evening with another beautiful sunset as Billy came into the house.

'I thought we would take the time and watch the sun go down, my darling. Jesse is coming over with Lily, and I have a few things set up outside on the veranda.'

Billy came to her. 'Grasshopper, something special?' He kissed her forehead, gently running his fingers down her cheek. 'Maybe,' said Lisa with a hint of a smile as they stepped outside.

In the distance, a big copper horse galloped towards them. Lily was driving the horse towards them while Jesse clung to her waist. Their laughter could be heard on the winds. 'It could be us, Billy. That was us.'

'My boy, he like da Lily. She take his heart,' Billy said.

'I think the feeling is mutual. Anyway, they're joining us as Jesse said he and Lily wanted to speak to us both,' Lisa smiled. 'You know when you throw a stone in a pond, the concentric waves spread out further and further. You never know what to expect.'

Jesse took Lily's hand as they all sat down, and it was clear love was in the air. Something had shifted between them.

'What is it?' asked Lisa. 'I get the feeling...'

It was Jesse who spoke. 'I asked my Lily to marry me. She makes me so happy.'

'Oh my goodness, that is wonderful news. Billy, did you know about this?' asked Lisa.

Billy nodded. 'Jesse tell me last week.'

'And you have kept that news from me for this long? I mean a week?' Lisa laughed. 'You men.'

'But,' interrupted Lily, as she looked sheepishly at Lisa.

'But what?' asked Lisa.

Jesse laughed as he took Lily's hand. 'My Lily, she is with child.'

Lisa couldn't wipe the smile from her face. That's the best news, Jesse. Oh my, we're going to be grandparents, Billy. A new life is coming to Woodside!'

They all hugged and cried and celebrated into the night.

◊

As Lisa and Billy lay in the stillness of the night, she felt his body turn as his arms came around her.

'Do you think they're too young, Billy?' Lisa asked softly.

'No, we were young, Lisa, young like dem. Jesse know what he wants. Dey have da strong love.'

Lisa breathed him in. It was a full moon as she listened to his quiet breathing, the silvery light filling their bedroom.

'Our world is changing, my darling.' She tenderly traced Billy's face with her fingers.

'Always change, Lisa.'

'I have some news too. I thought about saying something this evening, but I wanted Jesse and Lily to have their special moment.'

'What is your news, my grasshopper?' He kissed her mouth softly.

'I thought the willy wagtails would have gossiped the news. They're always around wiggling their tails and being nosy,' Lisa laughed.

'Tell me what?'

'It's been a long time coming, and I never thought it would happen.' Lisa's eyes filled with tears. 'I'm so happy, Billy.' Her voice was full of emotion as she took his hand. 'I am now three months pregnant. We're having a piccaninny. I so wish Mum Shirl was here for this news.'

Billy sat bolt upright. 'A piccaninny!' He threw his head back and yelled, a jolt of excitement running through his body. 'Piccaninny!'

As they lay together in the darkness, they knew the old life would continue at Woori but a new and different life spread before them as they entered the season of the heart.

THE END

ACKNOWLEDGEMENTS

Thank you to Dr Juliette Lachemeier (my wonderful editor and publisher) at The Erudite Pen, my brother Mark who supports me so unconditionally, Willo, (my gorgeous farmer), Merrie and Professor Louise for their help with the research into birthing and mental health. And mostly to my amazing *Splintered Heart* and *Sinister Intent* readers who sent so many wonderful comments that truly inspired me. My heartfelt thanks for your continued support and for enjoying my novels.

ABOUT THE AUTHOR

Linda Dowling grew up in the western suburbs of Sydney, Australia. During her childhood, she spent most of her time in rural areas and has continued to enjoy life in the bush or in areas with natural surrounds. Her aunt, a wonderful horsewoman, lived in Carinda, New South Wales and taught her a great deal about horses, riding and the outback. It was during her vacations with her aunt that Linda herself fell in love with the vast outback plains and the Aboriginal culture, their stories and their unique but simple way of living. Linda has a natural affinity with Indigenous peoples and was the only white girl selected to play for the Papua New Guinea softball teams at the Pan Pacific Masters.

In her professional life, Linda has established and managed four medico-legal firms, including her own. During the course of her career, she has been involved in reporting on coronial matters and inquests. She has also worked with the New South Wales Police State Crime Command Centre and in various Royal Commissions where she was exposed to the worst of human nature. Linda has drawn upon her professional and personal experiences while writing her Red Dust novel series, but the stories are a work of fiction and do not depict any person, living or dead. Her first novel in this series, *Splintered Heart*, was an award-winning finalist in the 2020 International Book Awards in the multicultural category.

Enjoyed the book? You can follow the author at:

Email: lsd777@bigpond.com

Facebook: facebook.com/authorreddustnovels

LinkedIn: linkedin.com/in/linda-dowling-10bb0635/